Forbidden passion

is the ultimate temptation . . .

"Trust me."

He drew her closer. So close that his breath whispered over her lips as he said, "I'm not going to let him hurt you—or Jake—ever again."

And then he moved closer, and closer still, until his lips pressed against hers. The contact was electric, sending a jolt through her, bringing every single nerve ending in her body alive.

It seemed to travel through him, too, because she felt him shudder. Then it was no longer a mere touch of lips. With a soft groan, he surrendered to it, opening to her, kissing her deeply, thoroughly. His hand slipped from her cheek behind her neck, bringing her into it with him, into a give-and-take that made her whole body reawaken and yearn for the touch it had once known. *His* touch...

Praise for the novels of Jennifer Haymore

Secrets of an Accidental Duchess

"4½ stars! Haymore's characters leap off the pages in her latest installment in the Donovan family saga. Written with gentleness and emotional strength, it's a creative romance readers will not soon forget."

—*RT Book Reviews*

"5 stars! Now this is a book worthy of its luscious characters with all their secrets and baggage on board... Jennifer Haymore has given us a wonderful Cinderella story that does have more than its share of pain but also has more than its share of passion. A wonderfully paced story that will take you from London to Gretna Green and back with a lush amount of sass, finesse, and pizzazz to keep you well satisfied like a cat in front of a bowl of milk. Just delicious!" —GoodReads.com

"Gripping...engaging...The writing allows the reader to get deeply involved and the emotional struggles of Serena are palpable...I'm looking forward to reading about the other Donovan sisters...*Confessions of an Improper Bride* is a great start to this series, and I would recommend it to all romance novel fans."

—TheRomanceReader.com

A Hint of Wicked

"Full of suspense, mystery, romance, and erotica...I am looking forward to more from this author."
—*Las Vegas Review-Journal*

"A clever, provoking, and steamy story from an upcoming author to keep your eye out for!" —BookPleasures.com

"Haymore is a shining star, and if *A Hint of Wicked* is any indication of what's to come, bring me more."
—FallenAngelReviews.com

"Debut author Haymore crafts a unique plot filled with powerful emotions and complex issues."
—*RT Book Reviews*

"A unique, heart-tugging story with sympathetic, larger-than-life characters, intriguing plot twists, and sensual love scenes."

—Nicole Jordan, *New York Times* bestselling author

"Complex, stirring, and written with a skillful hand, *A Hint of Wicked* is an evocative love story that will make a special place for itself in your heart."

—RomRevToday.com

"A new take on a historical romance...complicated and original...the characters are well crafted...surprisingly satisfying."　　—TheRomanceReadersConnection.com

"What an extraordinary book this is!...What a future this author has!"　　—RomanceReviewsMag.com

"Ms. Haymore's talent for storytelling shines throughout this book."　　　　—Eye on Romance

A Touch of Scandal

"Jennifer Haymore's books are sophisticated, deeply sensual, and emotionally complex. With a dead sexy hero, a sweetly practical heroine, and a love story that draws together two people from vastly different backgrounds, *A Touch of Scandal* is positively captivating!"

—Elizabeth Hoyt, *New York Times* bestselling author

"Sweep-you-off-your-feet historical romance! Jennifer Haymore sparkles!"

—Liz Carlyle, *New York Times* bestselling author

"Haymore discovers a second fascinating, powerful, and sensual novel that places her high on the must-read lists. She perfectly blends a strong plot that twists like a serpent and has unforgettable characters to create a book readers will remember and reread." —*RT Book Reviews*

"*A Touch of Scandal* is a wonderfully written historical romance. Ms. Haymore brings intrigue and romance together with strong, complex characters to make this a keeper for any romance reader. Ms. Haymore is an author to watch and I'm looking forward to the next installment of this series."

—TheRomanceReadersConnection.com

"A deliciously emotional Cinderella tale of two people from backgrounds worlds apart, *A Touch of Scandal* addicts the reader from the first page and doesn't let go until the very last word. Hurdle after hurdle stands in the way of Kate and Garrett's love, inexorably pulling the reader along, supporting them each step of the way. *A Touch of Scandal* is a surefire win!"

—FallenAngelReviews.com

"A classic tale…Reading this story, I completely fell in love with the honorable servant girl and her esteemed duke. This is definitely a tale of excitement, hot, sizzling sex, and loads of mystery." —FreshFiction.com

"These characters are just fantastic and endearing. I just couldn't wait to find out what happened on the next page."

—SingleTitles.com

"4 stars! Kate and Garrett were wonderful characters who constantly tugged at my heartstrings. I found myself rooting for them the whole way through...If you like historical romances that engage your emotions and contain characters you cheer for, this is the book for you."

—TheRomanceDish.com

A Season of Seduction

"4½ stars! Haymore uses the Christmas season as an enhancing backdrop for a mystery/romance that is both original and fulfilling. Her fresh voice and ability to build sensual tension into lively love stories...make this tale shine."

—*RT Book Reviews*

"Sizzling...an engaging historical tale."

—RomRevToday.com

"Each time Ms. Haymore writes a book in this series I think there is no way to top the one I just finished. I started this latest one and realize she has done just that and has proven to me how fresh this series can remain."

—The Reading Reviewer

"Jennifer Haymore strikes a good balance of strength, sensuality, drama, and intrigue in her characters...Becky is an independent, fearless woman except when it comes to opening her heart to another man. And Jack, while strong and passionate, shows great sensitivity under his 'rogue' persona."

—www.FictionVixen.com

Pleasures of a Tempted Lady

ALSO BY JENNIFER HAYMORE

A Hint of Wicked
A Touch of Scandal
A Season of Seduction

Confessions of an Improper Bride
Secrets of an Accidental Duchess

JENNIFER HAYMORE

A DONOVAN NOVEL

Pleasures of a Tempted Lady

FOREVER

NEW YORK   BOSTON

Copyright © 2012 by Jennifer Haymore
Excerpt from *Confessions of an Improper Bride* Copyright © 2011 by Jennifer Haymore
Excerpt from *Secrets of an Accidental Duchess* Copyright © 2012 by Jennifer Haymore

Forever
Hachette Book Group
237 Park Avenue
New York, NY 10017

www.HachetteBookGroup.com

Printed in the United States of America

First Edition: July 2012
10 9 8 7 6 5 4 3 2 1

Forever is an imprint of Grand Central Publishing.
The Forever name and logo are trademarks of Hachette Book Group, Inc.

The Hachette Speakers Bureau provides a wide range of authors for speaking events. To find out more, go to www.hachettespeakersbureau.com or call (866) 376-6591.

The publisher is not responsible for websites (or their content) that are not owned by the publisher.

For Lawrence, as always.

Acknowledgments

To Kate McKinley, who helps me keep my head screwed on straight. To Cindy Benser, who reads my books and catches all the mistakes I don't think anyone else in the world would ever find. And to my dad, Kelly Haymore, who suffered through all the "spice" and "touchy-feely emotional stuff" to spend hours talking to me about ships and sea warfare of the nineteenth century. Thanks especially to my agent, Barbara Poelle, and my editor, Selina McLemore, two amazing, brilliant, and talented women who've supported me through thick and thin. I'm blessed to be able to work with both of them.

Pleasures
of a
Tempted
Lady

Chapter One

William Langley gazed over the bow of his ship, the *Freedom*, at the rippling gray surface of the ocean. Though the seas had finally calmed, a slick of seawater coated everything, and half of his crew were still snoring in their bunks, exhausted from the exertion of keeping the ship afloat through last night's storm.

Will ran his fingers through the cold beads of water along the top edge of the gunwale. It'd probably be a month before they dried out, but they were no worse for wear. Now they could go back to the task at hand—seeking out smugglers along the Western Approaches.

In the nearly windless morning, the *Freedom* crept along in an easterly direction. They were about halfway between Penzance and the Irish coast, though the storm had certainly blown them off course, and they wouldn't get an accurate reading on their position until the skies cleared. God knew when that would be. In the interim, he'd keep them moving east toward England so they could patrol the waters closer to the shore.

"She did well, didn't she?"

Will glanced over his shoulder to see his first mate, David Briggs, approaching from the starboard deck, freshly shaved and calm, a far cry from his harried demeanor last night.

Will smiled. "Indeed she did." The *Freedom* was a newly built American schooner rigged with triangular sails in the Bermuda style, a sight rarely seen among the square-rigged brigs and cutters common on this side of the Atlantic. But Will's schooner was fast and sleek—perfect for the job she had been assigned to perform. And sturdy, as proven by her stalwart response to last night's storm.

She was, above all, his. Will owned a fleet of ships captained by various men involved in his import business, but since before the first planks were riveted together the *Freedom* had been his. Three years ago, he'd sent his carefully rendered plans to Massachusetts with detailed instructions on how she should be built. And now, with every step along her shiny planked deck, the satisfying twin prides of creation and ownership resonated through him.

The only area in which Will had relinquished control in the building of the *Freedom* was in the naming of the ship. The name he'd wanted for her would be too obvious. It would raise too many smirking eyebrows in London society. Even his best friends in the world—the Earl of Stratford and his wife, Meg—would frown and question his sanity if he'd given the ship the name his heart and soul had demanded.

So instead of *Lady Meg*, he'd agreed to the name suggested by the American shipbuilder—likely as a joke, since they knew well that he was a consummate Englishman. *Freedom*. It seemed everything the Americans created involved their notions of freedom or liberty or national pride. Yet, surprising himself, Will had found he wasn't opposed to the name. For him, this ship did represent freedom.

Being out here again, on the open sea, on this beauty of a vessel and surrounded by his hardy crew—all of it was freeing. The bonds that had twisted around his heart for the past two years, growing tighter and tighter, stifling him until he was sure he'd burst, were slowly unraveling.

Out here, at least he could breathe.

He glanced over at Briggs, who was scrubbing a hand over his eyes. "Sleep well?"

"Like the dead."

"You should have slept longer."

Briggs raised a brow at him, causing the angry red scar that ran across his forehead to pucker. "I could say the same to you, Captain."

Will chuckled. "Touché." Briggs was right. Will had achieved no more than two hours of sleep in the predawn hours. He could have slept in later, but he'd been anxious to survey the *Freedom* in the light of day. He was glad he had. The anxiety and energy that had compelled him into action since the beginning of the storm were gone now, and he felt . . . not exactly happy, but peaceful. For the first time in a long while.

"No sightings this morning," Briggs said.

"No surprise there," Will answered.

Briggs scanned the horizon with narrowed eyes. "Aye, well, it's bloody foggy."

"And we're too far offshore." Will had a theory that the

particular ship they pursued—a brig smuggling rum from the West Indies—remained close to the shore for several weeks at a time. Instead of using one cove as a drop for its cargo, it used several—depositing a few barrels of rum here and another few there so as to throw the authorities off its scent. The captain of this ship was wily, and he had proved elusive to the coast guard as well as the revenue cutters. They had a vague description of the man, but nobody knew his name—or, perhaps more accurately, no one was willing to reveal his name.

The *Freedom* was, in essence, a spy ship—with only four guns and a crew of twenty, they wouldn't stand in a fight against a fully armed brig with a crew of a hundred. Their task, instead of capturing the pirates, was to log the brig's activities and hand over the information to the revenue officers, who in turn would seize the ship and its illegal cargo, then prosecute the smugglers.

Will glanced over at Briggs and saw the muscle working in his jaw. He clapped a hand over the man's shoulder. "Patience," he said in a low voice.

Briggs was a few years younger than him, and patience had never been his strong suit. He was anxious to find the culprits, whereas Will preferred to take things slowly, as if they had all the time in the world. The best plan of action was probably somewhere in between the two men's methods. If they waited too long, the brig would be on its way back to the West Indies for its next illegal mission, not to be seen in these waters for at least another year.

Briggs turned to Will and nodded, the edges of his blue eyes crinkling against the glare of the morning sun's attempt to burn through the fog. "We've been out here a fortnight and haven't seen a hint of them."

The wind had picked up, and it ruffled through the other man's thick, tawny hair and sent wisps of fog swirling through the rigging behind him.

"We'll find them." Will squeezed Briggs's shoulder. Neither man said any more; instead both turned back to gaze out over the ocean. The sea and wind were slowly gathering strength after their rest from the gale, and the schooner sliced through the small waves at a faster pace now. Will took a deep breath of the salt air. So much cleaner than the stale, rank air full of sewage and coal smoke in London.

"What's that?" Briggs asked.

Will glanced at the man to see him squinting out over the open ocean.

"What's what?"

His first mate pointed straight ahead. "That."

Will scanned the sea. Could he have been wrong all this time? Might they encounter the smugglers way out here? Even as he thought it, he realized how unlikely it was. More likely they'd come across another legal English or Irish vessel.

Seeing nothing, he methodically scanned the blurred horizon once again, and then he saw it: the prow of a boat emerging like a specter from the fog.

Will frowned. The vessel was too small to be this far out at sea on its own.

After half a minute in which they both stared at the emerging shape, Briggs murmured, "Holy hell. Is it a jolly boat?"

"With a broken mast," Will said, nodding. "I don't see anyone in it. Can you?"

Briggs leaned forward, squinting hard. He shook his

head, but then frowned. "Possibly. Lying on the center bench?"

The mast looked like it had snapped off to about a third of its height, and half the sail draped off the side of the little boat, dragging in the water. No one was attempting to row.

The boat was adrift. And the *Freedom* was headed straight for it.

Will could see at least one figure now—or at least a mound of pinkish fabric piled on one of the benches. And then he saw the movement. Just the smallest shudder, like the twitch of a frightened animal, beneath one of the bench seats.

He spun around and shouted to Ellis, the helmsman, ordering the man to turn into the wind on his command. If they timed it properly, rather than barreling right over the little boat and reducing it to splinters, they could pass it on the larboard side without getting its floating sail tangled in their keel or rudder.

"Aye, Captain!" Ellis answered.

Will heard a shout. He turned to take stock of the other seamen on deck. There were six additional men, four of them clustered near Ellis, speaking in excited tones and pointing at the boat emerging from the fog. The other two had been at work swabbing the deck but were now gazing at the emerging vessel in fascination.

"Fetch the hook," someone shouted, and a pair of seamen hurried down the starboard deck where the telescoping hook was lashed.

Everyone else was still asleep, but Will could easily make do with the nine of them. The *Freedom* was sixty feet of sleek power, and one of the most impressive of her attributes was that her sails were controlled by a series of winches, making a large crew unnecessary. In fact, Ellis and three others could easily control the ship while Briggs, Will, and the other seamen secured the vessel.

"We'll draw alongside it on our larboard side," Will murmured to Briggs. Even after such a short time aboard his new ship, Will had impeccable timing when it came to the *Freedom*. Briggs and the crew often joked that the ship was such a part of him he could command it to do anything he wanted with a mere thought. The truth was, Will knew the *Freedom* intrinsically. He could predict with great accuracy how it would react to any manipulation of its sails and rudder—certainly a product of controlling everything about its design since its earliest conceptualization.

"Aye, sir," Briggs said. "I'll prepare to secure it larboard-side."

"Very good." Will turned back toward the jolly boat as Briggs hurried amidships. He could see the figure on the bench more clearly now, and he swallowed hard.

It was definitely a woman. The pink was her dress, a messy, frothy, lacy concoction spattered with the gray and black muck that constituted part of the inner workings of any sailing vessel. She lay prone and motionless on the bench. Beside her, the brownish lump wasn't entirely clear. A dog, Will guessed, probably half dead from fear, with its head tucked under its body.

He waited another two minutes, judging the wind and the closing distance between the two vessels. Finally he shouted, "Haul up!"

Ellis responded instantly to his order, turning the wheel so the *Freedom* sailed directly into the wind. The sails began to flap wildly, but Will heard the whir of the winches, and soon they were pulled taut.

The *Freedom* lost speed quickly as the jolly boat approached, and they drifted to a halt just as a seaman reached out with the grappling hook to snag the gunwale of the small vessel.

Will hurried to the larboard side while Briggs lashed the boat to the *Freedom* and one of the seamen secured a ladder. He had already descended into the jolly boat when Will arrived at the scene.

"There's a lady here, sir!" The seaman, Jasper, who was really little more than a boy, looked up at Will wide eyed, as if uncertain what to do.

"Can you heft her up, lad?" Will called down. The poor woman hadn't budged, and her matted hair and torn clothing covered her features. He hoped she could breathe through that thick tangle of blond hair. He hoped she was alive.

Jasper appeared rather horrified at the prospect of carrying her, but with a gulp that rolled his prominent Adam's apple, he nodded. Widening his stance for balance in the bouncing jolly boat, he leaned over and gingerly tucked his arms under the figure of the unmoving woman and hoisted her up.

Will sensed movement from the corner of his eye, and he glanced over at the lump he'd thought was a dog.

Two brown eyes stared at him from under a mass of shaggy brown hair. It was looking up from its position curled into a ball on the floor of the jolly boat, but it was no dog. It was a child, and he was creeping backward, as if he were considering escape.

Seeing that his first mate had looked up from his task

and had noticed the child as well, Will nodded at Briggs. "Go down and grab him," he told him. "Best hurry, too— looks like he's about to jump overboard."

Briggs vaulted over the side of the *Freedom*, his movements graceful. The man had a way about him on a ship—no matter where he was from the bilge to the top of the mast, he was inherently graceful and self-composed, even in twenty-foot seas.

Briggs's fast motion evidently frightened the boy, because he scrambled backward, and when Briggs stepped over the bench toward him, the child scurried up the side of the hull and leaped overboard. Briggs was lightning quick, though. He whipped out his hand, grabbed the urchin by the scruff of the neck, and hauled him back into the boat.

Without making any noise, the boy kicked and flailed, his hands gripping the strong arms around him and trying to yank them away.

"Feisty one, aren't you?" Will heard Briggs say above the slap of the waves against the jolly boat's hull. "But don't worry, lad. We're here to help you, not hurt you."

That seemed to calm the boy enough for Briggs to get a firmer grip on him, and Will turned back to Jasper, who was struggling with hoisting the lady up the ladder. The second mate, MacInerny, had climbed halfway down to help, and they'd managed to heft her most of the way up.

Will bent over and reached down for her, managing to grasp her beneath the armpits, and with the two men's help, he was able to maneuver her onto the deck. It wasn't that she was heavy—she was actually a slip of a thing. But the movement of the ocean combined with her dead weight and the frothy torn clothing combined to make it a cumbersome process.

Cradling her head, Will gently lay her on the deck.

"She's breathing," Jasper gasped as he scrambled up the ladder. "She lives!"

Will heaved out a sigh of relief.

Holding the little boy—who looked to be about five or six years old, though Will was certainly no authority on children—Briggs stepped onto the deck. The four men hovered over the woman. Crouched near her feet, Jasper cleared his throat and tugged the filthy hem of her dress down over the torn and dirty stockings covering her legs.

Something about those legs was...familiar.

With his heart suddenly pounding hard, Will raised his hand to push away the blond mass of hair obscuring her features. Her hair was dense with wetness and salt, but he cleared it from her face, his callused fingertips scraping over the soft curve of her cheek.

"Oh, God," Will choked, his hand frozen over her hair. "Oh, my God."

"What is it, Captain?" The question came from somewhere above him.

Will blinked away the water threatening to stream from his eyes. Was he overtired? Was he having visions? Had the intensity of the storm and lack of proper sleep caused him to have strange, perverse dreams?

No. God no, he was awake. There was too much color—the dewy flesh of her skin, the light brown spatter of freckles on her nose, the pink and white of her dress. Beyond the rancid smell of bilge water—originating mostly from the boy, he thought—he could smell her, too.

She'd always smelled sweet and pure, like the sugarcane from the plantation in Antigua where she'd been raised.

Was she a ghost?

Half fearing she'd evaporate like fog beneath his fingers, he clasped both sides of her face and turned it upward so she would have been staring at him if her eyes were open.

"You're real," he whispered. He crouched over her mouth and nose and closed his eyes as the soft puff of her breath washed over his cheek.

Jasper was right—she *was* alive.

This was impossible. She'd been lost at sea eight years ago—on the other side of the Atlantic. Had she been adrift all this time, like some sleeping beauty, waiting for him—her prince—to find her and kiss her awake?

Did he dare hope that this was a true miracle and not some cruel joke of fate?

"Meg," he breathed. The dewy feel of her skin beneath his fingertips swept through him like the stroke of a rose petal. "Meg? Wake up," he murmured. "Wake up, love."

The urge overcame him, and forgetting the men staring at him—at them—he bent forward and pressed his lips to hers.

Her mouth was soft and cool, with a hint of salt. God help him, but memories slammed into him. He remembered the feel of her lips against his, the feel of her body against his. And his body could do nothing but respond to the images rolling through his mind. The sweetness of her body tucked against him. Her trusting gray eyes . . . the way she'd looked at him. No one had ever looked at him like Meg had.

He drew back, his movement slow. She hadn't moved.

Keeping himself just over her, he held her precious face cupped in his hands. He couldn't bear to let her go. He couldn't bear to pull farther away from her. Instead, he touched her nose with his and reveled in the soft feel of her breath as it whispered over his forehead.

She was alive. Meg was alive.

"Captain?"

It was Briggs's voice. Will closed his eyes and waited until she exhaled once more, and then he dragged his face up to look at his first mate. Briggs still held on to the shoulders of the dark-haired little boy, though he'd stopped struggling and was staring at Will with wide blue eyes.

Was the child hers?

The thought nearly toppled him. He lowered a hand onto the deck to steady himself and said through his teeth, "Yes, Mr. Briggs?"

"Perhaps we should take the lady below?"

Will hesitated. Of course they should take her below, but where to put her? This wasn't a large ship—there was no sick bay or surgery, and none of the men possessed much in the way of medical expertise. There was only one reasonable place.

Rising to his feet, he let out a sigh that misted into the cold morning air. "Yes. Take her to my quarters."

Before anyone else could move, Jasper had gathered her in his arms and risen to his feet. MacInerny led the way to the stern, where he held open the door to Will's quarters.

Jasper hesitated, glancing back over his shoulder with his heavy brows raised in question.

"Lay her on the bed, if you will, Mr. Jasper."

"Aye, Cap'n." With infinite gentleness, he settled her on the bed. Jasper was a rough mountain of a man, born in the slums of London and raised by the Navy. Will wouldn't have expected tenderness from him in any circumstance. But here he was, behaving like the gentle giant with this lady.

With *Meg.*

Jasper stepped back and gazed at her as Will stepped to his side, and the rest of the men formed a semicircle around Will's bunk, all looking at Meg, all awaiting his next command.

Will glanced over at Briggs, who now held the boy's hand in a firm grasp. "All of you, back to your duties." As the men turned to go with muttered *aye, sir*s, Will added, "Briggs, you and the boy stay."

When the room was cleared, Will knelt in front of the boy. "What happened, lad?"

The boy didn't say a word, but his wide eyes fixed on Will as if he were entranced.

"Was your ship lost in the storm?"

No response.

Will gestured to Meg. His next words were taut. "Is that lady your mama?"

Again, there was no response, but the boy's gaze flickered over to Meg.

With a sigh, Will rose. "What do you think, Briggs?"

"No idea, sir." Briggs hesitated, his gaze sharpening. "Are you somehow acquainted with this lady, Captain?"

After a long, uncomfortable hesitation, Will nodded slowly. "I knew her. Long ago. You're probably going to think me mad, but..."

Briggs raised an expectant eyebrow, and Will found

himself unable to voice the truth. It would make him sound crazy if he said the lady had been lost at sea eight years ago. He glanced significantly down at the boy. "Later."

Briggs nodded, but his speculative blue gaze didn't falter.

Meg let out a soft puff of breath, jerking Will's attention to her. He hurried over to her. "Meg?"

She'd grown still again.

Briggs came to stand beside him, the boy at her side. "What's her name?"

"Margaret Donovan," Will responded instantly. Was it still her name? Had she married? He glanced downward, but the child stared at the unconscious woman without a change of expression, giving him no clues.

Suddenly, the lad tugged out of Briggs's grip and scrambled up the side of the bed, smearing his dirt and grime over the silk counterpane. Briggs reached out, intending to stop him, but Will held up his hand. "Let him go."

The boy tucked himself against Meg's body, slung his arm around her, and closed his eyes. Without waking, Meg wrapped her arm around the boy's thin shoulders and drew him close.

Will watched them for a moment longer. "Perhaps it's simply that both of them are exhausted from their ordeal."

"It seems that way," Briggs agreed.

Will's curiosity gnawed at him like a hundred mosquito bites begging to be scratched, but for now, Meg and the child needed to rest.

He could wait a few hours. Hell, he'd waited for Meg for six years before he'd learned that she'd been lost at sea. A few hours longer couldn't hurt.

He released a shaky breath. "I want them watched at all times. I don't want to see any more escape attempts from the little one. Or from the lady," he added as an afterthought. It seemed a reasonable assumption that she might try to escape. If she'd kept herself hidden from him for eight years, why on earth would she want to be found now?

Chapter Two

Meg hurt all over, but it felt like she was drifting on a cloud.

Where was she?

Her body didn't want to respond to her commands for it to open her eyes, but she managed to peel them open a crack.

Nausea overcame her so fast and so hard, her eyelids slammed shut again.

Slower. More slowly this time.

She was wide awake now. Jake's slumbering body was heavy and warm beside her—a familiar, comfortable presence. The ship rocked beneath them—and the every-day creaks and groans of the rigging sounded overhead.

She drifted off again but then came wide awake with a painful jolt.

No!

This wasn't right. She wasn't supposed to be on the *Defiant.* She and Jake had escaped. They'd been sailing for Ireland . . . and then it had begun to storm . . .

She couldn't remember what had happened during the storm. Obviously, something had gone terribly wrong. Caversham had found them.

Oh, God.

She kept her body very still, combating the choking sobs that welled in her throat. After all this time...she'd planned it so perfectly. She'd spent years planning it, for heaven's sake. It had been her and Jake's only hope of escape.

And now Caversham would punish them both. He'd make sure it never happened again.

She gathered Jake closer against her body, bending her head to bury her lips in the little boy's hair. The strands weren't as baby soft as they usually were—they were stiff with salt and reeked of the sea.

"Meg?"

She froze, not breathing. She didn't recognize that voice...and yet she *did*.

Her heartbeat pounding in her chest, she tried cracking her eyes open again. The cabin was bright and blurry, and she couldn't make out any shapes. Pain sliced through her skull, and she choked back nausea. She squinted, trying to discern the shadows and figures in front of her.

"Are you in pain?" The voice was soft, full of compassion. She wasn't used to male voices sounding like that. She was only used to the harsh, guttural noises of the men from Caversham's ships. And Caversham himself, coldly aristocratic. A shudder prickled her skin at the thought of his voice.

And then it struck her as she squinted harder and the blobs of color turned into the unfamiliar shapes of a cabin she didn't know: She wasn't on the *Defiant*. He hadn't found her.

Someone else had.

She didn't know whether to cry from relief or fear. Yet, whoever it was, surely it couldn't be as bad as Caversham finding them.

Jake's dark brown hair blocked her view of the room, and she struggled against the pain to raise her head. Jake grumbled softly and snuggled harder against her. She tightened her arm around him. Above all, she thanked God they were still together. She didn't know what had happened, but there were all sorts of scenarios in which she might have lost Jake. He was the most important thing. As long as he was with her, she could protect him.

She blinked hard. That seemed to clear her vision a bit, and she blinked again. She could see buff trousers tucked into shiny black Wellingtons, and a sea-blue waistcoat with a line of gold buttons—far finer than anything Caversham's men wore, although Caversham himself was quite the fop. This man, though—he filled out his clothing in a way Caversham never could. Powerful thigh muscles pressed against the wool of the trousers. The waistcoat cinched a narrow waist that widened to strong, broad shoulders. He seemed endlessly tall.

Finally, she was looking up into the man's face. The face was familiar, like his voice, but who was he? She frowned. Something about him...

He stared down at her; his lips parted as if he was about to speak but lost the words before he was able to push them free.

He blinked, and her gaze riveted to his eyes—dark as chocolate swirled with bits of amber. Beautiful eyes. Eyes that hadn't changed.

She must be dreaming. Having visions. The days in the *Defiant*'s jolly boat and the storm had muddled her mind. She was probably, at this very moment, lying on one of the jolly boat's benches as they drifted toward Ireland.

"Meg," the man whispered.

And his name—and all the memories associated with it—flooded through her in a powerful rush.

Commander William Langley.

She wrapped both her arms around Jake and gathered him close. The boy was her only link to reality. If she lost him, she'd have nothing. He shifted, and she glanced down to see that he was awake and gazing at her.

She looked back up at the man—no, *Commander Langley*. He was still standing there, pale and motionless, his dark eyes swirling with emotions she couldn't begin to name.

How should she address him? When she'd last seen him, she'd called him Will. But that was years ago. Surely it wouldn't be appropriate after so long. She swallowed hard against the lump that had formed in her throat.

"Commander Langley?" Her voice emerged low and cracking.

He released a hissing breath, and his hand covered hers over Jake's back, heavy and warm. "Yes. It's me. William Langley."

"How . . . ?" She choked on the word.

He hesitated, then gave her a tight smile. "We found you. Floating in a jolly boat with a broken mast. You've been unconscious since we brought you aboard."

"Jake?" She looked down at the boy again. "Are you all right, darling?"

"Mmm hmm," he said with a sober nod.

She struggled to raise herself into a sitting position, but the world swirled around her, her vision blurred, and she groped to hold on to the bed sheet.

Instantly, firm arms came around her shoulders, holding her steady. "There now. Lie down. I...we found a lump on your head—looks like you were hit quite hard by the mast when it fell."

"I think I...I'm going to..." Her body pitched forward. It was too much. Unthinkable that after so long she should be on a ship with—of all the people in the world—William Langley.

Unthinkable that she was about to vomit all over his fine silk bedspread.

"I'm sorry," she groaned, willing it not to happen. But it was. As if he knew he might be the target of the imminent disaster, Jake scrambled away from her.

"Hold on," Commander Langley murmured.

She closed her eyes tight and focused on the rapid thump of his boots over the wooden floorboards.

Within a few seconds, his hand was on her shoulder again. "Here. Lean forward. I've got you."

Opening her eyes, she saw the silver gleam of the tin bucket he'd placed in her lap. She leaned forward and released the sparse contents of her stomach as William Langley held the hair back from her face.

For years she'd fantasized about seeing this man again. Never once had the reunion of her dreams included bile, an overwhelming headache, and dizziness so pervasive she couldn't think straight.

When she'd finished, she leaned over the bucket panting, tears seeping from her closed eyes. "I'm sorry," she murmured. "So very sorry."

His fingers tightened on her shoulder. "There's nothing to be sorry about."

He took the bucket away, and when he returned, he drew a handkerchief across her lips and then pressed a glass into her hands. She opened her eyes and stared into the pink liquid, then up at him, her brows drawn in question.

"Watered-down wine," he explained.

She took a cautious sip. The wine flavored the water but wasn't overwhelming, and the concoction flowed smoothly down, ridding her mouth of the awful taste.

She offered a game smile to Jake, who had scuttled to the foot of the bed and was still gazing at her, terrified. She reached her hand out to him. "There's no need to be afraid, darling. We're safe now."

She glanced at William Langley and sent up a silent prayer that she was telling the truth. Eight years was a long time, but she had no doubt that the Will she'd known would have tried to protect her from a man like Jacob Caversham. She could only hope that time hadn't altered his character too much.

When Jake took her hand, she murmured, "I'd like to introduce you to this gentleman. His name is Commander Langley, and he's an old friend"—*an old lover*—"of mine. Commander Langley, this is Jake, my . . ." Her voice trailed off.

Once they'd escaped from the *Defiant* and were safely in Ireland, Meg had planned to pass Jake off as her son. William Langley was the first soul she'd seen since they'd slipped away several nights ago.

For some reason, she couldn't bring herself to tell him she was Jake's mother. She closed her eyes in a long blink, and when she opened them, she was thankful that the commander had chosen to ignore her unfinished sentence. Gravely, he held out his hand to Jake.

"Pleasure to meet you, lad."

"Hold out your hand," Meg murmured. "Like I taught you. Remember?"

Tentatively, Jake reached out. Commander Langley took the little hand into his grip and shook it firmly. "Good. Now that we're friends, I trust you won't try to leap overboard again?"

"Oh." Meg gathered the boy against her chest. Jake didn't speak much, he was easily frightened, and no one would dream of thinking him a "typical" boy. But Meg was convinced that while he would always be rather unusual, with proper love and care he might grow into a well-adjusted and capable man. It was what she wanted so badly to give him in Ireland. She looked up at Commander Langley. "I'm sorry. He's very easily frightened and was probably terrified when you brought us aboard."

He gave Jake an easy smile. "It's all right," he said to Jake. "Of course you were frightened, surrounded by unknown men and with your mama unconscious."

He'd placed a soft emphasis on the word "mama." She knew it was a question, and he paused, awaiting a confirmation or correction. She offered neither, instead looking down to hide the heat flaring in her cheeks.

Meg knew he would assume it was true now. It was as it should be. Just as she'd intended. Though she'd never intended to encounter this particular man when she'd been planning her escape from Caversham. She had been prepared to face the condemnation of society—society meant little to her now after all she'd been through. But to face the condemnation of William Langley . . . the thought of it made her stomach clench into a tight iron ball in her abdomen.

Looking down at Jake, she forced herself to speak. "You needn't be frightened anymore. I'm certain Commander Langley will help us."

When she glanced up at him, unable to hide the pleading in her expression, he gave a polite incline of his head, his expression completely unreadable. "I'll assist you in whatever way I can, of course. Shall I return you to your husband? Where—?"

"I am not married," Meg said quickly.

He raised a single eyebrow. "I see."

She'd intended to inform the world that Jake's father was dead, but once again the words snagged on the back of her throat, simply unwilling to emerge. She had learned to lie in the past years, and lie well, but lie to this man about such a thing . . .

She couldn't have conceived of lying to him about anything when they'd been lovers so long ago. More than anyone else, even her twin sister, Will had known the real Meg. To lie to him now seemed a betrayal of that.

But she knew she must. She'd already lied to him by omission, anyhow.

She took a deep breath and forced her lips to curl into a semblance of a smile. "It's just Jake and me now," she said softly.

"Ah. His father is gone, then?"

At the mention of his father, Jake had made a small whimper and clung tighter to her. She knew it was from fear of Caversham, but Commander Langley interpreted it as a confirmation.

"I'm very sorry," he said in a low voice. He patted Jake's back, attempting to comfort the boy. "Sorry, lad."

Not quite meeting his eyes, she gave a jerk of a nod. "We must get to Cork. My father's family lives near there, and they will take us in."

Will frowned at her. "What of the rest of your family? Your mother and your sisters?"

Her sisters. She'd dreamed about reuniting with her sisters—especially Serena—almost as often as she'd dreamed about seeing Will again. But if she went to her mother or her sisters, Caversham would surely find her, and they'd all be in grave danger. It was one fact she'd long ago come to terms with—to ensure their safety, she could never see them again.

Going to Cork to be with her father's relatives was different. Caversham knew nothing of that obscure branch of her family.

Blinking hard, she looked at the far wall, at the brass oil lamp bolted to the wall. It wasn't lit right now—sunlight aplenty streamed in through the row of windows along the back wall of the cabin. The room as a whole was downright luxurious, as ship cabins went. She realized with a jolt that she must be in the captain's quarters.

"Perhaps... perhaps I should speak to your captain."

For a second, he looked perplexed, as if her question had jolted him from his train of thought. Then a slow smile curved his lips. "I am the captain of the *Freedom*. I haven't been a commander for five years now. I own this ship, and I designed her as well."

For a long moment, they simply gazed at each other. Satisfaction welled sweetly within her. When she'd known him long ago, his dream had been to someday captain his own ship. It seemed he'd made that dream come true. She'd never doubted he would.

"I am happy for you," she said quietly, meaning it.

"Thank you." His gaze lingered on her face and then swept lower. Feeling suddenly shy, she resisted the urge to cover the front of her bodice with the blanket.

He frowned a little. "This is...difficult, I'm afraid. I've no lady on board to assist you with your needs."

She shook her head. "I've no need of help, but thank you for the thought."

"We haven't any clothes, nor have we the convenience of a bath for you. I'm very sorry."

"That's quite all right." Once Caversham had had a bath for her, Sarah, and Jake, but he'd had it thrown overboard before Sarah died. The bathtub had been one of the many things he'd blamed for causing Sarah's fever. Meg hadn't had a bath in months, but she'd become adept at bathing herself with a cloth and basin.

"All I can offer you is fresh, warm water."

"We'd appreciate that." Her body was covered in salt and grime, and so was Jake's. Squeezing a wet cloth over her face might help clear her muddled brain.

"I might be able to find some clothes for the boy." He tapped his fingers on his chin. "Guernsey, one of my sailors, is a dwarf and about the same height but a mite wide, I daresay. We'll have to cinch his belt."

She glanced down at Jake. His cherubic face was streaked with dirt, and his shirt was so soiled it was impossible to tell that it had once been white. She gave him a mock-stern look. "You were sleeping in the bilge again, weren't you?"

He nodded, and Meg sighed. Jake had been fearful of sailing in the small jolly boat, and whenever a bit of a wave splashed over the bulwark, he had squeaked in terror and dived into the bilge. The child was born at sea and had spent most of his life there, but despite the fact that his knot-tying abilities were as good as some sailors' four times his age, she had never known a soul less suited to be a sailor.

"I'm sorry I haven't any clothes for you, though." Captain Langley—no, he was and always would be *Will* to her—gave her a rueful smile. "In fact, I believe you're the first lady to ever step foot on the *Freedom*."

"The *Freedom*," she repeated, liking the sound of the ship's name on her tongue. "I'm honored to be the first woman aboard. But about the clothes, I'll manage." She thrust aside the counterpane that still covered her lap, swung her legs off the side of the bed, and when the dizziness faded and she was certain of her balance, she took stock of her dress. It was truly a disaster—her skirts were torn and streaked with dirt and grease, and the lacy overdress covering her bodice was in shreds. It was a near-hopeless cause, really.

By the look on his face, Will had come to the same conclusion. His brow furrowed. Then he met her eyes and said, very softly, "I don't want any man to see you like this."

She was too stunned by the words to point out the fact that it was likely that most of his crew had seen her in even worse condition when they'd brought her aboard.

"I'll find something," he added.

It had been a long time since anyone had made her feel shy. It was like the Meg of eight years ago, the Meg she'd thought long dead, was rising from a very long slumber.

"Thank you," she murmured.

Will reached out for Jake's hand. "Come along, lad. We'll find some hot water and some clothes for you."

Jake clutched Meg's arm and stared at Will, who gave him a kind smile. "Do you know what I had the cook bake today?"

Jake looked at Meg, then back to Will.

"Peach pies." Will winked. "He swears they stave off scurvy, but I just like the crust and the sugar sauce. Do you like peach pie?"

Jake nodded, and to Meg's surprise, he slowly reached out to take Will's hand.

"Good," Will said. "We'll give your mama some time alone, but we'll return directly, all right?"

Jake nodded again.

Meg winced. *Your mama.*

Well, in a way, it was true. She was all Jake had now, and she'd make good on her promise to Sarah. She'd be a mother to him, no matter what.

"Come along." Will glanced at Meg. "We'll talk more later. For now, I think it's most important for you to get cleaned up and feeling better."

Will led Jake out to the deck. Meg stared at the door for a long moment after it closed behind them. She didn't think she'd ever seen Jake go off with a stranger so easily. Usually, and for good reason, it took him weeks to warm up to a person.

Then again, Jake trusted Meg like he'd never trusted another soul, and she'd told him that Will was a good man. He'd believed her. And Will's gentle, friendly demeanor hadn't hurt matters.

The ship pitched gently over a wave, and Meg rose on unsteady feet. Not because she'd lost her sea legs, but because of the brutal nausea that still hadn't faded. For a long moment, she just stood there, studying the space she found herself in.

William Langley's space.

The bed she'd just left was larger than the cot she shared with Jake on the *Defiant*, and built into the corner of the large cabin. Beside the bed stood a counter with a recessed porcelain basin under built-in shelves holding folded white towels. A large navigation desk dominated the center of the room. Organized wooden bins bolted atop the desk contained rolled-up charts and other nautical tools.

A cushioned bench chair was built against the back and far walls, partially encircling a fine mahogany dining table. Behind the chair on the wall opposite to Meg hung three small portraits. She stepped closer to study them.

She'd seen the first one before. It was a painting of Will's house in the English countryside, a pretty, small white Palladian mansion on the banks of the River Till. When he'd first shown her this picture, she had dreamed about living there after their marriage.

She'd since learned that dreams never came true. Life threw at you the opposite of what you expected, the opposite of what you wanted. She suppressed a small snort and moved to the next painting.

This one was of a ship—clearly a naval vessel. It looked like the one she'd seen anchored in the Thames just before she'd left London. Will's naval ship.

The third portrait was of a pretty, dark-haired young woman with two boys tucked near her skirts, the younger holding a small dog. That one, she was sure, was Will. She could see the amber glint in his eyes that he hadn't lost as an adult. The older boy was probably Charles, a lieutenant in the Army who'd died at Waterloo when Will was still a youth. The woman was Will's mother, who'd succumbed to an illness shortly after Will had joined the Navy. His father, who wasn't pictured, had died when Will was very young.

Meg stared at the portrait for a long while, wondering who Will's family was now. He'd lost his parents and only brother. Had he ever married? Did he have children and a wife waiting for him in England? The thought made something clench hard in her chest.

There were certain things she was best off not knowing. She'd been aware of this truth for a long time. Years ago, she'd come to the conclusion that pining after Will, after her twin Serena and her other sisters, would only drive her to madness.

As a woman placed in so many situations in which she'd found herself utterly helpless, she'd learned to focus on the present and on the few things in her life she could control. For the past several years, her reality had consisted only of Sarah and Jake.

And now, even though Will had come back into her life—in a very odd way—Jake was still her priority. He was a little boy with needs only she understood, and above all, she loved him. She'd made Sarah a promise. She'd do right by them both.

She turned as the door opened to see Jake enter, followed by Will and two other men. She smiled at Jake, whose mouth was covered with what appeared to be sticky orange syrup, and crumbs were scattered over the front of his soiled shirt.

"From my recent experiences with children," Will said in a low voice as he came to stand beside her, "I have learned that promises of sweets from adults can go a very long way in winning a child's affection."

She nodded. Had those recent experiences with children involved his own offspring? She tried to banish the thought, but she couldn't seem to let it go, even though she knew it was ridiculous. It had been eight years. A very long time. It was natural that he'd have a family of his own by now.

The two sailors walked in carrying steaming buckets of water, one of which they poured into the basin. They diligently kept their eyes averted, making her wonder if Will had ordered them not to look at her.

Will handed her the clothes for Jake, then he held up a pair of trousers and a clean white linen shirt that looked like they would fit a small adult. "I probably shouldn't even offer these, but they look as though they might fit, and perhaps offer more . . . coverage than the dress."

She took them gratefully. "They will, thank you. And if you have a needle and thread, I can mend the dress."

He looked relieved. "Yes, of course. I'll have them brought straightaway."

The men hurried out of the room without glancing in their direction, and Jake wandered over to the basin to draw his fingers through the water.

"I'll leave you to your toilette, then," Will said. "Afterward, I'll have some food brought. If you're hungry, that is."

"Yes. Thank you again." Despite the fuzzy head and the nausea, she felt half starved. She'd eaten very little in the past few days. They hadn't had the time to steal much from the *Defiant* before they'd escaped, and she'd given most of it to Jake.

"And then we'll talk," Will said, his voice low.

He'd ask questions, demand details about why she and Jake had been sailing alone in a jolly boat in the middle of the Irish Sea. And after saving her and assuring her safety, he deserved answers.

The question was, could she manage to tell Will all the lies she'd planned to tell?

Chapter Three

W ill stood on the stern of the *Freedom*, barely registering the sun as it slipped behind the layer of clouds and fog that separated the horizon from the sky. He fought to keep his feet stationary on the deck, to prevent himself from striding back into his quarters and demanding answers.

Meg intended to go to Ireland. *Why?*

There was so much Will didn't understand. Why wasn't she looking for her family, for her sisters? And Ireland, of all places? He knew her father was Irish, but her mother's people, the branch of her family with the most connections, were in England. As were her sisters.

When he'd known her, Meg had adored her four sisters. Now, she didn't even speak of them, and when he'd brought them up, she'd grown vague and distant.

Meg was different. Changed. More reserved, more guarded than she'd been before. She'd grown up. Her innocence of so many years ago had vanished. As his own had.

She was still so damn beautiful. The differences between her and her twin, Serena, were subtle. They were almost completely identical in looks, except Serena had been in society for over a year now, and her skin had lightened and her body had filled out. Meg was thinner but not frail, and she had obviously been outdoors more—the splash of freckles across her nose had become more pronounced rather than faded, like Serena's had. Her hair, too, was a shade lighter than her sister's, bleached by the sun.

Personality-wise, the years of separation had seemed to bring them closer rather than further apart. Eight years ago, Meg had been the shy, demure one. He still saw that sense of shyness in her—that tendency toward reticence and to blush and look away when something embarrassed her. But she was a woman now, and it was clear to him that she had a goal she didn't intend to stray from.

What was that goal?

Will wasn't the sort of man who demanded answers. He always bided his time and waited. Hadn't he, just this morning, chided Briggs for his impatience?

But, God, he wanted answers. He needed them.

And he wanted to look at her again. To touch her and make sure she was real and not some extended fantastical dream.

He squeezed his eyes shut, welcoming the image of the little boy who'd refused to speak but wouldn't remove his grip from Will's hand as he gorged himself on peach pie.

Meg obviously loved her son. Perhaps the boy was at the root of her change. With a son to protect, she would fight for his needs now; when before she was so easygoing he'd had to remind her to ask for what she really wanted rather than constantly allowing other people to make her choices for her.

"Changing course, eh?"

Will opened his eyes to see that Briggs had come to stand beside him.

"Yes. I intend to take Miss Donovan"—how was it that he didn't know whether that was still her name?—"to her family in London. She and I will disembark in Plymouth. You'll replenish our supplies, and then I want you to continue to the search for the smuggler off the coast between Falmouth and Penzance."

Briggs merely raised a brow at this information, and Will continued, "I'm leaving you in command of the *Freedom*, Briggs. I'd appreciate it if you didn't sink her."

Briggs's lips twisted. "If you're worried I'll sink her, perhaps you shouldn't leave me in command."

Will chuckled softly. "I'm not worried. You know I trust you." As a sailor, he trusted Briggs more than anyone. Will could count the number of gentlemen he trusted on one hand, and Briggs was among them—even though his first mate wasn't technically a gentleman.

Briggs was a middle son in a long string of Briggses. A hard worker but entirely ignored by his family, he'd struggled through the ranks of the Navy on his own. After his near-fatal injury in the battle of Gramvousa two years ago, he'd gone home to recover, but his parents had both died since he'd joined the Navy, and he was politely turned away at his brother's door and given the excuse that the house was full.

He'd returned to London, where Will, having just left

the Navy himself, took him in, helped him heal, and hired him into his fledgling shipping company.

Briggs looked out over the gray waves, his face etched in severe lines, his scar wind-reddened. Will couldn't fathom what weighed so heavily on Briggs's mind, but Will himself was still engaged in the battle to refrain from rushing back to Meg.

After a moment, Briggs asked, "How is it that you know Miss Donovan, Captain?"

Will hesitated. It wasn't something he liked to talk about. But Briggs was a trusted friend, and the truth of Meg's identity would be common knowledge soon enough. In any case, it was better that Briggs learned it from him than someone else.

"I intended to marry her eight years ago."

Briggs cut him a look of astonishment. "*That* woman?"

"That very one."

Briggs let out a whistling breath. "What happened?"

"It's a long story," Will warned.

Briggs shrugged. "We've got all night, haven't we?"

They didn't, really. Soon, enough time would have passed that Meg and Jake would have completed their toilette and he could bring them their dinner. He slid a glance toward Briggs.

"Her twin sister is the Countess of Stratford." That would probably confuse the hell out of Briggs, but it would also bring to light the monumental nature of Meg's reappearance into the world.

Briggs was silent for a moment, but Will watched as his lips slowly turned down into a frown. Finally, Briggs said, "I see two impossibilities in that. The first is that, if I recall it right and if the gossip is correct, the Countess of Stratford's twin perished some years ago. Second, isn't the countess's given name Margaret? How is it possible for twin sisters to have the same name?"

"I told you it's a long story."

"Perhaps you should tell it from the beginning, then."

Standing there, with the cold breeze ruffling his hair and the waves slapping against the hull of his ship as it forged toward England, Will told Briggs all of what had happened between himself and the twin sisters whose lives had become inextricably entwined with his own, Meg and Serena Donovan.

Well, he told Briggs *almost* the entire story. He left out those moments—so many of them—that would always be for him and Meg alone.

"Meg and her twin sister came to England eight years ago," he began. "They were raised on a sugar plantation in the West Indies, but their father had died some years earlier, and their mother sent them to London for a Season with the hope they'd find husbands. Meg and I . . . grew very fond of each other."

He hesitated, trying to calm his pounding heart. Even now, speaking of that time made his blood heat and surge through his veins. Taking a deep breath, he continued. "During the same period, Serena made the acquaintance of Stratford. While Meg and I tried desperately to be discreet, Serena and Stratford put little thought into discretion. In the middle of the Season, they were caught in an . . . ah . . . *extremely* compromising position at a ball, and a tremendous scandal ensued."

Briggs frowned. "I'm not part of all that *beau monde* stuff and nonsense, but even I recall that scandal."

Will tightened his fingers over the gunwale. "Serena

and Meg were sent back to Antigua in disgrace. On their journey home, Meg fell overboard and was lost at sea. But since they were perfectly identical and since Serena's reputation was ruined beyond repair, their mother believed that if Serena took on Meg's identity, she might still be able to find a proper husband. Everyone knew of Serena's disgrace, and Mrs. Donovan felt that if Serena didn't become Meg, her future was in true peril."

Briggs's lips parted in shock. "And she agreed? To steal the identity of her twin?"

Will gave a grim nod. "Eventually. She wasn't offered much of a choice. By the time Serena learned about it, her mother had already sent news of 'Serena's' death to England. Serena herself was placed in a thorny situation—if she told the world the truth, she would compromise her family's reputation. However, it was difficult for her to pretend to be Meg, whose personality was very different from her own."

"Damned if she did, damned if she didn't . . ."

"Exactly," Will said. "So she returned to London two years ago, pretending to be Meg. And a few months later, she married the Earl of Stratford."

Will left out the bit about the short time he'd been engaged to Serena, thinking she was Meg. Briggs had already heard about his failed engagement, but he knew Will well enough to know that it was a forbidden subject. Even now, Will had no desire or intention of speaking about that painful time.

Briggs mulled over the story for a few moments. Then his brows climbed toward his hairline. "Does Stratford know her true identity?"

"He does."

"And who else knows, besides you two?"

"Only her sisters. And now you."

Briggs shook his head. "Good God. What a deception."

"It has succeeded thus far, although Meg's reappearance will no doubt complicate matters."

"And yet you intend to take her to London to reunite her with her family."

"I do."

"Where she'll learn that her identity has been stolen by the sister she once admired."

"Undoubtedly." Meg would forgive Serena, surely, once she learned about the impossible position her twin was forced into. Still, an uneasy feeling stirred in Will's gut.

Briggs snorted. "I'd like to see the looks on all those fine lords' and ladies' faces when they discover there are, in fact, two Meg Donovans."

"Ultimately, the matter of identity will work itself out. The point is, she needs to be taken to her family. They need to know she is alive, and I think she needs their help."

"Do you believe this has something to do with the smugglers?"

Will glanced sharply at Briggs, wondering where he intended to go with this train of thought. "I don't know. I hadn't considered it. Why? What are you thinking?"

"Perhaps she's involved somehow."

Will coughed out a laugh. "With the smugglers? I don't think so."

"Why not?"

He gazed at the widening path of wake the *Freedom* left in its trail. "Because," he bit out, "I know her."

"You knew her long ago. People change. What has she

told you about her whereabouts for the past... How long did you say? Eight years?"

"Not much," Will admitted, his voice grim. "Just that she is running away from someone." And she hadn't even openly told him that—he'd inferred it from what he'd seen and heard from her and the boy.

"What is the name of her captor?"

Will didn't answer for a moment, but then he replied, "She hasn't said."

Briggs arched his brows. "Why not?"

Will crossed his arms over his chest and slid his first mate a cold look. "This is not the Inquisition, Briggs. She's guilty of nothing, and I won't treat her as though she is."

Briggs shrugged, then spoke so quietly that Will could hardly hear him over the sound of the waves slapping against the hull. "But how can we be so sure she's guilty of nothing, Captain?"

Will shook his head in absolute denial, but Briggs didn't know when to stop.

"Uncovering the truth seems simple enough. Ask her. If she has nothing to hide, then she should tell you everything. However, if she's in league with the smugglers—"

"Enough," Will growled. There was no way in hell Meg could be in league with rum smugglers. That Briggs would accuse her of such a thing made his blood boil.

For a long moment, he struggled to calm himself. When he'd retained some composure, he spoke in a calm voice. "I am taking her to her family in England. We will help her."

"Perhaps she doesn't want your help," Briggs said.

"I'm helping her if she needs it. Regardless of whether

it's welcome." Will turned his glare on Briggs. "And now this subject is closed."

Briggs gave a grim nod. One of the sailors working on the halyards behind them had been humming, and his song came to an abrupt stop mid-verse. Will turned to glance at the man and saw him staring openmouthed in the direction of the captain's quarters. When Will moved his gaze to his door, he saw the flash of the descending sun on Meg's loose blond curls before his gaze traveled lower.

Holy hell. She was wearing the shirt and trousers he'd given her. The clothes belonged to his cabin boy, a sixteen-year-old stick of a lad, but they didn't make Meg Donovan look like a stick. The fabric clung to the feminine curves of her breasts and hips, sending sensual signals ricocheting through Will's body like wild billiard balls.

As she spun toward him, he caught his breath and took a second to glance around at the men in viewing range of what just might be the most erotic vision any of them had ever experienced.

The man working on the halyards seemed to have sensed Will's dark look and snapped his gaze back to his task. Another man, who'd been oiling the deck lanterns when she'd emerged, was staring at her, mouth agape, oil can dangling from his fingertips. Feeling Will's scorching glare, he cast a guilty glance toward his captain, who had warned all of them earlier to go on about their duties and ignore the lady on board, and then turned—rather hesitantly—away.

Will cursed under his breath. The *Freedom* was no place for a woman. He had to get her off this ship.

Briggs had turned around and was looking at Meg,

too, but his gaze wasn't a lascivious one. Instead, it was filled with dark suspicion.

"If you give the lady anything less than the high level of respect she deserves," Will said in an undertone to his mate, "you will have me to answer to. Do you understand?"

"Aye, Captain." Clasping his hands together behind his back, Briggs walked away.

Meg marched toward Will, alarm blazing in her gray eyes.

"We're heading southeast," she told him.

"Yes, we are."

"Ireland is to the north."

"It is."

"I told you, I must go to Ireland." She licked her lips, a habit Will knew was a product of nervousness, yet he found it wildly erotic, remembering how he'd tasted those very lips so many years ago, how he'd licked and nibbled and sucked... God, he wanted to kiss them again. Right now. He didn't care whether his crew watched—in fact, he wanted them to. Some primitive, feral part of him wanted to mark her with his ownership.

God, he'd loved her for so long. Too damned long. Only in the past year had he begun the difficult process of healing from the pain loving her had wrought upon him.

Shaking off those thoughts, he tried to make sense of what she was saying.

"I thought you had agreed to help us... that you would take us to Ireland before you continued on with your... assignment." She frowned. "Whatever that might be."

"Listen, Miss..." Donovan? Was that still her name? She said she wasn't currently married, but that didn't mean she'd never had a husband. "Er... Mrs...."

"Miss Donovan," she said quietly. "I have never been married."

So the child had been born out of wedlock. As soon as he had that thought, he pushed it from his mind. "Miss Donovan. I am still acquainted with your sisters. They believe that you died years ago, and they have been mourning your loss for a long time. They'll be overjoyed to see you. Whatever trouble you're in, I promise, they'll do whatever possible to help you."

As will I, he vowed silently. He'd failed to keep her safe so many years ago. And even though he didn't know her anymore, even though he didn't have the first idea where she'd been or what she'd been doing for the past eight years, he'd be damned if he'd let her drown again—even if it was only a symbolic drowning.

"My sisters are not in England, sir."

So she believed they were still in Antigua. "Yes, Meg," he said softly, "they are. They are in London for the Season. All four of them."

She bowed her head, her shoulders trembling beneath the thin linen shirt.

Instantly, Will wrapped an arm around her and drew her against him as if she could absorb some warmth from him. "You are cold. Let's go to my quarters, where it's warmer."

She held her ground, though. With a sweep of her hand over her eyes, she looked up at him with a shiny gaze. "No, thank you, Captain. Jake is asleep, and I don't wish to wake him. And I don't wish to move until I have your assurances that you'll leave my family out of this. If you must go to England"—a shudder rippled through her thin frame—"then just deposit me at the nearest port, and Jake and I will find another means to get to Ireland."

Briggs had stopped close by and had been inspecting the halyard the seaman was repairing. Will had no doubt he'd heard the entire conversation.

"Why Ireland?" Will asked her.

"Because my family is there."

"Your family is in *England*."

She pulled away from him. "That part of my family is one I have no wish to disturb. Or involve..." Her voice trailed off.

"Involve with what?" Will asked, the seeds of frustration beginning to take root.

Turning and approaching them, Briggs bowed at Meg. "If you'd like a warmer location to converse," he said, his words and expression so polite that Will could find fault with neither, "please feel free to use my quarters."

Will looked from his first mate to Meg, who had her arms wrapped around her thin body. She'd catch her death out here. His tone was a touch more curt than he intended as he took her by the upper arm. "Come with me, Miss Donovan."

Meg tried not to grimace as Will led her to his officer's cabin. Of course he'd wonder why she wished to go to Ireland instead of to her sisters, especially if her sisters were in London.

When had they gone there? And Serena, too? But after the scandal, their aunt had promised Serena she'd never step foot in England again.

For the first time, Meg wished it hadn't been William Langley who'd found her. As much as she'd wanted to glimpse his face once more in her lifetime, his presence now made everything so much more difficult.

And what could she possibly tell him?

She entered the sparse, tidy space—about a third the size of Will's quarters—and turned around as Will closed the door behind them. She made a show of rubbing her arms briskly. It had been cold outside, and the wind had seemed to slice right through her skin, but that seemed inconsequential compared to her desire to go to Ireland.

"Meg," Will said.

She jerked her head up, unaccustomed to the sound of her proper name coming from a man's mouth.

The lines around that handsome mouth softened, as did his dark eyes. "Please, tell me what happened. Tell me why you don't want to go to your family. Why this desperate urgency to go to Ireland?" His voice was low and gentle. "I've just discovered that you're alive after eight very long years. I keep having to convince myself that you're real, not a ghost. Please help me, Meg. Help me understand how it came to be that I found you in the middle of the Irish Sea."

Meg's knees weakened, and she glanced around the tiny room for a chair. There was one, pushed beneath the table bolted to the far wall under a porthole that lent light to the small space. She took one step to it, then jerked it out and lowered herself into it.

Her shoulders deflated, and when she spoke, her voice was nearly a whisper. She clamped her hands in her lap and stared down at them. "I planned to lie about it." She looked up at him. "I planned an elaborate lie. But I can't lie to you, Will."

He stared at her as the sound of his name filled the cabin. Here they were, after eight years, calling each other by their given names. She'd been so easy with him then. She had been herself with him, open and raw, and most of all, honest. Could it be that easy?

No. She had Jake to think about. His safety. For heaven's sake, Will's safety, too, and that of her sisters.

The temptation to see them again was so strong, like a golden cord pulling on her heart, guiding her across the ocean to London.

For a brief moment, she closed her eyes and imagined her sisters: Serena, her twin and best friend; Olivia, so frail and lovely; Phoebe, witty and sharp; and Jessica, her loyal youngest sister, the most beautiful of them all. She pictured them all dressed in the height of fashion and dancing at glittering balls with handsome gentlemen.

And here she was, thin and dark as a heathen, wearing the trousers and the linen shirt of a cabin boy. Which, in her opinion, was far better than the awful pink frilly dress. She hated it. Not only because it was horribly ostentatious, but because it symbolized Caversham's dominion over her. Jacob Caversham had commanded every bit of her life, right down to her pantalets, for the past eight years.

"If you can't lie to me, then tell me."

Meg opened her eyes to see Will on one knee before her, the anguish in his eyes fathoms deep. Had she done this to him? After all these years, how could he care so much?

She swallowed hard. "I will tell you some. But I can't...I can't tell you everything. It's too dangerous."

Will looked as though he were about to argue with her, but after staring at her face—which she'd set into hard lines because she wasn't going to concede this point—he relented.

"Very well," he said softly. "Tell me what you can."

What I can.

That was precisely the challenge. What, exactly, could she tell him without endangering him further?

The most important thing was to convey that she couldn't be seen in London. She couldn't draw attention to her sisters.

"Someone will be looking for me," she said in a low voice.

"Who? And why?"

She couldn't say who. She *couldn't*. But the why... yes, the why she could answer.

"I fell overboard eight years ago, on my way home from England with my sister Serena."

"I know," Will murmured. "The crew searched for you for hours, but they weren't able to find you. What happened?"

"I was dragged under by the weight of my clothes. I nearly drowned before I was able to get my shoes and cloak off. By the time I rose to the surface, they had traveled some distance away."

"Thank God you knew how to swim," Will said with feeling.

"Yes." She and Serena had often played in the ocean when they were younger. Swimming was not a common skill among people of their class, even among sailors, although she remembered that Will also knew how—long ago, he'd told her that his older brother used to take him swimming in the nearby creek when they were young.

"I called out... but the ship had turned in the wrong direction and was traveling farther away by the minute."

She took a deep breath, remembering her desperation,

how her voice had grown hoarse after she'd screamed and screamed, and the despair she'd felt when the ship had disappeared into the fog.

She'd wanted to live. Her sister had needed her. And she'd been so in love with the man who now knelt before her.

"They didn't hear me," she continued. "The sea was rough, the wind was strong, and the fog was thick. But I knew they would arrive in Antigua that afternoon. I didn't know what else to do but try to swim in that direction. It was unlikely I'd be able to swim that far, yet I had no choice but to try.

"I swam until the sky cleared and the ocean calmed. I was exhausted, but I thought I could see land. It was too far. I knew I couldn't swim that far. And then I saw something bobbing on the surface of the ocean, not far away." She smiled, thinking of the elation she'd felt when she'd seen the rotting piece of wood. "It was a long, heavy log. Using the last of my strength, I swam to it and draped myself over it.

"I think I lost consciousness. The next thing I remember was opening my eyes to a calm dusk. There was a ship bearing down on me. Certain they would rescue me, I called out in my weak voice. But they'd already seen me. They drew alongside me and brought me on board.

"The men were rough, very unlike the friendly sailors on the ship I'd taken from England. I was taken before the captain."

"Who was this captain?"

Here was where things became difficult to describe without revealing too much. She looked Will directly in the eye and didn't answer his question. "He kidnapped me and threatened me with dire consequences should I try to escape. Those threats never subsided. I am finally free of him, but if I went to my sisters now, he'd find us easily, and he wouldn't show mercy to me or my family. I cannot risk their safety. I won't."

Will's face darkened, and his hand pressed over her knee, squeezing with more power than was gentle. "Who is he, Meg?" His voice vibrated with some emotion she didn't dare name.

She shook her head.

"Did he hurt you? Did he... or any of those men... touch you against your will?"

Her face went instantly hot, and she jerked her gaze away from him.

"No," she breathed. "No, it wasn't like that. The captain wouldn't let any of the men touch me or his wife, on pain of death."

Caversham was obsessed with decorum and politesse. Even though he could be violent to the point of madness, nothing was more important to him than the portrayal of himself as a proper English gentleman—no, *more* than a gentleman—as good as, if not better than his half brother, the Marquis of Millbridge. Any of his men touching Meg or Sarah would soil the image, and he wouldn't have that. Though she could hardly forget the leers the men made at her behind Caversham's back, nor the lascivious touches. Not once in eight years had she failed to remember to lock her cabin door at night.

Will gestured in the direction of his quarters. "Then... the boy...?"

"The captain had a young wife, a year younger than me. She was American and baseborn, and beyond anything, he wanted her to be someone he could present as a lady. As soon as he heard me speak, he knew I was educated, and he pressed me for my pedigree, which I— stupidly—revealed to him. He tasked me with turning her into a proper lady. I was her companion for almost eight years…" She hesitated to calm her suddenly roiling emotions. Together, Sarah and Jake had been her lifeline, her saviors, her sanity, her only joys. Without Sarah to love and protect, Meg would have done whatever possible to escape from Caversham years ago.

But now Sarah was gone forever. "She died this past winter," she murmured in a shaky voice.

Will's fingers over her knee squeezed a touch harder. "I'm sorry."

She gave a tremulous nod. The look on his face prompted her to offer more information than she'd planned. "Jake was Sarah's child. But I am his mother now that she is gone."

Will released a slow breath. "And his father is this captain you speak of?"

She nodded.

The muscles in his jaw tightened, but the rest of him remained perfectly still. "Meg." His voice was quiet. "Do you understand that you have no legal right to take a child away from his father? That's considered kidnapping?" He hesitated, then added, "It's a hanging offense."

"I know." Meg would keep her composure; she would not crumble under the weight of the horror dawning in Will's eyes. She'd never wanted to disappoint Will. He was the person she respected above everyone else. "It's one of the reasons I cannot return to England."

When he didn't respond, she continued, "I had to take him away. Jake won't survive with his father. And I won't survive with him, either. We had to escape from his cruelty and violence."

Her voice was hard, with only a slight waver in the words. Caversham's brutality had increased tenfold since Sarah's death. In his warped way, he'd loved Sarah, and she'd kept his sanity in check. Now . . . Meg shuddered.

"Who is he? I'll find him, bring him to justice—"

"No." Meg couldn't even begin to explain how impossible that would be.

Stalemate. She and Will stared at each other.

Finally, he murmured, "Do you miss your sisters, Meg? Because they still grieve for you."

She clasped her hands even more tightly in her lap. Her knuckles had turned white. "I miss them more than anything. But I won't knowingly put them in danger."

"And I can't imagine going to them and telling them that you're alive and that you chose to hide in Ireland rather than go to them for help."

And the truth was obvious: he would, in fact, do just that if she went to Ireland. And, though eight years had passed, she knew her sisters. She knew Serena best of all. Serena would come looking for her. She'd probably lead Caversham right to them.

"Don't . . ." Meg choked. "Please."

"You're alive, Meg. You're sitting in front of me. I can't keep that information from your family. You know I cannot."

Suddenly, the future spread out before her, ice cold and crystal clear.

After eight years living in misery but knowing that at least she was keeping her family safe, she'd failed. In attempting to save Jake, she'd thrown her entire family into peril. Will, too, and there was no way he could truly understand the extent of the danger to him.

She didn't dare to explain it to him. It would endanger him even more.

She let out a low groan and covered her face with her hands.

"Meg?"

"I'm so afraid," she whispered, shutting her eyes tight.

His fingers tightened over her knee again. "You're not alone anymore. Your family is powerful, and they will stand behind you. I'll stand behind you. There's no reason to be afraid."

She let her fingers slide down her face, and she gazed at Will through bleak eyes. He had no idea.

Chapter Four

A few days later, they anchored at Plymouth. Will left the *Freedom* in Briggs's capable hands, but he couldn't resist gazing at his schooner where it sat anchored in the placid bay as he, Meg, and Jake drove away from the dock. He'd hired a carriage to take them to Exeter, where they'd sleep at an inn tonight before continuing on their way to Southampton and then London.

When a row of buildings blocked his view of the ship, he glanced at the woman and boy sitting across from him in the forward-facing seat.

For the past few days, Jake had taken to trailing behind Will as he went about his duties on the *Freedom*. Will had ignored him after the first several times he'd attempted to make conversation only to scare the boy back into his quarters and the safety of Meg.

There was something odd about the boy. Something decidedly different. Will knew he was capable of speech, for he'd heard the child utter a few words to Meg. But as far as Will could tell, he hadn't spoken to anyone else on the ship. He kept to himself, and while those wide blue eyes seemed to take in everything, he was skittish as a colt, and it was clear that he trusted Meg above all others.

It was clear he *loved* Meg.

For her part, Meg had spent most of her time diligently mending her dress so that it would be acceptable to wear in public. She'd done a fine job, but Will still thoroughly disliked the thing. It was inappropriate for her. It wasn't that it was out of fashion—no, it was acceptable enough in that sense. But it didn't seem right for Meg. It was far too ... *pink*. When he thought of clothes for her, he thought of straight lines and elegance rather than lace and frippery.

Will was doing his best to forget their old relationship and treat her as a new acquaintance. It was clear they'd both changed; they were different people now. Still, something about her drew him like a lure, just as it had before. It was something innately Meg, something her twin had never shared with her, something that hadn't disappeared in eight long years.

And his body hadn't forgotten her, either. When she was near, he lived in a perpetual state of arousal. After suppressing the hotter side of his nature for so long, it was disconcerting and embarrassing. He could only hope no one had noticed it, but from Briggs's raised eyebrows in the past few days, he was fairly certain at least one person had.

He didn't think Meg noticed. Most of the time, she studiously attempted to keep her attention on things other than him. He didn't know why, but it made him want to reach out, cup her face in his hands, and make her look at him until he drew her face closer and bent down, and touched his lips to hers.

The carriage rattled over a pothole, jerking Will's attention from the fantasy.

He moved into a more comfortable position, subtly adjusting himself in his seat, praying to God that she didn't lower her gaze. Smiling at them, he said, "You'll see your sisters again soon."

There was little enthusiasm in her tone when she answered. "Yes."

He gazed at her, realizing that she truly had no idea what she was heading into. Since she hadn't known her sisters were in London, her knowledge of them must be extremely limited. She couldn't be aware of her heightened social status due to her sisters' marriages or that Serena had married Stratford.

"How much do you know of your sisters' current situation, Meg?" he asked gently.

She pursed her lips, then said in a clipped voice, "Nothing at all."

Jake tugged on her arm, and she looked down to his questioning gaze. "Do you have a sister, Meg?"

"I have four sisters, Jake. Serena, Phoebe, Olivia, and Jessica. Serena is my twin. She looks just like me. People used to confuse the two of us all the time."

"I didn't," Will said before he thought better of it. Her gaze jerked to him.

"No," she said softly. "You never did."

"Did you know that Serena has married?"

Her eyes widened. "No."

"She married Jonathan Dane."

"*What?*" she gasped.

"Yes. They married last year. He's now the Earl of Stratford, which makes Serena a countess."

"Oh, my," she murmured. "Oh, my goodness." She looked out the window at the passing scenery of the Devonshire countryside. When she turned back to him, she was smiling. "I suppose that means she forgave him, then?"

"She did. Although," he added, chuckling, "it took some spectacular groveling on his part."

"I am so very happy for her—for them. Serena loved Jonathan very much. She was devastated when he cut her and we were sent back to Antigua. I thought she'd never smile again."

"She smiles now," Will said. "Often."

"I'm just glad Serena didn't reject him out of spite, though I imagine she was inclined to."

Again, she looked down at Jake. "My twin sister is married to an earl, Jake. Which means, she's not just Serena anymore. She's *Lady Stratford*." She said the title with reverence, and her smile finally reached her eyes, shining there like polished silver.

Will took another strengthening breath. *Tell her. Tell her now before you're in London and it's too late.*

"Meg, you must know—" He hesitated, not knowing quite how to say this. "Well, you need to know that Serena . . . Well, she no longer goes by that name."

She frowned. "What do you mean?"

Oh, God. This was more difficult than he thought it would be. She was so beautiful, looking at him with that slight crease between her eyes. He wanted to press his thumb to it and make it smooth again. Instead, his news would probably deepen her concern, and that crease.

"She's . . . taken on your name."

She stared at him uncomprehendingly.

"Her name now is Margaret Dane, Lady Stratford."

Meg's expression didn't change. She didn't understand.

"Everyone calls her Meg," he continued. "Even your other sisters."

She shook her head. "I don't—"

"For the past two years," he blurted, "she's pretended to be you."

Meg sucked in a breath, then she wrenched her head to the side for long, silent moments. This time her eyes were vague and unfocused and he knew she wasn't seeing the countryside. He remained quiet, allowing her to process the information, fighting with himself to keep from reaching for her and offering comfort.

Bored with the conversation—or, rather, lack of conversation—Jake turned to his window and began to point at the grazing sheep they were passing, his lips moving as he counted in an undertone.

Will remained still, quiet, sitting straight and stiff as the carriage rolled along beneath him. As much as he hated to be the bearer of this news, there was more that she wouldn't like. So much more, and most of it would make him look like a fool in her eyes. No, more than a fool. A complete ass.

He sighed, resolute and determined, as she turned back to him.

"Why?" she asked, her voice quavering.

Pain radiated in those stormy gray eyes, so sharp and compelling that Will couldn't stop himself from touching her. He leaned forward and gathered her hands in his own, squeezing gently. "She was forced to. She was placed in an impossible situation—told that as Serena, she'd never be able to return to London, never make a good marriage, and worse, none of your sisters would have the opportunity, either."

"My mother told her this," Meg said. It wasn't a question, but Will answered as if it was.

"Yes."

"Where is my mother now?"

"Serena brought all your sisters to London, but your mother has remained in Antigua."

"So Serena...became me." Meg blinked hard.

"Yes."

"So who am I, Will?"

"You're Meg." His answer was automatic, because who else could she be? He squeezed her hands in his own, running his thumbs soothingly over her palms. She had small, delicate hands, but for the first time, he saw the calluses and redness of her skin. The sight of those beautiful hands marred by work made him want to throttle the man—that unnamed captain—who'd done this to her.

"I'm sure London society won't look approvingly on twin sisters with the same name." Her chest rose and fell on a heavy sigh, and she lowered her voice. "This isn't a good idea. Please. Stop this folly, Captain Langley. Stop the carriage and allow me to go to Ireland like I'd planned."

Will glanced at the boy. His head rested against the back cushion, and he was still gazing outside, but his eyes were half closed. He was nearly asleep.

He turned back to Meg. "Call me Will," he murmured. "Like you did before."

She tore her gaze away from him. A blush crept across her cheeks. He wanted to touch her, to kiss away that warmth there. God, she was beautiful. Even more so than she'd been years ago. He'd thought her the most beautiful woman in the world then, but now...He couldn't even pinpoint what it was about her. Everything, from her gold curls and the smattering of freckles across her nose, to her gray eyes and slender but curvaceous form, appealed to him.

He'd grant her anything. Anything but what she'd just requested.

"I'm not stopping this carriage. You need your family, and they need you." He leaned forward, and his voice was firm, filled with the confidence that he wouldn't fail her this time. "I know you're afraid. But I'll protect you. I promise."

She closed her eyes. "You don't understand."

He fought off the annoyance that filled him at those words, and his voice was calm, matter-of-fact, when he said, "That's because you've explained very little to me."

"Please know that that's for your protection. I promise you. Please trust me."

Such anguish glowed in her eyes that his anger drained away instantly. "I do trust you, Meg," he said softly. "The problem is, I don't believe you trust me."

Will was right. She didn't trust him. Through no fault of his own—he was the strongest, most steadfast man she'd ever known. But she'd spent so many years trusting only herself, Jake, and Sarah, that she'd forgotten how to let anyone else in. She'd forgotten how to trust. It wasn't as simple as just opening up to him, either. She just might do that if she didn't have Jake to worry about.

Will cleared his throat, and when she glanced at him, he said, "There's something else..."

The obvious distress in his expression turned her blood cold. "I thought learning that my sister had stolen my identity would be enough for one day."

His brows rose at the cynical tone of her voice. She'd surprised him—the side of her that was a cynic hadn't existed back when he'd known her.

"It can wait," he murmured, "but not for very long. It's best I tell you this before we arrive in London. I'd prefer you hear it from me rather than..." His voice faded, and he glanced at Jake. Meg looked toward the little boy. His head had lolled forward uncomfortably. She plumped one of the carriage pillows on her lap, took Jake into her arms, and laid his head onto it.

The boy shifted, and his eyes fluttered open, but she murmured to him, "Sleep, dearest," and gently combed her fingers through his hair. Soon he drifted off again.

"You care for him," Will observed quietly.

"He is everything to me." Meg looked down at Jake, and love for him surged through her. He was so innocent, despite all the horror he'd experienced in his short life. And while most people thought him an idiot, Meg knew the opposite was true. She hadn't known many children other than her younger sisters years ago, but in many ways his mind was more advanced than other children of his age. Surely few six-year-olds could work the difficult mathematical operations Jake could solve.

She looked back up at Will. "He likes you."

Will shrugged, but his pleasure at her statement was clear in the tipping of his lips and the brightness of his dark eyes as he glanced fondly down at Jake.

"Whatever it is, you should tell me," she said, stroking the silky strands of the boy's hair. "I might as well leap into the lion's den as prepared as I can possibly be."

He flinched subtly at that. "Your sisters and their husbands aren't lions."

"Their husbands?" Meg frowned. "My other sisters have married, too?"

Will nodded gravely. "Phoebe is married to Mr. Sebastian Harper—he was once well known as a rake about town, but she has, much to my surprise, tamed him."

Meg could tell that Will had been involved in their relationship. How close was Will to her sisters, anyhow? Eight years ago, Serena had known him only on the most formal terms.

"And Olivia is married to the Duke of Wakefield."

Jerked from her thoughts, Meg choked on the air she'd been inhaling. "What? Olivia?"

He nodded, and she slumped back in her seat, her fingers stilling in Jake's hair. "Sweet Olivia," she mused. In truth, she'd been afraid to ask about Olivia. After a bout with malaria as a child, Olivia's health had never been strong. And to think she'd married. To think she'd married a duke! "A duke?" she murmured. "Now that is something…"

Will smiled. "It is indeed. They are very happy together, too."

"How long have they been married?"

"Only three months. But they are famous in London." He chuckled. "Your sister's illness has gone public, and contrary to expectation, people have gloried in the romance of it all. It's said theirs is the most romantic society match of the century."

"Really?"

Will nodded.

"And what about Jessica? She's only nineteen. Is she married, too?"

"No, not Jessica. Although your brothers-in-law have been fighting off suitors by the horde."

"Well, that's not a surprise." Jessica was not only the most beautiful, but she also possessed the most outgoing, gregarious nature of all the Donovan sisters. Meg had always predicted that when Jessica came of age, it would be a struggle to keep her free from scandal.

"I'm glad she's not married," Meg murmured. "She's too young."

"You sound like your sisters," Will said. "But no one's worried. No man has struck Jessica's fancy yet."

Meg narrowed her eyes. "You seem very well versed in the goings-on in my family, Captain Langley."

"I am well versed in the lives of all of your sisters."

"How did that come to pass?"

"Well..." He gave her an uncomfortable smile. "It has to do with that bit of news I think you should know." He hesitated, then asked, "Are you certain you want to know? Are you sure it's not too much for one day?"

Meg's body tensed all over. Jake felt it and mumbled in his sleep. She put a comforting hand over him and looked at Will. "Just say it."

Will took a deep breath. "Nothing came of it," he said. "Nevertheless, it's public knowledge and therefore something you should be aware of."

She nodded, hoping he would continue, because she had no idea what he was talking about.

"After you and Serena left London eight years ago, I waited to hear from you for months. I finally received a letter. It was from you."

"But... I didn't send you any letters," she whispered. She'd wanted to. Lord, how she'd wanted to, especially at the beginning, when she'd dreamed nightly of freedom.

Will shook his head. "No. I know that now. It was..."

Mrs. Donovan. Your mother. She was already planning for Serena's future. In the letter, she wrote that your sister, Serena, had been lost at sea." His Adam's apple moved as he swallowed. "Several years later, I sold my commission. I thought you were still alive, Meg. You and I had been communicating for years. I really believed it was you, not your mother..." He clasped his hands tightly together in his lap. "Two years ago, I was ready. I was free of the Navy, wealthy, and finally in a position to—" He stopped abruptly and stared at her with eyes brimming with grief. Each word emerged with clear effort. "I wrote to you and asked you to be my wife."

She simply stared at him, on the verge of being unable to understand. How could it be? She'd always dreamed of marrying him. He'd as much as promised marriage during their liaison, but they'd both known it would be years before he would be in a position to marry. She'd been willing to wait.

He'd finally proposed to her. And yet, he hadn't really proposed to her. He'd proposed to her *mother*, pretending to be her.

Nausea twisted in her gut. "Oh, God."

"You answered my letter, saying yes, you wished to marry me, that..." He bowed his head. "...that nothing would make you happier. Six months later, you arrived in England."

"But I didn't..."

"You didn't. Serena did."

"Oh, God," she repeated, her voice a raw whisper. "And Serena was pretending to be me." Misery rushed through her, a flash flood of bitterness. "You were engaged to my sister, then. But you didn't end up marrying her. Did anything...? Did you...? How...?"

"I knew right away that something wasn't right, and Serena felt extreme guilt about her deception. She finally told me the truth, and we called off the engagement, which sparked a tremendous scandal. Her subsequent marriage to Stratford added fuel to its fire."

All these years, she'd wished for nothing but the best for her four sisters. But now Meg was furious. She was a forgiving person, but to hear in the course of a few moments that Serena had taken everything that was hers... her identity, the man she loved...

She glanced at Will and then away. He wasn't the man she loved any more than she was the woman he loved. That had been long ago.

In any case, Serena hadn't married him.

"How long did the engagement last?"

"About two months."

There was that, at least. Meg couldn't even begin to think of how it would have affected her if Serena and Will had actually married.

She took a shaky breath. "I'm glad you didn't marry her."

"So am I, Meg. We would have both been miserable. Stratford is the only man for her. And you..." He broke off.

How had he intended to finish that sentence? *You're the only woman for me?* But was she? Neither of them could know anymore. She wasn't the same Meg who'd loved him so long ago.

But she remembered him. Her body remembered him. He sat on the squabs, his bearing straight, so tall his head nearly brushed the ceiling. His hair matched his eyes—dark as chocolate but highlighted with streaks of amber. His face was narrow but masculine, with sculpted cheekbones and a straight nose. She liked his eyes the best, though. Those amber-tinged eyes had always melted her all the way through to her heart.

"All of it is past," he said. "Years ago, after you and Serena left London, Stratford and I became good friends. None of that has changed, and I've had the honor of befriending all of your sisters as well."

"I see," she murmured. Despite the vast distances separating them, she'd never felt so separate from the Donovans—and even from Will—in the past eight years as she did right now. With a sudden pang of longing, she missed Sarah. Sarah had been her confidante, her best friend. Her *sister*.

Her real sisters were strangers to her now. They seemed like a distant dream, unreal and unattainable. And Serena, her twin and once the closest person in the world to her, had stolen the essence of who she had once been.

How could Meg face her now?

Chapter Five

That night, they stayed at an inn at Exeter. Meg's nerves were taut and bristling. The day after tomorrow, she'd be in London. She'd see her sisters. Soon, Caversham would discover her whereabouts ... and then ...

She needed to find a way to ensure Will and her family's safety, as well as Jake's. But try as she might, she couldn't think of one.

Perhaps she should have run away from Will when she'd had the chance. But with him so close, she couldn't think in the ruthless way she'd learned from Caversham. It was difficult to contemplate running from Will, the man she'd wanted to run *to* for so long.

They secured two rooms—one for Meg and Jake and another for Will. Jake had been quiet and well behaved. She hadn't quite known what to expect from him—he wasn't used to long carriage rides through green countrysides, but he'd surprised her with his relative calm. She supposed she shouldn't have been surprised. Until now, Jake had lived a life of unpredictability—he, as well as his mother and Meg, had never remained in one place for more than a few months at a time. Always, Caversham would take them somewhere new—somewhere they wouldn't be found.

She lay beside Jake now on the inn's narrow bed, stroking his back and humming low, as she did every night.

"Meg?"

"Hm?"

"I miss Mama."

She sighed. "I know, darling. So do I."

Poor, sweet Sarah. She was a fisherman's daughter from Maine. Utterly beautiful, with raven-dark hair and obsidian eyes but skin as pale as ivory. Mesmerized by her beauty, Caversham had asked her father for her hand in marriage. When the man—a fair judge of character—had refused to give his approval, Caversham had kidnapped her by force. No one said no to Caversham and got away with it. Meg had learned that lesson quickly.

Caversham had found an ordained minister who, when presented with enough money, had agreed to marry him to Sarah. When Caversham had discovered Meg floating in the ocean a year later, Sarah was seventeen, just a bit younger than Meg. But there was an enormous difference between the two young women. Despite her innate beauty, Sarah was a rough country girl who'd had little schooling and was nearly illiterate. Meg, though circumstances had forced her family into genteel poverty, was an English lady. Her grandfather had been a viscount, her aunt was a countess, and her mother had ensured her daughters were raised to be proper young debutantes.

When she'd recovered from her ordeal at sea, Meg had begged Caversham to return her home to Antigua. But as soon as she opened her mouth and the cultured English accent emerged, an idea had formed in Caversham's head.

He'd wanted a lady wife, but no real English lady would ever have him. He dreamed of bringing Sarah back to England and parading her about like a prize. She was beautiful, that was true. But the moment she opened her mouth, her rough American drawl would give her away as what she truly was—a nobody.

So he assigned Meg the task of turning his wife into a proper lady. She was to educate Sarah and instruct her on the etiquette of London society.

Sarah tried, but she'd never understood the point of Meg's teachings. It wasn't natural for her to curtsy or titter like a well-bred English girl, and her forthright American nature would forever set her apart from the *ton*.

"You won't leave me like Mama did, will you, Meg?" Jake asked, yanking Meg out of her memories.

Meg slipped her arm around the boy's thin waist. "Your mama didn't want to leave you, Jake. She was sick and she died. She wanted nothing more than to be with you until you were big and strong and could take care of yourself, but God decided to take her early. Only He knows why."

Jake didn't seem convinced. "I don't think she wanted to take care of me. Not like you do."

Meg flinched. There was some truth to his words. Sarah had spent the last years of her life in a haze of pain and fear. While Jake's birth had given Meg a reason to fight and be strong against Caversham, it had seemed to deplete Sarah. When Jake was a toddler, she'd become thin and sallow, and days went by in which she didn't get out of bed. When she finally died—of unhappiness even more so than the fever, Meg thought—she was just a shell of the girl she once was.

"Remember how I told you that different people love in different ways?" she said to Jake. "Well, that's the way it was with your mama. She showed you love every time she smiled at you. Don't you remember?"

Meg did. Sarah had the widest, most beautiful smile of anyone she'd ever known.

"Yes." Jake snuggled closer to her. "But I like the way you love me better."

She kissed the back of his head but didn't respond. She understood, but it made her uncomfortable that Jake favored her over his own mother. She supposed it was common among children who spent the majority of time with particular caregivers rather than their natural parents, but she wished it was different. She wished Jake had been able to heal Sarah like he'd healed her. She wished Jake could have known the true nature of his mother, of her sweetness and kindness, of how she'd kept Meg sane in the early days.

But that would never be. Not now.

She held him until he slept, taking deep, peaceful breaths beside her, and then she eased out of the bed and sat by the window, gazing down over the street below. It was not yet nine o'clock in the evening, and there were still a few pedestrians and dusty carriages making their way down the cobbled street.

She needed a plan. In London, in the public eye, with her twin having the same name she did—

She bowed her head, resting her forehead against the cool glass. Serena would be in grave danger. God, what was she going to do?

If Caversham...or his brother...came across Serena, she would certainly introduce herself as the Countess of Stratford, not Meg, and so much time had passed that Meg and Serena probably weren't as identical as they'd once been.

Beyond separating herself physically from Serena, there wasn't much Meg could do. By showing her face in London she would be plunging everyone she cared about into peril.

Meg chewed on her lower lip. The best thing she could do was keep her reappearance as secret as possible. Maybe she could mislead him somehow—make Caversham think she'd escaped elsewhere. Or that she'd been lost in the storm. After all, the poor little jolly boat had barely made it through.

A soft knock sounded at the door. Rising, she hurried through the small parlor area and answered it, not wanting to awaken Jake.

Will stood at the threshold. She looked at him, one eyebrow raised, and he gave her a rueful smile.

"I was worried about Jake. Did he settle in well?"

It warmed her that he cared for the boy's welfare. He had seemed to from the beginning.

Her gaze wandered up his tall, strong frame, scanning the narrow hips and the way his waistcoat hugged his broad shoulders, until she met his dark eyes. A shudder started at the base of her spine, rushing upward in a warm flush.

The way he looked at her—it had always heated her. That hadn't changed.

"He's settled in just fine," she replied.

"He's adaptable, that one."

She smiled, glancing over her shoulder at Jake. In the dim light, he was a small lump beneath the blankets. "He is."

"Well . . . I just wanted to check—"

"Stay." The word popped out before she had time to think about it. Her voice was breathless. She gave a shaky laugh. "Just for a few moments. It's early yet, and I'm not tired."

"Neither am I." He stepped inside, his movements tentative, and she shut the door behind him, then walked a few steps to close the door leading to the bedroom, leaving it slightly ajar so she could hear Jake if he awoke.

She turned back to Will. "Please sit down." She gestured to the chaise longue pushed against the wall beside the tall window. The room was too small to allow anything more than that one piece of furniture.

He lowered himself onto the striped chintz and then gestured for her to sit beside him.

Her heart began to pound. For the past few days, she'd kept her distance from him for a reason. She was afraid of getting too close, of remembering, of being confused by all those old feelings.

"Sit." The word was a soft command, and memories flooded through her. Will was kind, fair, and generous. A gentleman through and through, but he had been an officer in the Navy, and he knew how to command men.

Meg lowered herself beside him. The chaise was small, and their thighs brushed. Such a subtle touch, but it resonated through her. It had been so long since she'd sat next to a man . . . and this man . . . the only man she'd ever loved . . . She almost felt dizzy from the reality of it.

After a moment of silence, she said, "I've been

wondering why you left the Navy," struggling to keep her voice—and her emotions—steady.

He stared at her for a second and then tore his gaze away to look at the large, dusty portrait of a nondescript countryside on the wall in front of them. "I wish I'd brought us a drink," he murmured, "but I didn't..."

She began to rise. "Oh, I'm sorry. You're thirsty. I didn't think—"

He laid his hand on her thigh, lightly pushing her back into the cushion. "No, Meg," he said quietly. "It's just... Well—" He pushed his fingers roughly through his hair, then squeezed the back of his neck. "Well, the reasoning behind everything I've done for the past eight years makes me appear to be such a damned fool."

"A fool?" she asked, confused. "You're not a fool."

Will grimaced. "I sold my commission because I wanted to give you a stable home after we married. I didn't want to marry you and then be apart from you three-quarters of the time."

Perhaps he hadn't changed so very much. He'd told her something similar eight years ago.

"So I quit the Navy and bought a shipping business in London," he finished.

"How does that make you sound like a fool?" On the contrary, it confirmed some of the traits she'd always admired about him. She'd met many gentlemen during that short Season she'd spent in London with Serena. Most of them looked to be searching for a wife to stick in some country house and bear their children while they went on their merry way, taking mistresses, carousing, and traveling without the company of their lonely, home-bound wives.

She'd never wanted that kind of a husband. She wanted a partner. A friend. A lover. Someone who'd remain by her side through everything. Will would have been that man.

"It makes me sound like a fool," he said, "because I was never going to marry you. I spent six years planning for an impossible future." His lips twisted in self-recrimination. "The world sees me as the man who wasted years of his life waiting and planning for the woman—the marriage—that would never be."

"I don't see you that way," she said softly. "I see you as noble. I wish…" She broke off, took a deep breath, and continued. "I wish that I had been there. I… would have waited for you. If I was in Antigua, it would have been me making those plans with you. Not my mother." Her voice cracked on the last word. She'd never, ever forgive Mother for what she'd done to Will. *Ever.*

"How is it possible that no one knew you were alive for all that time?"

She clasped her hands together tight in her lap. "I attempted to communicate with you, and with my family. I missed all of you so much. I wanted my old life back so badly." She closed her eyes. "I ran away once, a month after Cav—after he'd plucked me out of the ocean. We were in Haiti, and I thought if I could just get to Port-au-Prince, I might find someone to help me."

"What happened?"

"He found me," she said simply. But it hadn't been so simple. He'd stripped off her drawers and whipped her until she'd bled. Then he'd thrown her into the room she shared with Sarah, and Sarah had nursed her wounds. She swallowed. "There were a few more attempts in the months after that, but I never got as far as I did the first time."

His hand covered hers. "I'm sorry, Meg." Gently, he squeezed her fingers. "If I knew his name, I could send people after him. We'd find him, and we'd—"

"No," she said, interrupting him. "It's not that easy. He has too many connections. He knows too many powerful people."

"I wish you'd let me be the judge of that."

She shook her head stubbornly.

Will sighed, relenting for now. "Did you give up in your attempts to run away?"

"Eventually. I knew it would be no use. And Sarah didn't have the strength to run. She needed me, especially after Jake was born. And Jake needed me, too."

"You were a prisoner, and you were trapped."

"Exactly."

"What finally convinced you to try to escape again?"

"After Sarah died, he grew...worse." She took a moment to find her breath. "He'd kidnapped her and forced her to marry him, but he loved her in his own way. Her death snapped the final string of his humanity. After that, I truly feared for myself and Jake. Especially Jake." Wrapping her arms around herself, she shuddered. "And then, two years ago, he began a smuggling scheme between the West Indies, Ireland, and England. Between his increasing violence and our proximity to home, I couldn't resist the opportunity."

Will stiffened beside her. "You say he was a smuggler?"

"A smuggler and a pirate," she admitted, the misery thick in her voice.

Will studied her, as if by staring hard at her he could somehow delve within her and absorb the answers he sought. "The *Freedom*'s mission was to capture a smuggler who's been running rum into Cornwall this time of year for the past two years."

Meg looked away. She couldn't tell him she was glad he hadn't found Caversham. He wouldn't understand. "No one told me that was why you were at sea," she said softly. "I've kept you from your duties."

His hand, which still lay over her clasped ones, tightened, and his other hand moved up to cup her cheek, gently turning her head to face him. "It's not important. Compared to returning you to your family, it's nothing. In any case, Briggs will pull anchor tomorrow. He'll head back to Cornwall to patrol the coast."

She hoped Mr. Briggs didn't find Caversham. Caversham would crush the man under his boot heel.

She'd seen it done. Caversham's ships were vessels of war, first and foremost. She'd heard the boom of cannons and seen fiery ships slip below the ocean's surface. She would never forget the screams of dying sailors.

He'd always locked her, Sarah, and Jake in their quarters when they were pirating. In his arrogant way, he had assured them they'd be safest there, that his own ship was not in danger. And it never had been.

She'd often gazed out the porthole at his victims, half hoping they would capture Caversham's ship, even sink it. But no one had ever boarded one of Caversham's vessels unless he was specifically invited by its captain—or captured.

"Look at me," Will said. There it was again—that soft command.

She realized her eyelids had slipped shut. She forced them to open.

His hand was soothing and warm on her cheek, and

it didn't move as he gazed deep into her eyes. "I know you've been taught to fear this man. I know eight years with him has made you distrustful and afraid. But you must remember, he's only a man. Just like the rest of us, he cannot be infallible. You must trust me. Trust that I will help you, and trust that I will keep you safe."

She stared at him, unable to answer, unable to fathom how he could be so certain in his desire to help her. But then, he'd always been that way. Noble to a fault.

"Please, Meg."

"But he's not just a man. He has...allies..."

He drew her closer. So close that his breath whispered over her lips as he said, "I'm not going to let him hurt you—or Jake—ever again."

And then he moved closer, and closer still, until his lips brushed against hers. The contact was electric, sending a jolt through her, bringing every single nerve ending in her body alive.

It seemed to travel through him, too, because she felt him shudder. Then it was no longer a mere touch of lips. With a soft groan, he surrendered to it, opening to her, kissing her deeply, thoroughly. His hand slipped from her cheek behind her neck, bringing her into it with him, into a give and take that made her whole body reawaken and yearn for the touch it had once known. *His* touch.

She slipped her arms behind his back. His muscles rippled beneath her hands. He tasted like salt and the sea, and like Will. His taste—sweet, musky, and all male—was something she'd never forget.

Gently, he drew back, his breaths harsh in the quiet of the room, and touched his forehead to hers. "I still want you, Meg." His voice was low and infused with wonder.

"After all these years, after all that has happened, I still want you."

God, she wanted him, too. But she drew back, remembering Jake in the next room, her cheeks flooding with hot shame. She closed her teeth over her lower lip, then took a deep breath. "I must think of Jake. He comes first."

Will flexed his hands, then looked away from her.

"Please understand. I'll do anything—*anything*—to prevent Jake's father from taking him away from me."

His chest rose and fell as he inhaled a deep breath. "I understand. If Jake's safety is important to you, it's important to me. We'll keep him safe. Together."

The next day consisted of more long hours of travel. That night, they slept in a hotel at Southampton, and the following morning, the three of them were breakfasting when a loud screech assaulted Will's ears. He plunked down his coffee cup to see a large, round woman bearing down on their table, her focus on Meg. She was clothed in an orange dress, which made her look rather like the citrus fruit.

She blustered to a halt, her voluminous skirts swirling, and bent down until she was almost nose to nose with Meg before straightening again.

"Why, Lady Stratford, it *is* you! I mightn't have recognized you in that dress, but I'd know your face anywhere. I told Mildred, 'Look, there is Lady Stratford,' and she said, 'Of course it is not. Lady Stratford doesn't wear pink, or…'" Here the woman hesitated, then glanced at Jake and quickly covered with, "'…have a child.' But I said, 'Yes, indeed, Mildred, it is Lady Stratford, and I shall prove it.'"

"You were right, Barbara." A shorter, thinner lady

wearing spectacles came up behind the woman. She inclined her head toward the table. "Good morning, Meg."

Oh, hell. These women were friends of Serena's. The thin woman's gaze rested on Jake for a second and then moved to Will. Fortunately he didn't know either woman. Maybe he could get them out of this.

The large woman clapped her hands to her voluminous bosom, making it jiggle. "What on *earth* are you doing in Southampton, my lady? Why, you just arrived in London two weeks ago, and you told me you planned to stay for the duration of the Season!"

The lady paused, waiting for Meg to respond. Meg gazed up at her, blank eyed, pale faced, and speechless, her lips parted in shock.

Patting his napkin to his lips, Will rose. "I'm so very sorry, ma'am, but I'm afraid we've no idea who you're talking about. We're not acquainted with any Meg or Lady Stratford." He glanced outside and found their carriage parked at the curb waiting, thank God. He bowed toward the ladies. "Now if you'll excuse us, our carriage awaits, and we must hurry away if we want to be in London before dark. Come along, lad."

He bustled Jake and Meg out of the hotel, leaving their breakfasts half eaten and the two ladies standing in place, gawping after them like a pair of hungry goldfish.

Chapter Six

At dusk, the carriage pulled in front of a tidy house in St. James's Square. Meg didn't move—she just stared bleakly out the carriage window. "I know this place."

Will hadn't taken his eyes off her since they'd stopped. "Yes," he said softly.

She tightened her fingers around Jake's hand. They'd stopped not directly in front of, but very near to Meg's aunt Geraldine's house. Aunt Geraldine was the one who'd forced Meg and Serena to leave London in disgrace. She'd said Serena was a slut, an embarrassment to the family, and she never wanted to see either of the twins again. She'd effectively shoved them onto the first ship back to Antigua.

"I'm not taking you to your aunt's house," Will reminded her gently. "Stratford lives next door. It was his father's house once, but it's his now."

"Of course." Meg tried to smile, but it emerged as a pathetic quiver of her lips.

Will stepped out of the carriage, lifted Jake and set him onto the pavement, and then handed her down. The three of them hesitated before the steps leading toward the front door, Meg renewing her tight grip on Jake's hand.

Finally, Will looked down at her. "Are you ready for this?"

She didn't look at him. Staring at the house's large front door, she nodded. "Yes."

It was a lie. She hadn't seen her sisters in eight years. They'd thought she was dead for all that time.

She'd never be ready for this moment, no matter how long she took to prepare for it. And it wasn't any comfort to her to reflect on the fact that they were even less prepared for the reunion than she was.

"Let's go, then," Will said.

He led them to the front door, where he raised the knocker and let it fall. She heard the boom of it reverberating inside.

"Ow!" Jake complained, trying to wiggle from her grip.

"Oh, Jake, I'm sorry," she breathed. Her fingers had wrapped around his in a tight squeeze. Forcibly, she relaxed her hand. "Is that better?"

He didn't have time to answer. The door swung open. A red-haired man dressed in fine livery stood before them. "Captain Langley!" he exclaimed. "Welcome home."

His gaze moved to Meg and he froze, then blinked. "My lady?" He glanced back into the house as if Meg had disappeared from some location inside and then magically reappeared before him.

She flinched. First the incident in the hotel this morning, and now this. Perhaps she still looked as identical to Serena as she once had.

The servant's gaze moved to Jake, then Meg's hand clasping Jake's, and his confusion deepened. "Uhm...?"

"Your master and mistress will explain it all to you later, Patrick. For now, will you let them know that I am here? With... a surprise for them."

The man's blue eyes went wide, but he managed to maintain his composure. "They're at dinner, but they always welcome a visit from you, Captain. Please do come in."

He held open the door, and the three of them stepped into an elegantly tiled entry hall. On the wall in front of them was a recent portrait. Meg stared at the likeness, recognizing it right away. It was a painting of Serena and the earl gazing at each other, looking very much in love.

Serena did still look just like her, if the artist's rendition was accurate. Meg swallowed down the hard lump forming in her throat, and Jake started wiggling again. "Sorry, darling," she murmured. "Sorry."

He'd be fine—better, probably—if she let him go. But she couldn't.

"Are you all right?" Will murmured.

She jerked her head to him. "I don't know," she managed.

He drew in a breath and said in an undertone, "I know this is difficult. But it's a happy moment. Your appearance tonight is going to bring great joy to your sisters, especially Serena. I promise you."

She wanted to ask how that was possible. Serena had taken Meg's identity, and now Meg had come back to reclaim it. Wouldn't her reappearance ruin everything? If nothing else, it would surely throw Serena's elegant countess's life into chaos. How could that possibly make her happy?

She didn't have time to ask Will, however, because the butler returned with three people following him.

Jessica was first. She'd been lovely at eleven years old, but now she was absolutely exquisite. Despite the fact that the little girl had turned into a woman—a beauty—Meg would have recognized her anywhere. She'd never forget the spark of mischief and the dash of stubbornness in those blue eyes. Meg stood absolutely still, gazing at her youngest sister, only mildly aware of the comforting presence of Will on one side of her and Jake on the other.

Jessica was curvaceous but with no extra fat, with a perfect oval face and big, deep blue eyes fringed by dark lashes. Her hair had just a hint of red in it, but it was more brilliantly blond than red, piled in loose curls of shining gold with a dash of copper.

She stepped into the entry hall and stopped short as her gaze fell on Meg, her mouth falling open.

Serena jerked to a stop just behind Jessica, yanking Meg's attention to her.

It was true. They still looked the same. Serena probably weighed half a stone more than her, and her skin was a touch paler, but no doubt people would have just as much difficulty telling them apart as they always had.

Pressure built in her lungs, and Meg realized she'd forgotten to breathe. She let out a slow, trembling breath as she stared at her twin, Serena's chest fell at the exact same time. A man's hands—they must be the Earl of Stratford's, but Meg didn't look at him—settled comfortingly over Serena's shoulders.

Everything seemed frozen, locked in a stare of surprise, a moment of dreamy disbelief.

Will finally spoke, his voice seeming loud in the

uncanny silence. "I found her and the boy in a disabled jolly boat halfway between England and Ireland."

Serena's eyes flicked to Jake, but in a flash they were on Meg again. She blinked once, then blinked harder, as if she expected the vision of her sister to clear. And then she cried out, "Meg!"

She ran to Meg, nearly toppling her before wrapping her in her arms and bursting into tears.

Another person's arms were around her, Jessica's, Meg thought, and the tears welled in her throat and she was crying, too.

Dinner forgotten, they gathered in Jonathan's enormous drawing room. Jonathan and Captain Langley sat in opposing armchairs while Jessica and Serena took the sofa with Meg between them and the little boy sitting on her lap, gazing at Serena with a fascinated expression.

Jessica stared at her older sister. She'd been so young when they'd lost Meg, and her memories of her older sister had begun to fade, but now they came rushing back to her in a torrent. When she was very little, it was always Meg who'd comforted her when she scraped her knee or had a bad dream. It was always Meg who'd told her she was smart and capable after Mother had yelled at her for being a hoyden.

Jessica wiped a stray tear and laughed. "The three of us have turned into watering pots. We could keep Sherwood Forest green!"

"No doubt," Serena said shakily. She blew her nose again.

Jessica couldn't even begin to imagine what Serena was feeling right now. She'd never stopped mourning

Meg. Not for one second since Meg had fallen overboard off that ship so long ago.

Meg wrapped her arms around the little boy, looking happy but mildly uncomfortable. Jessica supposed she couldn't blame her. All this was so overwhelming—for all of them.

"Captured by a pirate," Jessica mused out loud. Captain Langley had just finished a brief retelling of where Meg had been all these years. "It sounds terribly romantic, but I imagine it must have been awful for you."

"At times," Meg said. Each time she spoke, her gentle voice brought back more memories. She'd always been good at soothing people—and animals, too. She and Serena had kept Father's stables clean and the animals happy, even as they were sold off one by one. Jessica remembered running between their legs in the stables, jumping on hay bales, daring them to catch her.

They'd laughed back then. Far more than they'd laughed after Serena had returned—alone—from England.

"Sometimes it wasn't so bad," Meg said. "I had a friend. Her name was Sarah, and she was Jake's mama."

Jessica glanced at Serena, then at Jonathan, wondering if they'd thought what she had—that the little boy was Meg's. If they did, they showed no sign of it.

"His mama is gone, so I am his mama now," Meg said.

Finally, the child turned his gaze from Serena to Meg. "You're not Mama. You're Meg."

"Of course you're correct, Jake darling. But now that your mama is no longer here to care for you, it's my job. You needn't call me mama, though. You can call me Meg forever, if you like."

"I'd like," Jake said. Apparently finished with that conversation, he fixed his attention on Serena again.

The child was a bit on the odd side, Jessica decided.

"What is the pirate's name?" Jonathan asked. "We'll find him. Langley has the ships and I have the resources. We'll prosecute him to the full extent of the law."

Meg didn't respond. She simply looked down at Jake, shaking her head.

"She won't reveal his name," Captain Langley explained. "She feels it's too dangerous."

"Of course." Serena squeezed Meg's hand, then awkwardly drew away when Meg showed no response. "None of us can possibly comprehend how afraid you must be of that awful man."

At that, Meg looked up, her gray eyes shining. "I'm so happy for you, Serena. So happy. I never believed you'd love anyone like you loved Jonathan Dane." She smiled at Jonathan. "And thank you for coming to your senses, even after too many years had passed, and marrying my sister. I know you never really believed she was below you. That was your father putting you in an untenable position."

"That it was," Jonathan said softly. "When I thought Serena had died I could never forgive him...or myself. The way I'd behaved toward her was inexcusable."

Serena gave a dismissive wave of her hand. "All that's in the past. All that matters is that we're together now, and I thought nothing could be better...until today. Oh, Meg"—and *she* was crying again—"I'm so glad you've come back to us."

Jessica was certain that in the history of the world, there had never been a tearful reunion quite like this one.

"The goal now," Captain Langley said, "is to keep the boy and Miss Donovan safe."

"Oh, surely you cannot still be in danger," Jessica exclaimed. "You're safe here with us now."

Meg grimaced.

"She is in grave danger," the captain said, his voice grim. "The pirate will undoubtedly want his son back."

The boy made a strange, choking sound and clung to Meg, who wrapped her arms around him and tucked his head under her chin. "Don't worry," she said, speaking to him in a soothing tone. "I'll never let him touch you, Jake. Never again."

She flashed a warning look at Captain Langley, and he abandoned the subject, instead looking to Jonathan. "For now, it's important that no one discovers they're here. We need to devise a plan to keep her—both of them—safe."

For the next fortnight, Meg remained within the shelter of her brother-in-law's house in St. James's Square. She had no intention of going outside—not until she devised a solution to her dilemma. If she left the house, one of two things could happen. The first, and less worrisome, possibility was that people might mistake her for Serena. She was less adept than her sister at pretending to be someone she was not. Meg simply couldn't pretend to be Serena. As a countess married to the man she adored, Serena had become a mature, confident woman, and she glowed with happiness. Meg was only being honest with herself when she gazed into the looking glass and saw a frightened mouse there. The years with Jacob Caversham hadn't been kind to her confidence.

Second, someone might recognize her as Lady Stratford's—"Meg's"—dead twin sister. Which would be inevitable if Meg and Serena went out and about together. But Serena was a popular, fashionable lady about Town now, and knowledge that Meg hadn't drowned would inevitably create gossip. If that happened, Caversham or his brother, the Marquis of Millbridge, would find her post haste, she'd be thrown into prison for kidnapping, and Jake would be back in his father's clutches.

So she couldn't go outside. She couldn't step past the doors of the Earl of Stratford's opulent townhome. She often sat, as she did this morning, on one of the silk-upholstered chairs clustered between the majestic Ionic columns that flanked the drawing room window. From here, she could watch the bustle of the square beyond through the crack in the curtains.

She'd loved London on her last visit. It was so vast, so endlessly marvelous after a quiet childhood on a small, sparsely populated island. There was so much to see and do. And the people—so many of them, of all shapes and sizes, of all colors and social statuses.

But now, all she could do was look out the window and watch them.

Beside her, Jake sat on his heels on the carpet, examining the torn-up pieces of paper scattered around him. Jake's new obsession, now that he couldn't follow Will around all day, was puzzles. Using the earl's pen and ink, Meg would draw a picture of a house or countryside on a sheet of parchment, then tear it up into tiny pieces. Jake would spend hours putting the puzzle together, mixing the pieces up, and putting them together again.

Outside, three young women walked by, their heads close together, laughing at something one of them had said.

Meg had spent a great deal of time trying to reacquaint herself with her sisters. Will came every day and sat with her as she did so. Olivia and Phoebe, whom she'd reunited with the morning after she'd arrived in London, made daily visits from the Duke of Wakefield's house to see her.

In the afternoons, they'd all sit in the drawing room with her, talk to her, reminisce with her. It seemed to Meg that they were unconsciously trying to form her into the dear sister they'd once known. All their effort only served to remind her that she wasn't that person anymore. She still loved them. She was glad that they were happy here in London, with their newfound status and riches. But the past years had formed her into a different being. Serena, Olivia, Phoebe, and Jessica were obviously sisters, of one mind and spirit, and Meg stood apart, the proverbial black sheep.

In a way, being with them was worse than dreaming about them, remembering them. Now, in their presence, she realized that at some point in the past several years, the connection between her and them had been severed. She wasn't a true Donovan. Not anymore.

Suddenly, Jessica burst into the room. "There you are!"

Meg smiled up at her sister. "Good morning."

Jessica gave Jake a friendly smile, but he didn't pay her any attention. Sighing, Jessica plumped down on the chair beside Meg's. "What do you think, Meg?"

"About what?"

"Well, Lord Marsden has asked me to walk with him today. Serena is insisting that she come along. I think that's absurd."

"Why?"

Jessica huffed out a sigh. "For goodness' sake. I'm not some virginal maiden in need of protecting. I'm nineteen years old!"

Meg raised a brow. "You're not a maiden? You're not virginal? Is that what you're saying?"

Jessica had the presence of mind to blush at that. Then she scowled. "I wish I wasn't." She looked directly into Meg's eyes. "Virginity is a pest a lady is best rid of as soon as possible, don't you think?"

Meg stared at her sister. Then she simply shrugged and looked down at Jake, who'd ignored the entire conversation. He was busy mixing up the pieces of the puzzle for the hundredth time.

Jessica gave a low chuckle. "That would have truly scandalized the old Meg."

The old Meg. Her sisters often talked about "the old Meg" and how her demeanor had changed so much from that perfect, idealized young lady.

"Would it?" Meg murmured. "You were only eleven years old the last time you saw me. How could you remember how the old Meg would have reacted to such a statement?"

"Because I scandalized you all the time then. Don't you remember?"

Meg frowned. "No." In truth, she hardly remembered anything of that Meg. Except that she had possessed so many romantic notions and dreams. She had known so much less about the world than she did now.

"Well, it doesn't matter," Jessica said. "But honestly. What does Serena think I'm going to do? Lie with Lord Marsden in the middle of Hyde Park? Goodness, I don't even like him very much. I doubt I'd let him kiss me."

"Why not?" Meg asked, bemused.

"His nose is too long. And he's thirty-one. Far too old." She gave a mock shudder.

"I see," Meg said gravely.

Jessica's blue eyes suddenly widened. "I've a brilliant idea! Why don't you come with me instead of Serena? You can walk far behind us, and we'll hardly know you're there. You'll be far less bothersome than Serena, I know it."

"I don't think so," Meg said.

Jessica's lips turned down in a little pout. Good Lord, but her youngest sister was lovely. And she knew it, Meg thought, watching the sparkle in those intelligent eyes. She knew how to manipulate with her expressions and her looks. But it wouldn't work with Meg—at least not when it came to her going out among people and the risks that would entail.

"I can't leave the house, Jessica," she said. "You know that. It's too dangerous."

"Pfft. You can't stay imprisoned in this house forever."

That was true enough. A plan was forming in Meg's mind... It wasn't ideal, but it was the only one she had. The only thing that might protect all of her loved ones.

She'd talk to Serena and the earl about it. Tonight at dinner, perhaps.

The thought of it—of leaving her family *again*, and this time voluntarily—made a hard lump form in her throat.

She glanced meaningfully at Jake. All her sisters knew that she'd taken Jake illegally. Thank God they hadn't condemned her for that.

Jessica glanced down at the boy, then bit her lip and

sighed. "I understand." Clasping her arms over her chest, she leaned forward. "I appreciate your need to protect him," she said in a low voice. "I truly do, Meg, because you consider him family. I would protect any person in my family to the best of my ability, too. And that includes you, you know."

Meg's heart softened toward her younger sister. "Thank you," she murmured. She'd heard about how Jessica had befriended Lady Fenwicke last winter, and when she'd discovered how Lord Fenwicke was beating his wife, she'd convinced her to leave the horrid man.

As beautiful and delicate as Jessica appeared, she possessed an inner core of solid steel. It felt good to Meg to have such strength on her side.

Jessica's blue eyes studied her, and though they still contained that mischievous spark, they were serious. "I know you, Meg. Even though you think I cannot remember your true character, and even though you think you have changed irrevocably, I do know you. And above all, I know you wouldn't have"—she glanced at Jake again and lowered her voice, even though he continued to ignore them—"taken a child from his father unless it was truly warranted."

Meg closed her eyes, and with a shudder, she remembered the time Jake had been trailing after his father—just after his mother had died—and for no other reason than his rage over Sarah's death, Caversham had grabbed the child by the collar and tossed him overboard. If not for the quick thinking of one of the sailors, who, by some God-given instinct, had torn off his jacket and jumped in after the boy, he surely would have drowned.

The crew had turned the ship around to fetch the boy

and the sailor, while Caversham had stalked to his quarters and drunken himself into a stupor. No one saw him for two days after that, when he returned to the deck, pretending like none of it had ever happened.

That incident had only been the beginning. It had been bad enough with the drunken rages and beatings when Sarah had been alive. But afterward...Meg shuddered again.

She bent forward and ruffled Jake's soft brown hair. He was safe now, and she'd keep him that way.

"If there's one thing I've ever done right in my lifetime," she told Jessica, "it was taking him away from that man."

The door swung open, jolting Meg's attention. Even Jake's head riveted toward the sound.

It was Serena and the earl, followed by one of the maids. Serena smiled, first at Jake. "Jake, Molly is here with me. She wants to take you into the kitchen for a sweet. Would you like that?"

Jake didn't answer. He stared at her, then looked at Meg, his blue eyes flaring with panic, and gave a vigorous shake of his head.

Meg tried to give him a reassuring smile. "I could go with you," she murmured. "Would you like that?"

The earl cleared his throat. "There are a few things we'd like to discuss with you, Meg."

She glanced sharply at him. The way he and Serena stood side by side, it looked like they did intend to have a serious discussion with her. One they didn't want Jake present for.

She didn't want him present for it, either. But being away from him made her anxious—even when he was safe asleep in her bed and she was awake somewhere else in the house. Whenever she was apart from him, she worried. He felt the same. This was a new world for him, and his fears tended to overwhelm him unless Meg was within viewing distance.

Jake was only six years old, but he understood a great deal, not the least of which was why they'd escaped from his father. She sighed and looked up at her brother-in-law. "Jake would prefer to stay here. Whatever we need to discuss can be said in his presence."

The earl leveled a look at Jake, who ignored him, having already gone back to his puzzle. He tended to focus so intensely on his current obsession that he usually didn't listen to the drone of adults, anyhow.

Serena glanced at her husband and nodded. "Very well." After turning to dismiss Molly, she took the seat beside Meg on the opposite side of Jessica. The earl sat on a cream-striped silk chair across from them.

Her brother-in-law opened his mouth to speak, but Meg held up her hand. "Please," she said. "I believe I know what you're going to say. This situation is truly impossible, and it has been horrible of me to disrupt all of your lives this way—"

"Nonsense." Serena sounded cross. "Really, Meg. Don't be absurd. We're your *family.*"

Meg clasped her hands in her lap and looked down at them, watching her knuckles turn white. She chose her words carefully so as not to upset Jake—if he was listening. "The truth of the matter is that I cannot stay in London. I'm positive he'll be coming for us. I can't allow that to happen."

Serena nodded thoughtfully. "Jonathan and I have spoken about this. We want to help you." She leaned forward in her chair and spoke earnestly. "We are so happy you've come back to us. We all wish we could keep you here, have you close, so that we can be sure you're all right. We want you with us so badly. But the fact of the matter is that you're in danger here in London, and we cannot continue to selfishly keep you here."

It was a relief, really. Serena and Lord Stratford already understood why she needed to go away.

"I should go to Ireland," Meg said. "It is where I had originally planned to go, before Captain Langley—"

Serena shook her head. "No," she said, her voice flat. "It's too far away. Plus, the Donovan side of the family was never happy with Father for leaving Ireland to begin with, don't you remember?"

"Of course, but I don't think they'd turn me away." Meg had met her grandparents and aunts once, on a visit to Ireland before they'd gone to Antigua. They had seemed to be kind enough people, if a little distant. But wouldn't anyone feel distant from a son who'd been gone for a decade, a daughter-in-law they'd never met, and five young and very English granddaughters? "Even if they did turn me away," she continued, "I'd manage."

Again, Serena shook her head. "This is where our idea comes into effect."

"Phoebe's husband, Sebastian, has a house in Prescot, in Lancashire," Lord Stratford said. "We've used it as a safe house before."

Jessica, who'd been sitting quietly to this point, snorted. "Not very effectively!"

"True," Lord Stratford said. "But in the past, the various people who found it were able to easily discover our connection to the house. This time, it won't be so easy."

"The first time, it was Phoebe," Serena said. "She ran away with Sebastian and they lived there for a few days—until we found them. Jonathan knew it was Sebastian's only property, so he assumed correctly that it would be the logical place for them to go."

"And then it was me and Beatrice." Jessica blew out a breath. Beatrice was Lady Fenwicke—the sweet lady who'd escaped from her abusive husband. She was currently their houseguest and had been for some time.

"That time it was a bit more insidious," Serena explained. "Lord Fenwicke had employed a spy in our household, and he learned the girls' whereabouts from her."

"I think it will be safe for you," Lord Stratford said again.

"No one knows of your existence except the man who's after you," Serena added. "You could go to one of Jonathan's or Max's other properties, but surely anyone would search those before looking in Lancashire. It just *feels* like the safest option for you, Meg."

Meg nodded, relieved. They really did understand the danger to Jake. They wouldn't demand that she stay in London and parade herself about Town.

Serena leaned forward and squeezed her hand. "I need to remain here," she said quietly. "It would raise too many questions if I were to go with you."

"I'll go," Jessica said.

Serena shook her head. "No, Jess, you must stay as well, along with Beatrice. Too many people will notice if you leave London now."

Jessica rolled her eyes heavenward and sighed heavily but didn't argue.

"I can go alone," Meg said quickly. "Jake and I will be fine."

"A full complement of my most trusted servants will accompany you to Prescot. You'll have a coachman, a footman, a maid, and a cook at your disposal," Lord Stratford said. "And we'll supply you with an unmarked traveling carriage with lanterns so you can travel through the night without having to repeat the awkward experience you had on your way to London."

"Thank goodness Barbara and Mildred are harmless," Serena said.

Jake looked up at that. "Barbara looks like an orange," he said, before going right back to his puzzle.

Meg nodded gratefully, feeling a flush rise in her cheeks at the remembered embarrassment of those women believing she was Serena.

Serena brought Meg's knuckles to her lips and pressed a hard kiss on them. "I know it's been difficult for you here. I wish you could stay here with me—with us. I wish"— she blinked, her gray eyes, so much like Meg's own, glistening—"I wish we could be as close as we once were."

Meg turned her gaze to her lap. That was her fault. She was too quiet, too reserved. She'd withdrawn too much from them.

"But we have time," Serena added, her voice quiet. "When this is all over. When you come back to us and this affair is all straightened out and"—she glanced down at Jake—"you're safe."

Jessica nodded vigorously. "This will be over soon, and we'll all be together again. I *feel* it," she proclaimed.

Meg wasn't so confident. Her family still didn't know Caversham's identity—they'd given up pressing her for it—or his relationship to the Marquis of Millbridge. They didn't know that Caversham would never give up.

Still, she nodded and tried to give her sisters and Lord Stratford a game smile. "When shall I go?"

"We'll plan this carefully," Lord Stratford said. "We must take great care in obtaining everything required to ensure your safety."

"Next week?" Serena asked.

"Next week is perfect," Meg said. It would give her time to prepare Jake for the journey.

She looked down at him, her expression softening as she watched him mix up the pieces of the puzzle, then shove them to the side to clear a space to put it back together again. Dear, sweet Jake.

Someday, she promised him silently, we'll have a home where we will live, without moving, until you're old enough to *want* to move away. And you'll never have to worry or be fearful ever again.

Chapter Seven

Will sat in the alcove that served as his breakfast room. Laid out before him on the round oak table were his coffee, toast, poached egg, and an ignored copy of the *Times*.

He hadn't touched the egg, and he held his half-eaten toast between his fingers as he stared out the window into the small, grassy courtyard behind his house.

He'd lived alone for a long time now, but in the past fortnight his house had begun to feel so...*lonely*. So quiet. Before he'd encountered Meg in the Irish Sea, he'd considered this his place of refuge, but now it seemed so cold and sterile. He hadn't read the *Times* since he'd arrived in London—extremely out of character for him, a man who liked to keep informed. Every day, he rushed through his breakfast and abandoned it half uneaten simply so he could leave his empty house.

No, that wasn't completely true. It wasn't so simple. The truth was, he rushed to get out of here every morning because he missed her.

Will dropped the toast onto its plate and pushed a hand through his hair. It didn't make sense. He'd managed for so long without her. Why did his skin ache when he was apart from her? Why couldn't he stop thinking about her? Why did he make excuses every day to leave his offices early so he could visit Stratford's house? He'd never been a man to shirk his duties or make excuses...but he was becoming that man.

He'd begun to obsess about the reappearance of the man who'd captured her. Every day, when he rushed to Stratford's house and after he made sure she'd managed without him for the past several hours, he surreptitiously stood guard over her. When he left at night, he couldn't help but to remind the butler to check the locks before he retired, and he always took the time to scan the square before entering his carriage.

Will drank the dregs of his coffee and then set down his cup and stared at his half-eaten toast. If it was possible, Meg had become even more remote since they'd arrived in London. And she wasn't remote only with him—her sisters had noticed it, too. She and Serena were always polite and kind to each other, but he'd seen them together eight years ago. He'd borne witness to their closeness, their understanding of every subtle nuance of each other, their way of communicating without speaking a word. That all seemed to be gone now—crumbled beneath the heavy weight of all that had happened to both of them.

The permanent bleakness that had overtaken Meg's expression made his gut twist. He wanted her safe. He wanted her happy. Most of the time, both of those seemed unattainable goals.

He pushed back from the table, the chair legs scraping

over the wooden floor. God, he was tied in knots. He wanted the old Meg back; he wanted to once more be the recipient of that smiling splash of sunshine that had been her personality.

She would hate it if he told her that.

Perhaps he was still pining for a ghost. With a sigh, he rose. His presence was required in his offices this morning. And even though he really needed to be there all day, he knew he'd end up leaving in the early afternoon to go to Stratford's, just like he had every other day for the past fortnight.

He met his servant at the threshold of the breakfast room door as the man was raising his hand to knock.

"What is it, Dunn?"

"Mr. Briggs is at the door for you, sir."

Concern froze him in place, his hand still on his chair. "Show him in."

In a few moments, Briggs entered, and after Will offered him coffee and they were both seated at the table, Will frowned at him. "Where is the *Freedom*?"

"She's in Plymouth, safe. MacInerny is sailing her to London as we speak, and she should arrive at St. Katharine's Docks in a few days' time."

Briggs had well-honed intuition when it came to his captain's preferences—one of the many attributes that made him an excellent first officer. He'd known that Will would want the *Freedom* close. Will blew out a breath. "Good."

"We anchored in Plymouth Harbour day before yesterday," Briggs continued. "I didn't want to wait the length of time it would take for the *Freedom* to sail to London, so I took the mail coach."

Will narrowed his eyes at his friend. "Why the hurry?"

Briggs shook his head. "Don't worry, Captain. Nothing awful has happened. In fact, I received word that our pirate has left the area. And I did learn something else of importance: his name."

"What is it?" Will asked.

"Caversham."

"Caversham," Will repeated slowly, testing it on his tongue for the first time. The name wasn't familiar to him. "And how did you come by this information?"

"We encountered a fisherman—a Mr. Retallack—at Penzance, who's had dealings with him and his crew. Doesn't like the man, says the bastard's black-hearted as they come, so he agreed to give us information in return for our assurance that he won't be implicated in any wrongdoing."

Will nodded. He would have made the same deal with the fisherman. The Cornish people had been so tight-lipped about their villain—out of fear of both sides, he'd wager—that he'd been growing desperate. "Did you learn Caversham's given name? What he looks like?"

"He's dark haired and of average build. Retallack could tell us little more than that, and we already knew that much, in any case." Gripping his coffee cup in both hands, Briggs leaned close. "However, he did tell us that Caversham anchored in a cove near Penzance a week and a half ago. He dropped the remainder of his promised shipment there, rather than spreading the contraband along the coast, which Retallack confirmed is what he's been doing. Caversham was in a hurry. He was searching for someone—one of the crew told the fisherman they were looking for 'a kidnapper' and were heading straightaway to Ireland. Seems he is Miss Donovan's captor, and he's looking for her."

"And he's Jake's father," Will murmured.

"Aye."

Will sat still, allowing the information to sink in.

"The *Freedom* arrived in Penzance two days after Caversham pulled anchor and sailed north," Briggs said. "We just missed them."

"He's looking for Meg." Will rested his elbows on the table and bent his head into his hands, rubbing his forehead. "He'll find her family in Ireland and learn she hasn't appeared. He'll either think she and the boy drowned in the storm or that she changed her mind and headed to England. You say he was in Penzance ten days ago?"

"Aye."

"He'll be in Ireland by now."

"He'll want his ship hidden, so he'll choose to anchor it in some obscure place where nobody's looking for him. Or somewhere busy where the vessel will be overlooked, like the port at Dublin."

"So that gives us some time," Will said. "How long before he comes sniffing for her in London?"

"I'd say it'll be another fortnight, at least."

Will nodded, then frowned. "But how did Caversham know she was headed for Ireland to begin with?"

"Good question," Briggs said, then he gave a one-shouldered shrug. "Maybe she told him?"

Will looked at Briggs in disbelief. "That wouldn't make any sense whatsoever. Good God, David, don't tell me you are still suspicious of her."

"It just seems odd to me that she'd run off with the man's child."

"She cares for the boy. She is trying to protect him, that is all. I don't think anyone will disagree that Caversham is the bigger villain here."

"And yet, she could be prosecuted as a kidnapper," Briggs said. "That's a hanging offense."

Will ground his teeth. "I am aware of that. It is why I intend to protect her—and the boy—to the best of my ability until the man has been brought to justice."

Briggs met his eyes evenly. "Are you certain she isn't in league with him?"

Will nearly choked on his coffee. "What?"

"Think about it. She was with the man for eight years and didn't try to escape—"

"She did try to escape."

"That is what she claims."

Will stared at Briggs, narrow eyed.

Briggs held out his hands in a conciliatory gesture. "All I am saying is that something doesn't quite fit. Her story could be a tool by which to manipulate you."

Will rose from his chair. His voice was colder than he'd ever heard it when he said, "Watch yourself. I'll not have you speaking ill of her."

Briggs returned his gaze evenly. Slowly, he rose, too, until they were facing each other across the table. "I'm not speaking ill of anyone, Captain. I am doing what I can to look out for you. The woman has kept crucial information from you, information that you could have used to help her. For God's sake, she wouldn't even tell you the man's name. I don't believe you are looking at this objectively."

"Of course I'm not looking at it objectively!"

"Look at you," Briggs said softly. "You're not yourself. The woman has you tied up in knots."

Will gave him an icy stare.

"The Captain Langley I know is the epitome of calm. Even in life-or-death situations, like that storm the night before we found her. You never raise your voice. You always think with calm rationality on everything before you make a decision. You're the most patient man I know."

Will shook his head. "Clearly you don't know me very well, then."

"That's not true," Briggs said, "and you know it. Why are you like this, Captain? What has she done to you?"

Will turned away. It was no use trying to explain something he couldn't fully understand himself.

He stalked over to the window and put his hands on the sill. It was a beautiful, clear, warm day. The daffodils planted in the corners of his courtyard had begun to bloom in bright yellow clusters.

He trusted Meg. He believed everything she'd told him.

Because the thought of not trusting her made him sick.

"Her reappearance is a miracle—no one will question that," Briggs said, his voice gentler now. "But just because she's returned from the grave, it doesn't mean she's the same woman you knew long ago. She might have changed. Become someone else. In fact, it seems to me that anyone whose life altered in the way she has described to you would change irrevocably, especially when the change lasted for so many years."

Will shook his head. "I'm not going to speak of this with you," he said wearily. "I ask you to trust my judgment."

"I do trust your judgment, but because you trust her blindly doesn't mean I must. I'll continue to be wary with

Miss Donovan, since to be any other way would be a form of deceit."

Will blew out a breath. At least his first mate was being honest. "I can live with that," he said. "But I'll not have you slandering her to me or to anyone else."

"I've no intention of slandering her."

"Good." Turning from the window, Will asked, "Then may I ask for your help in getting to the bottom of this?"

Briggs had practically been born on the sea—his father had occupied a high rank in the East India Company, and his brothers had all held various positions in the Navy and on merchant ships. Despite being estranged from his brothers, he had connections throughout the London maritime community.

"Of course you can, Captain."

"I'd like you to remain in London," Will said. "I'd like you to find out whatever you can about Caversham. I'll talk to Meg and see if she'll tell me his Christian name, although we must consider the possibility that he might be using an alias."

Briggs nodded. "Yes, that's possible."

"I'll have Dunn make up the guest room for you."

"Thanks."

They rose, and Briggs went upstairs to begin writing letters for his information-gathering mission, while Will left the house on foot and headed toward his office.

It was a fine spring day, and though Will's office wasn't close to his home in Cavendish Square, it made for a good long walk. Today he used it to take the time to sort out the ways his life had so suddenly, so thoroughly changed in the past month.

She'd come back.

She was alive.

Those words still went through his mind with healthy doses of awe, disbelief, and amazement. When he looked at her, there she was. When she stood beside Serena and they gazed at him with those twin pairs of gray eyes, he wondered how he could have mistaken Serena for her for even a second.

Yes, they were very much alike, but he could pick out Meg every time. Something about her made his blood sing. Serena had never done that to him.

When Serena had first arrived in London, engaged to him, pretending to be her sister, his first reaction had been one of panic. Meg didn't make him feel the same way she had years ago. Had something altered the chemistry between them? Had time and distance eroded the love they'd shared?

Of course, that hadn't been the case. She'd been Serena, pretending to be Meg and failing at it, an ultimately obvious scheme to those who knew the sisters well.

And now Meg was back, in the flesh. The *real* Meg. Time and distance had certainly altered what she and Will had once shared, but the question was, in what way?

His blood still sang whenever he was in her presence. And he still wanted her. His body hadn't forgotten what she felt like beneath him.

And yet, time had passed. They'd both changed.

She kept secrets from him.

And he kept secrets from her, he thought miserably.

He walked the rest of the way to his office with pain tightening his chest.

Chapter Eight

At dusk, after a long morning of work followed by an afternoon meeting with Briggs, Will arrived at Stratford's house. The butler announced him into the drawing room, a space that had once been sparse and austere, but Serena had done much to improve it. Although still elegant with cream silk furnishings, a carved and tiered ceiling, and Greek-inspired columns framing the windows, it was comfortable, too, with an assortment of chairs and sofas in sets near the window and the fireplace. Adjacent to the chairs and sofas were plenty of small tables upon which one could set his brandy glass or his newspaper.

Meg was sitting alone in one of the small armchairs near the fire. She laid her embroidery in the basket at her feet and rose to greet him, smoothing down her skirt. She wore another new dress Serena had purchased for her, but it was of a simpler design than what one would expect of a countess's sister. It was just a shade away from white, a color that brought out the slight pink tinge in her complexion and those freckles he loved so much, and contained no decoration except for the ruffle at the bottom and matching lace trimming the bodice. The lace drew the eye to the creamy skin of her chest and made his fingers itch to stroke along that skin, to feel its warmth, its vivacity. Even after all this time, a part of him still couldn't believe she was real.

The dress was simple enough to make most women appear plain, but not Meg. It made her look lovely. Elegant, and beautiful.

She greeted him with a smile that didn't reach her eyes, and he clenched his fists at his sides, resisting the sudden urge to shake her.

He was trying to be patient. Hell, just this morning Briggs had told Will he was the most patient man he knew. But God, how he wanted that beautiful smile to reach her eyes. He wanted to be the one to bring it to her. He wanted her to smile at him like she used to.

Instead of shaking her, he returned the smile, wondering if his own expression appeared as manufactured as hers. "Where is everyone?"

"Serena, Jessica, and Lady Fenwicke are upstairs changing into their ball gowns. Olivia and Phoebe have returned to Olivia's house to ready themselves for tonight's festivities. Lord Stratford is in his office working. I just put Jake to bed." Her smile faltered. "I do hope he doesn't wake."

"Has he been having difficulty sleeping?"

"He has nightmares." She didn't meet his eyes, instead looking at a point on the wall somewhere beyond his shoulder. "I've got a maid keeping an eye on him. If he wakes, she'll come get me."

He took a step closer to her. "What about you, Meg? Have you been having nightmares?"

She turned away from him and lowered herself into the chair she'd been seated in when he'd arrived, clasping her hands in her lap. "Sometimes. When I can sleep."

He'd seen the gray shadows beneath her eyes when he'd first entered the room.

"I'm trying to help Jake forget, but it's not working. How can it, when I cannot forget, either?"

"You've only been away from his father for less than a month. It will take some time." He settled into the ivory-silk-upholstered chair beside hers.

Looking down, she nodded, then her gaze rose to meet his. "Do you think that there's something a natural mother can give a child that no substitute ever can?"

Having heard details here and there about Jake's mother, Will had thought for some time that Meg had probably given Jake much more in terms of mothering than his true mother ever had.

"No," he said firmly. "Consider the children who are taken in by families that can care for them better than their natural families. Those children usually fare much better than they would with their real parents."

"But maybe a part of them—a tiny part—would always know that they're not with their true flesh and blood. And that part would always be empty."

"Is that how you've felt?" he asked. "For the past eight years, have you felt like a part of you has been empty because you were not with your family?"

"Yes." She didn't meet his eyes. "But I'm not sure if that's just me, just because I had a twin and we were so close once, or if it's that way with younger children who don't know the difference as acutely."

"I believe that adoptive parents have the ability to make children just as happy and fulfilled as natural parents do."

She sighed. "Then why can't I seem to make Jake happy?"

"He loves you, Meg." That was patently obvious.

"And yet, he's not a happy child," she said. "My sisters and I suffered through hardships when we were children. Yet we were always happy. We always smiled and laughed, but Jake never does."

"Maybe he needs a friend," Will said. "Someone his own age to play with. To laugh with."

"He's never had a friend before," Meg murmured.

He looked away, his fingertips running restlessly over the ridges of the carved armrest. For a long moment, he gazed into the low flames of the fire, knowing what he had to do. Knowing he couldn't be a coward forever.

In a low voice, he said, "I know you don't like leaving this house, but do you think you and Jake would like to come to my house tomorrow? It will be good for both of you to get out, even if just to another house, and I'll take precautions to make sure neither of you are seen."

She didn't answer him for a long time. She turned her head to look between the columns. The drapes were open, but a filmy gauze curtain had been left over the window. The constant flow of traffic and pedestrians looked like dark shadows moving behind a screen.

"I haven't left this house once since I arrived." Her head swung toward him, and then she was looking at him, her eyes shining silver. "Sometimes," she murmured, "I think I'll go mad if I stay inside one more day."

"You cannot remain trapped here forever, Meg. That would be exchanging one prison for another."

She shook her head stubbornly. "No. Nothing would be worse than him finding us."

"I won't let him hurt you," he said, perhaps for the hundredth time.

One of the many changes that had affected her in the past eight years: she had become stubborn. He couldn't blame her for it, but it hadn't been one of her traits when she was younger. Serena had always been famous for her stubbornness; Meg was known for her easygoing nature.

"It doesn't matter." She shrugged. "We decided this morning—I'm to leave in one week's time."

Everything in him went still. "Where will you be going?" She hesitated, and anger flared in him, hot and fast. "You're not going to tell me?"

Her cheeks turned a bright pink. "I am. I mean, of course I am, Will. It's just—"

Rising from the chair, he blew out a breath through clenched teeth. He turned away from her and stalked toward the window.

So she was going to leave London. Without any input from him. And she clearly didn't want to tell him where she intended to go.

But who was he to have proprietary feelings over her? Good God. Leaning against a column, he closed his eyes. He couldn't keep up with his own feelings about this woman. Everything she said or did seemed to pull a new emotion from his chest. He sighed, forcefully reining himself back into control. "I'm sorry. I shouldn't have snapped at you."

But his voice emerged strained, even angry. Briggs had been right—Will *was* known for his composure, for his lack of emotion. In the past year his stone-faced existence had become a source of rumor and speculation. But this woman—everything about her—rattled him.

She didn't respond to his apology. He couldn't really blame her.

"Will you tell me where you're going?" His voice was soft and controlled.

She didn't hesitate this time. The words tumbled out of her, as if she spoke quickly, she'd somehow prove that she trusted him. "My brother-in-law, Sebastian Harper, has a house in Lancashire. Lord Stratford and Serena have suggested I go there."

"I've been there." For God's sake, Stratford believed she would be safe *there*? Only a few months ago, Jessica and her friend, Lady Fenwicke, had been kidnapped from that very house. "Will Stratford accompany you to Lancashire?"

"No. He and Serena must stay in London along with all my sisters, lest rumors start about their disappearance from the balls and parties they're expected to attend this Season."

Will pushed off from the column and stood very still, watching her. He intended to have words with Stratford the next time he was alone with the man. "Who will protect you, then?"

Her gaze settled on him, and her back straightened. "He's choosing several trusted servants to accompany me to Lancashire. Jake and I will be safe—at least for now."

That was the moment her sisters and Lady Fenwicke chose to pour into the drawing room.

Will walked forward to greet the ladies. Jessica looked lovely in a gown of deep red—her favorite color—with outrageously puffed, but fashionable, sleeves. Serena was dressed a touch more austerely, in a blue-trimmed seal gray, and he exchanged a real smile with her—defying all odds, they had become good friends after calling off their engagement.

Beatrice, Lady Fenwicke, was a widow, a voluptuous, pretty young woman, but there was a sadness in her demeanor that Will understood quite well—her husband, who'd died only a few months ago, had been a brutal man, and she hadn't yet recovered from his abuse. She was dressed in black silk, and her excitement was more muted than that of the other two ladies.

Serena grinned at Meg. "Beatrice and I were wagering as to how many dance invitations Jessica will receive tonight. Care to place your wager?"

"I couldn't begin to guess," Meg said, her tone kind but not containing the exuberance her sisters' held.

Jessica put her hands on her hips and turned her nose up in the air. "I shall only dance with handsome men. If they're ugly, they don't count, because I will refuse them."

Lady Fenwicke gave one of her rare smiles. "Does that mean we shall have to revise our wagers, Jessica? Not how many gentlemen will ask you to dance, but how many *handsome* gentlemen will ask you to dance? Isn't that a rather subjective choice, though? Who will decide whether the gentlemen are handsome enough to count?"

"I will, of course," Jessica said.

Serena made a scoffing noise. "They will all be handsome. After your antics last Season, I doubt any of the ugly ones will have the gumption to ask you."

"Really, Serena, I wasn't *that* awful."

"Apparently, though, you're planning to be awful to the gentlemen who don't meet your approval this year," Serena said, but there was a smile on her face rather than disapproval.

"Well, I need to be selective, you know. I'm nineteen. Certainly not getting younger. I'll be on the shelf in the blink of the eye." Jessica snapped her fingers for emphasis.

Meg and Serena groaned, then looked at each other, surprised by their simultaneous identical responses, and laughed softly. Or, rather, Serena laughed, and Meg gave the ghost of a smile. Serena narrowed her eyes at her youngest sister. "Watch yourself, Jessica. You're among old biddies here."

"Not true at all!" Jessica slung an arm around Lady Fenwicke's waist. "There's always Beatrice."

Serena rolled her eyes heavenward, and Meg looked thoughtful. "Well, I never thought of myself as on the shelf, but I suppose I really am." She frowned. "Now that's an odd thought."

Jessica and Serena sobered.

"We always believed you'd be the first to marry, Meg," Serena said.

Will took a tight breath. He had believed she'd be the first of the Donovan sisters to marry, too. He'd expected she'd marry him.

Meg shrugged and smiled, but the bleakness in her eyes never faded. "Ah, well. Fate has a way of asserting itself in surprising ways, doesn't it?"

Just then, Stratford entered and informed the ladies it was time for them to go. The sisters hugged good-bye, and Serena kissed Will's cheek and told him to look after her sister while they were gone. Will cast a glance in Stratford's direction and gave him a look that said, "We need to talk." Stratford gave a terse nod, and then they all fluttered away, glittering like people their age and class should, leaving a penetrating silence in their wake.

After a long moment, both of them staring at the closed door, Meg said, "It's growing dark."

The fire was already burning strong, but she went around the room, turning up the lanterns and using one of the flames to light the wall sconces.

When she had finished, she turned back to him. "You needn't stay, you know. Jake and I are perfectly fine here alone. Lord Stratford has an endless number of servants in this house. Honestly, I've no idea where he keeps them all."

He met her gaze and held it in his own. He wouldn't be comfortable leaving her and Jake alone tonight, servants or no. And it had been a long day—longer than he'd anticipated—and he'd missed her.

"I'll stay."

Just then, a knock on the door sounded, and a footman opened it. "Dinner is served."

She nodded, then she clasped her hands together in front of her. "Are you hungry?"

He'd had nothing to eat since his mostly untouched breakfast. "I am."

He slid a glance at her as they walked toward the door. "After dinner, would you like to play a game of cribbage?"

"That sounds nice. I always enjoy cribbage."

"I remember," he murmured, the corners of his lips tilting up in a smile.

She was so beautiful, in her shyness and sudden

embarrassment. God, how he wanted her. How could it be that he'd never wanted another woman even an iota of the way he wanted her?

She was everything to him. Even though she'd remained mostly quiet about the past years and she'd obviously changed in so many ways, she was still everything to him.

She'd wanted him once, too. Did she still? If so, she'd given him no indication...

No, that wasn't right. She had: When he'd kissed her in the inn that night, she'd kissed him in return. She hadn't pulled back, hadn't pushed him away. She'd wrapped her arms around him and kissed him, just as hungrily as he'd kissed her.

Surely that meant something, especially coming from a woman as composed and controlled and self-contained as Meg was.

They walked to the dining room, where dinner awaited them. They ate and drank, speaking sparingly. Even though the dining room was vast, with seating for at least twenty, somehow the servants had prepared it in a way to make it seem intimate. An elongated vase filled with jonquils and tulips cut off their end of the table from the rest, and the candles in the crystal chandelier were lit to pour golden light over their place settings, while the remainder of the room was bathed in a far dimmer and softer glow.

Will was comfortable here, dining with Meg. He wasn't much prone to conversation during eating—in the Navy mealtimes had been a chore that he'd accomplished with perfunctory attention before returning to more important duties, and since he'd sold his commission, it had never seemed natural to turn eating into a social activity. Though he had, on occasion, done so out of politeness, it wasn't his preference. Eating with Meg, however, he was content just to watch her.

The meal was simple for a dinner in an earl's home: turtle soup and salmon followed by a roasted pheasant, then frosted apples and a date tart and an assortment of cheeses. Meg only tasted the various dishes offered, and when a footman took the cheese course away, she twirled her fingertips in the perfumed water of her finger glass. Her hands were pale, the fingers long and slender. Moments later, cherries, grapes, strawberries, and tiny bowls of cream and sugar were laid in front of them.

"Oh, my," she murmured. "Strawberries."

Her gaze caught on to his and held. Years ago, Will had brought a bag of sugared strawberries to her aunt's house. They'd walked through St. James's Square, feeding them to each other. Later that night, they'd made love for the first time.

Not breaking his gaze from hers, Will took one of the strawberries from his plate. He dipped it in the cream then in the sugar. Leaning across the table, he held it toward her mouth. She moved forward and captured it with her lips. He remembered the feel of them, their softness and warmth, under his own.

She chewed the strawberry, then her pink tongue flicked out, catching a drop of strawberry juice staining her lip. "Mm," she said softly, her eyes half-lidded in an expression of ecstasy. "So good."

Will's body went hard as she dipped one of her strawberries in the cream and sugar and held it out to him.

He grasped her wrist in both of his hands on the pretense of holding it steady. He brought her fingers close enough so that he could take the strawberry between his teeth. He chewed and swallowed the sweet fruit, taking his time, without letting go of her hand, her fingertips close enough that they brushed against his lips. After he swallowed, he licked the strawberry juice from her fingers, then released her.

He sat back, glass of Madeira wine in hand, his lips curving at the flush spreading over her cheeks. Using his free hand, he offered her another strawberry.

He remembered how gaunt she'd looked when he'd taken her from that jolly boat. Obviously, her sisters had been attempting to feed her well. Though she hadn't seemed to eat much at dinner tonight, she'd gained a few pounds, and her skin, though still tanned by the sun, seemed to have more luster to it.

He took a deep swallow of his Madeira, then set down his glass as she held out another sugared strawberry to him.

They continued on in this way until the strawberries were gone, and the blood was pounding beneath Will's skin.

He couldn't stand without making his arousal patently clear, so he took his time finishing his drink in silence. Still flushed, she nibbled on grapes and cherries and sipped at her Madeira, and when her glass was empty and she seemed to have had her fill of grapes and cherries, Will asked, "Are you ready to return to the drawing room?"

She nodded and rose, and he rose along with her. In the drawing room, she took a cribbage board and cards from a gold-trimmed Oriental cabinet wedged in one of the corners opposite the window. She set the board on a small round black wood table, and he helped her to pull it between the two armchairs they'd occupied earlier.

She sat, then began to shuffle the cards. "We've both changed so much," she murmured out of the blue, her focus on the cards.

"You still like cribbage. We both still like strawberries," he pointed out, taking the seat across from her.

"True." The cards slapped together as she shuffled again. "But we've changed in deeper, subtler ways, I think."

"How?" Will asked, the challenge obvious in his voice. He didn't want to think of how they'd changed. He wanted to think of how they were the same. Of how she still made him feel the same way she used to. Hot. Wanting her so much he ached.

"You're so serious now."

"Am I?"

"Yes." The sweetness in her voice pierced through him. Her voice certainly hadn't changed. "You used to be quite lighthearted."

"Was I?" he asked, bemused. He'd never thought of himself as particularly lighthearted. His mother had always laughingly told him he'd been born staid and even-tempered.

She nodded, laying the cards back on the table without dealing. "You've changed," she repeated. "There's... well, there's a darkness in you now."

He choked out a bitter laugh. "Perhaps that had something to do with discovering the woman I loved was lost at sea."

She leaned on the arm of her chair, considering him seriously. Then she cast her gaze downward. "Was that really all it was, Will? If it is, I'm sorry. I...I didn't want to be the cause of your darkness."

"*All* it was? God, Meg, how could you think losing you—and in that way—could have been insignificant to me?"

With a jerky movement, she stood. He stood along with her, the movement an instant response to a lady rising from her chair.

"I wish...I wish you'd found someone else." She clasped her arms over her chest. "I wish...more than anything, that my family and I hadn't caused all your unhappiness."

She was close, close enough to touch—to pull into his arms. And he did just that, moving around the small table and tugging her against his body, biting back a primal groan at the feel of her soft, supple body against him.

He'd experienced moments of weakness since she'd left London so long ago. But they'd been few. He'd quickly—too quickly—learned from his mistakes. For the most part, his existence had been an ascetic one. Touching her now, feeling her slight, warm body against him, her breasts pressing against his chest, nearly tore down all the control he'd so carefully constructed in the past eight years.

"It's not your fault." He bent down to press his lips into her hair, her soft, silky blond hair. She smelled like lavender soap with the ever-present sweetness of sugarcane beneath. He ran his hands up and down the soft muslin covering her back. "You had nothing to do with any of it, Meg. You had no control over what happened to me."

"It *was* my fault," she whispered, her voice muffled by his chest. "If I hadn't fallen overboard. If I'd found a way to escape from him earlier—" Her slender body shuddered in his arms, and he held her tighter.

"Shh." He hesitated and then spoke into her hair. "So many years, Meg. So much has happened...to both of us."

There had been his two brief naval engagements while he'd served as Post Captain in the Navy. He never talked about those, but he would never forget the blood of the pirates flowing, like a strong current, over his hands.

Knowing that Meg was waiting for him had been his connection to peace and happiness. She had kept him going through those hellish times.

If he'd known the truth then—that she'd been lost at sea and was presumed dead—chances were, he'd be dead now. After that year he'd spent in the Aegean, he'd come home and the first thing he'd done was send that letter proposing marriage to her. He couldn't wait to hold her in his arms. After so many years, to bury himself within her and forget.

But that moment had never come. He'd never been offered that peace he'd longed for. When he'd learned of her "death," he'd believed he'd never achieve it.

Now, holding her close, he dared to hope again.

Slowly, Meg raised her arms and slipped them around Will's waist. He stood there, hard and firm, a steadfast pillar in her world of danger and uncertainty.

If only her mother and Serena hadn't hurt Will so terribly with their scheme to change Serena's identity. And now, she wished with all her heart that she hadn't involved him in the danger that Caversham would invariably bring.

She wished . . . well, she *almost* wished she'd never met William Langley. But she was too selfish for that. If she'd never met him, she would have never experienced love. And for so many years, the happiness of the few weeks she'd spent with Will had kept her going in her darkest days. She couldn't wish that away.

"If wishes were horses," she murmured, "beggars would ride."

He pulled away, looking down at her. "What do you mean?"

She wanted to tug him back against her, feel the hard length of his body against hers again, but she controlled that primal urge, instead looking up at him through the sting in her eyes. "I wish so many things, Will. Most of all, I regret what I've done to you. I wish..." She swallowed hard. "I wish someone else had rescued Jake and me. I wish it wasn't you."

Some raw emotion twisted his face, and he held her arms hard. "Why?" he asked gruffly. He shook her lightly. "How could you wish for such a thing?"

Letting her go with the suddenness of dropping a hot poker, he turned away and prowled the length of the room. He reminded her of a panther, sleek and strong and deadly, and so beautiful he made her ache. "God, Meg. *Christ*."

Will was always controlled. He rarely cursed; rarely showed emotion. Yet this was twice in one night that she'd angered him.

Even his anger tempted her. Oh, how she wanted everything to be as simple as it had seemed eight years ago.

She wrapped her arms around her body. "It's not what you think," she whispered.

He spun around, his dark eyes flashing. "What, then, am I supposed to think? You were gone for eight years. I thought you dead—everyone thought you dead. Then you appear like an angel from heaven, and I've never felt such...such..." He swung his head away, and she saw his throat move as he swallowed. "And your family, too.

We loved you. We *mourned* you. And you wish we hadn't found you?"

"No—I mean...yes!" she exclaimed. "Don't you see? I caused you pain. All of you, but you worst of all. It was my fault you were led along, blind, for years, thinking I was writing love letters to you, thinking I would marry you, thinking Serena might be me. And now, I bring you nothing. I'm not that girl you fell in love with. I've changed. I have Jake now, and he's all that matters. I have nothing to offer you except more pain. And danger."

"And you think that by keeping the villain's name from us that you'll keep us from harm?"

"I'd hoped to, but even that isn't enough."

Will straightened. "Did you know Caversham is currently looking for you in Ireland?" He said the name slowly and deliberately, studying her reaction. "Briggs and I believe that it's only a matter of time before he begins to search in London."

Meg's mouth dropped open. She was shaking so hard, her knees wobbled. She leaned heavily against one of the columns. "I've brought trouble to you," she choked out. "To all of you. And when he finds us, I fear we're all going to pay."

The shining look in Will's eyes turned hard. His fists clenched and unclenched at his sides. "Do you have so little trust for me, Meg? I've been beside you since I took you off that damned little boat. I've never wavered in my vow to protect you with everything I have."

He stared at her, and she stared back at him, her lips pressed tightly together. She had no answer for him. What could she say? How to explain that, yes, she trusted him, but she feared Caversham more. Caversham in a rage was like nobody and nothing she'd ever seen. Caversham in a rage with the force of the British government behind him—now that was something she never wished to see.

Finally, she said in a small voice, "I've kidnapped his son, Will. He'll come after me with everything. *Everything*."

He spoke through clenched teeth, white flashing between his lips. "He's a criminal, and I'll see him hanged before he has a chance to go after you at all."

She shook her head bleakly. "What do you know about him?"

"He's a smuggler. For the past two years, he's been smuggling rum into Cornwall."

She waited for more, but that was apparently all he had. God, he knew nothing. She closed her eyes. "How did you learn his name?"

"Briggs is in London. After he left us in Plymouth, he sailed the *Freedom* to Penzance. A man there gave him the information." He took a step toward her and said in a low voice, "Information we could have learned from you, but you refused to tell us."

She'd told him again and again it was for his own good, but it seemed useless to do so now, so she kept quiet. She gazed down at her blue slippers poking out from underneath the plain muslin dress she wore.

"No more evasion, Meg. You must tell me about him. Tell me everything you know. I need something to work with. I can't protect you—or myself—against a specter."

She looked up at him. He was right. What she was doing wasn't fair. Will was in trouble now, and the least she could do was offer him as much information as she could so he could arm himself.

"Very well," she whispered.

She staggered to the chair nearest the fire and sank into it. Heat from the flames licked at her toes through her slippers as she stared at the cribbage board without really seeing it. He stood for another long moment, tall and so handsome in the perfectly fitted dark waistcoat he wore, but she waited patiently, and finally he sat in the chair opposite.

She brushed away an errant tear and gazed into Will's dark eyes. "Jacob Caversham," she began, "is the Marquis of Millbridge's half brother."

Chapter Nine

The Marquis of Millbridge was Jessica's third dance partner for the evening. It was a waltz, which meant they were to spend the entire dance together—there was no exchanging of partners in a waltz.

Jessica took a final sip of her punch and then set it on the tray of a passing servant as she saw the marquis approaching.

"Remember," Serena whispered behind her fan, "he's not a 'Your Grace,' and for heaven's sake, do not call him Mr. Millbridge! It's 'my lord.'"

"Right," Jessica breathed. Her heart was doing a little pitter-patter in her chest. True, she'd had many associations with the aristocracy—she had a duke and an earl as brothers-in-law, after all. Still, she was notoriously gauche when it came to English titles.

"Yes, my lord," she muttered. Serena gave her a sharp look as the marquis stepped up to them. Smiling, he gave them a regal bow, and they curtsied in return.

That was it—there was something about *this* marquis that rattled her. He was tall and powerful in demeanor and in position. Whereas Max and Jonathan were perfectly comfortable remaining quiet in politics, she'd learned that this man had very high political aspirations indeed.

He was handsome, too, enough so that Beatrice, who'd been standing beside Jessica when the marquis had asked her to dance, had murmured, "Well, there was no question about that one, was there?" when he'd walked away.

He was much older than she—perhaps twice her age. That bothered Jessica, but as Serena had told her over and over, men matured differently than women. He was an imposing man, with sculpted facial features, somewhat thin lips but a wide mouth, and very thick dark brown hair.

"Are you ready for our waltz, Miss Donovan?" he said in that cultured voice of the English aristocracy.

She gave him a brilliant smile. "I am."

As he led her onto the dance floor, she glanced over her shoulder to grin at Serena, who was watching them go and gave her a little wave.

The marquis found a spot for them, and as the music began, he took her into his arms. Jessica loved to dance. Dancing was the one thing her mother had taught her that she wholeheartedly enjoyed.

So she slipped one arm around the Marquis of Millbridge and allowed him to take her gloved hand in his own. The music swelled, she inhaled, smelling the pungent odors of perfume and the crowd of humanity present tonight, and they began to dance.

"You're a very good waltzer!" she exclaimed as he swept her into a wide circle.

He chuckled. "So are you. It takes two to waltz."

She grinned up at him, and he smiled down at her, his dark eyes twinkling. They danced in silence for a while, then he said, "So, I hear you hail from the West Indies. Where, pray, did you acquire such excellent dancing skills?"

She laughed. "Hours of practicing with my sisters—mostly my sister Phoebe. We both love to dance."

"Oh? How many sisters do you have?"

"Four... well, three. The eldest is Meg. She's married to the Earl of Stratford. Then Phoebe—Mrs. Harper—and Olivia—the Duchess of Wakefield."

His dark brows drew together in a frown. "But you said four, at first."

"Yes." Her voice shook a little as they spun in another circle. Goodness, this man made her feel like she was flying! "Once I had four. But my eldest sister, Serena, died long ago."

"Oh, I am sorry." There was a pause as they danced around another couple. "How did she die?" he asked softly.

Jessica swallowed hard. Even though she knew now that it wasn't true, it still hurt her to say it. "She was lost at sea. Presumably drowned."

He stared at her, his dark eyes boring deep, as if he were trying to dig under her skin with his gaze alone. "Presumably?"

She shrugged. "Well, not *very* presumably. She was lost at sea and has been missing for eight years. Unless she was rescued by mermaids..." She allowed her voice to trail off. She didn't love to lie. Other than Phoebe, none of the Donovan sisters had ever been good liars. She hoped Meg would agree to revealing herself soon. Then the world could rejoice with Jessica and her family that Serena and Meg were both alive.

"But have you searched the seven seas for her? Perhaps she *is* alive." Jessica looked up at him, and he grinned, showing pearly white teeth that were a bit too small for the size of his mouth. "Perhaps," he said, "she was rescued by pirates and she escaped and is living somewhere, alive and well."

Jessica tore her eyes from his, suddenly scared to death they would give her away. The marquis's words were disturbingly close to the truth.

A realization struck her, and for the first time in years, she stumbled in the middle of a waltz. Fortunately, the marquis had not lost his composure, for he righted her quickly and continued on. "Forgive me," he said in a low voice. "I didn't mean to upset you."

"Oh, you didn't upset me." She chewed on her lip a moment, debating what to say. "That would be lovely, wouldn't it? If she were rescued, I mean."

"I shall hope that is what has happened to your sister. And I hope the pirates will return her to her family soon." He squeezed her hand, and compassion showed in his eyes. "If she does return, you will let me know, won't you?"

"Oh, of course," Jessica exclaimed. "We'd be so excited, we'd publish it in every newspaper in England!" That was the truth—too bad Meg wouldn't let them do that. Ultimately, Jessica understood Meg's predicament, and she wouldn't tell the Marquis of Millbridge—or anyone—that her sister was alive, but oh, how she wanted to!

They spoke of more mundane things—like the weather and the next ball both of them planned to attend—and then the waltz ended. The marquis returned her to Serena, they bowed to each other, and then he disappeared into the crowd.

"Well?" Serena asked as Beatrice joined them. "How did it go?"

Jessica frowned after him. "Very well, I think. But he seemed overly interested in our long-lost sister."

Serena glanced at the marquis, her brow furrowing. "That's odd."

"Very," Beatrice said.

Jessica shook off the uncomfortable feeling that had settled over her. There would only be a minute or two until the next dance, and she'd promised it to the very handsome Mr. Trenton. "Never mind. He's just an odd one, that's all." She turned to Beatrice. "You must tell me, Beatrice, how was your waltz with Sir Folsom?"

Will paced back and forth across the spacious drawing room, his mind roiling. "So Caversham's illegal activities are filling the Marquis of Millbridge's coffers."

"That's right." Meg had not moved from her chair. Her hands were clasped in her lap, her shoulders were tight, and her face was pale.

"But for what purpose?"

Slowly, Meg shook her head. "I don't know, exactly. Caversham is extremely careful about who he reveals information to, and he certainly never deliberately revealed anything to me. But after hearing bits here and there for eight years, I began to piece some of it together. The Marquis of Millbridge is a great supporter of the Duke of Cumberland."

Will nodded. Cumberland was the king's younger

brother, and third in line to the throne after the Duke of Clarence and Princess Victoria. The king was currently on his deathbed—he wasn't expected to survive the summer—and everyone believed the Duke of Clarence would be crowned King William IV by this time next year.

The populace mumbled, though. Worry had settled over Britain. The Duke of Clarence was old and suffered from poor health, and Princess Victoria was a child yet, too young to take on the duties of a monarch, not to mention the fact that she was female.

Will nodded at Meg. "Go on."

"Well, I believe the Marquis of Millbridge is using these ill-gotten gains to somehow advance Cumberland's power in England."

Will frowned. "But for what purpose?" Cumberland was already extremely powerful. He possessed a strong voice in the House of Lords, and, though he'd recently suffered a major defeat in the passage of the Catholic Relief Bill, he still was a force to be reckoned with in Parliament.

Meg shook her head. "That, I don't know."

Will leaned against one of the Grecian columns and studied Meg. Her gaze was fastened on the fire. Wisps of blond hair, lit bronze by the firelight, tumbled around her face. Just looking at her heated his blood.

Now he could understand, at least a little, her hesitance in telling him all this. It wasn't good news. The criminal he'd been after for the past six months was heavily entangled with a marquis and possibly the man third in line to the throne. Two of the most powerful men in England.

But why? What was Millbridge using those funds for?

Meg turned her head and looked up at him, her gray eyes dark and sad. "Caversham hates those who are not like himself, those he considers less than himself. He is the son of a marquis, but he is illegitimate. It is the worst sort of a curse to him, and a fact that will haunt him until the day he dies. He envies Millbridge, who is his younger brother by two years, but he also loves him. He has always wanted to prove he's more than simply the bastard sibling. He married Sarah out of lust more than anything, but he kept me prisoner in hopes that I would mold Sarah into a wife he could introduce to the marquis with pride."

Will returned to his chair and sank into it. "Did you succeed?"

She shook her head, her eyes glistening. "Not really. Sarah was born to a poor family in America. She was who she was, and she couldn't change—she never really wished to. Caversham punished her for that, though. Over and over, until he utterly broke her."

"Did he beat her?" he asked, remembering Lady Fenwicke and how brutal her husband had been to her.

"Sometimes."

"Did he beat Jake, too?" he asked, thinking of the boy's ever-serious expression and his somber blue eyes.

Meg wrapped her arms across her chest. "Once in a while. But...mostly...well, you've probably noticed this about Jake—he's different."

Will nodded.

"He's not simpleminded or mad, but sometimes people mistake him for an idiot. And that infuriates Caversham beyond reason. Jake withdraws, and in turn Caversham mocks him, scorns him, berates him, uses cruel words in an attempt to draw the boy from his shell."

"Does that work?"

She flinched. "It does, sometimes. But only in the

moment. Fear of his father only makes Jake withdraw further and for longer periods of time."

Will shook his head. "Why, if he thinks so low of his son, will he pursue him?"

"Because Jake is the only bit of Sarah he has left. He loved her in his way. Despite his cruelty, his jealousy, his obsession with her, he loved her."

"I see," Will said, although he didn't, not really.

"And Jake is his only legitimate son," Meg continued. "Caversham has always blamed Sarah and me for spoiling him. He believes that with proper discipline, he can turn Jake into a son worthy of bearing his name. And without Jake, who will take on Caversham's legacy after he's gone?"

"His legacy?" Will asked.

"As the modern-day pirate. The man who breaks every law he can and reaps a fortune. The man who owns a fleet of ships scattered through the Pacific and Atlantic oceans. The man who is, when all is said and done, even more powerful than his marquis brother."

Will's brows rose. "A fleet of ships?"

Meg nodded grimly. "I believe there are between fifteen and twenty."

Good God. "Are all of them engaged in illegal activity?"

"No. He maintains a façade of respectability with the few ships he uses for legal trading at any given time." Her lips twisted. "The others are either piratical or smuggling vessels."

"In the West Indies?" Surely if that were true, he'd have heard more about Jacob Caversham by now.

"Only one or two are in the West Indies at a time. The others are scattered around the globe."

"Does he keep any ships in England?"

Meg frowned. "I was never allowed to go ashore or show my face when we were in English ports. Nor was the crew allowed to discuss navigation in our presence. But I did overhear some of Caversham's discussions, and Sarah's cabins usually had a porthole. I was able to teach her some of the geography of the United Kingdom when I recognized certain ports of call where we were anchored."

"Where?" Will asked, prepared to commit the names to memory.

"Belfast. Bristol. Brighton. Blackpool." Her lips twisted. "They've been easy for me to remember, since they all begin with B—except Glasgow."

"Have you sailed on any of his other ships?"

"Yes. We moved from ship to ship. When we'd reach a port—one of the 'B' ports—we'd always swap ships. He did it mostly to throw the authorities off his scent, but he also wants to keep track of the condition of each of his ships at all times. He loves all his ships equally—each one is special to him, and complete control over each of them is very important to him."

Will slumped back in the chair, feeling the need for a glass of brandy. He didn't usually crave spirits, but there had been too many revelations this evening. He rose. "Would you like a drink?"

Her gaze jerked up to him, and she blinked. "I . . . suppose so."

"Some claret, perhaps?"

She shook her head. "No. I'll have whatever you have."

He nodded tersely and then went to the sideboard to pour their drinks. He returned with a tumbler full of amber liquid for each of them. He sat, swirled it around in his glass, watching the flames catch and refract on the crystal, and then took a long, fortifying drink.

Lowering his glass, he slid a glance at Meg, who swallowed hers with nary a flinch. He gave her a twisted grin. "Impressive."

A fine line appeared between her brows. "What do you mean?"

"No sputters, no coughing, and not even a little bit of a gag. Looks like you've drunk your fair share of brandy."

She gazed at the liquid in her glass. "Not brandy," she said softly. "Rum. Sarah and I did a bit of our own smuggling. It's a bit different. Harsher, I suppose. This is... fruity, in comparison."

He chuckled. "That it is."

After a moment of silence, both of them sipping their brandy, she asked, "Will?"

"Hm?"

"Before we leave London, Jake and I would like to see your house. I mean, if the invitation you issued earlier still stands."

He blew out a breath and took another long swallow before he answered her. Then he gazed into her eyes. "It does."

She gave him a small smile. "Thank you. Lord Stratford's home is lovely, but it would be nice to call on at least one other person before I leave town."

For the first time in a long while, Meg rose from her chair, extending her long, glorious limbs in a stretch. She walked to the sideboard to deposit her glass, her hips swaying in a delicate motion that mesmerized him.

"You're more beautiful than ever."

She froze, her hand still curled around the crystal. Then, slowly, she lowered the glass and turned to face him.

He rose, and his feet carried him to her before he had an opportunity to think about what he was doing.

When they were within arm's length of each other, she tilted her head up, looking at him, her eyes silver in the fire's glow.

"Don't be afraid," he murmured. "I understand your fear now. But we'll find a way. I will keep you and Jake safe."

"Jake and I will be leaving for Lancashire in a few days' time. We're not your responsibility."

"I want you to be." His voice was little more than a rough whisper.

"Why?"

He reached out and grasped her shoulders. "I want to try it again. I want to be with you. I want...I want to marry you."

He blinked. Even he hadn't expected to say that. But through his surprise, he realized it was the truth. He still wanted her in his life. Permanently.

Her eyes widened, and he shook his head at her expression of disbelief. "Listen to me...I still care for you, Meg."

She licked her lips, a frantic gesture, and her eyes darted to both sides of him as if searching for a route of escape. Her shoulders shuddered beneath his hands before her gaze finally returned to him. "You can't know that for certain, Will. You don't know me. I've told you this before. I've changed. I have Jake to think about now."

"Don't hide behind Jake."

Her eyes narrowed. "Do you think that's what I'm

doing?" She jerked out of his hold and backed up several steps. "How dare you pretend to know how I feel? I've spent the last six years protecting Jake, nurturing him to the best of my ability. And you dismiss all that and say I'm hiding behind him? Damn you, Will Langley."

Crossing her arms over her heaving chest, she turned away from him and stalked toward the door. Will thrust a hand through his hair. "Meg, stop. I'm sorry."

He closed his eyes as she hesitated.

"Don't be angry with me." He pushed out the words.

"Please. Don't do this," she said with her back to him, anger still resonating in her voice.

He shook his head. She was confusing the hell out of him.

She lowered her head into her hands. "This is too much. I just want to survive the next few months. I can't... I don't know how to face... you, or these... these *feelings* I thought were long dead boiling up inside me." He opened his eyes to see her turning back to him, halfway across the room from him. "I have spent so long trying to survive, trying to help Jake and Sarah survive... and I failed with Sarah. I am so afraid I'm going to fail with Jake, too. And if I let these rekindling emotions push aside my concentration on Jake, I fear..." Her shoulders shook visibly now.

"I'm so afraid, Will," she choked. "I remember you, but I don't know you anymore. I know myself, and I know Jake, but I don't know you!"

He strode across the room and pulled her into his arms. "You do know me, Meg. Let yourself know me again."

She'd kept him—and her family—at arm's length because she had a single-minded purpose—to keep

Jake away from his father. Will understood that and he respected her for it, but if she let him in, he could help her even more.

He pressed his lips into her hair. Digging deep within, he found the patience that her reappearance into his life had seemed to obliterate. "I'll wait. I'll give you time. As long as you need."

Minutes passed. It was hard to tell how many—Will couldn't judge the passage of time when he held Meg in his arms. Finally, slowly, her arms reached up and slipped around him, and she laid her cheek against his chest.

"Thank you," she whispered.

He closed his eyes and breathed in sugarcane. He wanted her. But she wasn't ready.

"I'll protect you always," he murmured. "And that's why I'm coming to Lancashire with you."

Chapter Ten

An unmarked carriage arrived at Lord Stratford's house late the following morning. Jake had been waiting, peeking out the drawing room's front window, and he squealed when Will disembarked from the carriage.

"Captain Will is here, Meg! Captain Will is here!"

Meg calmly put her sewing into her sewing basket and glanced up at her sisters and Lady Fenwicke. Serena had been reading a Shakespearean comedy, Jessica was attempting to embroider a scarf, Olivia was writing a letter, and Phoebe and Lady Fenwicke were rifling around in the drawer holding the pianoforte music.

"Well, here it is," Meg said. "My first outing."

Jessica snorted. "Not really an outing if you refuse to spend any time outdoors. And it's too bad, really, because it's a beautiful day and the trees in Hyde Park have finally decided to bloom."

Meg just shook her head.

Phoebe sighed. "Jess, you must stop badgering poor Meg to go outside."

"Someday I will go outside, Jessica," Meg promised.

"Someday soon, I hope," her sister said.

A footman came in to announce Will, who greeted Meg's sisters before turning to her. He held out a gloved hand to her, and she realized he hadn't removed his hat or his coat. "Are you ready to go?"

She grasped his hand with her own bare one and allowed him to help her up from the chair, smiling at him. "I'm ready." She slid a glance to Jake, whose brown hair was sticking up at odd angles all over his head. He had a habit of vigorously rubbing his hair whenever he was nervous or excited. "Jake is more than ready."

He gave Will a brilliant grin. "My tooth is loose, sir. Would you like to wiggle it?"

"Jake!"

He cocked his head at her, frowning. Meg knew what he was thinking: "I said 'sir,' just like you told me to."

"I'm sure," she said in a gentler voice, "Captain Langley doesn't wish to be poking his fingers into your mouth."

Jake ignored her. Instead, he walked up to Will, bared his teeth, and pointed at one in the top front. "It's that one," he said, his voice slurring.

Will smiled at Meg, then down at Jake. "I should love to wiggle it." He reached out, grasped the tooth between two fingers, and moved it back and forth. "It is quite loose. I daresay in a week or two, you'll have an enormous hole just there."

Jake smiled, pleased, and Meg took Will's arm. But as they turned to leave the room, Serena murmured something. Meg turned back to her. "What was that?"

Serena's cheeks instantly turned a shade of deep pink. "Before you go, there's something I'd like to tell you. All of you," she added, glancing back toward the window, where Jessica stood with Olivia and Phoebe.

She folded her hands in her lap and looked down at them. "I'm with child," she said, her voice little more than a whisper.

"Oh, Serena!" Jessica exclaimed, slapping her hands to her chest.

Will released Meg, and he went to Serena. He took both her hands in his own and helped her to stand before he gathered her into his arms, then pulled away and kissed her on the cheek. "Congratulations," he murmured. "Does Stratford know?"

She nodded up at him, beaming. "He does. This time, he was the first person I told."

Olivia, Phoebe, Jessica, and Lady Fenwicke all hugged Serena. Meg approached them but hung behind Will, feeling unaccountably shy. She knew Serena had suffered a dangerous miscarriage last autumn, and she'd been wanting to have a child badly.

Jessica clapped her hands. "When will the baby be born?"

"Sometime in October."

"Babies cry all the time," Jake announced from beside her, as if he were an expert.

"Not always," Meg said, smiling down at him. "You, for example, were the sweetest, quietest baby ever." She turned back to her sister. Not knowing what, exactly, to do with her hands, she clasped them in front of her. "Congratulations, Serena. I'm so happy for you." And she was. If the babe was due in October, that meant she was already a few months along, and the most dangerous part of the pregnancy, as far as miscarriages were concerned, had already passed.

"Thank you." Serena dropped Will's hands and hugged Meg. Meg wrapped her arms around her twin, glad she'd taken the awkwardness away. After congratulating her again, Will, Meg, and Jake finally left the drawing room.

They went down the corridor and exited through the kitchen from the back door, where the carriage had come up into the mews and there was less of a chance of anyone seeing her and Jake.

Will lifted Jake into the carriage, then he handed her up, stepped inside, and closed the door behind him before taking the backward-facing seat across from her and Jake.

Will rapped the ceiling and the carriage started with a jolt. Heavy curtains covered the windows, only allowing in a scant amount of dim light. As Will settled across from them, Meg wondered about the tightness in his expression and the stern press of his lips.

She slid her hand over Jake's and squeezed. Jake squeezed back and turned to peek out the curtains.

She tensed, then relaxed. Surely it was safe enough for him to look outside. No one would recognize him driving by. Truly, there were only a few people in the world that would recognize Jake, and according to Will, those people were still far away, in Ireland.

Still, she watched Jake for a long moment, chewing her lip.

Will raised a brow at her, but she shook her head. "He's all right."

Will nodded but didn't say anything. They sat in silence for long moments, Meg fighting not to fidget.

"What's wrong?" she finally asked Will.

In the dim light, she could see his dark brows snap together. "Nothing."

"You seem very . . . on edge," she said.

His lips twisted into a smile that didn't seem quite genuine. "Nothing's wrong. Nothing at all."

She didn't believe him for a second.

It wasn't long before they arrived at Will's house in Cavendish Square, but to Meg, sitting in a dark carriage with a very somber Will in front of her, the ride had seemed interminable.

Will gave them another of those false, twisted smiles. "We're here."

His voice sounded odd, too.

They'd arrived at the back of the house, and there wasn't much to see except the white-painted back walls, a pair of tall, narrow windows, and a wide brick chimney. Will helped them out, and keeping Meg's hand in his own, he opened the back door of the house and entered, Jake following close behind him.

The kitchen was small, but two women were working. One was kneading dough and another stirring a savory smelling mixture on the stove. They both stopped and bobbed curtsies at Will and Meg, with mumbled, "Good afternoon, sir, ma'am," before returning to their work.

"They're preparing a luncheon for us," Will murmured. "It should be ready shortly."

"Oh, that's lovely," Meg said politely.

They left the kitchen, and Will led them through the simple but elegant entry hall, where they deposited their coats, hats, and gloves, and down a short corridor that ended at three closed doors. Will opened the first one.

"This is my office and library."

It was a compact space, reminding Meg of Will's quarters on the *Freedom*. A large mahogany desk occupied the center of the room, with two narrow, high windows behind it—the ones she'd seen from outside, Meg realized. To the right of the desk, a large bookshelf teemed with books. There were relics of life at sea everywhere: compasses, clocks, thermometers, and even a sextant sat on one of the shelves. Paintings of ships lined the walls—Will's ships, Meg realized. The room smelled of a not unpleasant combination of old leather, musty books, and salt. Holding on firmly to Jake's hand, she smiled at him. "It's lovely."

"Thank you." Will hesitated. "I spend quite a lot of time in here."

"I can imagine," she murmured. He'd always been a hard worker. Ultimately, she wasn't at all surprised he'd made a name for himself in the London shipping industry.

They moved on to the next room—a dining room brightly lit by the late-morning sunlight streaming through the bow window that faced the street. The dining room table was of the same mahogany as Will's desk, and surrounded by six chairs, and a marble fireplace dominated one of the walls.

After they left the dining room, Will led them into the drawing room. It wasn't as grand as her brother-in-law's, but it was elegant and simple, in Will's style. A large window draped with elegant blue-striped curtains dominated one wall of the room and looked over a blue silk sofa and two chairs facing the fireplace. A plastered nautical motif—shells and dolphins—had been carved in the recessed square in the ceiling.

After Will saw her and Jake seated on the sofa and went to stoke the fire—something Lord Stratford always relied on servants for, she'd noticed during the past few weeks—she said, "Everything in this house reinforces your independence and your love of the sea."

He turned to look at her over his shoulder. "Does that bother you?"

She shook her head. "Not at all." She hesitated. "I was always ambivalent about the sea. I was surrounded by it for most of my childhood in Antigua, but then it took me from my family. During the years on Caversham's ships, it was my prison, but it was also very much a solace."

Indeed, even sitting here now, within the blues and whites of this room, and inhaling the faint salty smell of the ocean, she felt comforted.

"I understand." Brushing his hands, Will rose to his feet just as someone knocked at the door. "Come in."

It was a maid. She bobbed a curtsy and then asked, "Are you ready, sir?"

Will hesitated, then nodded. "Yes. Bring him in."

Meg glanced inquisitively at Will, who kept his focus on the maid until she closed the door behind her. Then, slowly, he turned to her, his face suddenly awash with anguish.

He glanced at Jake, who was fidgeting beside Meg on the sofa, and then looked at Meg. "I fear I've done this all wrong," he murmured. "I'm so sorry."

"What do you mean?" she asked.

"I should have told you...warned you. Prepared you...I don't know what I was thinking."

Jake scurried off the sofa and walked to Will, his hand in his mouth. "It's looser now, sir."

Will blew out a breath and looked down at Jake. "Is it?"

"Will you pull it out for me?"

Will's eyes widened. "I don't think it's quite ready for that."

"Meg said when it's very, very loose, we can pull it. It's verrrrry loose."

Will wiggled Jake's tooth. "Well, I'm not certain, lad. I think it'll be a few days yet before it's ready to go."

"I want it out. Now."

Meg stood, mild alarm growing within her. Jake was prone to tantrums, though he'd learned it was no use to have them among people like his father and his men. But he'd been obsessed with losing his tooth for a few days now, and he was growing impatient.

"How about this?" Will said. "When we arrive in Lancashire, at Mr. Harper's house, we'll pull it then. It can be our celebration of our arrival."

Jake's blue eyes widened. "You're going with us to Lancashire?"

Will smiled. "I am." He glanced at Meg, his brows raised as challenging her to deny it.

She wouldn't deny it, though. She'd already grown to like the idea of him being with them in Lancashire. She had to admit it was mostly for selfish reasons—the truth of it was, she wanted him close.

Maybe, just maybe, she could let go of her distrust and fear, and believe that Will did want to marry her—not the memory of her, but *her*. Perhaps she didn't need to be so afraid of Will taking over that place in her heart that Jake possessed. Perhaps they could both reside there; they could both be safe and happy there.

In the past few hours, the seeds of hope had begun to sprout within her.

The door opened, and the maid stood there with a boy—a year or two older than Jake and several inches taller.

The boy grinned. "Papa! You're back!"

He rushed at Will and threw his arms around Will's middle. Awkwardly, Will patted his back while he gazed at Meg, a raw sort of apology in his eyes.

Papa. She'd been a fool. Will *did* have a family here in London.

"Thomas," he said in a low voice as the maid retreated, "these are my friends. Miss Donovan and Jake. Miss Donovan, Jake, this is Thomas. My son."

"Good afternoon, Thomas," Meg said. "It's very nice to meet you."

Jake just stared at Thomas, who turned in Will's arms and stared back.

"How old are you?" she asked him.

He flicked a glance at Meg before returning his gaze to Jake. "Seven," he said sullenly.

"I see." Seven? Good Lord . . . Will had gotten a woman with child not long after she'd fallen overboard, then. Pain lanced through her, but she kept herself steady, doggedly keeping her gaze off Will. "Jake, darling, can you tell Thomas how old you are?"

Jake didn't move from his position on the sofa. Meg knew he wouldn't answer, so she answered for him. "Jake is six years old."

"Hullo," Thomas said.

Jake frowned at him, and Meg smiled at Thomas. "Jake hasn't known very many other little boys," she explained.

"Why not?" Thomas asked.

"He's been on a ship most of his life. There were no other boys there."

Thomas looked intrigued. "A ship? I like ships." He glanced at Will. "My papa is the captain of a ship."

Jake scowled.

"He says someday I will be a captain, too. Right, Papa?"

"That's right," Will said. "If that's what you wish to be."

The way he looked at the boy with such a gentle expression—it made something clench deep inside Meg. Once, she had believed she'd be the mother of Will's children. But this handsome child was proof that that wasn't to be.

"Papa bought me a fleet of model ships to play with, and big tubs that I sail them in," Thomas said. "Would you like to play with them with me?"

Jake's expression didn't change, and he didn't answer.

"Where are your ships?" Meg asked Thomas. It was miraculous that she was managing to hold a conversation, because the gears in her mind felt like they were whirring at a thousand miles an hour.

"They are upstairs, in my bedchamber. Papa created an entire ocean for them up there!"

Meg raised a brow at Will. "Well, that's something I'd certainly like to see. May I join you?"

"All right."

"Jake, would you like to see Thomas's ships?"

Without breaking his frown, Jake nodded.

They all went upstairs, Thomas leading the way. When he opened the door to his bedchamber, both Jake's and

Meg's eyes widened. "Goodness!" Meg exclaimed. "It is like an ocean."

A wide, deep trough ran along two of the walls. Several small replicas of ships floated in the calm waters. One looked very similar to the *Freedom*.

Will cleared his throat and gestured toward one end of the trough. "There is a drain leading from the bottom to the sewer. We drain and fill it often to keep it clean."

"It's amazing," Meg said. What little boy wouldn't love to have such a wonderful toy?

Jake pulled away from her and strode to the *Freedom* replica with purpose in his step. Cautiously, he reached out and touched one of the canvas sails. *"Freedom,"* he whispered.

"Yes!" Thomas exclaimed. "That's my papa's newest ship!"

Thomas went to stand beside Jake, and as he began to point out the features of the *Freedom*, Meg watched Jake relax. Even though her pulse still fluttered unevenly and unshed tears stung behind her eyes, something inside her softened. Jake needed to make friends.

Will and Meg stepped back and watched the boys as they grew more comfortable with each other. After about a half hour, when Jake was captaining the *Freedom* and Thomas another of the ships, Will murmured, "Shall we return to the drawing room?"

Meg hesitated. Jake was likely to panic if he found himself alone in a strange place without her, yet he seemed more than happy at the moment. "Jake," she said, interrupting his order to his imaginary sailors to haul up, a command he'd heard thousands of time in his short life, "would you mind very much if Captain Langley and I returned to the drawing room?"

"I want to play," he said.

"You may continue to play, but we'll be downstairs. All right?"

"You'll be here?"

"Yes, I'll be here in the house. Just downstairs."

"All right," Jake said simply, and went back to his maneuver.

Meg nodded to Will, and they returned downstairs. As they neared the drawing room, a maid intercepted them and told them that luncheon was ready.

"Do you think the boys are hungry?" Will asked.

"I think they're likely to play till sundown without one twinge of hunger."

"Why don't we eat first, then have a maid bring a tray up to them?"

"That sounds fine," Meg said.

Will nodded, then opened the dining room door for her. He held out one of the chairs for her to be seated in, then he took the chair beside it, at the head of the table.

The servants quickly cleared away the two extra places that had been set, and Meg registered the fact that Will had planned to eat with the children. She knew from experience that many upper-crust families segregated the children and the adults at mealtimes, and she'd never understood that practice. Her family in Antigua had always eaten together—it was something their father had been adamant about.

"How can ye be a family in truth," he'd ask in the Irish brogue all of them had loved, "without discussin' yer day at the table?"

Their mother hadn't complained about this practice, because it gave her the opportunity to teach her daughters excellent table manners, a task she took very seriously. After their father died, their mother had become stricter and she'd grown even more convinced that her daughters needed to be raised to be aristocratic ladies. Nevertheless, eating together as a family was one practice she'd never abandoned.

The meal was light: a mix of breads, cheeses, and two soups to choose from. As had become their practice, they ate in silence. Meg wanted to speak. There was so much she wanted to say, to ask... And perhaps it made her a shrew, but there were certain accusations tumbling around in her mind, and she had to bite her tongue not to snap them out at Will.

"You must have many questions," Will said quietly. He wasn't eating, she realized, just watching her with sad eyes.

She jerked her head up to face him and swallowed hard. "I do."

He pushed away his plate. "I should have told you sooner, but it never seemed the right time. We've had so many other things to discuss, to work out. But I couldn't keep him a secret from you, Meg."

"I can tell you've been a wonderful father to him. He seems like a very well-adjusted child." Each word felt caustic on her tongue.

"No. I have been a very poor father. I didn't see him at all until a year and a half ago." He looked down at the table. "I've been attempting to make it up to him ever since."

"Ah." She supposed that explained the extravagant ship models and ocean upstairs.

"Fortunately, though, he had a good fatherly role model to look up to before I came into his life. Stratford."

Meg's eyes went wide. "My brother-in-law?"

"Yes."

"Who is the child's mother?"

"I should tell you the whole story, from the beginning."

She nodded.

"I fear it will make you hate me."

The food suddenly felt like a lump of coal in her stomach. She was unable to answer, unable to guarantee that she could never hate him. Could one love someone and hate them at the same time? Perhaps, she thought. If she could name the contradictory feelings roiling inside her right now, those two words might appear.

She, too, pushed away her plate.

Will sighed, seemingly resigned. "Come into the drawing room with me?"

"Yes," she said, her voice as thin as her composure.

He helped her from her chair and then followed her to the drawing room. She took one of the blue armchairs, avoiding the sofa because she didn't want to risk him sitting beside her.

From the first moment she'd recognized him after all these years, she'd tried to distance herself from him. First it was for his own safety, and she'd failed with that. Then it was because she felt they were strangers to each other after all the time that had passed. Now, she realized she didn't really know this man, and perhaps she never really had. The Will she'd known had been so constant. Never— not for one second—would she have second-guessed his fidelity.

Before he sat, Will poured two brandies and handed one to her. She took it but set it on the small carved wood table beside her chair without taking a sip.

Nursing his own brandy, he began to speak.

"After you left London with Serena eight years ago, I was due to go to sea with the Navy. However, at the last minute it was discovered our ship required repairs and our departure would be delayed by at least a month.

"You hadn't been gone long, but I already missed you, Meg. I didn't know if I'd see you again; if I'd die at sea or in a battle; if I'd eventually lose you to some other man before I felt myself worthy of asking for your hand in marriage.

"I was depressed because you'd left, and I despaired of ever seeing you again. Stratford was also feeling low, though his depression ran to deep shame, because it was his fault you'd gone to begin with, his fault that Serena was ruined, and his responsibility for shunning her. In our mutual despondence, we became friends. I learned that despite what he'd done, Stratford loved your sister. His own actions had filled him with such indescribable regret, I found myself doing whatever I could to help him.

"He and I began to devise a plan whereby he would sail to the West Indies, where he would beg your sister's forgiveness and ask for her hand in marriage. However, before he could make good on his plan, word came that your sister had been lost at sea."

Meg flinched. If not for her own mother's machinations, Will would have heard the truth—that Meg had been lost at sea, not Serena. Lord Stratford would have gone to Antigua and married Serena long ago. Both of them would have been spared many years of unhappiness.

Not for the first time, Meg was glad her mother wasn't here. She couldn't bear to be in the woman's presence after what she'd done to all of them.

"When Stratford heard of her 'death,'" Will continued, "he lost his mind with grief. He blamed himself and considered himself a murderer. Guilt tore him apart. He fled London and went to Bath. I accompanied him there, determined to watch out for him, to ensure he didn't do anything foolish."

Will downed the rest of his brandy. When he looked at her again, his eyes were shining. "He did behave foolishly in Bath. But I was even more foolish."

Meg clutched the arms of her chair and stared at him, unable to speak.

"There was a young woman at the inn where we'd found lodgings. Her name was Eliza Anderson. We thought she was a barmaid."

Abruptly, Will rose and went to fetch himself more brandy. Meg waited, staring at the place he'd vacated, not moving, not speaking.

When he returned, sitting heavily on the sofa, he continued. "She wasn't a barmaid, though. She was the daughter of a local magistrate. She'd climbed out the window of her bedchamber to meet her friends at the tavern.

"Stratford and I had been drinking steadily for the entire evening, and we were both quite drunk. After we watched her and the barmaids sing a song, Stratford pulled her aside, and—" He stopped abruptly.

"And what?" Meg's voice was steady, quiet.

"He propositioned her. On my behalf."

Meg blew out a breath.

"She was young and wild, and she wanted to get out of Bath and go to London. She thought Stratford and I might be the means for her to do that."

He drank most of his brandy in one gulping swallow

and continued. "They gestured to me, and I staggered over to them. She took my hand and led me upstairs."

Will popped up off the sofa again, and Meg jerked in surprise at his abrupt movement.

He pushed both hands through his hair. "I didn't realize where I was, what I was doing, until the next morning, when I woke up beside her."

Meg moved her hands from the chair arms, certain she'd scratched permanent marks into them, and clasped them in her lap, looking down at them.

"You believed I lived," she whispered.

"Yes," he choked. "It was the stupidest thing I've ever done. The most foolish, the most cowardly. The most unforgiveable."

"Yes," she agreed.

He stumbled to her and dropped to his knees in front of her. "I'm not a rake, Meg. I'm no scoundrel. I don't pursue loose women. I never touched another woman after Eliza. The following morning I knew how deeply I'd erred, and vowed to myself I'd never repeat the mistake. And I didn't." He swallowed hard. "Meg, there is only one woman in the world I ever wanted to have children with, and that woman is you."

She just stared at him. It was impossible to just blithely forgive him on that statement. She couldn't.

Her tone was cold. "You have said you planned to marry me at that time. Yet you bedded someone else. How long had I been gone?"

He looked down, away from her. "Less than four months." His tone was flat.

She tightened her clasped hands, and they both sat in

silence for several minutes. Finally, she asked him, "What do you want from me?"

He looked up at her. "Surely you know the answer to that?"

"No."

"Your forgiveness. Not today. I know it's far, far too much to forgive in one day. But I want—I hope—that you will give me the chance to prove myself to you."

She stared at him, unable to answer, but as if she had responded, he nodded and rose to his feet.

"Where is she now?" she asked. "Thomas's mother?"

He groaned softly. "My foolishness didn't end that night. Not completely."

"Tell me what happened. I want to hear it all. Why didn't you marry her?"

Marrying her would have been the right thing to do. The *Will* thing to do.

Standing before her, he clasped his hands behind his back.

"We left Bath early the morning... after. But a few days later, I came to my senses. If word had spread, and I was sure it had, because most of the people in the tavern had seen us, I would do what I could for her. Short of marriage." He shook his head. "I couldn't, in good conscience, give her that. At least not yet. Because"—he licked his lips—"I wasn't sure about you. For all I knew, you could have been with child. We'd..."

She raised her hand, because she couldn't bear for him to remind her of the night they'd lain together just before she'd left London. Both of them—or so she'd thought—had been so bound by duty and honor, that night had meant everything. At least it had to her. Obviously it had meant far less to him.

"Yes, well—" Will cleared his throat. "I couldn't very well propose to Eliza when I didn't know your...status." He flinched at his own awkward usage of the word.

"I knew you would be devastated by what I'd done. But you were so beautiful, so lovely inside and out, that I knew you could do better than an inconstant bastard like me. Once I heard from you and assured myself that you were not with child, I planned to offer for Eliza. Even though she didn't love me, and I'd make a poor husband to her. It was to be my penance for what I had done.

"I went to Stratford and told him my plan, but he was adamantly against the idea. He, more than anyone else, knew how much I loved you. Knew how much my mistake had destroyed me. He'd made a terrible mistake, too, you see, with your sister.

"Stratford formed a new plan. *He* would return to Bath and take responsibility for Eliza. In a state of utter weakness and cowardice, I agreed."

Meg looked up at Will. His face was flushed a deep red, and his eyes still shone. His hands were still clasped behind his back as he stood before her, head bowed.

"He didn't find Eliza in Bath," Will continued. "But he continued to search for her, even after I went to sea. He finally found her in a workhouse, several months gone with child. Her father had thrown her out as a wanton whore and she had gone to London, where she'd quickly run out of funds."

Something constricted in Meg's chest. "Oh, Will." The story seemed to get worse and worse.

"Stratford provided for her and Thomas for several years, until a year and a half ago, when Serena discovered them by accident. By then, Stratford had grown very close to them both, and he remains so. But your sister needed to know the truth—that the child wasn't Stratford's, and it was then that I finally, belatedly, took responsibility for them and acknowledged Thomas as my own."

"What about Eliza?"

"We've come to an agreement whereby we each care for Thomas half the time. He arrived just this morning, and he will remain with me for the rest of the Season."

"You did not marry her," Meg mused. "Even believing I was dead."

"No. Although...I asked." He closed his eyes and continued. "I felt it was the honorable thing to do. She knew all about you by then, and she said no. She won't marry a man who doesn't love her and who she cannot love. When Thomas was an infant, she might have done so, for his protection, but now, it's too late. Thomas is seven years old, and he knows full well what he is."

Will didn't say it, but Meg knew he was thinking it: *a bastard.*

Will opened his eyes. "So there it is. He is my son, he is a good child, and he has brought a little happiness into my life. I continue to provide for Eliza, and I will do so for as long as she has need of my support."

"I see," Meg said quietly.

"I know you might disapprove of me continuing to support my one-night mistress, but I feel it is the proper thing to do. The only way I can compensate for my mistakes in some small way."

Meg shrugged. "Why should it matter to me what you do with your mistress, Will? I have never had any real claim over you."

Oh, but wasn't that the truth? Everything she'd felt for him, everything she'd thought she'd known of who he was, was false. She rose from the blue chair, no longer feeling comfortable here surrounded by all these things that resonated of Will.

"I think it's time for Jake and me to go home."

Chapter Eleven

The following night, Lord Stratford invited Will and Mr. Briggs over for dinner. Meg wasn't looking forward to the evening at all. Nevertheless, she hadn't told him not to come. As much as her reasoning mind told her to push him as far away as possible, for some reason, when it came to her speaking the words of rejection she knew she must say to him, they just wouldn't emerge.

After she'd hurriedly dressed for dinner and left Jake in the kitchen, which had become his favorite room of the house—he loved to gaze at the motions the servants made of chopping and kneading, and he even enjoyed watching the scullery maids scrubbing the dishes—she knocked on the door to Serena's dressing room.

"Who is it?"

"It's . . ." Meg hesitated, then said, "me." The servants knew who she was and who Serena really was, and Serena promised that they were trustworthy, but she still had a difficult time saying her name was Meg when the world knew her sister by that name.

"Come in," Serena called.

Meg opened the door to find her twin standing before a tall looking glass with her red-haired maid standing behind her, tugging on the strings to her stays. Serena glanced over her shoulder at Meg. "I'm getting fat," she announced. "This thing is tighter every day."

"Nonsense," Meg said. Serena possessed healthy, womanly curves, but no one would consider her fat. Her weight was ideal, a weight Meg wished to be. On Caversham's ship, food had always been simple and often scarce. Here, the heavy, richly seasoned foods the earl's cook made weighted Meg down and made her feel out of sorts, but she'd tried to eat and had managed to put on a few pounds.

"Besides," she added, "you are with child. Gaining weight is inevitable, you know."

"But not this early on," Serena said with a groan.

Meg reached for the strings from the maid. "May I help?" she asked, suddenly feeling shy. She and Serena had dressed each other from the time they could walk. But now, it seemed... awkward. Serena had someone else to do it for her.

Serena's gray eyes flitted toward her. "Of course," she said quickly. "You may go, Flannery. I will call for you if I need anything else."

"Yes, my lady." With a shy smile in Meg's direction, the maid exited from the room.

Meg worked on Serena's stays in silence. She managed the strings with practiced ease—she'd spent many an hour helping Sarah with her stays, too.

"Is something wrong?" Serena asked after a few minutes.

"What makes you say that?"

Serena's grin was wry as she looked at her sister in the mirror. "You don't make it a habit of coming into my room while I'm dressing."

Meg felt even more awkward. Her hands stilled on the strings. "I'm sorry," she said softly. "Should I go?"

"You should not."

Looking down, Meg tugged on the strings one final time, then began to tie them. "Remember how we used to help each other dress?"

"Of course I do. How could I forget?"

"I don't know. It was so long ago, it all feels like a dream. It doesn't even seem real anymore."

"Oh, it was real."

Meg turned to fetch Serena's petticoat, which was lying over a nearby chair. As she helped her sister into it, she said, "I came... Well, I wanted to ask you something about Will."

Serena nodded, but her shoulders stiffened. Serena had been rather tight-lipped when it came to Will. It was obvious that she and Will cared about each other, but Serena rarely spoke of him in Meg's presence.

"What about him?" The petticoat settled around Serena's shins, and she reached for her blue silk dinner dress hanging from the nearby clothes press.

"Why didn't you tell me about his boy?" Meg couldn't help the edge of despair that colored her tone.

Serena's empty hand dropped. Slowly she turned to face Meg. "You know about Thomas?"

"I do."

"Did he...tell you about him? Introduce the two of you?"

"Yes." Meg gazed down at the Persian carpet cushioning her feet. "Both."

"I'm glad."

Meg didn't know what to do with her hands, so she clenched them at her sides as she looked back up at Serena. "Why didn't you tell me about him sooner? Why did you let me find out...that way?" The words seemed to be emerging faster than she could control them. "How could you have let me continue on so long blind to the fact that Will has a child?"

Serena sank into the chair her petticoat had been lying over. "Oh, Meg. I am sorry. I just...it was his secret to tell you...or not. It wasn't for me to reveal such a thing to you."

"I didn't want to hear it from him, Serena."

"I'm sure you didn't want to hear it at all."

Meg gave her sister a bleak look. Serena sighed. "Meg...surely you see it. He is devoted to you. He still looks at you the same way he used to."

"Perhaps most women believe it is all right to turn a blind eye to unfaithful lovers," Meg said quietly. "But I fear I cannot do that. Perhaps I am too weak."

"No. You're not at all weak. If Jonathan did something like that..." Serena failed to hide her shudder. "Well, I don't know what I'd do. You have every right to feel hurt and upset."

"Even though it happened so many years ago? Even though we were both so young, and I truly had no claim over him besides a few promises murmured in the heat of the moment?"

"Even so."

Meg closed her eyes. "The worst of it is, he believed I was alive when he did it. He'd promised me nothing short of the moon only a few months earlier. And then...for him to go and betray that so soon..."

"I know." Serena's eyes were dark with pain, as if she truly did understand. "I thought Thomas was Jonathan's child at first. I cannot begin to describe to you the depth of the anger and hurt and betrayal I felt."

Meg stumbled around to the chair near Serena's and almost fell into it. "What am I going to do?"

"You still care for him?"

"How could I not? We not only have a past, but he saved me. He's been so...kind to me. And...well, I still find him...attractive. More so than I did before, if that's even possible."

Serena raised one eyebrow. "Well, I wouldn't have thought that was possible. You thought him Adonis personified before."

"And yet he was inconstant," Meg said, hardly hearing her sister. "He is not the man he's shown to me. There's someone else lurking beneath that surface I have always admired so much. It's someone I cannot like or respect."

Serena studied Meg for a moment, then she sighed again. "Meg, I don't want to influence you. I love you so much, and no matter what happens, that will never change. You're my sister and my twin. I want so badly for you to become part of our family again."

"But?" Meg asked, her tone and expression grim.

"But I love Will, too," Serena said. "Not in a carnal way," she added quickly. "It's never been like that between us. But I do love him, and my first instinct will be to defend him. Will has made mistakes. We have all made mistakes."

At Meg's skeptical look, she amended that last comment. "Some of us have made worse mistakes than others. But despite the terribly hurtful nature of the error he made, he's a good man, through and through. I truly believe what you see is the true Will. He's not hiding a wicked side underneath his honorable exterior. He *is* honorable—"

"How can you call inconstancy honorable?" Meg choked out.

Serena closed her eyes. "It was a mistake," she said again. "One he repented for and never repeated again for all those years. Even after he discovered I was not you, he never took another woman into his bed. Goodness, he's never even looked at another woman the way he looks at you now."

"I want to believe you so badly, Serena. I want to be able to forgive him. I'm just not sure I can."

Serena's look softened with sympathy. "Did you meet Thomas today at Will's house?"

"Yes."

"And Will told you the story?"

"Yes. As difficult as it was to hear." Meg grimaced.

"Thomas is a good boy. He and Jonathan are still very close. And Will has done so well with him over the past months. Like you have with Jake."

"Except Jake is not mine."

"He might as well be." Serena studied Meg for a moment, then took a deep breath. "Meg...you've been here for a while now...and I feel I must ask you...What's wrong with Jake?"

Instantly, Meg stiffened all over. She could virtually feel the brick wall stacking up between her and her sister. "What do you mean?"

"He's a very unusual child, Meg. Surely you know that."

"He's not stupid, if that's what you're saying." That's what all the sailors had called him, to his face. With Caversham's blessing. Caversham believed that if they called him an idiot often enough, he would try harder to not behave like one.

Serena looked taken aback. "I didn't say he was stupid. Just...different. Quieter than most children...and more...*extreme*, I suppose is the right word."

"He is," Meg said shortly. "It is his way."

"Has he always been like that?"

"He has."

"I see. I was wondering if this was new, brought on by his recent trauma."

Meg gave her sister a flat stare. "His life has been riddled with trauma, Serena. And yes, he has been this way for the whole of it. He didn't even utter his first word until just after he'd turned four...But it doesn't mean he is an idiot. He just shows his intelligence in different ways."

"I've seen that, too," Serena said softly. "Not many small children could fit together those tiny puzzle pieces you cut for him."

"I want to give him constancy. I want to give him a good, stable life so that he can grow up and integrate into society as much as possible."

"Of course you do."

"People have called him mad. They have called him a simpleton and an idiot." Meg wrapped her arms across her chest. "And I won't hear any of it. I'd rather take him far away than languish in a place where people speak of him like that."

"I wouldn't allow it in my presence, either. I never said he was mad or a simpleton, Meg. I only saw that he was different."

"He is different. He is special."

Serena nodded. Then she rose from the chair. "Will and Mr. Briggs will be here soon. I should get dressed." Giving Meg a hopeful look, she added, "Will you help me?"

"Of course."

Meg finished dressing her sister in silence, finding the familiar chore surprisingly calming to her pulse, which had rioted during the conversation they'd had about Jake. When she'd finished, they went downstairs, and just in time, too, because just as they reached the ground-floor landing, someone knocked at the door. The butler entered from the servants' wing behind them and gave Serena a questioning look.

"Bring them to the drawing room," she told him.

"Yes, my lady."

Jessica, Lady Fenwicke, and Lord Stratford—*Jonathan*, Meg said to herself, he'd asked her to call him Jonathan—already awaited them in the drawing room. After they entered, Serena went to her husband, slipped an arm around his waist, and gave him a peck on the cheek. "Our guests have arrived. Are you hungry?"

He kissed her on the lips. "Very," he said in a soft, husky voice.

Meg turned away, feeling the heat rush to her cheeks. She felt quite certain her brother-in-law wasn't talking about food.

• • •

"Oh, you are going to *love* dinner tonight." Jessica clasped her hands at her bosom. "With Beatrice's help, Cook has prepared a truly wonderful meal."

"Oh, I hardly helped at all." Lady Fenwicke blushed, and Jessica threw her an indulgent smile.

"She is *far* too modest. She planned every bit of this meal. Cook helped with some chopping and stirring."

"It's bound to be delicious, then." Serena smiled at both of them, her cheeks still flushed from Jonathan's kiss.

The butler opened the door and announced Captain Langley and Mr. Briggs. Introductions and greetings went around, but Jessica hardly heard any of it. Her attention was drawn to Mr. Briggs.

He wasn't handsome in the traditional way—not refined, aristocratic looking, and tall like Captain Langley, and not roguishly handsome like Jonathan. He was rough, with a jagged red scar that crossed his forehead and sliced his eyebrow in two. He had longish sandy-brown hair tied back in an old-fashioned queue. Why on earth didn't he grow his hair to cover that terrible scar? Jessica wondered. Certainly she'd reject this man for a dance at any ball, even if he was the only gentleman present!

His eyes met hers, blue and piercing, and Jessica quickly looked away. But...oh dear, Captain Langley was introducing them.

"Miss Jessica, this is Mr. Briggs, my first mate on the *Freedom*."

She glanced up at him, then quickly away, afraid he'd know her eyes were drawn to that wicked scar. She bobbed a curtsy. "Good evening, Mr. Briggs."

"Miss Jessica." His bow was stiff. Pompous, almost. She raised a subtle brow at him. Captain Langley had never been pompous in the least, toward her or any of her sisters, so certainly his first mate had no right to behave that way.

"And you already know Meg," Captain Langley told him.

"Aye, I do." He bowed again, equally stiff.

Now both of Jessica's eyebrows were raised, and she had to restrain herself from crossing her arms over her chest and confronting him. How rude! No polite, "Nice to see you again, Miss Donovan," or anything like that. He'd practically cut Meg! In their sister's drawing room, no less.

What an awful man.

Strangely enough, no one else seemed at all perturbed by Mr. Briggs's rudeness, but Jessica steamed over her claret, keeping quiet and watching him out of the corner of her eye. He was also quiet, speaking only when spoken to and answering tersely, keeping to monosyllables whenever possible. He kept glancing at Meg, and if you were to ask Jessica, she'd say those glances were *hateful*.

Jessica stood suddenly, and the men scrambled to set aside their beverages and rise as well. "Oh, I'm sorry," she exclaimed. She waved her hand in her face. "But...I...I feel I need some air. I'm going to fetch my maid and take a turn about the square. Would anyone care to join me? It's not quite dark yet. It might be dark by the time we return, but rest assured the streetlamps will light our way home."

She looked at Meg first, who'd just returned into the room from putting Jake to bed. She shook her head "no," not surprisingly. But no one else seemed inclined to go for a short, brisk evening walk either. With a sigh, Jessica turned to go fetch her maid.

"I'll go."

Jessica spun toward the man she had intended to avoid. *Oh, wonderful.*

She forced a smile. "That would be lovely," she said in a clipped voice. And then she left the room to find her maid, hearing his soft footsteps as he followed behind her without a word.

Within a few minutes, the three of them stood in the entry hall and Mr. Briggs was helping her with her rose wool pelisse. She buttoned the two large round buttons, reached for her gloves on the narrow table against the wall, and tugged them on. Mr. Briggs did the same with his own well-worn brown leather gloves, and before she drew on her second glove, Jessica squashed the mad urge to stroke the buttery soft-looking leather.

They went outside onto St. James, and Jessica sucked in a deep breath of the cool evening air. As her maid hovered behind them, Jessica and Mr. Briggs crossed the street, heading toward the park.

Jessica had walked with many gentlemen in the year since she'd arrived in England. When they crossed a busy street such as St. James's, most men would offer her their arms. Not Mr. Briggs. Watching him covertly out of the corner of her eye, she wondered what his first name was. Mr. Uppity Briggs. Mr. Snobbish Briggs... She smiled to herself. Wouldn't it be nice if parents named their children after their personalities?

What would she and her sisters be named, in that case? Serena would be Bossy Donovan, for certain. She was the oldest, only minutes older than Meg, and she had always used that as an excuse for ordering all of them about as if she were the queen.

Meg…Looking up at the darkening sky, Jessica wondered what Meg's name would be. Quiet Donovan? Reserved Donovan, or maybe Keeps-to-herself Donovan? And though Meg had certainly changed from how Jessica had remembered her, those three names would adequately represent her both then and now.

Olivia would be Sweetheart Donovan—because she had the sweetest heart Jessica had ever known, not to mention that was the endearment her husband had christened her with. Phoebe would be Thinks-she-knows-everything Donovan. Jessica made a small scoffing snort at that.

"What is it?"

She turned to Mr. Briggs to see him frowning at her.

"Oh. Nothing. Sorry."

"Very well," he said, and continued walking, looking straight ahead, his face expressionless. Except his eyebrows were drawn together in a frown, making that awful scar bulge.

"I wasn't"—oh, what was a ladylike way to describe a snort?—"making that noise at you, you know."

"Ah."

"Although I was tempted to earlier."

"Were you." He said it more as a statement than a question.

"Indeed I was," she said primly, then she pointed toward the center of the square. "I take the path through the square this way. Do you have any objections?"

"None at all."

"Well, good." She turned into the square garden, a green, grassy area crisscrossed by graveled paths. There were a few small trees peppering the square and a huge bronze statue of an English king whose name Jessica wouldn't have been able to remember even if her life depended on it.

Jessica's aunt Geraldine, who'd lived in the square forever, had said that once the square had consisted only of a large area of plain paved space with an ugly, dirty pool of water in its center. Jessica could vaguely remember seeing the square when she was a little girl and thinking it very bleak and unwelcoming indeed. It was much improved now.

She usually bisected the square on her walk, and sometimes she'd stop in the middle, close her eyes, and smell the trees, dirt, and flowers above the pungent odors of coal and city sewage and grime. Even though she could still hear the distant shouts of street vendors, the clomp of horses' hooves, and the rattling of carriage and cart wheels, she'd imagine she was in a quiet forest somewhere, alone and not surrounded by thousands and thousands of other souls.

As she and Mr. Briggs began to walk through the square on a path lined with low bushes, she glanced at him. "Don't you want to know *why* I wished to make that sound at you earlier?"

He shrugged and looked away, as if she wasn't worth looking at when he responded to her question. "Not particularly."

Her face instantly went scarlet—she could feel the burn of the blood rushing to her cheeks. Oh, what an insolent, ugly man he was!

"It was because you're very rude," she snapped.

He glanced at her, one side of his mouth curled

upward. It looked like a cross between a smirk and genuine laughter.

In all fairness, she had to admit he had a handsome mouth. Lovely, soft-looking lips, too.

"Forgive me," he said, sarcasm lacing his tone. "But I'm no London dandy who's going to simper and grovel to every pretty female who passes by."

Had he just called her pretty? She'd never been complimented in such a maddening way before. "Nevertheless," she said, "there is still a measure of politeness everyone should strive to achieve."

"Oh, is there? Then I suggest you strive a little harder, Miss Jessica."

"What?" Her flush deepened, if it was possible. She clenched her hands at her sides to prevent herself from shoving him. "I. Am. Always. Polite," she bit out.

"The way you were staring at me in the drawing room—well, it was difficult to restrain myself from raising my fingers with the sign to defend myself from the evil eye."

"Oh, what nonsense!" she cried. "I wasn't looking at you in any such way."

He shrugged again. "If you say so."

Furious, she glanced back to see if her maid was hearing any of this. Apparently not—she was several paces behind them and humming to herself, a faraway look in her eyes.

She turned back to glare at him. "If you're worried about the evil eye, perhaps you should think of the way you were looking at my sister Meg."

"Which Meg?" he asked dryly.

"The *real* one."

"Ah." He didn't elaborate.

"Why don't you like my sister?" she asked. "Surely you know her, don't you? You spent time with her on Captain Langley's ship."

"I was the one who first spotted her and the lad adrift in that jolly boat."

"And then she was on the ship, in your presence, for many days."

"Aye, she was. Along with the lad. Odd sort, that boy."

"So?" Jessica asked, not wanting to discuss Jake, whom she didn't understand at all. She was always kind to the child, but he was so standoffish, she never quite knew what to do with him. Instead, she kept her focus on Meg. "How can you possibly not like her? Meg is a lovely person and certainly not deserving of anyone's dislike."

He looked straight ahead. "It's not that I dislike Miss Donovan."

"Then why look at her like you do?" Jessica pressed. "You look at her as if you *despise* her."

Mr. Briggs hesitated. Then he said, "Takes some time to earn my trust, is all."

"So it's not that you dislike my sister, but you don't *trust* her?" The man was obviously not quite right in the head. Meg was so guileless—how could anyone not trust her?

Mr. Briggs made a noncommittal noise, and she looked sharply at him. "Why not?"

"As I said"—Mr. Briggs spoke with such strained patience he might have been speaking to a slow child—"I'm not one to throw out my trust so easily. Not like Captain Langley."

"Why not?"

He gave her a wry smile. "I suppose I've been betrayed one too many times."

"Do you trust anyone?"

"Of course I do."

"Who, then?"

He took a moment to answer. Finally, he said, "Langley."

Jessica waited for him to add more names. When she didn't, she asked, "Is that all?"

"Aye."

She blinked. "What about your family? Your parents? Brothers and sisters?"

"No."

"Well," she murmured. "I find that very sad."

Again, he shrugged.

They walked in silence for a few moments, then Jessica said, "So, you don't trust my sister, and you feel that Captain Langley has offered his trust to her too lightly."

"Close enough."

"But what could Meg possibly do to harm Captain Langley? What do you think her evil motivations could possibly be?"

"I don't know. But if she has any, I hope to expose them."

Jessica made a wide gesture with her arms. "So you've no idea how or why she'd possibly betray the captain, yet you consider her guilty until proven innocent."

He looked at her, again with that strange half smile. "I like that, I think," he said, a musing tone in his voice. "Guilty until proven innocent."

"Well, I don't," Jessica snapped.

"It's a safer way to approach the world. Thinking of all human beings as guilty until they prove themselves worthy of your trust..."

"I should think it's a lonely way to approach the world. Looking at everyone with such dark suspicion—like you were looking at my sister—" She shuddered.

"Well. To each his own, I suppose."

"Or her own."

He looked at her, eyebrows raised, scrunching the red scar to a higher spot on his forehead. "You're a feisty one, aren't you?"

"Not at all," Jessica said stiffly. "I am known, however, to be forthcoming to a fault."

"And defensive. Of a sister you hardly know."

"Oh, I know Meg."

"Do you? I wouldn't be so certain about that. In the short time since I arrived at Lord Stratford's house, I have already sensed a separation between her and the rest of you."

"There is no separation. She is..." Jessica didn't know how much of Meg's danger Briggs knew, so she chose her words carefully. "She has been away for a long time, trapped against her will and in a foreign place. And now she's been thrown out of the frying pan and into the fire of London. Of course it will take some time for her to adjust to her new life here."

"That's a mature assessment for someone so young."

She felt the band of muscle tighten all the way from one shoulder across the other. "I am *not* young." And she was dashed tired of all her sisters and brothers-in-law treating her like an infant.

"Really? How old are you? Seventeen? Sixteen?"

She ground her teeth. "Nineteen years old, thank you

very much." She puffed out her chest, hoping to give the illusion of having a more womanly bosom than she actually had.

"Really?"

"Of course. Why would I lie to you about my age?"

"I'm sure I can dream up many reasons," he murmured.

"Oh, right. I forgot about your distrustfulness," she scoffed.

They'd reached the middle of the square. Out of habit, Jessica paused there. He took a few steps forward and then looked over his shoulder at her. "Coming?"

"No. Not yet."

He looked around in the dimming light of the most woodsy area of the park, frowning. "Is something wrong?"

She sighed. "You do like to ruin a calm moment, don't you?"

"I don't know what you're talking about."

"I always stop here. To take some breaths and calm myself. To, just for a few moments, pretend I am alone in some vast forest."

"Ah." He paused, allowing her to close her eyes and take several deep breaths.

Deliberately, she relaxed all her muscles that he had so successfully coiled within her body. *There.* She felt better already. She took another deep, deep breath, and opened her eyes.

"Finished?"

Already, she could feel those muscles starting to coil tight again.

"I am." She stood tall as a princess, staring him down.

They began to walk again.

"Why do you imagine yourself alone in a forest?"

"Because the thought is calming to me."

He raised his brows. "The thought of wolves? Snakes? Other dangerous creatures?"

"I may look like the kind of maiden who would simper at the mere mention of those animals, Mr. Briggs, but I assure you I am not."

For the first time, he smiled at her. It was a real smile, that reached his eyes and—amazingly!—made him appear very handsome indeed.

"I was raised on a small island in the middle of a violent, unpredictable ocean, with an overbearing mother and four older sisters. My father died when I was very young. We lost Meg. My sister Olivia has been ill for the majority of my life. We ran out of money, and we learned how to work to keep food in our mouths. We survived malaria, cholera, two hurricanes, three droughts, and a flood. I'm rather inclined to think that after all that, if I was indeed a simpering maiden, I'd be quite dead by now."

She'd surprised him. She could tell by the slight raise of his brows.

"Well," he said softly. "I suppose it's true."

"What's true?"

"Looks can be deceiving."

Jessica grinned. "Tell me, Mr. Briggs, how do I appear to you?"

"Like a beautiful, spoiled English lady who's never seen a day of hardship in her life."

He wasn't the first man who'd called her beautiful. But somehow, it seemed more meaningful coming from his lips. Why? Perhaps because it didn't seem like a word he'd toss around lightly, unlike so many of the other men who probably used it to coax kisses from young ladies on a weekly basis.

"I suppose you're right, then," she murmured. "Looks often are deceiving."

And maybe his were, too.

Chapter Twelve

The next afternoon, Will, Briggs, and Meg's brothers-in-law Stratford and the Duke of Wakefield sat in a tense circle in Will's drawing room. The *Freedom* had arrived on the tide this morning, but Will was going to turn around and leave her again. The plan was for him and Meg to depart for Prescot at the beginning of next week, but he felt that might be too late. Serena had relayed to them Jessica's odd experience with the Marquis of Millbridge, and Will was convinced Millbridge was on the hunt for Meg.

Jessica had managed the situation with the marquis well, but since then, a strange man had accosted Stratford's cook at the market, asking about the sisters. Though flustered, she'd managed to say nothing to give Meg away. But this ruse couldn't go on forever.

As much as Stratford trusted the members of his household, people could be forced to talk. Will trusted Meg when she said that Jacob Caversham would use any means necessary to glean information about his son and his "kidnapper." For everyone's safety, the servants hadn't been told where Meg and Jake were traveling.

"What we must do," Stratford said, "is have enough evidence on hand to stop him before he becomes too desperate."

"We have evidence related to his smuggling activities, and at least one witness," Will said. "But until Meg told me, no one comprehended the extent of those activities."

"We do have Meg's testimony against him," Wakefield said thoughtfully.

"No. I want to keep her out of this," Will said. "It's too dangerous."

Stratford nodded. "Agreed. Plus, since he'll be accusing her of kidnapping, her accusations may be dismissed as simple retaliation."

"Ultimately," Will said, "the evidence we have gathered thus far is negligible, and probably not enough to interest the authorities."

"At least not yet," Briggs added. "I'm gathering information on the ships he owns and where they've all sailed. I think I can retrace his steps for the past few years, but I believe I'll eventually need to travel back to Cornwall to collect evidence." He gave them all a grim look. "If it's there, I'll find it."

"Take the *Freedom*," Will told him. "You will have all my resources at your disposal." Will would be with Meg and Jake in Lancashire, unable to lend his support in other ways.

"We need to learn more about Caversham's connection to the Marquis of Millbridge." Stratford was leaning forward, his elbows on his knees and his hands clasped under his chin.

"Yes," Will said, "and we'll be better off not involving the Crown or the authorities until we know exactly how deep this goes."

The men sat quietly for a moment, no doubt thinking of the implications of this, considering Millbridge's involvement with the royal family and with the government itself.

"Since Millbridge is here in London," Wakefield finally said, "I can look into his affairs here." He shrugged. "The activities of the London Season are so tedious, and this will be a good distraction. And, of course, I want to do whatever I can to help Meg."

"I'll speak with my solicitor," Stratford said. "He might be able to help us build a stronger case against Caversham. We wouldn't want to accuse the man and have the suit fall apart due to some annoying esoteric legal matter." Stratford tapped his chin with his fingertips. "However, Millbridge might be a little more difficult to pin down. He's a peer and an esteemed member of the House of Lords."

"If his activities are as illegal and immoral as I think they are..." Briggs hesitated.

"Then we'll see him hang," Will said coldly.

The four of them sat in silence. Will imagined the Marquis of Millbridge swinging from the gallows. The thought made him vaguely nauseous but more determined than ever.

He would see Caversham brought down before he could get to Meg and Jake. And if Millbridge was involved, Will would bring him down, too. He stood abruptly and then looked down at Stratford. "We need to leave."

Stratford raised his brows in confusion. "Who?"

"Meg, Jake, and I. Not Monday." He paced the length of the long, narrow room. The fact of the matter was that Millbridge was close—too damn close—and Caversham would be here soon. He needed to get Meg out of London. "Tomorrow."

"The carriages aren't ready—"

"Who gives a damn about the carriages?"

The men shifted in their seats, clearly uncomfortable. Stratford frowned. "Are you all right, Langley?"

"No, I am not all right. Millbridge is in Town—Christ, he lives in Mayfair, doesn't he? The man is less than a mile away. It's obvious he's hunting for Meg, and when he finds her—"

"Wait a moment." Wakefield held up his hand. "That encounter with Jessica could have been coincidence."

"It wasn't," Will said flatly.

Stratford's brows climbed toward his hairline. "How can you be sure about that?"

"Intuition."

"When did you start acting on intuition, Langley?" Stratford asked in a low voice. "You need to think about this logically. Even if he was digging for information about Meg's whereabouts, he didn't succeed in obtaining any."

"How can you be sure about that?" Will asked, tossing Stratford's words back at him.

"We've no evidence that anyone knows about Meg's existence besides the men in this room, her sisters, and Stratford's servants," Wakefield pointed out.

Will shook his head. There was no turning back. Now that he'd made the decision, he knew it was the right one. "To hell with logic. To hell with evidence. If we have to stay up all night preparing the servants and packing the carriages, then that's what we'll do. But I'm leaving London tomorrow, and Meg and Jake will be with me."

Meg convinced Will to bring Thomas along with them to Prescot. The boy's mother was traveling in France, and Meg couldn't bear to think of him alone in London with only a few servants for company. So, at the very last minute, when they were literally mounting the carriage steps, she'd requested that he join them.

Will's hesitation had been palpable. Meg couldn't imagine why he was so loath to bring his son with them, but speaking in low tones to him in an unmoving carriage while Jake squirmed with impatience, she'd finally drawn out the truth.

Will harbored concerns that the child would remind Meg of his inconstancy. That had just made Meg shake her head. "Even if he does, Will, even if it does cause me a soul-deep pain every time I look at him, I won't see you reject him for my 'comfort.' That would be infinitely worse."

"I'd never reject him," Will had said. "But how could I subject you to him if he causes you pain?"

"Listen," she'd said softly. "If there is to be anything between you and me—even friendship—ever again, then I must learn to be with Thomas. I won't have you hiding him from me. He's too bright a child not to recognize what you're doing. That would hurt him beyond repair. Above all, Thomas is innocent of any wrongdoing, and a child certainly shouldn't be punished for someone else's mistakes."

Will had finally relented, and he, Meg, Thomas, and Jake had traveled to Lancashire together. They'd taken two carriages—one for the four of them and another for the four servants Jonathan had insisted Meg bring along. The journey had been uneventful. Besides Meg and Will constantly striving to entertain two very active, restless boys, there was little else for them to discuss.

Still, Meg had silently observed Will as the carriage rumbled through the English countryside. His patient tone with his son made her heart ache, but at the same time, it was comforting to her. It had taken him years to take on the responsibility, but unlike so many other men of his station, he'd sacrificed pride, reputation, and probably the opportunity for a good marriage in favor of an obvious and open devotion to his son.

He also seemed to be developing a bond with Jake, who still worshipped him. Will never made Jake feel left out or awkward or different. Very few people were capable of those feats with the young boy.

By the time they arrived in Prescot on the third day, and the carriages pulled up to the house—a box-shaped white structure—late in the morning, Meg was softening toward Will. She had never been one to hang on to anger and bitterness. What was the point when neither of them could change the past?

In any case, it was the Will of today who mattered, not the Will of eight years ago. And she had no reason to believe that the Will of today would repeat such a mistake—in fact, all of his actions since he'd found her led to the opposite conclusion.

"We're here!" Meg told the boys, both of whom had been looking glumly out the window for the past hour and a half after Will had told them that if they didn't stop saying, "Are we there yet?" they'd be sent to bed tonight without any dinner—or any of the candy sticks he'd bought for them in Prescot.

"Finally," Thomas groaned.

"Candy!" Jake exclaimed.

Meg and Will exchanged a smile. The coachman opened the door and pulled the step, and the boys scrambled out, leaving Will to help Meg step down.

The house was very small and pretty, with trimmed yew box hedges lining the path to the front door.

Benson, their man-of-all-work, had the keys, and he opened the doors for them. The place wasn't as cold and musty as one might expect of a vacant house. Instead the air smelled fresh, the furniture appeared recently brushed and cleaned, and the floors sparkled.

Will watched her looking it over and grinned. "Harper told me he'd sent word ahead and ordered the place cleaned for us."

"They did a lovely job," Meg murmured. Between the spotlessness of the house and the group of servants filing in behind them carrying their luggage, how on earth would she keep herself occupied in this place?

The boys had already run upstairs, and Meg lifted her skirts and hurried after them, Will following closely behind. Jake appeared at the landing above her. He pointed to his left. "Thomas and I sleep there." He swung his pointing finger to his right. "And you and Captain Will sleep there."

"Ah"—Meg quickly assessed the two doorways at the top of the stairs—"No, I don't think so. I'll sleep with you, and Thomas will sleep with Captain Langley." Reaching the landing, she maneuvered Jake toward the smaller of the two bedchambers, ignoring the buzz that seemed to vibrate through her body in response to the boy's innocent suggestion.

Jake pouted. "I want to sleep with Thomas."

"I know, darling, but it's just not going to work. Perhaps when we return to London." *Whenever that might be.*

She looked over her shoulder at Will. "But where will the servants sleep?" she whispered.

"There's a loft in the stable for the men, and there's an area off the kitchen where there's a pallet for the women."

"Is that enough space?"

"It'll have to be."

Meg sighed. Clearly this house had not been built with the expectation of housing four servants.

They spent the next few hours settling in—unpacking their luggage while stowing away the fragile items around the house that two active young boys might break. Two servants were sent into Prescot to buy enough food from the inn there to sustain them until the next market day— which they discovered was the day after tomorrow.

They'd eaten dinner by eight o'clock, and in an effort that was met with much celebration, Will had successfully pulled Jake's loose tooth with a string one of the servants found in the stable. When they had the boys settled in their respective rooms and the servants had disappeared for the evening, an exhausted Meg and Will sat on the velvet sofa in the small parlor together, sharing a bottle of wine.

Meg glanced at Will. "Would you mind very much if—" She hesitated, then sighed.

"If...?" He took a sip of his wine, his dark eyes meeting her gaze over the rim of his glass. "I can't readily think of you doing anything I'd mind, Meg."

"Oh, goodness, you must be sotted. I can think of several things."

"Such as?"

"Falling overboard in the Atlantic, for one."

He sobered. "Yes." He reached across the small space separating them and gathered her hand in his own. "I'd mind that very much."

She gave him a faltering smile. "My feet...they hurt terribly. Would you mind if I took off my shoes? Just for a moment," she added hastily, not knowing how to interpret the serious set of his mouth.

"Why would I mind that?"

"I...don't know." She looked toward the fireplace—a simple brick hearth. The fire burned with an orange glow, emitting a lovely heat that washed over her body. "Caversham...he would become enraged if I ever behaved as anything but a perfect lady in his presence. He threatened to toss me overboard and find a real lady to properly teach his wife."

A breath hissed through Will's teeth. "I'm not Caversham."

She met and held his dark eyes in her gaze. "When I last knew you, I don't believe I behaved as anything but a perfect lady."

"You didn't... Well, except..."

She tore her gaze from his. "Right." Stupid of her to forget *that*.

"Take off your shoes, Meg."

Feeling awkward, she did as he said. Sitting in the carriage all day had made her feet swell a little, and her shoes had been pinching her feet during all the running up and down the stairs this afternoon. She couldn't resist a groan of pleasure as she curled her toes and they gave a few appreciative—but very unladylike—cracks.

Will leaned down and gathered one of her feet in his hands, pulling it up to his lap.

"What are you doing?"

"Relax," he murmured, and then he began to rub her aching feet. Meg could do nothing but make little moans of appreciation when he pressed the worst of the aches away.

"Oh, that feels so good."

He rubbed one stockinged foot for several minutes and then kissed her toes and gently lowered it and retrieved her other foot, beginning the process all over again.

"Thank you, Meg," he said, his voice so quiet she hardly heard over the crackle of the fire.

"For what?"

"For being kind to Thomas. Most women in your position . . . wouldn't."

"Thomas is a lovely child," she said truthfully. "He's becoming a good friend to Jake."

Still rubbing her feet, he looked up to gaze at her, his face infused with the softest expression she'd ever seen. She relaxed back into the sofa, her eyes half-lidded.

"Better?" he murmured, focusing on his task again.

"Infinitely."

"You're tired."

"Yes."

He continued his blissful rubbing in silence for several more minutes. She was half-asleep when she felt him lowering her foot and then scooping her into his arms. She clung to his neck as he carried her upstairs, where he gently deposited her into bed beside Jake.

He smoothed back her hair, tucked the covers up around her, and kissed her on the mouth. His lips were so soft and warm, like the most comforting blanket. "Sleep well, my love."

She didn't remember him leaving the room, because by the time he reached the door, she was already asleep.

Jessica tore open the seal and let her poached egg grow cold on the table while she read the letter. Finally, she looked up, grinning. "They have safely arrived at their destination," she told Serena and Beatrice, mindful of not giving away Meg's exact location with the footmen hovering about.

Serena pushed out a relieved breath. "Thank the Lord. Now to keep them safe."

"Exactly."

"How is the house?" Beatrice asked. She'd spent a short amount of time in the same house with Jessica just last year. "Have they settled in well?"

Jessica nodded. "Very well, but she's afraid the boys will cause damage, and she thinks Sebastian might be angry."

"Oh, goodness. Sebastian has a child of his own. He understands how curious little ones can be," Serena said.

Jessica snorted. If you asked her brother-in-law about his own daughter, little Margie, he'd say she was the most intelligent, talented child in the world. More like the most spoiled, Jessica thought wryly, and more than capable of expensive destruction. In fact, just before they'd all left Sussex this spring, Margie had destroyed a vase that a friend of Jonathan's father had excavated in Egypt. Sebastian had just shrugged and cooed at her. Good thing the rest of her family was so tolerant, Jessica thought. Still, after that, Serena had stowed away most of the more expensive relics in the earl's house.

Serena set her toast down and leaned forward across the breakfast table. "Listen, both of you. I think the Marquis of Millbridge, and maybe some other people, will be sniffing around us, asking about Meg."

"Meg?" Jessica cocked her head. "You mean my sister, the Countess of Stratford? She's very well, thank you." She grinned.

"Oh," Beatrice added, "Meg is my bosom friend's older sister. She's married to the Earl of Stratford."

"Right. I'm Meg. We have no knowledge of any other Meg."

"Although our sister Serena, Meg's twin," Jessica said, putting on a sad voice, "was lost at sea when I was a little girl."

Serena nodded. "We can't let them know anything. I'll remind the servants again this afternoon. No matter how they try to trick us into revealing that Meg is here, we cannot allow anyone outside of our family to know."

"Except Mr. Briggs," Jessica said. The ever-so annoying—and annoyingly fascinating—Mr. Briggs.

"Right. Except Mr. Briggs."

After breakfast, Jessica and Serena went upstairs to change into their walking dresses. They planned to spend the afternoon shopping in Bond Street—Serena wanted a new pair of shoes and Jessica needed new evening gloves for the Season.

Beatrice cried off the shopping trip, as she usually preferred to stay at home. Today, she wanted to work in the kitchen with Cook—they were perfecting a new dessert that Beatrice planned to try on the family at dinner tonight.

When she knocked on her sister's dressing room door, Serena emerged in her new spring dress—a bright coral-colored confection that made Jessica blink in surprise. "Oh, my goodness."

Serena whirled, her voluminous skirts billowing. "Do you like it?"

"Of course I do. But truly, I think it's more me than you. Don't you?" Serena usually opted for more somber colors.

Serena shook her finger good-naturedly at Jessica. "Oh, no you don't."

"Don't what?"

"This is my dress. Order your own if you want one for yourself."

"Well, I will," Jessica said. It still seemed odd that Serena would tell her to order a brand-new, ridiculously expensive, utterly fashionable dress so flippantly. Jessica had to constantly remind herself that her brothers-in-law were a duke and an earl, and the Donovans would never suffer for lack of funds again.

She remembered the day Mother had slaughtered their last sheep, remembered how quickly the mutton had disappeared between four hungry sisters. Mother hadn't eaten any of it—it was right before Serena and Phoebe had left for England, and Mother had wanted them to look healthy and presentable to the *ton*.

Jessica would never eat mutton again.

"Well, you needn't have such a sour look on your face," Serena said crossly. "I was just saying that you've no need to pine after my dress."

Jessica closed her eyes, then looked at her oldest sister.

"I was just remembering the sheep. The *last* of the sheep," she said with emphasis.

Some of the color drained from Serena's pink cheeks. Of all of them, she had been most attached to the sheep—especially the lambs. "Ah," she murmured. Then she gave Jessica a curious look. "Why?"

"It's just..." Jessica shrugged. "Well, things are so different now."

"Yes, they are quite different."

Just then, one of the maids appeared, running down the corridor from the direction of the stairs. "Oh, my lady, oh, Miss Jessica. There's three constables downstairs talking with his lordship. They're going to search the house for Miss Meg!"

"What?" Jessica exclaimed. Serena was already hurrying down the corridor, and Jessica rushed after her, followed by Beatrice, who must've heard the commotion. In the entry hall, Jonathan was facing three uniformed men.

"What are you talking about?" he snapped at the men.

The one standing in the middle, a hairy, massive man with a thick black beard, held out two sheets of paper. "We've a search warrant and an arrest warrant here, sir, issued by the Privy Council, for the arrest of Miss Margaret Donovan."

"I am Margaret Donovan." Serena stepped forward with Jessica at her shoulder. Jonathan threw her a dark look of warning, but she continued. "At least I used to be Margaret Donovan. I am now the Countess of Stratford. What is this about?"

"Good morning, ma'am, miss." The constable gave Serena and Jessica a curt nod. "We were told this might be a problem. Apparently, there are two Margaret Donovans who look very much alike, one of whom is a newcomer to London and the other who married Lord Stratford. You're twins, I believe?"

Now Serena's face flushed red. "My twin sister drowned eight years ago, and her name was Serena, not Meg."

"Apparently, she has been using your name as an alias," the man said.

"That's absurd!" Serena snapped.

Beatrice slipped her hand into Jessica's and squeezed tight. Jessica glanced over at her friend, who stared at the men with an expression on her face that was utterly blank. Jessica nearly smiled—Beatrice had been so weak and so vulnerable for so long. Watching her show backbone like this was a welcome, wonderful sight.

Jonathan held out his hand, preventing the men from moving forward. "You're upsetting my wife, sir. I must ask you to leave."

The bear-like man shrugged, undaunted. "We will search this property, per our orders. If Margaret Donovan is not here, then we'll go on our way."

"I am—was—Margaret Donovan!" Serena exclaimed. Jessica, standing just behind her, laid a calming hand on her shoulder.

"Yes, ma'am," Mr. Bear-man said. "You are the countess. We're searching for a woman who looks like you and has attempted to steal your identity. Your twin. There is some speculation that you have been hiding her here."

"What utter nonsense," Serena spat.

"What crime is this alleged woman charged with?" Jonathan asked.

"Kidnapping," Mr. Bear said.

Jessica sucked in a harsh breath before she could stop

herself. Despite what Jessica had told him that night at the ball, something had caused the Marquis of Millbridge to suspect that Meg was here. If they found her...they'd arrest her. Prosecute her for kidnapping Jake. *Hang* her.

Thank the Lord she and Captain Langley had left for Lancashire a week early.

Jonathan turned to Serena. "We have nothing to hide here. Let them perform their search and be on their way."

Looking numb, Serena nodded. They stepped aside, and Mr. Bear-man gave instructions to the other two men. Jessica, Serena, Beatrice, and Jonathan stood in a tight cluster in the entry hall as the three men went in separate directions. None of the residents spoke. What could they say, after all, that wouldn't reveal they knew about Meg?

They stood there for several minutes, a span of time that felt like hours to Jessica. Dimly, she heard the men in the house questioning servants, who she prayed would hang on to their loyalty even when faced by the intimidating Mr. Bear-man.

They must have, because when Mr. Bear-man and the two smaller constables returned to the entry hall much later, he tipped his hat to them.

"I assume you found nothing," Jonathan said dryly.

"Indeed, sir. We will continue our search for the woman elsewhere. Thank you for your cooperation." With that, he and his two constables left the house, leaving Serena, Jonathan, Beatrice, and Jessica staring at each other.

As soon as the front door closed behind them, Jessica's hand flew to her mouth. "Oh, God," she whispered, "what if they find Meg?"

Jonathan released a breath. "I'd send Langley a letter, but I think we're being watched. I'll have Briggs find a way to send him a message. He will need to take her somewhere else. Somewhere safer."

"Who did this?" Serena whispered.

"It must have been the Marquis of Millbridge, if the Privy Council issued the warrant. Something must have tipped him off that Meg was here."

"We know he's been having the members of our household questioned," Serena said darkly. "Maybe he just received one too many awkward responses."

"I responded awkwardly," Jessica said. "I didn't mean to—"

"It's not your fault," Jonathan said. "He's just out-smarted us."

They'll find her," Jessica whispered. "And kidnapping is a hanging offense, isn't it? They'll hang her."

"No," Jonathan said firmly. "They will not. We will gather evidence on Caversham, and even if they do find Meg, she'll be able to prove that she took Jake away to protect him."

"But you haven't found any evidence yet, have you?" Jessica pressed.

"Not enough yet. But we will." Jonathan sighed. "Jessica, I promise you, Langley and I aren't going to allow anything to happen to your sister."

Langley and I. What about *her*? Jessica was Meg's sister. She should have a hand in keeping her safe.

"Now, we should all go about our day as we originally planned. You must go shopping. Above all, we can't draw attention to this family right now."

Serena nodded.

"Very well," Jessica grumbled, even though she didn't feel at all like shopping anymore.

They fetched their gloves. Since the day was so warm, they opted to forgo coats. As they went outside and turned down St. James, Jessica pushed her dire thoughts about Meg aside. Determined to behave normally, she tried to have a mundane conversation with Serena. "Truly, I am curious. Why coral for your dress? You don't usually choose such... bright colors."

Serena slanted her a look. "Is it too much?"

"Not at all. Just different, for you."

"I ordered it a few weeks ago, when..." Her voice faded and then she added, "I suppose I was feeling bright."

"I see." Jessica did see. Meg had come back into their lives a few weeks ago. Smiling, Jessica linked her arm in her sister's and squeezed her hand. "I was feeling bright, too."

"I hope she can come back to us soon," Serena said under her breath.

"Me, too."

Serena glanced behind them, then gave a wry shake of her head. "Here I am, breaking my own edict. Talking about things that I don't want people to overhear. Let's stop speaking of it."

"Of course," Jessica said amiably.

They walked in silence as they turned onto Piccadilly where Jessica stopped in a dressmaker's shop to look at the few pairs of gloves on display. Not finding any she liked, the two sisters moved on, turning into Regent Street from Piccadilly Circus. Jessica went into a shoe shop, and they emerged only a few moments later. Serena had already chosen her shoes, a simple pair of brown leather shoes with low heels, and had arranged for the shoemaker to send them to her house in St. James.

"Utterly dull," Jessica murmured as they left the store.

"The shoes or the shopping?" Serena asked.

"The shoes."

Serena chuckled. "I could tell you despised them by the look on your face."

"They're so bland," Jessica said on a groan, "and they're the color of—"

"They're sensible. They're comfortable. And no one ever sees my shoes, anyhow. They're always covered by the hem of my dress."

"*You* see them. That's enough."

"Oh, Jess, please. Don't be ridiculous."

Their conversation was cut short because they were passing a millinery shop displaying a pair of gloves in its window that fronted the street.

Jessica hurried in and found that it was a quite large shop with rows of lovely evening gloves for her to look at and try on.

She'd tried on five or six pairs, dismissing them as too tight, too dull, too loose, too heavily adorned, when she picked up a pair of simple white kid gloves with a row of delicate pearl buttons.

"Oh, Meg, won't these look lovely with my pearls?" Jonathan and Serena had given her a beautiful strand of pearls for her nineteenth birthday. She motioned to the shopkeeper to take them out of the case so she could try them on, and then she glanced over her shoulder. "Meg?"

Her sister was nowhere to be found. Quickly, Jessica glanced around the shop. Unless she was bent over something, she wasn't in here. "Meg?" Jessica called, a little louder, fighting the urge to yell "Serena!" at the top of her lungs.

She spun back around toward the shopkeeper, grabbed her reticule, and tugged it over her wrist. "Excuse me, please," she managed, and then she turned and dashed out of the store.

The street was busy, with thick crowds of pedestrians strolling, footmen lounging, and fancy carriages lining the curb. Jessica looked this way and that, then ran between two of the parked carriages, ignoring the horse that nudged her shoulder as she rushed by and into the street.

She looked up and down the street with no regard to the traffic that flowed around her or the dust that billowed into her face.

"Here now, gel, this street ain't for gawkers!" a driver yelled at her as his carriage passed by.

"Would ye like a ride, missy? Easier than walking about in this traffic, I daresay."

She ignored it all and looked frantically ahead of her and behind her, turning in a slow circle, her heart pounding so hard she thought it might bang right out of her chest.

And then she saw it. About a hundred feet ahead of her, a carriage pulled away from the curb with a bit of coral-colored fabric stuck in the doorjamb and flapping in the breeze.

"Oh, God," Jessica murmured. "No. Not Serena."

She spun, turning to the cabriolet driver who'd asked her if she wanted a ride. He grinned down at her from his perch on the right side of the cab. He had ruddy cheeks, bright blue eyes, and thinning blond hair, and she made a split-second decision to trust him.

Not that she had a choice.

She flung her arm out toward the offending carriage,

which was quickly gaining distance. "Yes, I need a ride. And I need you to follow that carriage!"

She ran around the horse and leaped into the interior of the cab, thrusting open the curtains so she could see out the front. She bent forward, out of the open front window, and yelled, "Hurry!" at the driver.

When he only stared at her, slack-jawed, she threw out her very highest connection. "My brother-in-law is the Duke of Wakefield. My sister is in that carriage." She didn't bother to mention that this particular sister wasn't married to that particular brother-in-law. "If you follow that carriage successfully to its destination, I promise you, the duke will reward you handsomely."

The man's round blue eyes only grew wider.

"Move!" Jessica roared. Then she blinked. She sounded so much like her mother when she'd yelled at the sisters to do something quickly and properly, it made her stomach twist.

The man swallowed, nodded, and then urged the horse into motion. Just as they pulled into the street, Jessica saw the carriage with the coral fabric sticking out from the door turning left with the curve of the street.

"Hurry!" she cried. "We're going to lose them!"

The man clucked at the horse, and they maneuvered around a slower carriage and turned, and she spotted the carriage carrying Serena making a right into the Haymarket. It was all she could do not to stand up, leap out of the carriage, and chase after her sister.

"Patience, miss," said the man in his scratchy voice. "I've got 'em."

Obviously the man didn't—couldn't—understand how impossible it was for her to be patient right now.

They turned into the Haymarket, and they gained on the carriage until they were just a few yards behind. When the carriage turned into the Strand, they were directly behind it.

The Strand became Fleet Street, and then Jessica lost track of the streets and began to worry that the coachman of the carriage in front of them, whose back she could clearly see, might realize he was being followed.

She drew the curtain to cover most of her body and face, and peeked out the top. "Do you think he knows we're after him?" she asked her driver.

"Nay, how'd he figure such a thing?"

Because he's a bad man, and he knows whoever is inside that carriage has done a bad thing, Jessica wanted to retort, but she kept her mouth shut. For the first time, she wondered what she'd do when the carriage in front of them stopped. How could she and Serena fight whoever was in that carriage? He might have a knife...or a gun, and all she had was her reticule. It would be ridiculous for her to come at the villains like a blood-lusting warrior brandishing a little silk embroidered purse.

Dash it all.

She glanced around the inside of the cab. Of course, there were no convenient weapons lying about. And from what she'd seen of the driver, he didn't have anything, either. But there was no harm in asking at this point, she supposed.

"Excuse me, sir?" she asked as the driver turned another corner.

"Aye, miss?"

"Have you any weapons?" she asked hopefully. "A gun, perhaps?"

She couldn't crane her head out to look at him for fear of someone in the carriage ahead noticing the movement, so she waited through the silence, chewing on her lip.

Finally, he responded, "Ah, no, miss."

Double deuce it, she thought. She blew out a breath. "All right. Here's what we're going to do. When they stop"—and hopefully they weren't intending to drive out of London, because she had a feeling the driver wouldn't be willing to take her much farther—"please continue on a short way. I'll tell you when to stop. Then I'll see where they've gone, and you can be on your way."

Another long pause. "That don't sound quite safe to me, miss."

"Well, do you have a better plan? My sister is in that carriage. She's been kidnapped, and dangerous or not, I must know where they're taking her."

"Well, then," the driver said gruffly. "I'll stay until such time as I knows you're safe."

"Thank you," she said with feeling. "That's very kind of you."

They kept going, and Jessica glanced around at the unfamiliar scenery. Here, the houses were gray and drab, with none of the sparkling green and pretty flowers that grew in Mayfair and St. James. The deeper they went into this part of Town, the stronger the ugly smells of sewage and rot became. The pedestrians, too, were dressed in drab, gray, brown, and black, a far cry from the lace, feathers, jewels, and bright fabrics she'd seen just a little while ago in Regent Street.

Then they made another turn, she glimpsed the river to the right, and she sucked in a breath. They were headed toward the docks.

Which ones, though? The London docks were vast, populated by hundreds of ships. Captain Langley kept his ship, the *Freedom*, at St. Katharine's, the new docks near his offices. She'd been there just a few days ago when she had cajoled Briggs into allowing her to come along when Jonathan had asked to see the *Freedom*.

This didn't look much like the area of St. Katharine's Docks, but she couldn't be too sure. She hadn't been observing the scenery when they'd driven to the docks that day. She'd been analyzing Briggs's terrible scar and envisioning the many ways in which he could have obtained it. Perhaps he'd fallen down some stairs as a boy and had landed on a rock on his face. Or maybe, since he was a sailor, he'd encountered a flying fish hook and it had flayed him in the forehead...

They drove for another mile or so, and as the scenery transformed, Jessica twisted her hands and gnawed on her lower lip behind the curtain, peeking out once in a while to make sure they still followed the black lacquered carriage that had taken Serena. She was growing to know the carriage very well at this point; it was no different from any of a thousand others on the London streets, except for the deep, ugly scratch above its rear axle.

Serena's dress was still there, still dangling from the closed door. She supposed no one had noticed that her sister's dress had been caught. It was probably the least of Serena's worries at this point.

Poor Serena, and in her delicate condition... Jessica tasted blood and forcibly opened her teeth. Her lip certainly had had enough abuse for one day.

"They've pulled to the side," the driver said in a voice so low Jessica hardly heard him.

Jessica glanced up, and sure enough, the carriage had drawn to a halt on the side of the road.

"Pass them, as we planned," Jessica murmured. "I'll tell you when to stop."

"Aye, miss."

She snapped the front curtains closed and sank back in her seat as they passed the carriage that held her sister. When she was sure they'd passed, she asked, "Where are we?"

"Just past the Wapping Dock Stairs."

She really wished there was a window in the back of the cab. "Can you see them still?" she asked the driver. "Have they got my sister out yet?"

There was a brief pause. "They's still sittin' there. A man's got out of the carriage, but no lady. Miss, we might stop here—ought to be a good place to watch 'em from in secret."

"Do it." Jessica made the decision quickly. She didn't want for him to drive too far from Serena.

The driver directed the horse to the side of the street, and Jessica stuck her head out of the curtain. "Is it safe for me to come out? Do you think they'll see me?"

"Nay, not if ye stay behind the cab."

He had already jumped down, and he helped her out, very gentleman-like. She gave him a quick smile. "Thank you."

He nodded, then looked over the roof of the carriage. "They be takin' her out now. And she looks none too pleased about it."

Jessica flinched. "No doubt," she murmured. But she didn't dare look. What if one of the men saw her...or what if Serena did? No, it was better for her to stay out of sight...for now.

"Where are they taking her?"

He looked over the cab roof again, his eyes narrowed. "They're pulling her along…" *Pause.* "They took her between two buildings. Toward the dock stairs."

"I have to follow." Jessica made to go after them, but the driver caught her arm and held her still.

"I'll be doing it, miss. You just sit tight right here."

"But…"

"I'll find where they're taking 'er."

"Please," Jessica whispered, and he slipped around the cab, pulling his hat low as he slunk along. Jessica peeked around the side of the cab and saw him turning toward the river.

She had to follow. She had to know where they were taking Serena. Lifting her skirts, for the cab had parked in muck at least three inches deep, she hurried to where she'd seen the man disappear and turned down a cobbled alleyway that stank of rotten fish and polluted water. At the end, she could see the opening to the dock stairs, but she couldn't see anyone descending them, nor any boats waiting at the bottom.

The driver reached the end of the alleyway and paused, craning his head around the corner to the right.

She hurried up to him. "What is it?"

He whipped his head around, then frowned down at her. "It ain't safe for you here."

"I don't care." She wasn't entirely stupid, though—she did keep her voice down.

He heaved a sigh and moved away from the corner. "Well, go ahead and look, then."

Cautiously, she moved forward and peeked around the corner.

Serena, flanked by two men holding tightly to her arms, was stumbling down a narrow walkway fronting the river. A sign reading "Wheatsheaf Wharf" in fading letters was nailed to a low post just close enough that Jessica could barely read it.

A ship was tied to the wharf, and as Jessica watched, the two men pushed and pulled her sister onto the ramp leading to the ship's deck. She nearly lost them among other men and the ship's rigging, and then they disappeared completely as one of them shoved Serena below.

Jessica swallowed hard and hesitated, her mind working fast. Finally, she turned to the driver. "I must ask you to take me to St. Katharine's Docks, please. It's not very far from here, is it?"

"Not at all," he said.

"Let's go." Lifting her skirts again, she sprinted back to the cab.

Chapter Thirteen

That afternoon, John, the coachman, and Benson had taken Thomas and Jake out on the two horses. Both boys found the animals fascinating. Thomas had never had the opportunity to get too close to a horse, though he'd always wanted to, and for Jake, who'd lived his whole life on ships, horses were something new and interesting to fix-ate on. He was learning everything he could about them, to the point of driving Meg and Will to distraction with all his questions.

Meg stood at the door watching Benson ride the dap-pled gray mare down the drive. The man had been raised on a farm and was an excellent hand with horses, and he held Jake snugly in front of him, the boy squealing in delight as Benson took the mare from a walk to a trot.

Meg turned and glanced at Will, who was smiling down at her. "I love that sound," she said. "The sound of him happy. I've rarely heard it, you know."

"It is a good sound," Will agreed.

The boys and servants turned out of sight. If their pattern held, they wouldn't be back for at least an hour. Just a few minutes ago, the cook and Molly had headed to Prescot for the second market day since their arrival. The realization struck Meg like an anvil: for the first time since they'd come to Lancashire, she and Will were completely alone.

Her heartbeat quickened. It had been ages since she'd been alone with Will.

He stood behind her, and she felt his presence keenly. Warmth emanated from his body. His hand skimmed her waist, then settled over it in a possessive, firm hold, and she felt the heat of his touch through all the layers of fabric separating his skin from hers.

"Remember how we met?" he asked in a low voice, his breath tickling her ear.

"Yes," she breathed. "The waltz."

She turned in his arms, letting the front door swing shut behind her, and he moved one hand from her waist to capture her hand in his own. She closed her eyes, remembering that moment just before the dance had started. Like now, his hand had been firm and warm on her waist. Even though she'd danced a dozen other waltzes with different men, the way he held her—then and now—had been so different from any of the others. He was firm and warm and strong, making her feel very feminine against his innate dark masculinity.

Every inch of her skin tingled in awareness as he leaned down and whispered in her ear, "Dance with me."

She gave a small laugh. "We haven't any music."

"We'll make our own."

And he began to dance. No matter what song one

waltzed to, the music always had a particular rhythm, and Will danced to that rhythm now, taking her on a smooth journey from the entry hall into the parlor, where there was a large enough open space between the sofa and the hearth that they could turn in a wide circle.

And then she began to hear it, too, in her mind. The swell of the notes as they carried over the dance floor. As he spun her in a tight circle, she laughed and gasped, "You're right. I can hear the music now."

He looked down into her eyes. "I knew, from the moment we started to dance, that there was something special about you."

"I knew the same about you. But how can that be? You see someone, you don't even know them... All you have to do is dance a few steps, and you just... *know*."

"I don't think it's that way with everyone," he said as they waltzed along the far wall in an arc so they wouldn't get too near the fire.

"No. Surely it's not," she murmured.

He turned her again, and she gripped his solid, strong back so she wouldn't lose her balance.

The only time she'd danced in the past eight years was in cramped quarters when she'd attempted to teach Sarah the basics of ballroom dance. She hadn't forgotten how to waltz, though. The oddest thing was, when she danced with him now, she still felt that inexorable pull toward Will that she had on the very first night they'd danced together.

Perhaps their relationship was fated somehow. Or maybe there was something innate inside of each of them that simply fit perfectly with the other.

"Do you like it here? Do you feel safe here?" His voice was a low wash of warmth that made her skin tingle.

"I do, on both counts. Thank you so much for seeing us here safely."

"I'd do anything for you, Meg."

She smiled up at him, and for the first time, it wasn't a tremulous smile. It wasn't full of questions, doubts, or fears. It was real, whole, and pure. She felt the truth of it in her entire face, and in her eyes. She believed him.

The music was loud in her memory. She remembered what she'd been wearing that night—her blue silk dress Mother had spent the last of the sugarcane harvest money on. Will had looked so strong, so handsome, in his Navy uniform.

His grip on her waist tightened a little, but he slowed his steps and finally stopped. With a gentle hold on her upper arms, he looked down into her eyes.

Her lips went dry, and the breath escaped her lungs as she gazed up at him. Lord, since that night at the inn, she'd missed his kiss. She'd lain awake at night with the memory of it buzzing across her lips.

"Please kiss me, Will."

Strong arms drew her close, and his lips touched hers and then began to move, at first soft, then deeper, coaxing her to open for him. She slipped her arms around him, pressing against the hardness of his chest.

He kissed her deeply, and she was dragged in, intoxicated by the press of his mouth upon hers, his musky, salty taste.

And for the first time, she believed these touches were meant for *her*. Not because he remembered some dream girl she'd once been. He was kissing Meg: the silent, fearful, distrustful one. He kissed her, warts and all.

Without taking his lips from hers, he lifted her into his

arms. So focused was she on his kiss, on his touch, that she hardly registered that he was climbing the stairs.

He laid her on her bed, lowered himself beside her, and pulled away, finally ending the long, drugging kiss.

She stared up at him, at his glistening lips, as he stroked her cheek and gazed at her. His dark eyes had gone deep with longing, but she didn't feel threatened. His kiss seemed to have finally finished unraveling everything that had been holding her prisoner.

"I'm sorry," she whispered, "so very sorry."

He seemed genuinely taken aback. "Why?"

"I haven't been fair to you, Will. I-I've been such a coward."

"That's not true—"

"It is, though." She swallowed hard. "I was afraid that you were looking at me and seeing someone else—someone I was long ago and who you wished I could be again. I was afraid that you couldn't want someone like the person I have become, that no one would want someone like me."

He trailed a knuckle down her cheek. "You possess all the traits I admire in a woman. You always have, Meg, but the years have drawn them into clearer focus."

No man had ever made her feel beautiful like Will did. And he meant it—she could hear the sincerity in his voice and see it in his eyes.

"There's something about you—your gentle voice, the softness in your gray eyes—that draws me in. No one else has ever been able to do that to me. No one has ever made me feel like you make me feel."

"Not Serena?" she asked, not to lead him, but out of

honest curiosity. After all, she and Meg possessed many of the same physical traits.

He shook his head. "No. Only you." He cupped her cheek in his hand, and it was so warm, so comforting, that she nuzzled against it. "You gave yourself to me long ago, Meg, and that moment..." His eyes shone down at her. "It was the...most..." He blew out a breath. "It was the most powerful moment of my life. I believe it held deep meaning for both of us. I know now that if it happened again between us, it would hold that same meaning for me, and when you decide you're ready, it will hold the same meaning for you as well."

Meg smiled tremulously at him. She didn't want to wait any longer. The temptation was too strong. She wanted the pleasure of him—of his body—again, after all these years.

Slowly, she turned over onto her side. She breathed a few deep breaths, and then she whispered, "Will you help me with my dress?"

She heard his breath catch, then felt his fingers as they moved over the buttons of her dress, then her petticoat, and finally, the laces of her stays. He took his time, as if he cherished the undoing of each button and the loosening of each lace. She held very still. His fingers felt different from those of her maid—there was more warmth, more heaviness, more masculine power in them. More sensuality.

He peeled back the material of her dress and petticoat, leaving her stays gaping open. Meg slid off the bed and let the layers of fabric fall to the floor. He moved to stand beside her, and, without a word, lifted off her stays, leaving her clad only in her chemise and drawers.

She was nervous. Anxious. But she wanted this. Really, she'd wanted it from the moment she'd awakened to see him gazing down at her on the *Freedom.*

She reached up and tugged on the string at the neck of his shirt. She plucked at the tie, and the shirt gaped open, revealing the hardness of the top of his chest.

He pulled his shirt from the waistline of his trousers and tossed it over his head, revealing his chest in all its masculine perfection.

He was so beautiful, it brought tears to her eyes. She remembered each muscular curve of that chest. She'd traced it with her fingertips when they'd lain together all those years ago, and she'd stored each strong curve and angle into her memory. She had recalled them in her darkest days, when she'd thought she'd never be free of Jacob Caversham.

Will hadn't changed very much. If anything, his chest had grown stronger, larger. It had lost that last bit of youthful softness and thinness. The dips and curves had become more pronounced, as if a sculptor had taken years to painstakingly chip off the hardest pieces of marble to create him.

His chest was hairless but for the thin trail of dark hair that descended from his navel and disappeared into the waistband of his trousers.

"Take off your chemise," he ordered, his voice gruff, his eyes steady on hers.

She obeyed breathlessly, still staring at all the perfect skin he'd just revealed to her. She pulled her chemise over her head and let it drop to the floor. Now she stood bare from the waist up.

His gaze skimmed her breasts, leaving a trail of heat

in its wake. "So beautiful," he murmured. "You haven't changed at all in eight years."

"But I have."

He just smiled and moved back onto the bed, motioning for her to join him. As soon as she crawled onto the mattress, he wrapped his arm around her waist and drew her underneath his body.

"You're so warm."

"For you, Meg. Warm for only you," he said, and kissed her again.

This time, the heat of his chest collided with hers, bringing warmth to her nipples that traveled deep inside her, coalescing into a mass of light and energy that tingled and burned, centered between her legs. She squirmed to relieve that ache of desire, but then she slipped her arms around Will and drew him even closer against her, because he was the only one who could warm her inside and out, the only one who could slake her need.

"So beautiful," he murmured. "My beautiful Meg."

His hardness pressed against her thigh, moving against her as his kisses traveled down her cheek, jaw, collarbones, and up the curve of her breast until his lips skimmed her nipple. She moaned, a low, needy sound, and he took her nipple into his mouth and reverently suckled first one side then the other until she was gasping and squirming wanting—no, *needing*—more.

"Please, Will," she whispered. "Please." She bucked up against the solidity of his shaft, and he slid his hand between their bodies to work the falls of his trousers. When they were loose, his hand moved away to fumble with her drawers until his fingers found the slit in them and skimmed her sensitive folds.

"Oh!" she gasped, arching underneath his touch, seeking more of it. He obliged her, stroking gently at first, then more firmly, his fingertips skimming her most sensitive spot until she was a writhing, panting mass of need, begging him for more.

This time, he didn't oblige her, not right away. He teased her to the brink of explosion, then brought her down, twice, three times. The desire was so powerful, she was sobbing with it, when she felt him tug on her drawers. She lifted her body, and he shimmied them off, sliding them down her legs, his callused fingertips skimming her thighs and making her nerve endings jump as he did so.

He kissed his way up her body again, the warm press of his lips seeming to dive beneath her skin as he kissed her toes, then her shins and thighs, and then his mouth pressed just over the mound of her womanhood, making her gasp with the wicked pleasure of it.

He continued moving upward, his lips caressing her hipbone and her stomach. He took his time at her breasts again, kissing the underswell of each before returning his focus to her nipples, gently scraping his teeth over each of them. She wrapped her hands in the soft strands of his black hair and held him against each nipple, her breasts so sensitive now that each touch of his lips and teeth sent sparks of sweet heat shooting through her.

Finally, he moved up again, his mouth brushing over her collarbones and jaw and finally coming to her lips, pressing against them softly as his knee nudged her legs apart.

The tip of his manhood pressed at her entrance, and she stilled at that first breaching push. He hesitated, then she arched up, meeting him, encouraging him with a low groan, and he slid all the way in, so deep and so hard, it stole her breath.

"Oh, Will," she whispered against his lips. "Oh, Will."

Opening his eyes, he looked down at her, his dark, questioning gaze so tender, she felt like she could devour it.

"Again," she pleaded.

He withdrew nearly all the way before plunging deep and hard back into her, making her release a sharp gasp of pleasure. His body was larger and even more powerful than she'd remembered. Every move he made was so strong but also so tender, so loving, that she wanted to weep.

Her body met his thrust for thrust, her fingers digging into the thick cords of muscle in his shoulders, her legs wrapping around his thighs and drawing him closer, tighter, harder.

He filled her so deeply and so thoroughly that he forced the air from her lungs with every thrust. Each time he entered her, then pulled back, the friction of their flesh moving together unraveled her, until once again, she was panting and writhing and begging for more. But this time it was no tease. He pushed her and pushed her, until her body arched upward and then undulated as she exploded into a thousand pieces and then floated back together.

But he wasn't finished. He thrust inside her, more exquisitely forceful, deeper, passion suffusing his dark eyes and mottling his chest with pink.

And then, he, too, came, holding her tight, his face buried in her hair as he emptied himself inside her.

He held himself there for several long moments, and then he slipped out of her and rolled until they lay side by side, keeping his arm wrapped possessively around her waist.

Meg's body hummed from the delicious sensations, and she reveled in them, not moving or speaking until they faded, leaving her feeling languid and content. Finally, she looked at him. He was gazing at her. He looked so young, so unsure of himself, her heart squeezed.

"I'm sorry," he whispered.

Her eyes widened. "Sorry? About what?"

He flinched. "It's been so long for me. Once I was... Once we were joined, I lost myself. Forgive me."

She held him tighter. "Oh, Will, no. You're wrong. You gave me so much pleasure, I—Well, I cannot even describe it."

He didn't answer, but some of the concern left his face, and he kissed her, the warmth of his lips sparking some of the embers still burning within her.

"I've been thinking about that," she murmured, stroking her fingers through the hair she'd tangled during their lovemaking. "Eight years of complete abstinence? Truly? I've heard that's not... Well, I've heard it's quite unusual for a gentleman."

Yet she believed it, because not only had Will told her he'd been abstinent for so long, but Serena had confirmed it.

A soft shade of pink suffused his cheeks. "I made one mistake," he said gruffly. "And that experience—it was so different from being with you. There was no love, no passion. It was only a physical act." In a very low voice, he added, "I promised myself it would never happen again. Not until there was as much love, as much caring, as much meaning, as there was between you and me."

"And you kept that promise?"

"I did."

"And there hasn't been that much meaning with any other woman?"

He looked steadily at her. "No."

"Even after you discovered Serena wasn't me and you thought I was the one who died?" Surely he'd felt free to explore relationships with other women then.

"I discovered that you were the one who'd fallen overboard almost two years ago. I learned that it was a ghost I'd been courting all that time, that you were lost at sea and presumed dead. The chances of you being alive were so slim..." He hesitated, and she saw his Adam's apple move as he swallowed. "How could any man think of bedding a woman when he's mourning the only woman he's ever loved?"

She stroked her hand up and down his back. "I wish you hadn't mourned."

"I wasn't the only one. Your family mourned you. Serena never recovered."

She closed her eyes tight. "I know. I wish none of you had had to suffer like that. Early on, I wrote a letter intending to let you know I was alive, but Caversham discovered me writing it. He dragged me on deck and made me watch as he tore the letter to pieces and threw it into the sea. He told me that's what he'd do to me if he ever caught me writing to my family again."

"Did you try again?"

"Yes." Her voice was a near whisper. "He didn't tear me to pieces...but he came close. Close enough that that was my last attempt."

The look on Will's face was murderous. "Mad bastard."

She stared up at the ceiling. "Some might call him mad, but I think of him as more...fanatical. He obsessed about making Sarah into a proper lady. He obsessed over his inability to be as powerful and influential as his brother, the marquis."

"But he's violent toward those who are weaker than himself." A trait, Meg could tell from the tone of his voice, that disgusted Will above all else.

"Yes," she admitted. "He's given to fits of anger—especially when his will is thwarted. Hence his rages at Sarah, Jake, and me when our behavior didn't meet his expectations."

Will leaned up on his elbow and looked down at Meg, his expression growing tender. "You're amazing, do you know that? After eight years of being under that man's thumb, of suffering your own pain from his rages and his abuse, you still retained your humanity. You retained *yourself.*"

"Sometimes I'm not so sure."

But even that was saying something. When she'd first arrived in England, she was certain she'd kept nothing of the Meg of eight years ago. Only in the past few days had she realized that she did, indeed, retain something of the girl who could finish her twin sister's sentences and who served as a substitute mother to her younger sisters. Something of that happy eighteen-year-old who'd come to London for the first time and had met the tall, dashing Navy officer, William Langley, and fallen madly in love.

"But sometimes," she continued, "I think about Sarah. How he took everything from her and left her a shell of herself. Sometimes, I, too, felt like a shell when I was under his thumb. But once I discovered a purpose, I felt like something close to whole again."

"And that purpose was caring for Jake?"

"Well, for Sarah, at first. Then, when Jake was born, both of them. For the last few months, it has been just me and Jake."

"You miss her," Will said softly.

"I do," she said. "But from the day I met her, her soul was so full of sorrow. I like to think that she's in a happier place now."

Will stroked the hair away from Meg's brow. "I am sure she is."

She gazed up at him in silence.

"Marry me, Meg."

She didn't move, didn't flinch. She just continued to look at him as thoughts reeled around in her mind.

Will didn't understand, not really. He didn't know Caversham, and he didn't know the marquis. To him, both men were ideas, specters. They were two bad men who might come after Meg and Jake, but Will intended to merely unsheathe his sword, play the knight in shining armor, and whip them into submission. He expected that they'd slink away with their tails between their legs, and he, Meg, Jake, and Thomas would live happily ever after in some sugar-coated castle.

That would not be how it went. In a way, she wished she were as much of an idealist as Will was. If she were, she'd marry him tomorrow, to hell with Jacob Caversham and his brother. But she wasn't an idealist. And she wasn't stupid.

"You don't wish to marry me." His voice was flat.

"It's not that," she whispered. "It's just that we've spent

the past few days pretending to have a home here—a family. We've behaved as though everything is as it should be, and it has been lovely. But everything is *not* as it should be. I am running away from Caversham, from his brother, and ultimately from the law. I've already involved you too much. If you married me, you'd have to run, too."

Will blew out a breath through his teeth. "We've been through this so many times."

"Yes, we have."

They stared at each other.

"Then I suppose there's nothing more to say." Pain was etched deep into the corners of his eyes.

A harsh ache settled in her chest. "I wish it wasn't this way."

"So do I."

"I love you," she said, an edge of desperation in her tone. It was the first time she'd told him those words since he'd found her on the jolly boat. And they'd come out wrong. Those three words should never be shrouded in panic and despair.

He sat still for a moment, staring at the far wall. Then he said, "Not enough," in a clipped voice. He rose from the bed and started to pull on his clothes, distancing himself from her in his silence.

She rose, too. She slipped on her chemise and stays, and without words, he came over to work the ties on her stays. When she pulled on her dress, he buttoned it without her needing to ask him.

She glanced at the looking glass on the far wall. Her hair was a mess of tangled curls. That was one thing she certainly didn't expect him to put back together, but that was all right. Even though Molly had been helping her dress and do her hair every day, she'd spent years performing both tasks on her own.

By the time they were both fully clothed, Meg heard happy-sounding noises downstairs and realized the boys were home. Without looking directly at Will, she murmured, "I'll just fix my hair."

"Of course," he said coolly. "I'll join the boys in the parlor."

With that, he left the room, shutting the door behind him with a snap. Meg straightened the covers on the bed, moving slowly, feeling the residual soreness from Will's lovemaking between her legs.

She paused, her hand flat on the pillow where he had lain. The silky fabric of the pillowcase was still warm and still smelled of him, and she closed her eyes, lifting the pillow to her face to breathe him in.

She hated that she'd hurt him. She hated that no matter what she did or said, he would never truly understand why Caversham and his brother were such a terrible threat. Not until it was too late.

She'd seen Caversham kill a man in cold blood. An image of Will lying in a red pool flashed through her mind, and her eyes flew open.

She'd been such a fool. From the beginning, she'd been aware of the danger. She'd lived with Caversham for years, and she knew him well. She knew how his mind worked. He wouldn't hesitate to kill Will or anyone who got in his way.

She loved Will, and the temptation of happiness with him had been so strong, she'd been weak when he'd insisted he could keep her and Jake safe. She'd basked in every stolen moment she'd been able to spend with him, because she never imagined she'd have that luxury ever again.

Stupid, stupid, stupid.

She loved him. And her own selfish stupidity might end up getting him killed.

Woodenly, she walked to her dressing table, retrieved her comb, and began to fix her hair.

Someday, maybe, she'd no longer be afraid of Caversham. But, for now, she knew better. And now, in the relative peace of her brother-in-law's house, she was going to find a way to keep Will safe.

Chapter Fourteen

When Jessica and her driver—she'd learned his name was Mr. Twining—reached St. Katharine's Docks, twilight had settled over the Thames. As soon as she saw the long buildings at the edge of the docks, Jessica knew her way.

"Here!" she cried as they neared the narrow opening between two of the buildings. Mr. Twining stopped the horse, and Jessica leaped out from the cab. Lifting her skirts, not caring who saw her, she hurried toward the wharf where the *Freedom* was moored.

She released a breath when she saw the ship rocking gently in the light breeze, one rear porthole glowing gold from lantern light within. She hurried up and mounted the stairs two at a time, only slightly tangling her skirts in the ropes as she fumbled onto the deck.

All was quiet on deck.

"Hullo?" she shouted. When there was no immediate answer, she hurried toward the aft cabin, where the captain's and mate's quarters were located. She went to Briggs's door and burst inside without knocking, praying that he'd be inside.

He was. And he was naked.

Well, she amended... partially naked. His wide, well-muscled torso was bare, but the tops of his drawers covered everything below his flat, tight stomach.

"Christ!" he exclaimed when he saw her. He jerked up the trousers he'd been pulling on and quickly did up the falls. Turning away, he grabbed a linen shirt and yanked it over his head, pushing his arms through in what must be record time.

And then he turned back to her, glowering. "What the *hell* are you doing on my ship?"

In the half second before she came to her senses, Jessica thought that it was a shame he'd reacted so quickly. She would have appreciated a far more extended view of his body. Truly, he was a spectacular specimen of a man.

She'd think about that later. Now... her sister.

"Serena's been captured," she said, all business. "I think Jacob Caversham has her. And," she added, "I believe this is Captain Langley's ship, not yours."

He ignored her last comment, because his thunderous look was changing into one of disbelief as he digested the first bit of news.

"Are you sure?"

She stomped her foot. "Good Lord, Mr. Briggs. Why would I be here if I wasn't certain? We were shopping in Regent Street when she was kidnapped before my very eyes. They forced her into a carriage, and I followed them to a wharf on the river where three men dragged my very unwilling sister onto a quite sinister-looking ship, one much larger than this."

She gestured to Mr. Twining, who'd finally caught up to her, as if his presence verified everything.

Instead, Briggs narrowed his eyes at him. "Who are you?" he asked, his voice brittle.

"How impolite," Jessica said sharply. "This is the driver of the cab I used to follow them. I would never have known where they went if Mr. Twining had not been so helpful."

Briggs's focus turned completely to Mr. Twining. "And you brought the lady here after you saw the other lady kidnapped and carried onto that ship?"

"Aye, sir."

"Would you be able to return there?"

"Oh, aye. Easily."

"Can you describe the location?"

"Of course, sir. Just downriver from these docks, tied to Wheatsheaf Wharf, she was."

Briggs pressed his lips together and nodded. He glanced at Jessica, then gestured to the single chair in the room, pulled up behind a small desk bolted to the center of the floor. "Sit there and wait for me."

Her mouth dropped open. "You must be joking. I will not sit! I must go rescue my sister!"

"No, you mustn't. You will sit tight until I say so."

"I will not."

"Do it voluntarily, Miss Jessica, or I will tie you down. You'll be safe here on the *Freedom*. I won't have it any other way."

Grumbling to herself, she crossed her arms over her chest, glaring at him.

He glared back with ice-blue eyes, not giving an inch.

With a long-suffering sigh, she sat.

Without sparing her another glance, he gestured Mr. Twining into the small cabin, then he leaned out the tall, narrow door leading to his quarters.

"MacInerny! I need you in here, now!" he bellowed so loudly that Jessica winced. The man had a voice like a bullhorn.

Within moments, Mr. MacInerny, whom Jessica had met on her previous trip to the *Freedom*, entered the cabin. Briggs quickly explained the situation to him, then assigned him the task of delivering a message, post haste, to Jonathan.

Jessica wasn't sure about that plan. Jonathan was quite protective of Serena, especially now that she was expecting again. She hoped his rage wouldn't inspire him to do anything stupid.

Still, Jonathan would want to know. It wouldn't do to keep such information from him.

Hands folded in a most ladylike fashion on her lap, Jessica raised an imperious brow at Briggs as soon as Mr. MacInerny had left the small room. "Are you sure that's wise?"

He frowned at her. "What's wise?"

"The Earl of Stratford is quite fond of my sister. He's liable to blast away half of London in his effort to retrieve her. I hope you'll know how to contain him."

Briggs gave her an odd look that lasted a few seconds, then he turned back to Mr. Twining. "Describe this Wheatsheaf Wharf to me, will you?"

As Mr. Twining did just that, describing the route both by land and by river, Jessica twisted her hands in her lap and worried about Serena. The men who'd been bullying her onto the ship had looked like the sort of men who would hurt her without a qualm.

Jessica jumped up. "Enough of this blethering!"

Both male heads swung toward her. Briggs had one sandy brow raised high, scrunching up his scar.

"I shall not wait here, impotent, while my sister might be getting hurt." Getting killed, she thought, but she couldn't say that out loud. Still, tears sprang to her eyes. "I'm going after her, and I don't care whether you help me!"

She pushed Mr. Twining aside, and he stumbled against the table. But at the door, she ran into a veritable tower of rock. Briggs's powerful torso—the torso that she'd admired just minutes ago—loomed before her, blocking her way out the door.

"Not so fast, Miss Jessica."

"Let me out!"

"Don't be a ninny."

She gasped. Phoebe had called her a ninny once, and she'd slapped her sister so hard and had made such a fuss, Phoebe hadn't dared to do it since. And now this pompous, headstrong man dared to call her such a thing? What a...a...

"You...*bastard*," she hissed. "Move out of my way. Immediately."

His eyes widened. Obviously he had finally realized that she was serious.

"I am not going to let those men hurt my sister, do you understand me?"

Reaching out, he grabbed her shoulders, shaking her lightly. "And I'm not going to let those men hurt *you*, do *you* understand *me*?"

Stalemate. She gazed up at him, tears burning her eyes.

"I'm calling for the earl. Mr. Twining has described her location, and when darkness falls, I will assemble a group of men to go after her. We'll use a barge and go by river—we'll take them by surprise that way. We'll find your sister and bring her back to you."

"What if—?"

He pressed a firm finger over her lips. "You are a woman. This is a man's job. You have been uncommonly brave, Jessica, but you've risked yourself too much already."

Jessica seethed inside, but a part of her—a bigger part than she'd like to admit to—saw the wisdom in his plan. She'd be a fool to bumble about on a strange ship's deck in her layers of skirts. It'd be wiser to go at night, when their movements would be more difficult to trace. But...

"But what if they hurt Serena?" she whispered. "Really hurt her?"

That affected Briggs. His blue eyes darkened, and he leaned toward her, gently pushing aside a strand of hair that had fallen over her eye. "I'm going to do everything I can to prevent that from happening," he murmured. "I promise, Jessica."

Though she was furious at being left behind, Jessica understood the necessity. So she sat—well, *paced* would be a more appropriate term—and waited while Jonathan, Briggs, and their men carried out their rescue. They'd employed Mr. Twining as well, for the older man was fascinated by the intrigue and had volunteered to do whatever he could to help.

She waited—*paced*—for hours, often glancing at the

door of Briggs's quarters to see that yes, indeed, the enormous young man they'd placed there to "watch over her" had not moved an inch.

It was late. Nearing midnight.

God, what if those awful men had hurt Serena? What if she had been raped? What if she'd been killed?

Jessica lurched to the door, and the man, a round-faced youth with an apparently cheerful disposition, rose instantly. "Did ye need aught, miss?"

"I should like to go home, Mr. Jasper," she lied. "It is late and I am tired."

His smiling lips flattened, and he frowned at her. "Sorry, miss. Mr. Briggs said ye must wait here."

She studied him, gauging her odds of simply slipping by and running. She assessed them as quite slim. Yet slim was better than nothing, wasn't it?

"They ought ter be back soon, miss."

"I know that," she said sourly. They should have been back an hour ago, and yet they weren't.

Turning, she crossed her arms over her chest, paced to the tiny window, and then turned back to Mr. Jasper. Six steps total. She'd go mad if she had to stay in this horrible room for one second longer.

Putting her head down, she dashed through the narrow opening between Mr. Jasper and the door. On the dark deck, she lifted her skirts and ran toward the ladder leading to the dock. But her foot caught on a rope, and down she went in a flurry of skirts, hearing the screeching sound of ripping fabric.

She lay there for a second, stunned, and when her senses returned, she scrambled to her knees, only to find herself staring into the formidable bulk of Mr. Jasper's thighs.

"Drat," she mumbled.

"Are ye hurt, miss?"

"No," she grumbled. "But I fear my dress is."

His hand emerged from the shadows to help her up. Grudgingly, she took it and allowed him to hoist her to her feet. When she was eye-level with him, she stomped her foot. "I want my sister."

"There now," he murmured, patting her head as if he were an elderly grandfather comforting a beleaguered child, when in fact, he was probably around her age. "Of course ye do. But the men'll be bringing her back shortly."

"I don't want her shortly. I want her now." Jessica knew she was behaving like a brat. But sitting still, completely powerless, was not in her nature. Unlike most of the women she'd met in London, she was a doer, a person of action, and not one to sit and patiently wait for things to happen. And the knowledge that her sister was in danger sent impulses of energy to all her nerves, making it impossible for her to be still.

Just then, she heard a scuffing noise, and then voices.

"Is that them?"

"May just be," Mr. Jasper said in a low voice. He gestured with his chin. "You go on to Mr. Briggs's quarters now, and I'll be seeing if it's safe, aye?"

She bit her tongue, and the rational part of her ordered her body to obey Mr. Jasper's command. She turned and retreated into Briggs's quarters. Mr. Jasper closed the door behind her, and she leaned against its inside panel as she heard his retreating footsteps.

She continued to stand by the door with her fists clenched at her sides and her torn skirt dragging on the floor, listening intently to the goings-on outside. There was a soft scraping noise, voices speaking in low tones. Minutes passed, and she stood there, stock still.

And then the door swung open. Serena stood there, looking tired and out of sorts, but in one piece.

"Oh, thank God!" Jessica launched herself into her sister's arms.

Serena hugged her tightly. "I'm all right, Jess."

She didn't sound all right. Her voice shook like a leaf in an autumn windstorm.

"I think we should all sit down," Jonathan said from behind his wife.

"Captain's quarters is the best place. There's a larger table in there." Briggs's voice came from the darkness somewhere behind Jonathan.

They arranged themselves in Captain Langley's quarters, Jessica and Serena sitting on the bench against the wall and Jonathan settling in one of the chairs. The lanterns that Mr. Jasper brought in lit the room cheerfully, and Briggs opened a bottle of wine for the four of them to share.

"What happened to Mr. Twining?" Jessica asked as she took her glass from Briggs.

"Gone home," Jonathan said. "We were done with him, and the man was exhausted."

"I promised him a reward for following the carriage Serena was in," Jessica said. "Without him, I would have never been able to find her."

"Good," Jonathan said. "So did I. I told him to call on me tomorrow. He'll be handsomely rewarded."

Jessica nodded and took a long draught of wine, satisfied that Jonathan would see to the man's welfare.

He reached across the table, taking his wife's hand in

his own and speaking gently to her. "Promise me again that you're not hurt."

Serena took her time answering. "They weren't kind men, Jonathan, but I'm not hurt. Not truly."

"Did they strike you?" Jessica breathed.

Serena flushed. "A few times." Seeing Jonathan's expression darken, she added, "But I suffered worse as a girl at the hands of our mother. It could have been so much worse."

Briggs finally took a seat, looking serious. "Will you tell us exactly what happened, my lady?"

Serena took a shaky breath. "Jess was looking at some gloves, and I suddenly... well, I felt like I needed some air. I've... often felt that way in the past two or three weeks."

Jessica understood instantly—her sister had been feeling nauseous due to her pregnancy.

"So I stepped outside for a moment," Serena continued. "The next thing I knew, someone was pushing me into a carriage. I fought them, but I was so surprised, so afraid... The next thing I knew, the carriage door was slammed shut, and we were moving along."

"That's how I knew to follow you," Jessica said. "They closed the door on your dress, and no one on Regent Street today was wearing the same color. I knew it had to be you."

Serena gazed ruefully down at her coral-colored dress, now torn and stained beyond repair. "I suppose it earned its keep in another way, then, since I'll have to throw it away after wearing it only once."

Jonathan, still holding Serena's hand across the glossy wooden table, leaned forward. "Who was in the carriage with you?"

"Jacob Caversham and two of his men." She looked

away, at a point somewhere beyond Jonathan's shoulder. "He's a sallow man . . . with dark hair and cold blue eyes. He smelled of pomade. He kept demanding I tell him what I'd done with Jake."

Briggs's eyes widened. "He confused you with your sister."

"Apparently."

"But you're so different from Meg," Jessica exclaimed.

Jonathan agreed, seemingly as surprised as Jessica, but Briggs shook his head. "No, ma'am. You and Miss Donovan look very similar indeed. I mistook you for her the first time I saw you. It's true there are subtle differences, but I am not surprised he believed you were your sister."

"How did he happen to know you were shopping in Regent Street today?" Jonathan asked sharply.

"Apparently, that happened only by chance. He said he and his men had been covertly watching the house and considered himself lucky when he saw Jessica and me walking out today. He followed us to Regent Street and took the first opportunity he could to grab me."

Jonathan's eyes narrowed, and Jessica couldn't blame him. The idea of someone spying on their house made her insides twist.

"What did you say when he accused you of kidnapping Jake?" Jessica asked.

"I told him I had no idea what he was talking about, that I knew no one named Jake. That I was the Countess of Stratford and my husband would be looking for me . . . And that was when he grew angry."

"What did he do?" Jessica asked breathlessly.

Serena swallowed. Looking away from the men, she said, "He threatened me. He said if I didn't tell him what

I'd done with his son, he'd kill me. He said he knew I was Meg, and to stop lying to him."

Jessica pressed her hand to her mouth. "What then?"

Serena took a moment to compose herself before she continued. "We drove for a long while. Then, we stopped, and they forced me onto the ship. They blindfolded me and locked me in a large area in the very bowels of the vessel—"

"The hold," Briggs supplied.

Serena looked at him thoughtfully. "Yes, I suppose it was. I sat there for a few hours. Another man came in to question me." She turned her gaze to Jonathan again. "I believe it was the Marquis of Millbridge—it was very dark and his voice was muffled, but he sounded familiar. Anyhow, he cut his questioning short when I insisted that I was Meg, the Countess of Stratford, and that I had no idea what he was talking about, that I knew nothing about this boy named Jake."

Jessica shuddered, remembering how she'd danced and flirted with the Marquis of Millbridge. The next time she saw him, she'd poke his eyes out.

"He walked out, locking me back in the room, but I heard him arguing with Caversham outside. He called him an 'idiot,' said I was the Countess of Stratford, and told him to set me free. Caversham said he couldn't, that it was too late. Their voices faded in and out, but from what I gathered, the marquis knew I was who I said I was, and he believed I knew nothing about the real Meg and Jake. He berated his brother for the debacle he'd begun by kidnapping me. Their voices faded as they went away, and then I heard and saw nothing. Not until you and your men appeared and freed me."

"How did you do it?" Jessica asked Briggs.

"We rowed to the ship Twining pointed out to us and used ropes to climb on board," he said.

"The place was quieter than I'd expected," Jonathan said.

"Because I learned one thing about Caversham today, and that is that he is cocky," Serena said in a shaky voice. "He didn't expect anyone would have any idea about my whereabouts, and he didn't think it'd be any problem to keep me. When he first brought me on board, I heard him dismiss the crew to go eat and drink their fill at the nearest tavern."

"There was only the one guard posted at your door," Briggs said.

Serena nodded. "And he only remained behind because Caversham was punishing him for losing a rope overboard yesterday, if I heard him correctly."

"How did you get past him?" Jessica asked the men.

"We took care of him." Jonathan's voice was brusque. "He was in possession of the key to the hold, so from there, it was easy to free your sister and slip away."

"Caversham will be angry," Serena said. "He might come after me again."

"He might come after all of you," Briggs said.

"We'll leave town," Jonathan said. "I'd intended to stay so as not to draw attention to the family, but now I think it'll be safer if we go. I'd rather you and your sisters were in a safe place before I bring that bastard to justice."

"Will we join Meg in Prescot?" Jessica asked.

"No. We don't want to draw any attention to her. We'll go home to Sussex."

Jessica sighed. So much for her Season, for all the dancing she'd planned, for all the suitors she was amassing.

Serena took her hand. "Jonathan's right. It's the safest option."

"What about Meg?"

"He'll certainly be looking for her now," Serena said. "Along with the authorities. It's probably a race to see who will find her first."

"We'll dispatch a warning tonight," Jonathan said. "They must leave Prescot as soon as possible."

Serena nodded. "But don't tell her and Will what happened here, please, Jonathan. This is exactly what she didn't want to happen. I know my sister. She'll feel responsible. And, really, nothing happened. I'm quite all right."

Jessica frowned at her sister. For all her "it was nothing" comments, Serena's hands were shaking and her eyes were unnaturally bright. Jessica was fairly certain the ordeal had affected Serena more than she was admitting.

"We'll talk about that," Jonathan said quietly. "For now, we should get home and get you to bed."

Serena gave a tremulous laugh. "Well...I don't feel tired. I doubt I'll be able to sleep."

"You need to sleep," Jonathan said softly. "For the babe, if nothing else."

She gave him a game smile. "I'll try."

They rose, and Jonathan escorted his wife to the door and out onto the deck. Jessica lingered behind. She turned to Briggs, partially closing the door behind her.

"Thank you for saving my sister, David."

She went right up to him, slipped her arms around his waist, and kissed him on the lips.

She'd meant it to be a friendly, thank-you peck. But his

lips were astonishingly warm and soft, and she lingered for one second, then two. When she did pull away, it took far more effort than she'd expected.

"Good night," she murmured.

Leaving him staring after her with a dazed look, she slipped out the door and closed it behind her.

Chapter Fifteen

Meg spent her days racking her brain in the attempt to conjure up a way to ensure Will's safety, but she came up empty.

She was stuck in the middle of England, ostensibly with everything she could ever want or need except a way to escape. Ironically, the people she wanted to escape from—her family and Will—were the only people in the world she could trust.

Every day, she stood in the doorway and watched the boys go off with the servants for their riding lessons, and every day she felt the truth pressing in on her. Caversham was coming for her, and she wasn't prepared. If he found Jake and she wasn't with him...

The feeling grew daily, and it became more and more difficult to watch Jake ride away with Benson. She needed to keep him close, to protect him from Caversham in case he suddenly appeared.

And then, one of Jonathan's personal servants arrived from London with two letters. One was a letter from Serena to her, and there was a companion letter from Jonathan to Will. Once they'd offered the rider—who said he'd left London under cover of darkness and had ridden without stopping—a meal and some rest, they sat down to read their letters.

Dearest Sister,

I miss you so much, and I wish you could be with us. But I have some news to impart—news that isn't very good, though I know you were expecting it.

J.C. is in London with his ship, which is docked in the Thames. The family has decided to head home, where it is believed we will all be safer. A few trusted agents will remain in London for the time being. They have gathered some additional evidence regarding J.C.'s illegal activities, but it still isn't enough to prosecute.

I am so worried about you. Although I don't believe anyone has revealed your whereabouts to J.C., the man is, by all accounts, very intelligent, and I am concerned that he will eventually find you.

We have been considering other locations for you to reside until this is all over. J is sitting next to me right now, also writing a letter, and I'm sure he's suggesting several potential places for you to go.

Everyone is worried and concerned, and we miss you deeply, but we are all well. Your other sisters send their love.

With Love,
S.

Her mouth dry, Meg looked up at Will, who'd finished reading his letter from Jonathan and was watching her.

"He's in London," she croaked out.

He laid the letter down and held out his arms to her. "Come here."

She went willingly, soaking up all the comfort she could from his embrace.

"Stratford suggested that we go to my house in Northumberland," he murmured.

"Once Caversham discovers we're together, that'll be the first place he will search," she said on a near moan.

"That was my thought, too. But I have another idea. Somewhere even your family didn't consider."

She looked up at him through shining eyes. "Where's that?"

"At sea."

She blinked at him, not responding right away. Of course. It made a lot of sense. She'd been on the *Freedom*—knew how fast the ship was. Caversham would never catch them, especially if the only ship he had on hand was the large and cumbersome *Defiant*.

But...

"Oh, Will, what are we going to do? Sail the seven seas, trying to avoid Caversham for the rest of our lives?"

"No," he said firmly. "It's just a matter of time before Briggs and your brothers-in-law find the evidence that will prove, once and for all, the kind of men Caversham and Millbridge are." He held her more tightly. "I just want to keep you safe, Meg. But this *will* end, eventually. And then you will be free from him."

It was then that the seed of an idea sprouted in her mind.

"To get on the *Freedom*, we'd have to travel back to London. Won't that be dangerous?"

"Well, I wasn't thinking we'd take the *Freedom*. I've another ship—a steamer—in a shipbuilding yard in Liverpool."

"A...steamer?" she repeated dumbly. Of course, she knew what steamships were—she saw them more and more in the various harbors she'd been in. But to her, Will would always be a sailor. She hadn't predicted that he'd join the steam craze.

"Yes." He sighed and gently disentangled himself from her. "We started building the *Endeavor* almost two years ago, and we were planning to launch her in September."

"That's months away yet!" By then, Caversham certainly would have found them.

Will shrugged. "She can be launched early. The ship and engine are in working order now—they're just making the finishing touches to the hull and the interior."

"A steamship, Will? I'd never have expected that of you."

"Steam is the future, Meg. My business won't continue to be profitable if I stubbornly resist newer and better inventions."

"How sad to think of all our sleek, quiet, beautiful sailing vessels replaced by those ugly, noisy, dirty steamships," Meg murmured.

"I know."

Slowly, Meg nodded. "Well...Liverpool is close, isn't it?"

"Just over an hour away by carriage."

She breathed out, her idea sprouting into a thin vine that wrapped around her heart and squeezed.

"When can we go?"

Will thought for a moment. "Well, Stratford said Caversham has only recently arrived in London. Most likely, it'll take him several days before he realizes you and Jake aren't there, and another several before he learns where we've gone. I'll need to get the *Endeavor* launched and provisioned with a crew and enough supplies for us to be at sea for some time. I will have to travel into Liverpool every day for a few days to make sure it is all done correctly." He hesitated, his eyes narrowed as he calculated. "If we start preparing immediately, I believe we can be ready in ten days' time."

"It's risky," she murmured. "If Caversham were to find us before we left..."

Will shook his head, somber. "He won't. It's simply not enough time."

And she knew what she must do. Her plan had grown and blossomed in her mind, now fully mature. Will might hate her for it, but it was the only way she could keep him safe.

Pain, regret, and love for him swirled within her, and she made no effort to resist any of it. She surged toward him, wrapped her hands around his neck, and pulled him down for a kiss. He kissed her back, then pulled away a little. "Meg—the boys," he whispered against her lips.

"They've gone riding. Didn't you hear them?"

"Mmm." This time, he initiated the kiss, and she wrapped her fingers in the silky strands of his black hair and kissed him back. But in a matter of seconds, he pulled away again. "The servants?" he asked in a hoarse whisper.

"Shhh." Taking his hand, she led him out of the parlor. Molly and the cook were in the kitchen laughing about something, so Meg turned to go up the stairs. She steered him to his room this time because she knew Molly would never dare enter Will's space without an explicit order to do so.

She pulled him inside, then shut the door behind them with her foot. She leaned against the door, looking at him through her lashes, wanting him so badly—one more time—that her body vibrated with need.

He was staring at her. "What are you doing, Meg?"

"I want you," she said simply.

He blew out a breath. She could see the ridge of his erection behind his trousers and knew that he was as aroused as she. And yet he didn't step toward her.

She kicked off her shoes, then shimmied out of her drawers. Slowly, she lifted the hem of her dress over her stocking until she showed him her bare thigh. "I want you," she repeated.

He stared at her thigh for a long moment, his gaze raw with hunger, then he slowly dragged his head up to look at her. She saw something else in his eyes, however, something deeper than hunger. Pain.

Her fingers loosened, and her skirt fell to the floor. Her heart swelled in her chest, on the verge of breaking apart. "What's wrong?" Her voice was a croaking whisper.

"I want you . . . God." He pushed a harsh hand through his hair. "But not like this." He took a deep breath, and when she was silent, he continued, "I've told you before— I don't want a liaison. I want something more. I want a partnership. A wife. Someone who will offer me her love and trust without boundaries or conditions."

She gazed at him, her eyes burning.

"I can't accept a partner who doesn't look at me

as I look at her. Who won't trust me, share her deepest thoughts and fears with me, and who won't turn to me first when something is wrong." He shook his head. "I cannot—I won't—do it."

She pushed off the door with her elbows and went to him, wrapping her arms around him and pressing her lips to his chest. She peppered kisses to his coat, feeling his pectoral muscle clenching beneath her lips. "You don't understand. I love you so much. So much."

"You might feel that way at this moment. But not forever."

She flinched, pulled away, and looked up at him, holding her hands flat against his chest. "I do want you forever," she whispered. "I...just...Marriage...it seemed like too much, too soon. Not when I'm running from Caversham. Not now."

He stared at her for a long moment, his eyes dark. "And when it's all over with Caversham?"

She pressed her forehead against the hardness of his chest and closed her eyes. Her cynical side threatened to rear its ugly head, screaming, *It'll never be over! You'll always be under Caversham's control! You'll always be running!* But she refused to heed that voice right now. "We can try to build the partnership you're talking about."

"There will always be a Caversham, Meg. There will always be something or someone trying to get between us. There are always challenges. But a real relationship succeeds when partners work together to overcome them."

"I didn't mean to hurt you." But she had. She'd kept everything to herself in a weak attempt to protect him. Why was it that she just seemed to cause more pain wherever she went, when her only goal was to save the people she loved from pain?

She wanted to be with him. She wanted to have the kind of life they were pretending to live, and she wanted a partnership. But she couldn't stop herself from thinking it was all one vast illusion, a pretense, a screen temporarily blocking her from the harshness of the real world.

"I want the kind of marriage you're talking about. I do." Maybe, just for a moment, she could be a dreamer, like he was.

He pulled away from her, took her by the shoulders, and stared down at her, his eyes dark as coal. "Is that the truth?"

"Yes." It was a simple word, and she wasn't lying. One day, when all of this was over and Caversham was no longer a threat, maybe they could marry and have the kind of marriage he was talking about. That would be heaven. Bliss.

He groaned softly and crushed his mouth to hers, his kiss hard, possessive, consuming. After a moment, he pulled back. He didn't speak, but the question—the vulnerability—was there, deep in his eyes.

She kissed his lips, his cheek, and his chin, his afternoon beard scraping against her mouth. Her hands moved lower, stroking over first his back and then his backside, and her lips moved lower, too, kissing his chest over the linen of his shirt.

There was no time for shyness. No space for being tentative. She had to show him, had to prove that every word she'd said was the truth. Because unless she proved it to him now, when she left him, he'd think she didn't care.

She was doing it to keep him safe. Not because she didn't care, but because she did.

She tugged at his shirt, pulling it from the waistband of his trousers. Her hands moved up again, this time beneath his shirt, stroking up and down his back and then moving to the front. He shivered when her palms rubbed over his chest.

Her fingers found the ties of his falls, and she worked them, finally tugging them open and pushing the waist of his trousers down, revealing everything to her as she knelt, pulling his drawers and trousers along with her. When she reached his ankles, she nudged him aside, and he stepped out of them.

When he was free of his trousers, she looked up at him, now naked except for his shirt. Reaching beneath it, she stroked the long, hard length of him, feeling the silkiness of his most private skin beneath her fingers. Slowly, she kissed her way up his legs. Her lips traveled around his hips and abdomen over his shirt, and then she pressed a kiss to his shaft.

He jerked beneath her. "God, Meg," he gasped. And she knew, with certainty, that this wasn't only a first for her. He'd never had a woman's mouth on this part of him before.

That fact gave her confidence to explore further. Nudging under his shirt, she swiped her lips up and down him slowly, learning the shape of him, testing with her tongue. She kissed him all over—small, soft kisses that covered him up and down. And then she was at his tip again.

Pausing, she glanced up at him. His eyes were half-closed, and a look of utter ecstasy softened his features. *Yes.* Sarah had told her that men adored this, that it gave them extreme pleasure, and now she knew that her friend had been right.

Slowly, she opened her mouth and took him in deeply, as much of him as she could hold in her mouth, pressing her lips against him just as the entrance of her body might press against him. When she had him as far as she could take him, she pulled back, keeping up the pressure, sweeping her lips and tongue over his silky length.

Encouraged by his low groan, she kept moving her lips over him, following with her fingers, rubbing and stroking. Her own body heat rose from the inside out, as if having him in her mouth was sending a message to the rest of her, preparing her body for his ultimate invasion.

His fingers tangled in her hair, coaxing her closer, deeper. She complied, but within moments, he pulled his body away from her with a gasp. Before she could blink, he'd clasped her arms and hauled her to her feet. Drawing her against his body, he held her and kissed her deeply, thoroughly, and she realized he was moving forward and pressing her against the door.

Wrapping one hand behind her neck, he grabbed handfuls of her skirts with the other, yanking them upward. Crushing the fabric between them, he opened her legs with his knee and drove into her.

She hadn't expected this—not so fast. But her body gave way to his, filling her with such a powerful, exquisite sensation that she cried out. He bent down and covered her mouth with his, muffling the sound.

She wrapped her arms around his shoulders and wantonly hooked one leg around his thighs, tugging him tighter against her. He thrust into her, pinning her to the door, and pleasure stormed through her, a veritable flood of sensation. They exchanged mad kisses, covering each other's faces, their necks, their collarbones, their lips ravenous.

All the while, Will thrust his long, thick length into her over and over again. The friction of his skin against hers sent streams of pressure that built, with every deep penetration, into a torrent.

She gripped him hard, digging her nails into his muscled shoulders through his shirt. Her skirt rustled all around them with their frantic movements. She kept kissing him, wanting to inhale him, to take his masculine, salty essence in and keep it for herself.

His thrusts grew impossibly deeper, impossibly stronger. The streams of pressure coiling inside her built and coalesced. And then the dam burst, and pleasure streamed through her. Opening her mouth in a silent scream, she arched backward, her body undulating as Will continued to move powerfully within her. He held her tight, keeping her safe, keeping her whole, as she tumbled over the waterfall, diving into the warm pool of pleasure that covered her, suffused every inch of her body.

Soon after, Will joined her, tensing as he held her tight, pressing his lips to her forehead as his body hardened all over. And then he released in his own wave of pleasure, trembling as he spilled his seed inside her.

They stayed there, without moving, for several minutes, sweet aftershocks rumbling through them both, neither willing to relinquish the pleasure while it lasted. But eventually the tremors died away, and Meg's leg lowered from Will's thigh and her arms slid from his neck. Her skirts fell as he slipped from her body and moved away. She slumped against the door, watching him as he fumbled for his trousers, sat on the edge of the bed, and pulled them on, one leg at a time.

After he'd stood and fastened them, he looked across the room at her and smiled. It was a crooked, boyish smile, something she hadn't seen from him for eight long years. It melted her. He rose, and she moved into his arms. There they stood, simply holding each other.

Forgive me, Will, for what I'm going to do. You might hate me, but at least you'll be alive.

Jessica did not want to go to Sussex. It was for stronger reasons than she'd initially thought. She could do without the dancing and the suitors, after all.

She would be stuck at Stratford House in Sussex. Helpless. She'd rather be with David, helping him find evidence against Caversham and the Marquis of Millbridge. She desperately wanted both of them to hang for what they'd done to Meg and Serena.

Not to mention the fact that she very much wanted to stay near David Briggs.

In truth, she couldn't understand why she'd initially found that scar above his eyebrow so ugly. Now, it struck her as a mark of his masculinity, proof of his bravery, and something that added a great deal of character to his face.

She couldn't stop thinking about the softness of his lips.

When he came to see Jonathan to discuss the case against Caversham and Millbridge, she hovered nearby, serving them tea, listening to the conversation, and admiring Briggs's physique. He was neither too brawny nor too thin. He was hard all over, as evidenced by the firmness of muscle she'd seen when she'd stormed into his quarters and felt when she'd kissed him.

His eyes were a beautiful shade of blue, dark like the oceans he sailed upon, and they crinkled at the edges when he smiled. He had a strong nose and chin, and those lips, oh, how they made her knees wobble. The perfect bow, not thin like so many aristocratic men's lips, but plump, soft, and warm. And sweet. When she'd kissed him, it felt like honey had been pouring over her lips and straight through her.

He was—somehow—*more* than all the suitors she'd acquired in London ballrooms. More than all of them combined.

Unfortunately, though, he wasn't a suitor. And Jessica didn't have the first idea how to make him one. It might prove difficult if he really did despise her as much as his scowls and mumbled single-syllable words directed toward her might indicate.

Today, he and Jonathan were in the drawing room, discussing Caversham and Millbridge. Apparently, Caversham and his ship had disappeared a few days after Jonathan and his companions had rescued Serena. Briggs had stifled his urge to chase after the man and had instead continued his search for information in London.

Jessica had just served them tea and was hovering in the background like a servant instead of going upstairs and embroidering with Beatrice, who was expecting her. Jonathan looked up and gave her a pointed look, but she just frowned back at him. Sighing, he ignored her and went back to his conversation.

"It appears that Millbridge is using at least some of the funds to raise an army," Briggs was saying.

"What for?" Jonathan asked.

Briggs shrugged. "That's the question, my lord. No one knows. He has a large warehouse in the docklands packed to the gills with explosives."

"Good God, wouldn't the customs officials be aware of such a thing?"

"They've been known to turn a blind eye, especially when presented with enough blunt to quiet them."

Jonathan took a thoughtful drink of his brandy. "You make it sound like he's building an army to take over the country, or some such madness. But of course, he'd never succeed."

"No, he would not."

"And we cannot forget that one of his closest friends, the Duke of Cumberland, is a member of the royal family."

"Third in line to the throne, in fact," Briggs mused. "Perhaps he intends to use the weapons against a smaller entity?"

"Such as?" Jonathan asked.

Jessica thought hard. What would a man like the Marquis of Millbridge want to destroy? She knew from listening to previous conversations that Millbridge was extremely ambitious. But to what end?

It was all very confusing. In the end, she didn't care. She just wanted them to find enough evidence for the brothers to hang, so they'd leave her sisters and poor little Jake alone for good.

The men concluded their meeting, and Briggs promised to bring Jonathan any information he might find in the next few days. As he was leaving, he paused at the door.

"I've written to the captain. I think it might be best I continue my investigation in Cornwall. I believe I've reached a dead end for information here in London. There is more evidence to be found where Caversham and his ships have been located most often, and that is in the West Indies and in Cornwall."

"And he won't go to the West Indies now, not when he knows his son is somewhere in the United Kingdom," Jonathan said.

"True. I might encounter him in Cornwall. If I do"—Briggs paused—"I will be ready for him."

"It sounds like you ought to go, if you've exhausted your sources here in London. I'm certain Langley will agree."

"I'll wait to hear from him, then." With a nod to Jonathan, and pointedly ignoring Jessica, Briggs went out the door.

Anger flushed within Jessica, and she strode after him, ignoring Jonathan's soft warning. "Jessica—"

She shut the door against him and hurried down the passageway after David. "Wait!"

He stopped, hesitated, then slowly turned to her. He gave a formal half bow. "Miss Jessica."

She stopped in front of him, looking up into those lovely, stormy blue eyes. "You may call me Jessica. Forget the 'miss' part."

He raised a brow, said, "I don't think so," and began to turn away.

She grabbed his arm. "Wait!"

She heard the soft whistle as he released a breath through his teeth. "What is it?"

Her heart was about to pound right out of her chest.

She licked her lips. She was brave, always had been. She wouldn't falter now.

"I like you," she said in a soft voice. "But I promise to leave you alone, if you tell me to my face that you despise me as much as you pretend to."

His face relaxed from its unbreakable mask. "Jesus," he mumbled, looking up to the ceiling as if asking for deliverance.

They stood there for a long, silent moment, as he slowly leveled his gaze to hers.

"I don't despise you," he finally said on a near growl. He glanced over his shoulder and down the corridor beyond her. Apparently finding no one to overhear, he leaned toward her and murmured, "Damn it, Jessica. I can't stop thinking about you."

A warm flush of pleasure washed through her. So his behavior, the constant annoyance directed at her, was all an act. She'd known that, somewhere deep inside. She'd known he liked her. She grinned. "Why try?"

His blue eyes narrowed. "Are you mad?"

"Not at all."

"You are a lady. Untouchable."

"Oh, that's not true. I'm quite touchable indeed." She didn't mean to flirt, truly she didn't, but she couldn't help it.

His eyes were slits now. "Don't be stupid," he grated out.

"I'm not stupid, either. You should know that by now."

"You're nineteen years old," he whispered harshly. "You're liable to catch some earl or duke, like your sisters have done. You're the youngest, most beautiful, most eligible Donovan sister. Trust me, you don't want to ruin all that by being compromised by a man like me."

She stared at him, appraising. Was this an example of a man being noble? If so, she liked it very much.

She wanted to tell him, "Oh, yes, I certainly do want to be compromised by a man like you," but that would sound too flippant—even though it was the truth.

So she simply nodded. Raising her hand, she touched his cheek with her fingertips. "I like you, David Briggs. More than I like any duke or earl. And that's not going away. I may appear to be frivolous and superficial, but when I decide to go after something, I am loyal and constant, and I never give up."

He shook his head. "Your family would never approve."

"Nonsense," she said. Although it was partially true. Her mother and aunt would both have fits and probably swoon repeatedly from the disgrace of her being associated with a—*gasp!*—sailor. Her sisters and brothers-in-law, though they would be supportive, would worry for her.

"You're leaving for Sussex in a few days."

Pressing her lips together, she nodded. Even though Caversham had disappeared, Jonathan still thought it would be better for the family to retreat to Sussex. She hated the idea.

"And I'll be doing my duty for my employer, far away from Sussex. Give it a week, Jess. You'll forget about me once you're in the country."

Jess. Only her sisters called her that. But she liked how it emerged from his mouth. So smooth. So masculine.

"I won't forget," she whispered. "Will you forget about me when you're at sea?"

"Never."

They stared at each other for a long moment. Looking into those blue eyes, studying that rugged face, Jessica decided that he was truly the handsomest man she'd ever known.

Then, with a brief nod, he turned and left, leaving her standing alone in the corridor.

Chapter Sixteen

Will was determined to end Caversham's reign of terror over the woman he loved, and soon, before the damage the pirate caused was irreparable. Meg lived in fear, and it was tearing Will apart. She was so easily frightened. It had become so pervasive that if he, or anyone else, made an unexpected move, she'd jump in alarm.

Yesterday, she hadn't allowed Jake to go out riding with the servants. That had resulted in a temper tantrum that surprised Will—he'd never seen Jake react so strongly to anything. He'd punched and kicked and screamed, and Meg had just held him, serenely saying no, it was too dangerous. The boy hadn't understood, and it seemed like hours had passed before she was able to calm him.

Will had spent two full days in Liverpool, talking with the man in charge of the construction of the *Endeavor*, hiring sailors experienced with steam-driven vessels and outfitting the ship with all the supplies they'd require for a journey of unknown duration. The days were long and busy, and tonight when Will arrived at the house in Prescot, it was past midnight and the house was dark.

He led his horse into the small stables at the back of the house and brushed it down, murmuring to it as he did so. When the animal was comfortable in its stall, Will trudged back to the house, exhaustion settling over him. He hoped Thomas wouldn't thrash too much tonight. The boy was a wild sleeper—usually, Will either woke with the child draped over him or with his toes in his face.

Just inside the front door, a lit lantern awaited him. He took it gratefully and carried it upstairs to his room. He entered, seeing the still form of his son in his bed, and proceeded to undress, stripping off his coats and shirt, then lowering himself onto the edge of the bed to remove his boots.

There was a soft mumble às he depressed the side of the bed, and Will glanced over at Thomas, making sure he hadn't awakened the boy.

"Hm," he murmured in surprise.

Jake lay beside Thomas, one little arm flung over the older boy's torso.

Will was sitting, boots off, contemplating his options, when a soft knock sounded on the door. He opened it to Meg standing in her nightgown with a thin robe pulled over her shoulders.

"You're home," she whispered.

Home. He liked that word coming from her.

Taking the lantern, he stepped out into the small landing separating their two rooms and shut the door behind him quietly so as not to awaken the boys. "Yes. It was a long day."

She nodded. "I waited up for you. I can't sleep until I know you're home safe."

He gestured toward his room. "Jake?"

"He had another one of his tantrums today." She sighed. "About my not allowing him to ride. As a concession, I told him he could sleep with Thomas for a little while. I'll go get him."

She made to walk around him, but on impulse, he reached out, grabbing her arm. "Wait."

She gave him a questioning look.

"Will you . . . stay with me for a while?"

She didn't hesitate. "Of course. Come into my room. Should I go downstairs and fetch some wine?"

"Yes, wine sounds very good." Maybe it would loosen his knotted muscles and help him to fall asleep.

She took the lantern from him, and as she went downstairs to fetch the wine, he walked into her room, rolling his tight shoulders. There was only one chair in here—in front of her dressing table—so he sat on the edge of the bed.

She returned in a few moments, holding a wine bottle and two glasses. He took the bottle and poured while she held the glasses for him. When he finished, he set the bottle on the floor while she nestled close to him on the bed.

A sensation—new but already familiar—flushed through him. He knew it for what it was. Love.

Now, he had to heal her so that she could feel it in the same way he did. He needed to banish the fear from her heart and mind forever. Without the fear, she'd be able to trust him completely. Without the fear, she'd marry him.

He slipped his arm around her shoulders.

"Tell me about today," she murmured.

"I hired fifteen men. Sailors, all, and familiar with steam. I'm still looking for a first mate, though. Finding someone with the right kind of experience is proving difficult."

"How much of a crew will the *Endeavor* require?"

"At least twenty for a skeleton crew. I'd prefer thirty, though."

"Does the ship appear to be ready? You don't think the steam engines will break down, do you?" Under his arm, she shuddered slightly, and he knew she was picturing them adrift at sea.

"I don't think anything will break; however, if it does, I've hired an engineer who knows the ins and outs of repairing these kinds of engines. And if that doesn't work, there's always the option to sail."

The *Endeavor* was a side-paddle steamboat, with two masts and sails for use under ideal wind and sea conditions or when the boilers were unusable for any reason.

She smiled up at him. "I've seen steamships from afar, but I've never actually been on one."

"Well, you will be in a few days' time. I think you'll find it less disagreeable than you might suspect."

"I hope so." She hesitated, and her eyes shone as she looked at him. "I like this."

"What do you mean?"

"Being here with the boys. With you. At times it feels . . . *real*. Like we're a family." She blinked hard. "But it's all an illusion, really."

"We *will* be a family." Playing idly with one of her curls, he leaned over and kissed her cheek. "You'll be free of him soon, Meg. I promise."

He gazed down at her. The swell of her breast peeked

from the neckline of her nightgown. That plump, soft curve of skin evoked an instant reaction in his body. He took the wineglass from her hand and set it on the table by the bed, then returned to her side, this time lying down and pulling her against him. She came willingly and wrapped her arms around him. It was almost as if she wanted him as much as he wanted her, but he couldn't quite believe that. He still sensed that hint of reserve erecting that insidious wall between them.

Once Caversham was gone, that wall would evaporate. If it didn't... Will didn't know what he'd do. He loved her too much to consider failure.

He drew her in closer, feeling the soft press of her breasts against his chest, his cock a hard rod against her thigh.

"I want you," he whispered into her hair.

Her answer was simple. "Then take me."

They undressed slowly, almost languidly, their fingers gliding over each other's bodies as each item was removed. This time, there was little worry that the servants might hear or the boys might return from their ride. The household was fast asleep.

He lay over her, propping himself up on his hands to gaze down at her. She stared up at him, her eyes sparkling silver in the dim light.

"You're so beautiful," he murmured in a cracking voice, struck with awe at the way the lantern light played across her honey-colored skin. She possessed such a wholesome beauty. Such purity. There was truly no one like her.

He lowered himself to her breasts. He loved this part of her so much. They were symbols of her femininity, utterly soft, so delicate. He kissed them, reveling in their plump firmness. She gasped when his tongue touched their sensitive tips, teasing them into taut peaks that he rubbed his lips over, making her body arch with desire. For him.

All these years, and he'd been the only man to touch her thus. Something about that should shame him, he supposed, since he hadn't been so pure. Yet an elemental pride welled from somewhere deep within him. This beautiful, exquisite woman was his. She'd always been his, and his alone.

He slid his hand between her legs. She was already slick for him, and he smiled to himself, a smile of pure male satisfaction. The way he'd toyed with her breasts had aroused her.

He kissed her again, moving his hand between her legs as he did so. Beneath him, she responded, her breaths quickening, her hands stroking him all over.

He used his leg to push hers open and positioned his cock at her entrance. He hovered there for a long moment, her heat penetrating from the head through to his entire body. Then, slowly, he pushed inside. Her body accepted him, then squeezed him all around, a tight, hot, wet passage of pure erotic pleasure.

He took his time, sinking into her sweetness, allowing the blissful friction to encompass him.

As he moved inside her, he looked down at her to see her gazing up at him. Love shone in those seal-gray eyes. As much as she closed herself off from him, she did care for him. Her eyes couldn't lie.

Her body tensed gradually as she grew close, and then tightened all over. She gasped, and her back arched. Will groaned as her muscles clamped over his cock, but he repressed the urge for release and rode the storm with her.

When her tremors subsided, leaving her hotter and wetter than before, he increased his pace and the force of his thrusts. Pressure built at the base of his spine. He wouldn't last much longer. Still thrusting powerfully, he pushed his hands into her silky blond hair and buried his head into it, breathing her sugarcane essence into himself.

His orgasm was an explosion of love, of lust, of need, of desire. Everything he had poured into her in a silent, hopeful message.

Love me, Meg. Love me like I love you.

David had received a letter from Captain Langley approving his recommendation to sail the *Freedom* to Cornwall in the search for additional evidence against Caversham. Captain Langley had said that to keep her safe, he was taking Meg to sea in another of his ships, also suggesting they meet in a few weeks' time at Penzance.

Jessica couldn't see much of the logic behind the latter part of this plan. Wasn't Caversham known to frequent the area around Penzance? If so, how did the captain intend to keep Meg safe there?

Suddenly, Jessica didn't entirely trust Captain Langley. She *mostly* trusted him—after all she'd known the man for over a year now and knew something of his character. He was, perhaps, the most staid, somber man she'd ever known. But she, along with her sisters, had always thought him a good man.

Still, why on *earth* would he bring Meg to Penzance?

Well. She had her own plans to keep Meg safe.

David and the *Freedom* were leaving on the morning

tide, and by that time, Beatrice, the Donovan sisters, their husbands, and most of the servants would be bound for Sussex. The household had been in a flurry of preparation for the past few days—and no one spared much attention for Jessica. That was all for the better, as far as she was concerned.

Jessica had been in bed since seven o'clock—she'd skipped dinner, giving the excuse of a terrible headache, which was a technique she'd learned from her sister Phoebe, who'd used it quite effectively when she'd eloped with Sebastian.

She lay there wide awake until midnight, when the sounds of the house finally died down. She rose and grabbed the satchel she'd packed earlier. She'd no room for a dress, so she'd packed only the essentials. Her toothbrush, a comb, hairpins, some underthings, a bit of food, and a skin of water. She'd need those items for the few days she intended to stay in hiding.

She hesitated a second, thinking about Beatrice. She and Beatrice had been nearly inseparable ever since Beatrice had revealed the abuse she'd suffered at the hands of her late husband. But she'd healed significantly in the past several months. She'd be all right—and, probably better than anyone else, she'd understand why Jessica needed to do this.

She opened her desk drawer, took out the note she'd written to Serena and the others, and laid it on the bare surface of her desk. They'd find it right away, probably early tomorrow afternoon when they grew worried that she hadn't come down. She'd be long gone by then.

Slipping out of the house was easy, and finding a cab at this hour in St. James was little trouble. She gave the driver instructions, and, apparently familiar with young ladies slipping out on their own in the dead of night, the old man nodded and set the horses in the direction of the docks. When they turned onto Fleet Street, Jessica settled back, content that they were headed in the proper direction.

Several minutes later, the cab stopped at St. Katharine's Docks. Jessica stepped out and paid the driver, adding an extra-large tip because she was so thankful he hadn't given her any trouble.

She'd visited the *Freedom* three times and knew it quite well. But she'd never been here at midnight. The docks were quiet now, the sounds of slapping rigging and creaking wood the only noises—particularly eerie noises, in Jessica's opinion. Keeping diligently aware of her surroundings but staying in the shadows so as not to draw attention to herself, Jessica hurried toward the ship.

Captain Langley had hired a very sparse crew for the *Freedom*—according to David, a large crew of men wasn't needed for this particular vessel's new, advanced design. David spoke of the *Freedom* with such pride, one would think it was his own ship, yet it was obvious he was particularly attached to Captain Langley and considered him a true friend.

Tonight most of the crewmen would be at the nearby pub, celebrating their last night of being ashore in London. David said when they sailed tomorrow, half of them would be sick with drink, and it would be a particularly difficult journey down the Thames. Still, he couldn't begrudge them their last night of fun. He knew from his Navy days that it was a necessity.

She reached the dock and hesitated under an awning.

This was the most dangerous part of her scheme—she'd be in wide open space, visible to anyone who happened to glance at the dock. If someone saw her and wondered what she was doing out here—well, she'd be in a bit of trouble.

She looked all around and was about to make a run for it when she heard a soft scraping noise and then footsteps walking toward her from the direction she'd come. She sank back into the shadows and wedged herself between a barrel and the edge of the building. She stood stock still as the footsteps came nearer, and she saw the man—a dock policeman.

Well, she told herself, it could be worse. It could be some drunken sailor on the prowl for a bit of female flesh before he went off to sea.

She didn't move, keeping her breaths shallow and light as he walked past her and onto the dock. He was looking to the right and left as if hunting for a criminal, and when his gaze neared her hiding place, she held her breath so as not to make any movement that might draw his eye. Thank God her cloak was dark gray, a good color to melt into the gray brick of the warehouse.

His gaze moved right past her, and he continued on, beginning to whistle a jolly tune. He traveled down the length of the dock and walked up the steps leading to the far end of the building and then disappeared beyond it, his whistling growing fainter as he stretched the distance between them.

Jessica took several deep, gulping breaths. Well, the policeman had cleared the way for her. There was obviously no other soul on the dock right now. She tugged open her satchel and withdrew the one tool she'd brought—a picklock.

Pulling her satchel over her shoulder, she rushed forward and onto the dock, hurrying to the steps that led to the *Freedom*'s deck.

She peeked over the edge of the deck wall. The deck was completely abandoned. Apparently, there was no need to patrol the deck when the ship was empty of cargo, locked tight, and tied to a dock patrolled by the London dock police.

She scrambled onto the deck, her feet making the slightest *thunk* as she landed on the wood planking. She hurried to the back of the ship, where Captain Langley's quarters were. No one would be using his quarters, since he wasn't aboard for this mission. David wouldn't move there—she'd asked him. He preferred his own quarters, though she couldn't imagine why. They were a third the size of the captain's.

Grasping the tool, she pushed it into the lock and fumbled with the tumbler until she heard the telltale click. *Yes.* Sebastian, Phoebe's husband, had taught her how to do it when she'd been bored one afternoon at Stratford House in Sussex. She'd known the skill would come in handy one day.

She removed the tool and turned the door handle. It swung open easily, and she walked inside Captain Langley's quarters as if they were her own. Closing the door and locking it behind her, she turned to analyze the place that would be her home for the next few days, and she sighed. It was dark as pitch, and she didn't dare light a lantern—even if she could find the supplies to do so.

That had been easy, all things considered. She expected there'd be hell to pay from her sisters and brothers-in-law when they received her letter tomorrow, but by then she'd be long gone, and they'd all forgive her if she saved Meg.

Well, there was nothing to do except go to bed. Not that she could sleep—her heart was still pounding at a million beats a minute—but she might as well give it a try. She felt around until she found the wide bunk wedged into the corner of the room. A woolen blanket was folded at the foot of the bed. Jessica slipped out of her dress and stays, folded them as nicely as she could in the darkness, and wrapped the blanket around her.

Then she spent the hours until dawn staring up at the black, black ceiling. It wasn't until very late the next day, when they were well under way, that she was able to sleep a wink.

Chapter Seventeen

Jake had another fit on the day Meg had planned her escape. But he was nothing if not predictable—to her, anyhow—and it was all part of her plan.

Will had left before dawn. She'd heard him wake and had tiptoed downstairs to see him off. No one was awake, so she'd kissed him good-bye at the door, allowing the heat of his lips to singe into her memory. She'd thrown all her dreams into that kiss, hoping beyond hope that this kiss would reassure him whenever he began to doubt her in the next few days.

She'd watched him leave until he'd disappeared down the bend in the road.

It was market day in town, so Molly and the cook had taken the cart and one of the horses and left in the afternoon. They wouldn't be back until dusk.

As usual, Thomas had gone riding with the coachman, and as usual, Benson had offered to take Jake on the mare. She'd said no, as she had for the past week, and just like every other day for the past week, Jake reacted to this edict by throwing himself onto the floor and proceeding to scream himself purple.

Frowning down at him, Benson spoke loudly so she could hear him above the noise. "What if we were to keep in sight of the house at all times, Miss Donovan?"

She frowned at him, even while admiring his kind intentions. "You're not helping me, Benson. I said no."

"Yes, miss."

Jake screamed even louder, and she breathed a heavy sigh. "Very well," she said, kneeling beside him. "*I'll* take you riding."

Jake quieted instantly and looked at her with those big blue eyes, utterly shocked.

"Benson, would you mind saddling the mare?"

Benson stared down at her for long seconds, perplexity wrinkling his brow.

"He's safe with me," she explained, knowing her own logic didn't make any sense. But that didn't matter. Servants like Benson were well trained not to question the logic of their employers.

Jake frowned at her. "Do you know how to ride horses, Meg?"

"Yes, I do," she told him firmly. "When the Lady Stratford and I were little girls in Antigua, we rode all the time." That was true. She and Serena had loved the horses, loved riding. It had been their solace after their father had died and when Olivia was so sick from the malaria.

A year after their father's death, they had sold the horses. They'd needed the money. Both Meg and Serena had cried for hours the day the horses had been taken to a plantation on the other side of the island.

Jake grinned at her. "I want to ride with you, then!"

She squeezed him to her. "I want to ride with you, too."

Kissing the top of his head, she thought about how it would be a much longer ride than he expected. Jake didn't like being surprised, but she would have a few hours with him on horseback to work on keeping him calm.

She didn't have much money, but she'd collected all that she had earlier, along with a few other essentials for her and Jake, and packed it all into a saddlebag. In the middle of the night last night, she'd hidden the saddlebag under a tree about a half mile away from the house, under a rock outcropping near the road to Liverpool.

She'd planned ahead this morning and worn her plainest gray muslin dress—a dress that would help her blend in with the crowds in Liverpool. She took Jake's hand and led him to the entryway closet, where she tied her cloak around her neck and her sturdy straw bonnet under her chin. She pushed Jake's cap onto his dark hair at an angle that was jauntily askew. Then she led him through the back door and out to the stables, where Benson was saddling the dappled gray mare with the sidesaddle. Silently, she helped him, then accepted his boost up onto the saddle. When she was settled, he lifted Jake to sit in front of her, awkwardly due to the design of the saddle.

Jake frowned at her. "Why are you riding funny?"

She smiled at him. "I cannot ride like a man, Jake. I'm wearing a dress, so I must keep both my legs on one side of the saddle."

"That's crooked." He frowned, clearly disapproving.

Meg sighed. "Yes, it's quite crooked indeed." She wished she could ride astride, but she didn't want to draw any undue attention. With a nod at Benson, she turned down the road leading west around the town of Prescot and from there to Liverpool.

Jake giggled. Leaning down, he hugged the horse, his little arms attempting to wrap around the mare's powerful neck. He kissed the horse's brown mane and said, "I missed you, but Meg said we can ride today!"

He turned to look at her over his shoulder as she concentrated, keeping one hand firmly wrapped around his torso while she worked the reins.

"Will we find Thomas?" he asked.

"Maybe," she said. But they wouldn't. He'd been too busy with his tantrum to notice that Thomas and the coachman had ridden in the opposite direction.

"I'll look for him," Jake said. "If I see him, I shall shout."

"That is a good plan." Meg glanced back in the direction of the house and watched it as they progressed along the gentle curve in the road and it disappeared from view.

She'd enjoyed their time there. The easy friendship that had developed between Thomas and Jake had made her feel like she was doing right by him. She'd liked watching Thomas and Will together—so obviously father and son in the shapes of their faces and the curves of their lips. Their temperaments were similar, too—serious, studious, and easygoing—which were some of the many reasons why Thomas had adapted to Jake's idiosyncratic personality so easily.

Most of all, she'd enjoyed keeping house with Will. It was likely the closest to domestic bliss she'd ever come. The one night they'd slept together in her bed—she'd never forget it. It was etched in her mind alongside that final kiss they'd shared early this morning.

Thinking of the kiss, she almost missed the spot where she'd hidden the saddlebag. She stopped the horse with a jerk, nearly causing both her and Jake to topple.

"Sorry, Jake. It's been a while since I've been on a horse."

She jumped down and lifted Jake after her.

"What are you doing?"

"There's something I need to fetch back here." She led the horse off the road and to the outcropping. There the canvas bag lay tucked into a small crevasse, thankfully untouched. She strapped it onto the horse with Jake watching.

"Benson never picked up anything."

She smiled at him. "Well, I'm not Benson, am I? I ride differently from him, and I retrieve bags for us to carry."

"I like the way Benson rides better."

She blew out a breath. "I'm sorry. Let's ride again, all right? We'll ride for a long time, and it will be fun."

Jake gave her a doubtful look. "All right."

It took several attempts—she wasn't as agile as she'd been as a girl—but finally she hoisted herself up onto the horse then pulled Jake up behind her, tucking him tight against her body.

As they rode back onto the road, Meg wondered how she was going to break the news to him that they were leaving Will and Thomas, perhaps forever.

It was late afternoon when they reached Liverpool. Jake had been crying softly on and off for the last few miles— he was tired, he was hungry, his bum was sore—but now he was facing Meg and nodding off against her chest.

Her biggest fear had been the possibility of encountering Will himself on the road home, but he'd stayed true to form and apparently didn't plan on returning to the house until late tonight.

She stopped at horse stalls near the vast Liverpool Docks and sold the horse along with the sidesaddle for half their value, which was a good enough price considering she was a lone woman with a child.

The mare had been Lord Stratford's. She'd pay him back, in full, once she obtained the money to do so.

Although, where she would obtain the money was a whole different problem, and one she couldn't think about yet. She had bigger problems to deal with right now.

"One thing at a time," she mumbled to herself as she slipped the coin from the horse into the saddlebag she now carried slung across her back. She grabbed Jake's hand. "Come along, Jake."

He trotted along beside her, forgetting his exhaustion and captivated by the sights of the docks and all the ships. "Are we going to go on that ship?" he asked Meg, pointing at a particularly enormous schooner.

"Probably not."

"That one?"

"I doubt it."

"That one? That one?"

She answered his questions patiently while she went to the packet office and found that a packet was sailing for New York first thing tomorrow.

New York.

Well, by all accounts, it was a burgeoning city. Surely Caversham would have a difficult time finding her and Jake there.

She bought them tickets. There was no way she could

afford the thirty-five-guinea price for a cabin, so she bought the much-cheaper steerage passage for them both.

When they left the office, Jake pointed to yet another ship. "Will we be sailing in that one?"

She nodded. "Yes, I think that might be it." Their ship was the Liverpool Packet *William Thompson*. The pennant flying high atop its center mast—a black ball on a red background—matched the image on her passage receipt.

They had much to do before tomorrow, and twilight was coming on fast.

"A room first," Meg muttered to herself. Then, they'd have to go purchase the supplies they'd need in steerage—bedding and food to last forty days, for the captain of the *William Thompson* did not provide anything but space on the ship to his steerage passengers. At least they'd have access to the galley—when the cabin passengers weren't using it.

She went back into the office to ask about lodging for the night and was given the name of several inns near to their location at the Prince's Docks. Meg selected the Angel Inn, about a half a mile away, mostly because of its name. They could use an angel looking over them tonight.

They trudged in the direction of the inn. Jake was growing tired and whiny again. Meg would carry him when they went shopping later, but for now it was too difficult with the saddlebag.

It had all been easy so far. Escaping from the house, the travel to Liverpool without encountering a soul until they were almost in town, buying the tickets, finding shelter for the night.

However, by now the servants had probably notified

for her, and Liverpool would be the first place he'd look.

Will. The thought of him made her insides clench tight. She missed him already.

She glanced around, and relieved to see no sign of him, or of anyone who looked remotely familiar, she tugged Jake along. Within a quarter of an hour, they'd reached the inn, and a few minutes after that, they had deposited the saddlebag safely in the room she'd secured for the evening.

Poor Jake was ready to sleep, but their work wasn't done yet. She'd learned from the innkeeper that St. John's Market was open late tonight since today was a market day. It was only a few blocks away, and he'd said there were merchants aplenty there who would be happy to provide them with bedding and all the sustenance they'd require on their forty-day journey to New York.

"It's not very far, Jake," she reassured the exhausted boy as they descended the inn's stairs. "There will be so many fun things for you to look at. And if you're very good, I'll buy you a sweet."

That perked his step, and some of the brightness returned to his eyes as they exited the inn and turned into Dale Street.

Meg had accomplished the most difficult parts of her plan—leaving Prescot, selling the horse, securing passage to somewhere that Caversham could not find them. She had only fifteen more hours in England—an hour to accomplish shopping for necessities in a busy marketplace; thirteen hours in a locked room, most of which would be spent asleep; and the final hour on the *William Thompson* before the ship sailed with the tide tomorrow morning.

In forty days, give or take a few, she'd be in America—in New York.

Would she ever see Will again?

On the evening of their third day at sea, Jessica decided it was time to reveal herself to David. Surely he'd agree it was too late to turn back. Besides, she was famished, and even though Captain Langley kept a few books in his quarters, they were utterly dull, and she was about to perish of boredom.

She waited for most of the ship's sounds to die down. She knew there would be one or two men at watch on the deck, but beyond the creaks and groans of the *Freedom* as it swayed over the waves, she'd grown accustomed to the sounds of David preparing for bed.

Cracking open the door to Captain Langley's quarters, she peeked outside. All was dark and quiet save the single lantern lashed to one of the stays that sent an uneasy flicker of light to sway across the deck.

No sign of life. She cracked the door open a bit more, and way up near the bow, she could see the shadow of a man walking away from her.

Perfect.

She rushed out, closing the door behind her, and rapped loudly on the door to David's quarters.

"What is it?" he asked, rubbing his jaw with a towel as he opened the door.

He froze, his jaw slack as he stared at her, his hand dropping to his side and the forgotten towel falling to the floor.

"Well, that's a polite greeting," she said, pushing herself past him and closing the door behind her. She strode two steps into the room before the table stopped her from progressing any farther, and then she turned. "How about a 'good evening, Jessica'?"

He gaped at her for a moment longer, and finally found his voice, croaking and broken as it was. "Are you mad?"

"Mad?" She tilted her head as if considering his question for a few seconds, then she shrugged. "No, I don't think so."

His eyes narrowed, and the step he took forward brought him within easy reach of her. She held her ground, though. "What the hell are you doing on my ship?"

"I believe it's Captain Langley's ship...and I believe we've been over this before."

"Although this time the answer is different, no doubt."

He looked brilliant when he was angry, Jessica thought. So utterly handsome with his mouth compressed in a tight line and his eyes narrowed. It made her want to kiss those lips until they became soft and pliant under her own.

She gave him a game smile. "I thought I'd join you. You need my help to find the evidence you're looking for. And I want to be there when you meet with Meg and Captain Langley, to be sure everyone's actions remain in my sister's best interests."

He blinked at her, then scrubbed a hand over his face. His shirt was open at the chest, exposing a bit of tantalizing flesh. Ooh, but he was lovely.

"You believe you can help me find evidence? In the violent, piratical caves of Cornwall?"

"Absolutely."

"And you believe that Captain Langley and I will fail to make decisions in your sister's best interests?"

She crossed her arms over her chest. "I'm not sure about that. You see, Captain Langley is throwing Meg directly into the lion's den by bringing her to Cornwall. And you—well, you seem to take on a sneer every time you mention her name."

"I'm rather more concerned about her leading my captain into danger."

"That's ridiculous."

"How can you be so certain? Perhaps she has suggested that they travel to Cornwall in order to lead him into a trap."

"Surely you cannot believe such a thing! I'm disgusted that the thought would even cross your mind."

"Well, it has," David said tightly. "Countless times."

She tightened her grip on her arms and glared at him. "Well, even better that I'm here, then. You don't trust my sister, and I don't trust your captain."

He took a menacing step forward. "Women don't belong at sea."

She tossed her head. "Oh, what rubbish. I've crossed the Atlantic Ocean twice. Don't tell me I don't belong at sea."

"This is no passenger ship...there are no cabins..." He cocked his head, his brows drawing together in a frown. "Where have you been stowing yourself, anyhow?"

"In your captain's quarters."

He breathed out through pursed lips, studied her for a moment longer, and then he began to turn away. "Excuse me. I'm going to order a change of course."

She lunged forward, just one step, and grabbed his arm. "Where to?"

"Portsmouth. I'll hire someone from there to take you to London."

"You cannot do that."

"Why not? Your family will be furious. Your reputation will be in tatters—"

"My family will manage itself. It has been through worse scandals than this could ever be. And as for my reputation...Well, it doesn't matter overmuch."

" 'Overmuch'?"

She simply shrugged. She'd decided to forgo a life in London society. She didn't want that now. She wanted more. She wanted *him*.

He didn't look too receptive to those ideas at the moment, so she kept her mouth shut.

"I must take you home."

"If you send me to London, no one will be there. My family has gone to Stratford House in Sussex. You know that."

He didn't look at all convinced. "With you missing?"

She waved her hand. "Oh, I'm not missing. I left them a letter."

"A letter will prevent them from changing their plans?"

"Yes. I have explained to them where I am and what I have planned. I told them they must continue on to Sussex."

"And you believe they'll agree?"

"Of course."

"Why wouldn't they think I'd bring you straight back to London?"

She gave him a half smile. "I told them I didn't intend to reveal myself to you or the crew for several days, and then once I did, it would be too late for you to turn back to London. And if you didn't believe that, I'd convince you. My family knows I have extreme powers of persuasion."

He leaned back against the door. "So."

"So?"

"I'm expected to carry you halfway around England as a...guest?"

"I'd prefer to be looked upon as a crew member. A crew member with a rank equivalent to yours, of course."

He made a scoffing noise. "You are the most brash, impetuous woman I've ever known."

She frowned at him, not knowing whether he meant that as a compliment or as an insult.

"And the most beautiful." His voice was as low as the rumble of distant thunder, but she heard him, all right. And she melted from the inside out.

Closing his eyes, he rested the back of his head against the door. "God, Jessica. Do you realize what danger you're in by being here?"

"Do you mean from Caversham? Well—"

His eyes snapped open and he lowered his chin to look at her. "No. Not from Caversham. From me."

"From you?" She laughed softly. "I think not. You wouldn't hurt me."

He shook his head slowly. "Your virtue..." His voice trailed off.

"Is a pesky thing," she finished for him. "I'd like to be rid of it as soon as possible."

His eyes went wide, and then he bent over and laughed, great choking guffaws. She frowned at him. "Are you laughing at me?"

With effort, he rose to full standing. "No," he choked out, still grinning. "But I do have to say, Jess...I've never met a woman like you. Brash, impetuous, and absolutely one-of-a-kind."

"That's good...isn't it?"

He sobered a bit, but his eyes still shone. "It's good. It's...the best."

He reached out, snagged her around the waist, and hauled her into his arms. And his lips descended onto hers in a kiss so richly passionate, Jessica thought she might drown in its luxury. They swayed with the ship, but David remained firmly attached to the floor, keeping her from stumbling, his soft lips caressing, stroking, tasting. He tasted like wine, rich and full.

When he pulled away, minutes later, they were both breathing hard. And Jessica felt like squirming, like she wanted to climb right out of her twitchy skin and into his, which would certainly be warm and comforting.

She looked up at him, waiting. He'd ended it. Perhaps he had something to stay.

He stared down at her, his eyes soft. "By God," he said. "You're the most beautiful damned thing I've ever seen."

"You curse like a sailor."

"I am a sailor."

"I know." She pulled him into her arms once more. "It's one of the many things I admire about you."

"I cannot begin to comprehend what you mean by that." Idly, his fingers stroked through her hair, which she'd worn loosely tonight.

"Don't question it," she murmured. "Just accept it."

Jessica felt the breath releasing from his chest as he sighed softly. "I will, then."

"Good."

His lips nuzzled her hair. "You must go back to the captain's cabin."

"Yes...I probably should." She wasn't stupid. She

wanted him, yes. But they had time. She didn't want to rush things. They would go to bed together when they were both ready for it. Jessica wasn't quite ready yet, and even though she could feel the hard ridge of his erection against her hip, she thought he wasn't, either. He was still dealing with the implications of her presence on "his" ship.

She tilted her head up and with her fingers wrapped around his neck, pulled his down until his lips met hers. She kissed him softly, then spent a moment simply nuzzling him, drinking in his softness, before she whispered, "Good night, then."

"Good night, Jess." His voice was gentler than she'd ever heard it. "Morning mess is at eight o'clock sharp. Meet me here first, and we'll explain your presence to the crew."

"Does that mean you're going to allow me to join you on your mission?"

"It means you'll be sailing with us. If you're asking if I'm going to willingly place you in danger, the answer is no."

She sighed, then gave him an indulgent smile. "That's good enough. For now."

Squeezing her arms around him, she kissed him one last time and then slipped back into her own quarters—well, Captain Langley's quarters—to fall immediately into a deep, dreamless sleep, not remembering until morning how hungry she was.

Chapter Eighteen

Will arrived home at dusk, exhausted from a long day. He'd ridden nearly all the way to Manchester today in order to find the first mate who had come highly recommended by the *Endeavor*'s architect. Clifford Halliday hadn't been happy to have his holiday with his family cut short, and he'd been expensive, but if he was as skilled with oceangoing steamships as the architect had claimed he was, he was worth every penny. After much haggling, he'd agreed that after spending one last night with his wife and seven children, he would join the *Endeavor*'s crew in Liverpool early the following morning.

The *Endeavor* would be ready to launch in two days. Not perfectly outfitted, but stocked well enough, and with a competent crew. Will didn't want to delay their departure any longer. He had a sick feeling in his gut that Caversham was close.

As he neared the house, the feeling tightened and condensed into a hard ball. Usually, when he arrived home, a single lantern was lit in the entryway for him. Tonight, lights blazed in all the windows of the house.

The coachman met him at the stables, taking the reins. The look on his face confirmed Will's worry that something had happened.

"What's wrong, John?"

"It's Miss Donovan and Master Jake, sir. They've gone missing. I went to Liverpool to fetch you—"

"I wasn't in Liverpool today." Why hadn't he thought to inform the household where he was going?

"Yes, sir, the dockworkers told me you'd headed out to Manchester. By that time it was too late to pursue you there, so I came home to await your arrival and your instructions."

"You did the right thing. Come into the house."

Within a few seconds, he was striding into the house, closely followed by John. Thomas met him in the entryway and flung his little body into Will's arms. "Papa! Meg and Jake are gone. Gone! And they didn't even say good-bye!"

He knelt down to comfort the boy and looked up at Benson, who'd appeared in the doorway to the parlor. "Tell me what happened."

"Miss Donovan took Master Jake riding, and they didn't return. However, I don't believe they were taken, sir. I believe she left of her own accord. I found this in her room, addressed to you." He held out a piece of folded stationery.

Will closed his eyes. So, she'd left on her own. She hadn't been taken against her will by Caversham. The ball of fear in him tightened into something else, something bitter and painful.

Taking the letter from the servant, he looked down at Thomas. "Go with Benson, now, lad. It's past bedtime for you, isn't it?"

"I was waiting for you."

"I'm glad you did. But now it's time for bed."

Benson took Thomas's hand and led him away. After asking John to stay close, Will rose and walked with leaden legs into the parlor.

Will sank down on the sofa and turned the letter over in his hands before he broke the seal.

Dearest Will,

I'm sorry. But please understand, I cannot put you or my family in danger any longer. Please don't follow me. Please understand that the farther away Jake and I are from you and Thomas, the safer you'll be.

I will never forget the time we spent here. It meant everything to me.

Meg

He read the short letter three times, then crumpled it in his fist and tossed it into the fire. The fire was almost completely out, but it only took a few seconds for the paper to spark and flare into bright flames, and another few before it was reduced to ash.

"And that's what I think of your heroic efforts to keep me out of danger, Meg," he murmured to the hearth.

He rose, went upstairs, and kissed his son good night. Then he left the house, returning to the stables, where

John had begun to rub down his tired horse. "Saddle the gelding," he ordered. "I'm returning to Liverpool."

"Returning to Liverpool, sir? But why?"

Because, thought Will, where else could she possibly have gone?

Night had descended rapidly, but streetlamps lit the footpaths, and the roads were still busy with workers heading home for the evening.

Deep in her thoughts, and murmuring answers to Jake when he pointed out various features of the brick architecture that seemed to dominate Liverpool's streets, Meg heard a muffled noise behind her—just odd enough that it popped her out of her reverie. She bowed her head and walked faster, squeezing Jake's hand, not daring to glance back.

But it couldn't be Will! How could he have found her already? She'd been so careful...

The footsteps—several of them—came closer, and within seconds, men boxed her and Jake on all sides. There was no way out. She stopped in the middle of the footpath and looked up at the man facing her—a dark stranger wearing a menacing look.

The voice came from behind her, smooth and rich yet full of venom. "Why, it's the lovely Miss Donovan. Fancy meeting you here. In Liverpool, of all places."

Oh, God. Tears squeezed unbidden out of her eyes as she closed them. It wasn't Will—it was Caversham.

For God's sake, how had he found her? Gathering Jake, who was squirming to get a better view of his father, into her arms, she dodged under the arm of the dark man blocking her path and ran into the busy street.

But she was too slow. In seconds, Caversham had grabbed her arm and yanked her back onto the footpath.

She glanced around. Pedestrians were scattered about, and the traffic was thick. What would happen if she screamed?

Caversham jerked her around so she was looking into his pale face, into his cold blue eyes and the swoop of black hair he oiled straight and parted severely in the center. His face was narrow but sculpted, and his top lip so thin it was nearly invisible, especially when it was curled in anger, like now.

His blue eyes glinted at her. So like Jake's ... and yet so different. Narrow and hateful as opposed to wide and innocent.

So many people would agree that she'd done wrong by taking Jake from him. So many people would think that hanging was a just punishment for her. But they didn't know this man.

And there, right in the middle of the street with dozens of onlookers, he slapped her so hard, the breath whooshed out of her and spots scattered in her vision.

Jake cried out as she bent forward, and he slid out of her arms. But he was just as afraid of his father as she was, so he buried himself in her skirts as if he could make himself invisible in them.

She fumbled for him, trying to soothe, trying to keep him as calm as possible, even as her jaw throbbed and she tasted blood in her mouth.

"Pardon me, is there a problem here?" A man had stopped just behind Caversham and was glancing warily from him to Meg.

"Indeed, there is," Caversham said. "But I am taking care of it. Thank you for your concern, good sir."

The man glanced at the brutes, at Caversham, then nervously back to Meg. She bit back the "Please, help me!" that was looming on her tongue. All she needed was to bring yet another innocent into this.

It was difficult, though. She knew she must look horrid, with blood dripping down her chin and an expression of terror on her face. But the man glanced back at the thugs again and then turned to Caversham. "I believe you've injured this lady."

"You're quite mistaken, sir," Caversham said. Responding to the nod of his head, his men moved forward. One of them held a gun partially concealed by his coat. He pointed it at the man, who stepped back shakily, raising his hands in a gesture of defeat.

"I don't want any trouble."

"Oh, no," Caversham said. "Neither do we. Go along now, and we'll take care of this."

With one last guilty glance at Meg, the man hurried away.

"Well now, that was awkward." Caversham gestured behind them, and Meg realized a small black carriage was parked a few yards back on the road, its coachman and the horses poised for movement. "Why don't we go into my carriage and talk this through."

It wasn't a question, it was a command. But once he had her out of sight of the public, what would he do to her?

Jake whimpered and burrowed deeper into her skirts. Caversham glanced down at him and rolled his eyes heavenward but didn't comment.

Meg struggled to gain some control over her fear so

she could speak. Finally, she murmured, "How did you find us?"

Caversham's lips twisted into a mocking smile. "Why, it was almost too easy." Taking her arm in a bruising grip, he said, "Come. Let's walk a ways, and I shall tell you."

Not having any choice in the matter, she took Jake's hand and allowed Caversham to drag them along the footpath.

"It begins with you, my dear. Your foolish plan to escape to Ireland."

"How did you—?"

Caversham waved a dismissive hand. "Oh, please, Miss Donovan. Do you really think yourself so sly? Sarah told me years ago that you have family in Ireland. Knowing I might need to use them someday, I found that they all live in Cork, and I've kept a close eye on them ever since. When you disappeared from the *Defiant* in Irish waters, it was clear to me where you intended to go."

Meg nearly groaned. Even after all these years, she'd still underestimated Caversham.

"But alas, when I searched there, you were nowhere to be found. Which left me with two possibilities: either you perished in that nasty squall or you had gone to England instead.

"The heroic Captain Langley cleared up that confusion quite rapidly. I have known for years of his close ties to your family. First, he arrived in London out of the blue—a very odd appearance when my sources say the Crown had engaged him to search for smugglers along the Cornwall coast. Then, only a few weeks after his odd appearance, he left London suddenly and without any sort of explanation. When his builders in Liverpool began scrambling to complete work months early on his steamship, I knew without a doubt that all these strange behaviors must have something to do with you."

Meg shuddered. She should have predicted Caversham would find out all about Will. She'd been so stupid.

"I sent the *Defiant* on her merry way back to the West Indies for her next shipment while I hurried to Liverpool via coach," Caversham continued. "I intended to catch you when you boarded Langley's steamship. However, one of my spies saw you today at the packet offices buying passage to New York and then inquiring about inns in the area. By the time you left the Angel Inn tonight, we were already outside devising a plan to break in to your room. How easy you made it for me, Miss Donovan—you have eliminated the potentially embarrassing situation of me having to face your lover." He gave her a cold smile. "It seems you have used Captain Langley very poorly indeed. You seduced him, didn't you? You allowed him to think he was being the gallant and protecting you when you had plans to leave him all along. Either that or you knew I was close and you were making one final attempt to throw me off your scent." Lifting his thin, long nose into the air, he sniffed several times. "Alas, all your efforts were useless. Even in the stench of this city, I could smell your nearness. I'm like a hound, you know. Nay, better than a hound. I was so very close to you in London. Just a day or two behind, was I not? Even with the bit of confusion with your sister, it was only a matter of time before I caught up to you once and for all."

"Confusion with my sister?" she whispered.

"Ah. You didn't hear about that?"

Weakly, she shook her head.

He held tighter on to her arm but continued to walk at a leisurely pace. "My keen nose led me to your twin at her home in St. James's Square. Unfortunately, for a time, I believed she was you." He shrugged. "It was a minor inconvenience."

She groaned softly.

"Really, Miss Donovan, you never mentioned how very identical you and your twin are."

"We're not identical at all," she said instantly, and then regretted it. It was never wise to naysay Jacob Caversham.

He drew her to a stop and politely inclined his head, once again gesturing back to his carriage following behind them at a snail's pace. The brutes were back there, too, watching Meg closely, clearly daring her to try something.

"Now," Caversham said graciously. "My carriage, if you please?"

"What do you intend to do with us?" she grated out.

"Why, I intend to raise my son to be a gentleman."

Yes, like you, Mr. Caversham. Such a fine gentleman.

"And you"—Caversham's voice lowered, and the corner of his mouth quirked up in the semblance of a smile that made her blood run cold—"I'll deal with you once we're out to sea."

"Deal with you" meant that he planned to kill her, certainly.

He leaned forward, a gleam lighting his blue eyes in the darkness. "You know, Miss Donovan, Sarah once told me your deepest fear."

She closed her eyes. He'd always known her deepest fear; had used it to threaten her over and over. And now he was about to do it again, although this time she had the sinking feeling he intended to make good on his threat.

"I suppose it makes sense, since you would have drowned that day so many years ago had I not found you," he continued. "I gave you eight extra years of life, but I think that's enough. I think the best thing to do—the right thing to do—is to put you back where I found you. In the middle of the ocean. No land, no ships, no hope in sight." His smile widened. "Now, my carriage, if you please."

"No, thank you," she said, her tone as brittle as glass. "I believe I'd prefer to stay here. On dry land."

Caversham raised a single thin black brow. "What? You reject my hospitality? Come, Miss Donovan. I'm afraid you have little choice in the matter."

She hefted Jake onto her hip and looked him in the eye, realizing that drawing the attention of the nearby pedestrians was her last hope. "I'll scream."

He gave her a pleasant smile. "You'll regret it if you do."

She knew he spoke the truth. And yet, she couldn't— wouldn't—go willingly into that carriage and certain death.

She lunged off the footpath and onto the road, running as fast as she could, calling out, "Help me! Someone, please help—"

One of the brutes caught her arm, spinning her around to face him. She recognized the butt of the pistol a split second before it smashed down on her head.

It wasn't easy to find information about a single woman and child in a large town in the middle of the night. Where the hell had she gone?

Late that night, frustrated and empty-handed, Will returned to his quarters on the *Endeavor* and fell into a brief, restless sleep. At dawn he rose and began the search again.

His first stop was at the docks, where he scoured through the ships that took passengers and were leaving the area in the next few days.

And, finally, he found something.

The clerk at the offices for the Black Ball Line said he'd seen a woman and child of Meg's and Jake's description last evening, just before he'd closed the office. They'd purchased passage on the *William Thompson* bound for New York this morning.

Will rushed straight to the ship, which was scheduled to have sailed ten minutes ago but hadn't yet. Once there, he yelled up to the seaman tying off the shrouds. "Good morning, lad."

The boy tipped his hat. "Mornin', sir."

Will met the boy at the top of the stair leading to the deck. "I'm looking for a passenger on your vessel."

"Oh, aye? We've only a few this sailing."

"A lady—Miss Donovan, and a young boy."

"We've no ladies or lads aboard, sir. Sorry." He turned away.

"Wait!" Will called. "Are you sure?"

"Dead sure, sir. There's two couples what's married, and six gentlemen on their own." He frowned. "Though the cap'n did say we had a party that didn't show."

"Who?"

A sailor toward the bow called out an order, and the boy gave Will an apologetic look. "Sorry, sir, but I couldn't say. You ought to ask the cap'n."

He would. A seaman tried to stop him, but he talked his way past the man and found the captain on the bridge. The man looked him up and down disdainfully. "We are about to sail, sir. Please disembark immediately, unless you intend to purchase passage to New York."

"Forgive me for delaying your departure, Captain." Will knew how annoying that could be. "My name is William Langley. I need to know the name of your passengers who didn't show today. It's of the utmost importance, I assure you."

The captain's round face relaxed. "William Langley? Are you the Navy commander who distinguished himself at Gramvousa a couple of years ago?"

Will gave him a tight smile. "Yes. That was me." God, how depressing was it that his one claim to fame involved such carnage?

The captain clapped him on the back. "Well, welcome aboard, Captain. It's men like you who've kept the heathens from overrunning civilized society. I'm George Maxwell. It's an honor to meet you, sir."

"Er...thank you."

"Now, what can I do for you?"

"I only need a minute or two of your time. I'd like to see your passenger list."

"Well, then, you shall see it. It's below." He turned to the nearest seaman, a lanky young man who was all sharp points and angles. "Oy, Ogilvy! Go fetch the passenger list for Captain Langley here."

"Aye, sir." The man ambled off.

Maxwell squeezed his shoulder. "Tell me about it."

"Tell you...?"

"About Greece. Gramvousa."

"Oh." Will swallowed. "Well, not much to tell, really. We went in and occupied the fort, while the French patrolled the surrounding waters."

"And how did you rout the pirates?"

Will met the man's eager gaze. "We killed them," he said flatly. "All of them." And Will himself had done a fair share of that killing after Briggs and Pratt had been injured. Briggs would carry that scar on his face for the rest of his life. Pratt had died in Will's arms.

There was a moment of silence, and Maxwell's arm dropped. "Ah." He shrugged. "Well, you did no more than was required, I'm sure."

Right. They'd tried to run, tried to surrender. Will hadn't allowed it.

They stood in awkward silence until Ogilvy returned with the passenger list. And there it was, last on the list: Margaret Donovan. He pointed at her name. "Is this the passenger who didn't show?"

Maxwell frowned down at the list. "Well, yes. You can see, we note all the passengers who are present and accounted for." He slid his fingertip down a row of check-marks adjacent to the names, then glanced toward the dock. "Is she coming, or . . . ?"

Will blew out a breath. "No. No, I don't think so."

He thanked the captain and disembarked from the *William Thompson.*

Damn it. This could mean one of two things. Either Meg was leading him on a false trail, or someone else had found her first.

Will had a sinking feeling it was the latter.

But how the hell was he going to find them? He hesitated, looking out over the busy docklands of Liverpool.

Where would Caversham take Meg and his son?

The morning fog broke, and light slashed over the water of the dock basin, making it sparkle silver, like Meg's eyes, and the answer came to him.

Of course. Caversham would take them to sea.

Chapter Nineteen

David Briggs, when facing his crew, was an imposing rock of a man. Watching him, as he commanded obedience and doled out orders, was magnificent. Jessica sat primly, her hands clasped in her lap, as she listened to him speak to his underlings in the salon—a room adjacent to the galley and containing a long table flanked by two equally long benches.

"Finally," he said, glancing at her and then back toward the three men who were the top-ranking sailors below him, "you'll have noticed we have a passenger. It is our responsibility to see to her safety and comfort while she's on board."

She recognized young Mr. Jasper, who had been scowling at her on and off during the meeting. "If you'll excuse me, sir, but where'd she come from? We haven't seen her these past four days since we set sail."

David sighed. "She is, in fact, a stowaway. She has

been with us since we left London, but she was hiding in Captain Langley's quarters."

More scowls turned on her.

"But," David continued, the note of warning in his voice so dark even she wouldn't dare disobey it, "you will treat her as her station requires. With respect and deference. That's an order."

The three men mumbled, "Aye, sir."

"Furthermore, if you see any man regard Miss Donovan with anything less than the utmost respect, you will report that man to me, do you understand?"

"Aye, sir."

"Good. MacInerny, effective immediately, you will join us for our meals in my quarters."

Suddenly, MacInerny looked like he was fighting off a grin. "Aye, sir," he said gruffly.

Now, why had he done that? Jessica thought, feeling petulant. She'd been looking forward to long meals with him, alone together in his quarters.

Well, drat it all. He'd effectively put a damper on the romance she'd planned for all those intimate moments together.

And why on earth was MacInerny smiling about it?

Oh, Lord, she was pouting. She forced her face into a more neutral expression.

"Dismissed," David said. The men all left as she stood, balancing herself on the floor planks. The sea was rougher today than it had been on their journey so far.

In two strides, David was beside her, holding her arm to steady her.

"There now," he murmured in a whisper that sent chills tumbling down her spine. "Are you all right?"

She smiled at him. "I'm perfectly fine, thank you."

"I'll escort you back to Captain Lang—*your*—quarters."

"Thank you, but I'd prefer to take some air on the deck for a while."

He sighed. "You're just asking for trouble, you know that?"

"Are you speaking of my virtue?" She smiled. "Because I'd say it's hardly in peril. You just gave an order that every sailor must treat me with respect and deference, and only a fool would disobey you."

"Especially in that matter," he said, his voice a near growl.

"I sense...possessiveness," she murmured, looking up at him from under her lashes.

"Miss Donovan, as usual, you are pressing your luck with me."

"But aren't you supposed to treat me with deference and respect?"

"That was an order for my *men*."

"Ah, I see. It doesn't apply to you."

Leaning down to her ear, he spoke in such a low voice, she could hardly hear. "You have no idea how strongly you test me, Jess."

She raised a brow.

"It applies to me," he added, straightening. "However...unfortunately, I feel that I am the one most likely to break my own edict."

She gazed up at him. She felt such...*tenderness* toward him. Why on earth she felt such an emotion when he was essentially suggesting he might ravish her, she had no idea.

"Why did you do that, anyhow?" she asked, frowning.

"Do what?"

"Order Mr. MacInerny to dine with us."

"Good Lord, woman. Why do you think?"

She shrugged. "You're being difficult? You don't wish to spend entire meals in my company?"

He stared at her. "I can't decide whether you're sorely lacking in wits or just naïve."

"I'd choose naïve, probably. Though I don't think of myself as particularly naïve, I must say. I know all about coupling, copulation, French letters, com—"

His hand closed around her mouth. "Please. Stop." He pushed out a short, sharp breath. "The reason I wish MacInerny to dine with us is because I have no desire to have you alone with me in my cabin."

He dropped his hand from her mouth.

"Why on earth not?"

His eyes narrowed at her. "Ah. So you are naïve."

Honestly... why? She wasn't so very naïve, because she knew that if they were alone in his quarters, he'd want to seduce her... or vice-versa. What was so wrong with that? Didn't he *want* that? She did. She fought to keep from pouting again. She wasn't a pouter, but for goodness' sake, the disagreeable man made her want to pout and stamp her foot and throw a tantrum.

He leaned forward, looming over her. "The reason MacInerny needs to dine with us is because if you and I dine alone, I will cause serious damage to your virtue."

"Yes." She hesitated, then looked up at him, her brows drawn together. "And... you don't want to?" Honestly, he didn't make any sense.

"For God's sake." He took a predatory step toward

her. "I want you." His gaze raked her body, and the blue heat of his eyes prickled her skin from head to toe. "I'm not known as a patient man, Jess, but this—this is far too important. So, yes, I want you... but I *won't* destroy your virtue, your reputation, your innocence. Not until—" He cut himself off, and with a sharp intake of breath, looked away.

"Not until... what?"

He closed his eyes, then opened them, but he didn't meet her gaze. "Until I have your family's blessing."

She cocked her head, trying to imagine her family giving their blessing for him to ravish her. *That* would never happen.

And yet, from the expression of hope, of desire—goodness, of *love*—on his face, she knew he meant far more than ravishing her.

Oh, God. Her heart expanded, feeling full and whole, probably for the first time in her life. She reached up to smooth his brow, her fingertips stroking over the bumpy surface of his scar. "How did you get this, David?" she whispered.

He stood still, unmoving, but his eyes sank shut again as her fingers moved over them.

"In the Navy."

"How?" she persisted.

"A battle."

She frowned. "Surely there haven't been any major engagements for the British Navy in a long while."

His lips twisted. "I'm sure no one would say it was a major engagement."

"What happened?"

His eyes were still closed. She continued tracing his

scar, then moved on to touch the details of his face as he spoke, starting with his forehead, his hairline, his cheeks and nose, down to his jaw.

"Two years ago, the Greeks were having difficulties with pirates in the Aegean. They requested British and French help to contain an especially active pirate port at Gramvousa. We were to occupy the island and force the pirates out."

She nodded, her fingers hesitating over his cheekbones. "Go on."

Keeping his eyes closed, he continued. "Captain Langley's men were to occupy the island. The French would rout the pirates from the harbor and surrounding waters."

"A land battle," she murmured.

"Exactly," he said. "At first, the pirates had the advantage of us. They knew the tiny island well, and they ambushed us." He blinked hard. "A man shot one of our lieutenants, and I was running toward him, attempting to help him...and I heard a shout from behind me. I turned, and..." He gestured toward his forehead, his eyes now open and gazing at her.

"You were stabbed in...in the skull?"

"It was a bayonet—the blade swiped across my eyebrow and halfway around my head as I spun away."

"Oh. Lord." Jessica held her hand over her mouth.

"There's a scar across my scalp, but it's difficult to see because of my hair." He shrugged.

"What happened to the man who...attacked you?"

"I tried to fight him, but blood was running into my eyes, blinding me. Captain Langley..." David swallowed hard and gazed at a point somewhere beyond her shoulder. "Saved my life. He saved us all."

"He killed the man?"

David released a breath that sounded like it had been pent up for hours. His gaze flicked to her. "Yes. He killed the man."

"Well..." Jessica's knees felt a little weak. "I suppose now I understand why you are so loyal to him. You owe your life to him."

David's eyes, such a dark, ocean blue, gazed at her, imperturbable, indecipherable. "I do," he said softly.

Releasing a breath of her own, she hooked her arm around David's. "Come. Let's go above. The air will be fresher up there, and perhaps you will feel less seasick."

He raised a brow at her, and the scar she now understood wrinkled. "I'm not seasick."

"You look rather green about the gills."

"So do you."

She hesitated, then nodded. "Well... not because I'm seasick, though."

"Me, either."

She looked up at him, knowing what they were both thinking about. For a long moment, they gazed at each other, fully understanding. She wanted, so badly, to kiss him again.

But not now. Not here, where she might embarrass him in front of his crew. Instead, she tugged him out of the salon and up to the deck.

Caversham hadn't had time to bring his brig *Defiant* all the way to Liverpool. Furthermore, as far as Will knew, Caversham didn't keep any of his vessels in Liverpool. But Meg had told him that he did own ships frequenting the ports that began with "B." Blackpool was one of those ports, and it was nearby.

If Caversham had a ship there, then he would be sailing on it. Will would bet his fortune on that. He had nothing firm to go on, but he'd spent enough time on the ocean that he knew the minds of sailors and their ships. What he intended to do with Meg and Jake—especially Meg—was another question. One Will didn't want to think about.

He didn't head north to Blackpool. Instead, he went straight to the *Endeavor*, which was now afloat in one of the Liverpool locks in preparation of being launched day after tomorrow. His hired men were already working, even this early in the morning, and they paused to hail him as he walked by.

He went to the bridge and shouted to all within hearing distance. "Change of plans, gentlemen. We sail today."

His first mate, Halliday, rushed up to him. "Sir, we're not ready. I haven't even—"

Will raised his hand. "I won't hear any excuses. Do whatever needs to be done. We sail at noon."

Halliday's eyes bugged at him, and his mouth gaped open, but he shut it with a snap and turned away from Will, shouting orders. "You heard the captain. Get yer lazy arses to work, lads. We've a steamer to launch!"

Will went into his chart room and rolled open a chart of the area. Blackpool wasn't far from here, and if Caversham had sailed with the tide, he'd already gone out at the same time as the *William Thompson* earlier today. Will doubted he would have sailed north—the northern passage was too narrow and he'd be too easily sighted and caught. If he was traveling south—and Will would wager money on that—he'd have already passed Liverpool. That meant Will would be in pursuit of Caversham's ship, rather than on an intercepting course.

He had to trust the promises of his architects... they'd said the *Endeavor* would be the fastest thing on the sea—especially in calm conditions. It was calm this morning, but the wind always picked up in the afternoon...

He shook his head, flinging those thoughts from his mind. He couldn't dwell on the "what-ifs." He needed to follow through with his plan. If it didn't work, there'd be another plan, and another... until he found Meg and Jake, and Caversham no longer posed a threat to either of them.

He wanted them all to be together again. As a family. Without them—without Thomas, Jake, and Meg—he was a shell. They filled him—with love, with belonging, with a sense of fullness. He needed *all* of them.

Thomas. For now, he needed Thomas, and Thomas needed him. He couldn't leave his son alone and afraid in Lancashire—not now. And yet this mission was a dangerous one...

Will sucked in a breath. The *Endeavor* was faster and stronger than whatever ship Caversham might've had in Blackpool. Will wasn't going to let anything happen to Thomas. Or to Jake and Meg, for that matter. He was going to keep his family safe.

Turning to the closest idle-looking man, Will sent him on a mission to fetch his son and bring him back to the *Endeavor* in time for him to be aboard when it sailed.

A few hours later, the *Endeavor* left the Liverpool docks under its own steam power, black smoke puffing out of its smokestack. When the boiler first started, Thomas clung to him, and Will closed his eyes, imagining the soft whoosh of the *Freedom* as she slipped through the waves.

How different this was. Was this what the future was going to be like? Full of engines and noise? Even on land. The Manchester-Liverpool Railway would be opening at the end of summer. If they'd come to Prescot only a few months later, they could have taken a train instead of a carriage.

The future—full of foul-smelling smoke and the roar of engines. Was this the price they'd all pay for progress?

Despite his misgivings about the ugliness of steam power and progress, Will was grateful for how easy it was to get out of the harbor. They didn't require a favorable wind or tide, or a tow. They left when they pleased, and the *Endeavor* navigated the harbor waters easily without a concern about the direction and force of the wind.

"Sure sounds sweet, don't she?" Halliday yelled at him over the belching roar of the engine. "Smooth as silk."

Will thought it sounded anything but smooth, but he didn't say so as they chugged out of the harbor, deftly swerving around anchored vessels. Instead, Will ordered the course for the pilot to lay and stood at the bow with Thomas beside him. He'd explained to the boy that they were searching for a ship that had taken Jake and Meg away, and Thomas's little chest had puffed out.

"I'll find them, sir!"

So as the *Endeavor* emerged from Liverpool Harbour, Will and Thomas stood at the bow on the lookout for any other vessels heading south through the Irish channel.

The first thing to penetrate Meg's consciousness was that she had a horrible, skull-splitting headache. Clutching her head, she turned over, feeling her hip bone dig into the hard surface of a wood floor.

She opened her eyes to a weak light filtering through a grime-covered porthole. She must be in the bowels of the front of the ship. It smelled of rank salt water, and cold, dirty water seeped through the layers of her clothes, chilling her to the bone.

Jake was nowhere to be seen in the tiny V-shaped room.

Closing her eyes, she remembered—vaguely—the rattle of a carriage. Being dragged onto the deck of a ship she'd never seen before. Jake sobbing and crying her name. Men taking her by the armpits and dragging her down stairs, then literally tossing her into this room and locking the door behind her. Trying to pound the door, calling for Jake, then weakly crawling into a corner before she lost consciousness again.

She rose clumsily, holding on to her aching head as if to keep it attached to her neck, and searched for the door. She saw it—a faint rectangular shape in the dimness, and lurched to it, feeling for the handle.

"Jake!" she called, her voice scratchy and weak. "Jake?"

Of course he didn't answer. He was with Caversham, and Caversham wouldn't be found anywhere near the bilge on any of his ships. And, of course, when she wiggled the handle, she found that the door remained securely locked.

The ship swayed under her feet. Obviously, she'd been out for a while. They were under way.

Like an old woman, she hobbled back to the porthole and scrubbed at it with her skirt, slowly wiping away the thick layer of grime until she could see the blue sky, the ocean below, and the gray spray of the waves as they crashed into the hull. There was no sign of land, but that didn't mean anything. They could be very near to shore, and she wouldn't know unless she was looking from the correct angle.

She rose to explore the room more thoroughly.

It appeared to be an old surgery, the working space of a surgeon who no longer existed—or at least no longer used this space. A cot sat in the center of the room, presumably where the man had performed his medical procedures. The wall adjacent to the porthole held shelves full of half-empty and broken bottles, probably containing old medicines. Meg searched for one labeled with something akin to "cures a horrible headache," with no luck. But as she scanned the shelf, her attention moved from the intact bottles to the broken ones, to their sharp, jagged corners and edges.

Weapons. Or, at least, potential ones.

She found a particularly deadly looking large shard of glass—not from a bottle, but from a broken hand mirror—and carefully slipped it into a pocket sewn into the folds of her chemise. It might work—if she didn't flay her hand open in the process of trying to fight.

Good Lord. They were out at sea. If she did resist and by some miracle was able to get away, where on earth would she and Jake go? She'd have to fight off the entire crew to be able to launch a jolly boat. She'd had years to carefully plan that escape from the *Defiant*. Even then, the plan would have certainly resulted in her and Jake's deaths had Will's ship not happened by to rescue them.

Even through the fog of hopelessness that shrouded her, the weight of the glass in her pocket was comforting. It made her feel a little stronger. And right now, she welcomed whatever tiny bit of strength she could get.

After she explored every crevice of the room without

finding anything else that might be of use, she huddled back into the corner she'd slept in, tucking her knees against her chest, wrapping her cloak around her, and conserving her strength for the encounter that would invariably happen.

About an hour later, she heard a key scraping in the lock. She looked up from where she'd been resting her forehead on her knees, as one of Caversham's brutes entered.

Hesitating at the door, the man squinted, searching for her in the dimness of the room. Finally, his gaze stopped on her. "Hurry up, then. Cap'n wants you," he mumbled.

She hesitated, but it would be no use for her to resist. If she did, the man would drag her, kicking and screaming, to Caversham. And she still needed to conserve her strength.

Painfully, she rose to her feet. Leaving her cloak behind—it was wet beyond repair—she made her way to the door. The man grabbed her already bruised arm and pulled her through, then dragged her up the two sets of short, narrow stairs that led to the deck.

Meg clenched her teeth so she wouldn't whimper. Her head throbbed with every motion that her body made.

Taking shorter, shallower breaths, she straightened her spine. No matter what happened, Caversham would not see her cringe away or cower in fear. She'd been completely justified in taking his son away from him. He was an evil, despicable man. She would face him for the last time, and she'd be strong.

The man yanked her into the captain's quarters, where Caversham was sitting at a small, rather shabby and grease-stained table, his scowl deep, the parallel lines on his forehead and crevices bracketing his mouth more severe than usual. The state of the table would irk him, surely, she thought with a sinking heart. And right now, Caversham in a heightened state of annoyance would not help her predicament.

And then she saw Jake. He was seated in a chair behind Caversham, a gag tied around his mouth. His brown hair stuck up at all angles, tearstains streaked his face, and terror made his eyes wild.

"Jake!" She stumbled toward him only to be yanked back by the brute. His fingers tightened so hard over her bruised arm, she bit back a gasp of pain.

Jake's blue gaze locked on her. He made choking sounds through the gag as he struggled, and she realized that he'd been bound to the chair.

She turned hate-filled, accusing eyes on Caversham, trying with all her might to keep from hissing and spitting at him. "What have you done?"

He merely shrugged. "He was being inappropriately noisy, so I had him gagged. His arms were flailing about wildly and he scratched me like a wildcat." He gestured to a long, shallow cut on his arm and continued. "So I ordered his hands tied. And then he was running about like a lunatic, so I tied him to his chair, where he will learn to sit calmly and quietly, like a proper boy."

She gawked at Caversham for a moment, and then she couldn't hold her tongue. "You're a damned fool, Jacob Caversham," she grated out. "Release him. Immediately."

Caversham raised one thin, dark eyebrow. "Cursing now, Miss Donovan? And in front of an innocent child. *Tsk tsk*. And I blame you for his outlandish behavior. Clearly, you've allowed him to run amok."

"Let him go!" she shouted, trying to get to Jake again. The steely grip on her arms held her back.

"Please hush. I should not like to have to gag and tie you, too. Rest assured, I will release the boy in due time."

She went still, unscrambling the violent thoughts pouring through her mind. Was this what it was like to be a mother? To feel such a deep connection to a child that you'd do anything, *anything*, to keep him safe?

Yes, she thought. Jake was her son now, and she'd fight for him.

But right now, violence would not work. She could not overcome these men by force. There had to be another way.

"Sit down, Miss Donovan." It was a polite command but a command nonetheless, and even though her instincts told her to snatch Jake up and run away, she forced her feet forward and took the chair facing Caversham at the table.

"It's still going to be a few minutes before we reach the drop location, so I thought we'd have a little chat."

"The . . . drop location?"

"Indeed. Where you shall walk the plank."

Panic surged through her as she realized that he intended to play the part of the pirate to its fullest. She was a good swimmer, but this wasn't the Caribbean. How long could she swim in the icy cold waters of the Irish Sea?

Did it matter, though? She certainly wouldn't be able to swim to the coast, and it was ridiculous to hope that someone might happen by and save her yet again.

She let loose a slow breath, releasing those dismal thoughts along with the air. She would not think this way. She would somehow survive, and she'd save Jake while she was at it.

Caversham was staring at her, his cloudy blue eyes narrowed. "Did you really think you could get away with kidnapping my son?"

God, his pretense of caring for Jake didn't make sense. He'd never loved Jake like a real father. All through the boy's short life, he'd been attempting to form him into a small version of himself. He'd failed so far, and it had angered him to the point of beating Jake, tossing him overboard... and still he hadn't given up.

"I only want him to have a good life."

Caversham's eyes were slits. "And you do not believe I will offer him that?"

"I believe you could, but I fear you won't give it to him. He's himself, and you can't turn him into someone else, no matter how hard you try."

Caversham gave a low, humorless chuckle. "He's *my* son, and he'll be who I wish him to be."

She shook her head, despair gurgling through her like a thick black pudding.

"You truly are stupid." Caversham shook his head. "At least you could have had a laudable goal—such as kidnapping him with the intent to ransom him to my brother. But, no. You took him with some misplaced notion to save him from me. From his own father. How pathetic."

She didn't meet his eyes. She didn't care what he thought about her. She'd call *him* pathetic if she didn't know how useless the returned insult would be. Instead she glanced at Jake, silently encouraging him to be strong.

There was a soft knock on the door.

"Come in," Caversham said.

A sailor—a man Meg had never seen before—entered. "We've reached the dead center of the channel, sir."

That meant they were almost fifty miles away from the nearest landfall. There was no way anyone could swim so far.

"Excellent." Caversham rose from his chair. "After we deal with her, have Ingerson set a southwesterly course. I wish to stay well clear of the Welsh shore before turning east to Bristol. Not too far clear, you understand. My presence is required in Oxfordshire by the end of the month."

"Aye, sir."

Caversham and the sailor moved toward the door, but at the threshold, Caversham paused, turning to the brute who'd lingered in the shadows. "Remove her dress and stays, if you please. I don't want her drowning too quickly." Looking over his shoulder, he gave her a polite nod. "I'll await you just outside, Miss Donovan."

He closed the door, and the brute came forward. He took her by the shoulders and roughly turned her so that her back faced him. She heard Jake's whimper as the dagger cut through her dress, her petticoat, and the ties of her stays. The man pulled them off her body and arms, slicing fabric wherever he could to make the task easier, refusing to meet her eyes until the job was finished and she stood dressed only in her chemise, stockings, shoes, and drawers.

"Come along, then," he said gruffly. And in his voice, she heard it. A tiny glimmer of compassion.

Jake was sobbing now, and she turned to glance at him, then looked back at the brute. "Please let me say good-bye."

He considered for a moment, glanced back at the door, then shrugged. "Hurry up."

She hurried over to Jake. Kneeling, she took him—and

the chair he was tied to—into her arms. "It'll be all right," she whispered. She started to promise she'd come back for him, that she'd get him out of here, but she couldn't make a promise she might not be able to keep.

He was squirming, groping for her with hands that could hardly move. She covered them with her own, trying to calm him, and he pressed something into her hand.

He mumbled something that sounded like "bosun" through the gag.

She took it without question, closing her palm around it and feeling its shape—a long, uneven cylinder. If she had to guess . . . she'd say it was a boatswain's whistle.

"Oh, Jake," she whispered, blinking back tears. *You smart, smart boy.* "I love you so much."

He'd put it into the hand that the man behind her couldn't see, and she slid the whistle under her chemise and slipped it into the top of her knee stocking.

Jake couldn't speak due to the gag, but he laid his head against her shoulder.

She just held him until the brute pulled her away and pushed her toward the door. "Good-bye, Jake," she said one last time, watching him as she stumbled away. Finally, someone closed the door behind her and she could no longer see his wide blue eyes.

Once on deck, they turned toward the stern. Summer had arrived at last, and the morning sun shone brightly, sparkling off the small ocean waves and warming Meg through the linen of her chemise.

Meg's gaze scanned the wide curve of the horizon. There was no other ship in sight. No one to rescue her. Nowhere to run.

She was impotent to help herself or to help Jake.

Good Lord. She would drown. It seemed impossible, unreal. But it was happening.

They reached an opening in the deck wall, where a flat beam had been lashed so it protruded from the deck, lying parallel to the water. *The plank.*

The men around her hesitated, looking to Caversham for instructions.

He gave her a thin smile. "No need for long, drawn-out good-byes, I should think." Then he nodded at the three men who'd surrounded her. "Do it."

Before she could fight—before she could blink—they'd lifted her, and with one great heave, they pushed her onto the plank. She stumbled forward, fighting for balance, fighting to stay on the narrow beam. The ship swayed with a wave, and she wheeled her arms wildly, trying to stay upright.

But it was no use. She stumbled, then fell off. She was flying through the air, the skirt of her chemise billowing, then down, down...and with a great, painful splash, she hit the water, a sharp slap of cold covering every inch of her skin.

She sank instantly. Fighting the pain shooting through her head, she toed off her shoes and kicked to the surface.

As she broke through, gasping, she felt the weight against her leg and belatedly remembered the large shard of the glass mirror in the pocket of her chemise.

She hadn't thought of it in time. How could she have been so stupid? It had all gone so fast, she hadn't had time to think of using a weapon, hadn't had time to fight back.

She wiped seawater out of her eyes, opening them to see Caversham's ship already a great distance away.

And he had Jake.

"I'm sorry, Jake," she whispered. "So, so sorry."

Left alone, in the middle of a cold sea, half-naked, in pain, and losing hope rapidly, Meg could do nothing but tread water...and wait for death.

Chapter Twenty

The *Freedom* entered Mount's Bay and anchored in Penzance Harbour in the afternoon of a hot day in late May.

Jessica insisted she was ill, and the only thing that could cure her was dry land. David narrowed his eyes at her, clearly knowing exactly why she wanted to come with them and that it had nothing to do with her being sick, but he said nothing and gallantly handed her down into the jolly boat.

Once ashore, the men led Jessica to the outskirts of the town, along the coast to a string of poor fishing cottages. As they hesitated at one of them, David murmured, "This was the only person I could find who'd give me any information on Caversham. I'm hoping I can get something more out of the old man today."

She nodded, deeming it prudent to stay quiet. For now.

They knocked, and the door opened to a man probably in his midthirties. Not much older than David.

He looked them over, his face blank, not saying a word.

"Afternoon, sir," David said. "I'm looking for Mr. Retallack."

"That'd be me," the man said gruffly.

David shook his head. "No, ah...the elder Mr. Retallack. Your...father?"

"Dead," the man said shortly.

"What?"

"Aye, dead, I said."

"He was your father?"

"Aye."

"I'm very sorry."

The man shrugged.

"What happened?" David asked, leaning forward slightly. "I saw him a little more than a month ago, and he appeared in the prime of health."

The man's face darkened. "Well, not anymore. They called it an accident. Got himself caught up in the ropes, they said. But my da's been fishing his whole life. Half a century, that was. He wouldn't have got caught up in no ropes."

David frowned. "What do you believe happened?"

The man sneered at him. "Who'd you say you was?"

"I'm David Briggs. This is MacInerny and Jasper. And this"—he gestured toward Jessica—"is Miss Jessica Donovan."

Jessica gave an awkward curtsy, and the man raised his brows in surprise—as if no young lady had ever curtsied to him before.

"We're looking for information about a man named Jacob Caversham."

The man's face darkened further. "I don't know nothing about anyone by that name." He began to close the door in their faces, but David held out his palm, forcing it to stay open a crack.

David leaned forward. "Is he the one who killed your da?"

"Do you think I'd tell you if he were?" the man shot back in a harsh whisper.

David glanced around and behind him. "It's too open here. Let us inside, and we'll talk."

"You here to kill me, too?"

"No!" Jessica gasped. She ignored David's dark warning look. "We're here to help you. And to help my sister."

"What's this got to do with anybody's sister?" the man asked.

"Please, sir," Jessica said. "Please help us. He wants to kill my sister, like he probably killed your father and many others before—"

David cut her off. "Will you let us in before this foolish girl gets us all killed?"

With a bemused expression on his face, the man opened the door wider and stepped back.

They entered the tiny hovel, which contained only one spindly chair and a rough-hewn table by the hearth. A cot stood in the corner, and there was one window on the opposite wall that let in a very weak light. That was the extent of the place.

Goodness, Jessica had thought they'd been poverty stricken when she'd been growing up, but though they had neither the slaves nor the servants nor the livestock the other plantations had, at least they had a bright, airy, large, and clean house. This place was covered with soot, from the packed dirt floor to the rough low beams overhead.

She stood, squashed between David and MacInerny, hesitant. The man gave them a wry smile, barely visible in the dim light. "Welcome. Fifty years of working his arse off—sorry, miss—fishing, and here lies the sum of my da's riches."

"Why are you here?" David asked.

"I've come from town to settle 'is business."

"You're a fisherman as well?"

"Aye, I work the herring boats."

Jessica wasn't surprised. Indeed, the man himself reeked of herring. The whole hovel did.

He gestured toward the single chair. "Would the lady like to sit?"

Jessica raised her brows. "Me?" She glanced at David. At his encouraging nod, she took the chair, which was, surprisingly, very comfortable. The woven straw seat cradled her bum quite nicely.

"We're here searching for information on Caversham. He's a corrupt man, a murderer, and a criminal," David said. "We want him stopped."

Mr. Retallack studied them one by one, then he sighed. "I don't know a damn thing about 'im. I already told you that."

"Did your father tell you anything? Do you know anyone who might know something?"

Mr. Retallack shrugged. "Can't say as I do."

He was lying. Jessica could feel it. "Please," she said softly.

Mr. Retallack turned his gaze down to her, then looked back to David. "Makes me wonder—what's a society miss doing with seagoing folk the likes of you?"

"She was a stowaway on our ship. She's a notion that her presence here will save her sister from Caversham."

"How's that?"

Mr. Retallack hadn't asked her the question, and Jessica had been taught that a lady in the company of gentlemen should remain silent unless directly addressed.

She'd never been much of a rule follower.

"Jacob Caversham," she said, chin high, "kidnapped my sister, Meg, and forced her to be governess to his son and companion to his wife for several years. Caversham was abusing the boy . . . he came close to killing him more than once. So she escaped from his ship, taking the child with her. Now, Caversham is after her. He intends to have her arrested and prosecuted, but if he finds her first, I'm quite certain he'll kill her." She paused, then added in a whisper, "Perhaps like he killed your da."

Mr. Retallack crossed his arms over his chest and studied her for a long moment. Then he said, "P'raps you should run along home, miss, before you dig too deep into this bad business. This ain't a safe place for you."

"I won't leave without Meg," she said firmly. "Not until I know *she's* safe."

The man studied her for a moment longer, then he turned to David. "You didn't hear any of this from me, aye?"

"Aye," David promised solemnly.

Mr. Retallack took a deep breath and leaned forward. "Is your sister, Meg . . . Is she Catholic?"

Jessica shook her head. "No. Our father was Irish, but he was a Protestant. Why?"

Mr. Retallack shrugged. "Caversham hates Catholics. Was mightily irked when Wellington pressed that Catholic Emancipation Bill last year."

"Was he?" David asked slowly.

"Oh, aye. The bastard"—he glanced at Jessica and cleared his throat—"apologies, miss. Anyhow, Caversham was right pleased with the Duke of Cumberland's attempt to form a government entirely against Catholic emancipation."

David glanced at Jessica. "The Marquis of Millbridge was part of that." He turned back to Mr. Retallack. "But the Duke of Cumberland didn't succeed in his endeavor."

"Nay, and Wellington returned to Parliament and passed the bill. Caversham was here at the time, and in a fearsome temper. The village was abuzz with it—one of his sailors failed to follow an order quick enough, and he shot him dead, right there on our dock!"

Jessica shuddered.

So Caversham had been against the Catholic Emancipation Bill, as was the Marquis of Millbridge, his brother, and the Duke of Cumberland, the king's younger brother.

Was that what they were illegally raising money for? To somehow undermine the Emancipation Bill? But it was too late for that—the bill had already been signed into law.

Mr. Retallack's dark eyes scanned David, then Jessica. He chewed his lip, seemingly debating how much more to tell them. Jessica slid to the edge of her seat.

"Please, Mr. Retallack. My sister's life depends on it," she murmured.

He glanced at her, then at the single window in the cottage. Apparently not seeing anyone outside, he took a breath. "Before he died, my da saw something that worried him greatly."

"What was it?" Jessica breathed.

"Caversham has a cave full of booty not far from here." Mr. Retallack gave a solemn shake of his head. "Plans to use it for something bad, my da believed. Something...

traitorous. Was watching them—following them—on the sly. A fortnight after they left, he was murdered."

"Did they know he was watching them?" Jessica asked.

"Oh, aye, miss, for certain. My da was never one for stealth."

David frowned. "Will you take us to the cave?"

"Nay." Mr. Retallack's voice was flat, but fear had stamped deep lines into his face.

"Please tell us where it is, then," Jessica begged.

He hesitated, then said gruffly, "Aye. I'll be telling you where it is. Then you must leave this cottage, and you mustn't return."

A quarter of an hour later, they returned to the *Freedom* and fetched extra men and supplies, and two hours after that, they had dismounted from the hired horses at the druid clearing Mr. Retallack had described to them.

Jessica had insisted on accompanying them to the cave. David must have expected this, and he acquiesced with a sigh, which made her want to give him a smacking kiss on his cheek. Since he likely wouldn't approve of that in front of his men, she decided against it.

So she planned to kiss him thoroughly later. As the days went by, she liked him more and more. He was protective of her, but not overprotective. He allowed her to make her own decisions, and despite his gruff monosyllabic responses, he truly listened to what she said. He treated her as though she was an intelligent being. Very different from all those men she'd experienced in London, who'd viewed her as a potential pretty trophy to display in their home. David didn't look at her like that at all.

And he wanted her more every day. Every time he

looked at her, she could see the hunger in his eyes, and it made her skin prickle. She wanted him, too, badly, but as much as she flirted with him, as many kisses as they had shared, he'd forced himself to stop after a time, breathing heavily, hard all over, his gaze stark with need.

He held back because he was staying true, no matter what it cost him, to his promise to speak with Serena and Jonathan first.

He was a man of conscience, of self-control. Of honor.

Jessica was falling in love with him. Correction, she'd already fallen. *Madly* in love.

The sun was bright today, and warm, but there had been a recent rain, leaving the path treacherously muddy. She fumbled, her foot losing its grip on the slippery path. David, who was right behind her, caught her, his arm wrapping around her waist.

"Careful, now," he murmured in her ear.

She rested against him, just for a second feeling the hard press of his body against hers, secure and stable.

With a sigh of regret, she separated her body from his and moved forward at a slow pace, placing her feet carefully so she wouldn't fall. They'd been searching the area for half an hour and had found a few giant rocks and ruined piles of stones, but no cave.

From ahead of them, Mr. MacInerny gave a victorious shout. He was standing at the base of a small hill, his body partially obscured by brambles and tall grasses.

She and David rushed over to where he was pushing dead branches aside, revealing a door made of crisscrossed bands of iron. David knelt across from him, and together they heaved the door aside.

Jessica peered into the shallow hole. At its bottom, it

swerved at an angle so she couldn't see very far inside—but it was definitely a cave.

Mr. Jasper hurried up to them and busied himself with lighting a lantern.

David jumped into the hole and then reached up for Jessica. She slid down slowly, then let herself fall into his arms. He caught her waist easily and set her onto the rocky, uneven ground. Leaning forward, she peered into the dark depths of the cavern. She couldn't see far, but she could tell that the walls were made of smooth, flat stones. This was a man-made tunnel, then, not a natural cave. She wondered what the druids had used it for.

Mr. Jasper handed David the lantern, and he went in first, bending at the waist and knees since the entrance to the cavern was only about three feet high. Jessica followed, picking up her skirts out of habit more than necessity, since her dress was already hopelessly torn and soiled from her adventures so far.

The ceiling grew higher quickly, and the passage grew wider, until they could stand side by side. Jessica focused on finding her footing along the uneven floor, but when David stopped abruptly, she stopped, too, and looked up.

She'd expected barrels of rum, but this wasn't contraband of that sort.

No, it was weapons. Bayonets, cannons, crates labeled "gunpowder," and bombshells.

"Good Lord," she whispered. "What on earth?"

"What the hell does he plan to do with all this?" David murmured.

"Look at those cannons." She pointed to a pair of small, shiny guns mounted on wheeled carts. They appeared brand new. Certainly they'd never been used or fired.

"Not cannons," David corrected. "Howitzers. Smaller and more maneuverable than cannons."

A sick feeling curdled in Jessica's gut. These weapons, along with the explosives David had found in the warehouse back in London, could cause terrible damage to something...or someone.

"Mr. Retallack was right," she breathed. "Caversham is planning something very, very bad."

Only an instinctual desire for survival kept Meg afloat. She was tired. So tired. It had been calm, so that helped, but the wind was picking up and she wasn't going to last much longer. Her muscles ached. Her head ached.

But why did she bother? She'd been afloat for what must be hours now, with nothing to do but fruitlessly search for any vessels that might by chance encounter her and watch the sun make its slow crawl across the blue, blue sky.

She lay on her back, her arms outstretched, feeling the skirt of her chemise floating up around her.

Gazing up at the sky, she prayed. *Please, Lord, protect Jake. Whatever happens to me, please watch over him and keep him from harm. Please.*

She'd thought she'd find a way out, somehow, but it was sinking in. There was no way out. She was going to drown.

She thought of Will, of how he must have felt when he'd found her gone. Of how he'd feel when he realized, once and for all, that he'd never see her again. That made her close her eyes. *Please, Lord. Help Will to forgive me.*

She'd been so stupid not to trust him. What she wouldn't give to see him right now, to see his somber face, so full of love as he looked at her. He'd do anything for her. Anything to make her happy, and to keep her safe. Now, she recognized the raw truth of how he'd looked at her. Why hadn't she believed in it at the time? Her focus had been too narrow; her distrust of everyone in the world too strong.

Please, Lord. Help my sisters forgive me, too. Please help them to overcome the loss of their sister a second time.

Now, Serena, Olivia, Phoebe, and Jessica would have to mourn her all over again. Everyone had told her Serena had never gotten over her loss the first time. And she'd been so distant from her sister. So awkward and uncomfortable. She'd failed to open her heart to her family, just like she'd failed to open her heart to Will.

She closed her eyes, the sun heating her face as she bobbed in the swell of the ocean waves. Her skin from the neck down was numb with cold. Her face was chapped and burned from the wind and the sun, and she'd have terrible freckles from this day . . . but what would it matter now?

And then she heard it—the low drone of an engine. She'd only heard it a few times before, but the sound of a steam engine was a memorable one.

She struggled up, swimming. There, coming from the east, was the most beautiful sight she'd ever seen. A steamship, moving fast in her direction.

She fumbled in her stocking, taking out the whistle and shaking the water out of it. She'd had plenty of time earlier to analyze it, to experiment with it. It was a silver boatswain's whistle, the kind the men on Caversham's ships used to alert the crew of a watch change.

"Don't be too eager. Don't waste your breath," she murmured to herself. The ship was still too far away—there was no way they would hear her.

It drew closer, and closer, until it was about half a mile away, Meg estimated. She began to blow on the whistle. When she could see people standing on the deck, she alternated waving her arms, calling out, and whistling.

It drew closer, and closer still. A quarter of a mile away. It was headed in a direction that would pass her by several hundred yards unless the ship turned.

"Turn," she called. "Please! Someone see me!"

She whistled and waved and called.

No one saw her. No one heard her. More and more desperately, tears streaming down her face, she called until her voice was hoarse. She blew until she thought she might faint from lack of breath. She waved until her arms hurt and her legs could hardly kick hard enough to keep her afloat.

The ship plowed onward, its engine growing louder and louder, until it surged past her, still quite a distance away, and she was staring at its stern, at the trail of smoke the ship left in its wake, blowing in her direction.

"No!" she cried. "No! Please don't pass me! Please, come back! Please!"

No one heard her. The roar of the engine was too great. Even if she blew the whistle on its deck, she doubted anyone on board would hear her.

Oh, God. Why hadn't a sailing ship passed her? Why had it been a loud steamship? To taunt her? To offer her hope and then whisk it away, leaving only a trail of foul-smelling smoke for her to inhale?

It had been her last hope. And it had left her here.

Of course, no one would have heard her whistle. She'd been stupid to even try it.

She lay back, shivering, as lethargy crept, syrupy thick, through her veins. She'd been too long in this frigid water. She closed her eyes and waited for the exhaustion to overtake her.

Chapter Twenty-one

Will stared over the bow of the *Endeavor*, his heart sinking. The Irish Sea was a big damned ocean. Not as big as the Atlantic, or even the Caribbean, but bloody big. Finding a single ship in the fifty-mile-wide channel between Holyhead and Dublin—hell, he might as well have been trying to find a needle in a haystack.

And where would Caversham be taking Meg and Jake? Back to the Caribbean, where he could keep them hidden among the traders frequenting those ports? Where he could continue his rum-running activities for the benefit of his half brother?

Or somewhere else? Somewhere having to do with that warehouse full of explosives in London?

"Papa?"

Thomas had quickly grown bored with the endless study of the sea, so Will had given him his spyglass so that he could "practice" for his future role as captain of his own ship. "Yes, son? Do you see another bird?"

Thomas had been so excited upon making his first sighting of something besides the rolling sea that Will had thought for a moment that he'd found Caversham's ship. His hopes were dashed when Thomas's discovery proved to be a pair of puffins.

Thomas lowered the spyglass to frown up at his father. "No, Papa. There's nothing out there anymore but waves. But Mr. Halliday is calling for you."

With one last glance out over the bow and seeing nothing besides water clear to the horizon, Will sighed and turned toward the stern to see Halliday at the wheel, gesturing and calling out, "Captain!"

Will had been so focused on his search for Caversham's ship that he hadn't heard him. Not to mention the fact that he was unused to being hailed over the sound of the engine.

He took Thomas's hand, and they trudged to the stern, where Thomas stood at the rail and lifted the spyglass again while Will turned to Halliday.

"Wind's picking up, Captain," Halliday said. "I suggest we shut down the boiler and proceed under sail. We'll progress at the same speed under full sail, and we'll save the coal."

Will hesitated, glancing out again at the sea. It had been a calm morning, but now the wind was indeed rising, kicking up whitecaps on the tops of the waves at intervals. Turning back to Halliday, he gave a jerk of a nod. "Agreed."

Halliday tipped his cap, then turned to issue an order to a midshipman.

Will went to stand beside Thomas, his eyes grazing the horizon once again.

"Papa?"

"Yes, son?"

"There's something shiny out there." Holding the spyglass to his eye, Thomas pointed behind them and to the north.

Will squinted at the horizon for a long moment, and then he saw it. A flash of silver. A flying fish, perhaps?

"Do you see it?" Thomas asked excitedly, standing on his tiptoes now, with the spyglass still trained on the same position.

Will stared at the ocean's surface where he'd seen the glint. He couldn't see anything there but a bit of white—could be a whitecap, or . . .

"Thomas, hand me the spyglass, will you?"

The boy pressed the brass instrument into Will's hand, and he raised it to his right eye.

There it was, the glint again, as if the sun was refracting off some shiny surface . . .

"Good God," Will murmured as the form came into focus. "Halliday!" he bellowed at the top of his voice, still not moving his gaze from the woman floating in the water, her skirt billowing around her, her body limp, her arms outstretched. She wasn't moving, but something glinted again—it looked like something she held in her hand.

"Aye, sir?" Halliday asked from directly behind him.

Will pointed. "Turn this ship around immediately. There's a woman in the water back there."

Meg, Meg, Meg, his mind screamed. Caversham, that rotten bastard, had tossed her overboard. He'd tried to kill her.

Please, he begged. Let me not be too late.

Halliday and the rest of the crew flew into action while

Will kept the spyglass trained on her limp, floating body, making sure they didn't pass by her again.

The ship was turned, the boiler kept running even though half the sails had been raised, and they bore down on the woman.

Meg.

When they were close and he could see that it was indeed Meg—an unmoving, half-sunk Meg, he lost all patience with the men struggling to get the boat into the water. He tore off his coat and waistcoat, kicked off his boots, and dove off the side of the *Endeavor*, leaving Thomas with his eyes wide, asking, "What are you doing, Papa? Where are you—?"

The splash stung, but then the water washed over him and he could feel nothing but the painful pinpricks of cold. How long had she been in this? Hand over hand, his feet scissoring, he raced toward Meg.

He reached her just as her face dipped under a wave. Her eyes, those beautiful gray eyes, were closed, and her face was peaceful.

"Meg?" he cried, clutching her against him, kicking hard to stay afloat. "Meg, love, wake up. Please wake up."

Something fell from her open hand. It shimmered through the water, tumbling, sinking deeper, away from them. He didn't go after it, but whatever it was, he knew it had been what had caught the midday light and made Thomas see her.

A buoyed rope splashed into the water in front of them, and he grabbed on to it, thankful to have it hold some of their weight. There were shouts above him, someone on the ship, but he couldn't make out the words over the sound of the rotating paddle.

Meg's body was cold, her skin rubbery, and he couldn't see her chest moving with breaths. "Please, Meg," he whispered into her hair as he continued to hold her face above water.

"Please breathe. Please don't die. I couldn't bear it—not again. Please..."

He kept whispering to her, encouraging her, vaguely realizing the salt water running in streaks down his face was not from the sea. Eventually, hands were tugging at them, taking Meg first, and then pulling him into the boat. They rowed back to the *Endeavor*, which now drifted silently. Meg still hadn't moved. One of the seamen leaned over her, taking the pulse at her neck.

"Is she breathing?" Will choked out.

"Aye," the man said. "Weakly. Her pulse is weak, too"—he frowned—"and not quite right."

"What do you mean by that?" Will asked, desperately clawing his way through the surging panic.

"It goes fast, then slow, seems to skip a beat every now and then."

Will closed his eyes, forcing himself to think rationally. He didn't dare touch her. He was dripping wet, and he'd only make her colder. "She needs to be warm. All of you, take off your coats and cover her. Wrap her in them. Warm her up."

The four men in the boat complied instantly, and one of the seamen bundled her tightly in wool.

They struggled, as they had the first time on the *Freedom*, to get her limp form up the ladder and onto the deck. As before, Will had her laid in the captain's quarters. This time, though, he ordered everyone, including Thomas, out. He stripped her clothes off completely, tearing the delicate fabrics of her chemise and undergarments, and then he did the same to himself. He wrapped her hair in one of the blankets he'd had the cook warm over the fire.

By now, he was hot again. Sweating, actually, fear for her sending blood surging through him and making his heart race. Naked, he'd be a furnace next to her. If blankets couldn't keep her warm, he would.

He climbed into the narrow bed and drew her slight form against his, touching her cold, clammy body everywhere he could. He lay there against her, half the blankets on board the *Endeavor* covering them. When she cooled one side of him, he switched her to his other side.

"Please, Meg. Please wake up. I love you. So much."

I love you, Meg. You are my life. Please wake up, Meg.

Will's voice. Her beloved Will. Was she dreaming? Was this heaven?

Her lids were so heavy, it was almost impossible to raise them, but through sheer force of will, she did it. Though if anyone asked her to move a limb, she'd fail. Was she paralyzed? A wandering spirit?

She squinted at the form in front of her, blinking until it came into focus.

Will's face, drawn and haggard.

"Will," she whispered. But no sound emerged.

Will blinked, too, and she saw moisture in his eyes. He moved the hair, tangled and thick with salt, off her forehead. "Don't speak, Meg. Save your strength."

He turned away, then back to her, holding a bowl. "Here's some hot broth. Try it. You're cold, inside and out, and it'll help to warm you."

She couldn't speak to him, tell him she wasn't sure if

she could open her mouth, and if she could do that, how could she possibly find the strength to swallow? But he pressed a spoon to her lips, cracking them open, and then the broth, warm and comforting, slid down with hardly any effort at all.

She had so many questions, so much to say to him, to ask him forgiveness for. But she ate without speaking, focusing on rebuilding her strength.

Caversham has Jake.

She closed her eyes and swallowed another spoonful of broth. He fed her in silence, spoonful by spoonful, until the soup was gone.

Then, as the warmth swirled around in her belly, he set the bowl and spoon down and then turned back to her, drawing her close, skin to skin. For the first time, she realized he was naked. She didn't question it. She rested weakly against him, taking in his warmth, his salty male smell.

Will Langley. The man she loved. The man she'd always loved but had forgotten, for a time, *how* to love.

"Will," she finally whispered, her voice rough, cracking and breaking with every other word. "I am so sorry." Bowing her head, she tightened her arms around him. "I was so stupid. I thought it was the only way to keep Jake safe . . . to keep you safe, and I ruined everything. Please forgive me."

"Shh," he murmured, stroking her tangled hair, the warmth of his fingertips dancing over her back. "Hush. It doesn't matter now. All that matters is that you're alive. That you're going to be all right."

"When I left you, I thought I'd never see you again. I thought I'd never be whole again."

"You're tired, Meg. Sleep now. Rest and get warm."

She went limp, her muscles relaxing.

"But Jake..." Her voice was weak and whiny. She needed strength. She needed to find Caversham, fight him, get her son...

"I know. Caversham still has our boy. I'm going to find him, Meg. Trust me. Sleep now and get your strength back."

She did trust him. For the first time, she thoroughly trusted him. Will would do exactly as he said.

"He wants to stay well off the coast of Wales," she murmured. "But he's heading for Bristol."

"Good. Can you tell me anything about his ship?"

"It's a brigantine—maybe eighty feet? Caversham equips all his ships with cannon—I think"—she scrunched her forehead, trying to remember through the thickness that seemed to have shrouded her mind—"this ship has four or six six-pounders."

Warmth infused her forehead as he pressed his lips to it. "That helps me a great deal. We'll find him, and we'll get Jake back."

Secure in the knowledge that he'd save her little boy—no, *their* little boy—she dropped into an exhausted sleep.

Late in the afternoon, there was a knock on the door. Will turned away from a deeply slumbering Meg and called out softly, "Who's there?"

"It's Halliday, sir. We've sighted a ship." A short pause, then he added, "It's a brigantine like the lady described."

Gently, Will disentangled himself from Meg. After he quickly pulled on his trousers, he went to the door and opened it. "Is he flying a flag?"

"None that we can see, sir."

"Very well. Set a course to intercept."

"Aye, sir."

Will dressed and slipped out of the cabin, going directly to the cook and asking him to watch Thomas and to give him more warm blankets to lay on Meg. He posted a man at the door to his quarters with strict instructions not to allow anyone but himself to enter.

Then he went to check on the ship they were overtaking. It was beating a southwesterly course, and since Will had chosen to continue running on steam after they'd retrieved Meg, they didn't have to fight the wind to catch up to it. Halliday told him that on full steam, he thought they'd overtake it in less than half an hour.

Dusk was approaching, and they were losing light rapidly. But if this was Caversham, Will thought grimly, they'd sink his damn ship and everyone on it regardless of whether the sun lit their way.

He went to the galley to check on Thomas, who was happily playing a card game with the cook.

"Thomas," he said, interrupting their game. "There's going to be a battle."

Thomas's blue eyes widened. "A...battle? With cannons and—"

"Yes, son. And I want you to stay here with Gunnar, do you understand me?"

"But—"

Will looked at his cook. "Keep him safe, Gunnar."

"Aye, sir," the cook said soberly.

"Good. All will be well, Thomas. You do what Gunnar tells you to do, and everything will be all right." Will kissed the boy's head and left, trusting that his cook, who had young sons of his own back in Liverpool, would take good care of him.

It turned out that Halliday had underestimated how quickly they'd reach Caversham. By the time Will was back on deck, he could see far more detail through his spyglass. He and Halliday watched the crew mobilize to prepare to fire upon the *Endeavor*, and Will ordered his own crew to do the same.

Caversham's ship swung around, giving it the advantage of the wind. For the first time in his sailing career, that didn't matter to Will. He could maneuver however he wanted under steam power, giving him the advantage regardless of which of them had the wind on his side.

However, if one of Caversham's six-pounders were to destroy one or both of his paddlewheels, then it would be a different story altogether. If that happened, they'd be in trouble. Will ordered the sails readied, just in case they needed to make a rapid switch from steam to wind power.

In just under half an hour from Will's order to pursue, Caversham's ship made its first attack, launching a volley of cannon fire that fell well to larboard of the *Endeavor*'s bow. Instantly, the enemy ship turned slightly, making the correction that would give them better aim.

Will roared the order to fire, and a split-second later, the *Endeavor*'s two starboard cannons fired with deafening twin booms. One of the shots fell off Caversham's bow, but the other grazed the gunwale, showering the deck with wood splinters.

Undaunted, Caversham's ship glided forward. Its starboard guns fired again. This time, there was a giant exploding noise and a bone-shaking shudder as one of the cannonballs hit the *Endeavor*.

"Damage report?" Will shouted as men scrambled around him.

"Paddlewheel's been hit, sir," a midshipman cried out to him.

Will turned toward the starboard paddlewheel. Water spewed up over the deck, wood splinters flew into the air, and the screech of bolts wrenching free assaulted his ears.

"Shall I shut down the boiler, sir?" Halliday shouted.

Will glanced at Caversham's ship, heard another volley of shots, then looked up at his sails. The *Endeavor* was beginning to turn toward starboard as that paddlewheel slowed and the larboard paddlewheel kept thrusting forward.

He made several quick calculations. If they shut down the engine, they'd give Caversham a huge advantage in terms of maneuverability.

"No," he said to Halliday. "Full steam ahead. Release the spanker sheets. Unfurl the foresails."

"Sir—"

He turned away and shouted toward the helm. "Turn hard to starboard."

"Aye, sir! Hard to starboard!" the helmsman repeated without hesitation, though surely he saw where that would put them.

Will glanced back at Halliday and saw the man gaping at him, bug-eyed.

"Brace yourself for the impact, Halliday," he said grimly. "Because we're going to cleave that damned ship in two."

Meg came awake with a painful jolt as her body was thrown forward onto the floor of the cabin. She clutched one of the posts nailed to the floor holding the bed in place and held on, her head pounding as she found her bearings.

She'd been dreaming about pirates. About Caversham.

Through the years, she'd witnessed the atrocities he'd committed against honest ships and the people aboard them. Most of the time when Caversham attacked, the captains and crews knew that they'd been beaten and surrendered without bloodshed. But in the first year after she'd been taken, Caversham had boarded a ship, and to everyone's surprise, the captain refused to surrender. Caversham had laughed, called him an idiot, and then took his first mate aside and promised him his life if he told him what the captain's most beloved possession in the world was.

"His son," the mate had wheezed. "Lad's on board—he serves as cabin boy."

Caversham had called his crew, including Meg and Sarah, onto the deck and had made them watch as he denounced the mate as a traitor to his captain and then had proceeded to slit his throat.

Then he'd commanded his men to find the cabin boy, and there, on the deck of the other captain's ship with the man watching, struggling against his bonds, Caversham had slit the boy's throat, too.

Meg had never forgotten the look in the father's eyes, that expression of sheer horror, of such intense pain. She dreamed about that ship—the *Mary Ann*—and its captain, first mate, and cabin boy often.

She'd been dreaming about them now. It was the beginning of the engagement, that gleam in Caversham's eye when he was contemplating the kind of prize he'd take, and the loud, low boom of cannons and the sharp retort of firing guns.

After a moment of confusion as the dream faded, of the panic of not knowing where she was and what was happening, it all came flooding back.

Battle. Will had pursued Caversham. Obviously, he'd found him.

Men were shouting, their footsteps heavy as they ran past Will's door.

The ship wasn't moving in any way that made sense—not forward or with the swell of the waves, but rather like some giant fiend had grabbed it and was attempting to pull it apart, plank by plank. Metal screamed and wood splintered as the ship groaned.

She stumbled to her feet, needing to know what had happened, whether Will and Thomas and Jake were safe. She was naked, but her chemise, now only slightly damp, was hanging on a peg. Holding on to a post for support, she clumsily yanked the garment on over her head, then pulled one of the blankets from the bed and wrapped it around her like a large woolen shawl.

She opened the door to chaos. She pressed herself against the door frame to stay clear of the men running. Gunshots cracked all around. Thick, black smoke covered everything—so thick she couldn't even see to the side of the ship. The smoke scalded her throat and burned her nostrils and eyes. Loud shouts, pandemonium, but there was a strange sort of order to it all, with men calling out orders and obeying them.

Her first thought was that Caversham had sunk them, but that couldn't be true. Will had made her a promise, and she knew that he wouldn't break it.

"Miss Donovan?" A form of a sailor appeared through the smoke.

Shading her eyes, trying to make sense of the chaos and identify the man, she grabbed at his sleeve. "What's happening?"

"You ought to get back inside, miss. It's danger—"

Gunshots rang out again, whizzing by her ear and cracking wood behind her. Reflexively, she dropped to the deck. Smoke billowed, but when she looked up, she saw that the sailor had crouched down over her, as if to protect her from any flying debris. "Are we sinking?" she gasped at him.

His smile was grim through a face streaked black with soot, only his bloodshot blue eyes gleaming through the smoke. "Nay. But the enemy ship is."

He squinted down at her, then knelt so they were eye to eye. "Och, I'm sorry, miss. Terrible thing to wake to, I imagine. Here now, let's go back to the captain's quarters."

"But what's happened?" she asked, her voice breaking with desperation.

"We've rammed the enemy ship, and it's goin' down—"

"Sinking!" She surged to her feet, then stumbled as the ship made that strange shuddering, jerking movement again.

The man rose, caught her arm, and steadied her. "Aye, miss. We broke her right down her middle."

"Jake is there, Jake is on the ship. He was tied down—gagged...oh, God. I have to go..."

She struggled to break away, but he held on to her with a firm grip. "Now that'd be a foolhardy thing to do, given as the ship's going down," the man said, his voice gentle but stern.

She glared at him, knowing she was half-naked, her hair tangled and wild, and that she probably looked like she'd gone completely mad. "You don't understand," she said, her voice now steely. "He's my son. My *son*. I have to find him."

"Nay, miss," the man said, his voice still gentle. "Never worry. The captain has already boarded. He'll find the boy."

"What?" Meg cried. Losing Jake was unthinkable. Losing Jake *and* Will was . . . impossible.

"He'll be fetching the lad and bringing him to you."

Groaning softly, Meg stilled. She closed her eyes.

"Cap'n Langley's as determined a fellow as I've ever seen. You've got to trust him, miss."

Her knees went weak, and the man steadied her as she sank back down to the deck planks. "I trust him," she whispered. "I do."

Crouching on deck in the midst of bedlam, she found peace in her trust as she waited for her son and her beloved to return to her.

Chapter Twenty-two

Chaos reigned on deck, but Will heard Halliday and his other officers calling out orders, and he knew they'd take care of the *Endeavor*. Will had another mission: Caversham's ship was going down fast, and he had to find Jake.

From the starboard deck of the *Endeavor*, he leaped onto the shattered stern of Caversham's ship and rushed toward the poop deck, where the captain's quarters would be located. If Jake wasn't there, Caversham would most likely be near, and Caversham would know where Jake was.

He rushed toward the first narrow door, and as he laid his hand on the handle, a cold voice spoke from behind him. "Captain Langley, I presume. I suppose I have you to thank for destroying my ship."

Slowly, moving his hand from the door handle to the pistol holstered at his hip, Will turned and took a few steps forward.

"I suppose you do," he said, coming face to face with

Jacob Caversham for the first time. The ship lurched, making a cracking noise like the wrenching of nails being torn from wood. It was coming apart. He needed to get to Jake, and soon.

He narrowed his eyes at Caversham, his hand still on his pistol. "Where's the boy?"

Caversham raised one thin black eyebrow into an arched peak. "The...boy? One would think a child would be the least of your worries, good captain, since this ship—*my* ship—is preparing to go down and likely to take you with it."

"Not if I can help it," Will said.

Caversham gave him a watery smile. "You won't be able to, if I've anything to say about it."

The ship lurched again, and now the stern listed at a treacherous angle. God...there wasn't enough time for idle chitchat—certainly not enough time to stand here listening to Caversham's tripe.

Will stared at him for another second. This was the man who'd kept Meg from him for the past eight years. This was the man who'd tried to crush her spirit, taken away her trust and her hopes for the future.

Without any further hesitation, he drew his gun, aimed it at Caversham, and shot.

At the same time, Caversham dove at him. The bullet whizzed over the man's head and struck the mizzenmast, burying itself into the thick oak.

Caversham's weight barreled into Will's middle, and they both went crashing to the deck. Caversham rolled to the top, grabbing Will's coat in one hand, pummeling his fists into Will's face, his chest.

They tumbled about, grunting and cursing, the dull

sounds of connecting blows, of smacking flesh, renting the air along with the clashes and shouts of the men running and fighting around them.

Caversham pinned Will beneath him. Over and over he punched him. Blood flowed over Will's face. He struggled, but his movements turned sluggish. Then his arms dropped, limp, at his sides. His hand searched desperately for his other pistol, but it was pinned beneath Caversham's thigh.

On his knees straddling Will, Caversham kept hitting him, cursing, sweating, his face livid with exertion and rage. Then he wrapped his long, aristocratic fingers around Will's neck and squeezed.

Harsh choking noises emerged from Will's throat as he clawed at the bastard's arm, trying to get free. But Caversham was apparently made of steel. Heat flushed through Will's face as Caversham cut off all air, all blood flow between his neck and the rest of his body.

Vaguely, he heard a thin voice coming from behind him. "You let go of Captain Will! Let go of him! I hate you! I hate you, I say!"

Caversham's head snapped up, and he looked up toward the door of his quarters.

Will took advantage of the short distraction. His fist shot out and smashed into the side of Caversham's face, connecting with a sickening crack. Caversham crumpled over him but recovered quickly, jumping to his feet.

Will lurched up, grabbing the man's legs and making him stumble back as, with another explosive splintering sound, the angle of the deck increased by several degrees. Will wiped dribbling blood from his eyes with the back of his sleeve, then grabbed a nearby rope lashed to a deck cleat to keep himself from sliding into the sea.

He couldn't take the time to look at Jake, but sent a quick prayer that the boy had found something to hold on to. Around them, a few men dangled on ropes while others slid screaming down the deck, and splashes sounded as men and parts of the ship crashed into the churning ocean below.

Farther down the deck, Caversham was scrabbling like a crab, grabbing on to whatever he could find to lift and drag himself closer to Will.

Will raised his leg and smashed his boot into Caversham's already damaged and bleeding face. The man's nose shattered beneath Will's heel. With one hand clutching the gunwale, Caversham flopped over, howling in pain.

With a quick glance at Jake—who was sitting in what looked like a chair that was being kept from sliding down the deck by the door frame of the captain's quarters—Will unholstered his other pistol. Aiming it at Caversham, he carefully shimmied down the rope, which was now dangling from the cleat. When he reached Caversham, he pointed the weapon at the man's chest. Caversham's eyes shone blue behind the mask of blood covering his face. Blood dripped from a gash near his eye and gushed from his flattened nose.

"Surrender, damn you," Will hissed at him. "For God's sake, I don't want to shoot you in front of the boy."

Desperate eyes moved from the pistol pointing at his chest to Will's face. Caversham spat a mouthful of blood onto the slanted deck.

"Never...surrender..." he gasped, his voice a sickly nasal whine, nothing like the cocky, sneering confidence he'd approached Will with.

Clenching his teeth, Will cocked the pistol.

Caversham closed his eyes, and for the briefest of moments, Will thought he was waiting for the inevitable shot. But then he opened his eyes. His expression had softened from the coldly murderous glare to a gaze of defeat, his pupils dilated and his brows drawn together, causing deep crevices to appear between them.

In a voice so quiet, no one but Will could have heard, he said, "Don't want...to...go to gallows. Let me go. Down with my ship, as a captain should."

Another thunderous crack. The ship listed even more. If things kept going this way, the stern would soon be perpendicular to the ocean. Then it would be nearly impossible to keep from sliding off.

Uncocking his pistol, Will pulled it back and stuffed it back into his holster. "Go, then, Captain," he said coldly.

After another moment, Caversham closed his eyes again. His hand relaxed its grip from the gunwale, and he slid down the deck until he disappeared over the jagged edge of jutting, torn wood.

Will had no doubt that this was the last he'd see of Jacob Caversham. He knew the look of a man defeated. Of a man ready to die.

Hand over hand, Will climbed up the rope toward the dangling door to the captain's quarters.

"Captain Will! Captain Will!"

Will reached the cleat and grabbed the gunwale to hoist himself up the rest of the way. When he reached the cabin door, he held his hand out. "Jake, come to me, lad."

"I cannot!" Jake said, his voice small and thin. "My papa tied me here."

What? Why? Pressing his lips together, Will swung on the rope and grabbed the door frame, lifting himself into the cabin. Though most of the furniture was nailed to the floor to prevent it from tumbling about in high seas, all the loose items had slid to the front wall of the captain's quarters. Jake was half hidden in a heap of blankets, broken dishes, charts, books, and various other items.

"Good God." The child was indeed tied to the chair, his hips and arms lashed to it. A wad of wet material was wrapped around his neck—a gag he'd managed to spit out, Will thought. What kind of a father tied his child to a chair and gagged him?

Will threw aside broken plates, pillows, and papers, and he scrambled to untie the knots. Jake watched him critically. "You're bleeding, Captain Will."

"I know. But I'm all right. It's just a bit of a cut." It was true. He'd be bruised tomorrow, and he'd probably have a black eye, but right now, those were the least of his worries.

"Can you swim, lad?"

"Yes, I can. Meg taught me!"

Of course she had.

"Good." Finished untying Jake's hips, he got to work on his hands. "Then you and I are going to swim to my ship, the *Endeavor*. All right?"

Jake frowned at him. "You and me? Together?"

"Yes, son," Will said. "Me and you together."

Jake gave him a solemn nod. "All right."

The ship lurched again, and what had once been the cabin floor was now a solid wall in front of them. Something dislodged and crashed against Will's head, but he hardly registered the sting of pain. He was focused on the singular goal of escape. Of returning Jake to Meg. He'd made her a promise, and he had no intention of breaking it.

He gathered Jake into his arms. "Hang on to me," he said. "Wrap your arms and legs around me."

"Like a monkey?"

"Like a monkey."

Distractedly, Will realized that Jake had spoken more to him in the past few minutes than he had in the entire sum of their time together. He looked down into the little boy's blue eyes, and Jake looked trustingly back up at him.

Love surged through him for this innocent child. No wonder Meg had been so determined to keep him safe. Somehow, Will had acquired that same instinct.

He peered outside the door. This wasn't going to work. It wasn't a clean drop to the ocean below. There was the wheel, the mast, and treacherous-looking shards of ship breaking apart in the boiling waves below. If he and Jake jumped, they'd probably be hit by something and drown.

He drew back in, looking up at the three windows that had once provided light from the far wall of the captain's quarters. One of the windows had cracked under the strain of the ship breaking apart.

Below them, the ship shuddered and creaked, and the floor seemed to drop from beneath them. They were sinking—fast.

Will lowered Jake, grabbed a sheet and whipped it up, shaking it free of loose debris. He tossed it to Jake. "Cover yourself."

Without question, Jake did. Balancing atop the chair Jake had been tied to, Will grabbed a second chair that had tumbled down nearby. He thrust a leg of the chair at the window, causing a web of cracks to spread out from that first crack. On Will's second thrust, the window shattered. He ducked his head under the chair seat as glass showered down onto him. Then he used the chair leg to poke out the rest of the glass from the window frame, and he carefully lifted the glass-covered blanket off of Jake.

"Come here, son."

Jake reached for him, and he took the child into his arms and hoisted him up. "You crawl onto the stern and wait for me, understand? Don't go onto the glass—your weight might break it."

"Yes, Captain Will," Jake said, his eyes wide. The boy grabbed the ledge, and Will winced, hoping the glass was gone and he wouldn't cut his hands. But he scrambled up without complaint and disappeared onto the stern of the ship.

The gurgling sound of water, swallowing up the ship like an enormous sucking mouth, filled the captain's quarters.

Will couldn't reach the ledge. It was about a foot over his fingertips. He looked around, searching for something else to stand on. A ladder would be useful about now. Of course, there wasn't one to be found in the disaster that had once been the captain's quarters.

Frustrated, he glanced up to see Jake peering down at him over the ledge.

"You cannot reach," the boy said. It wasn't a question.

"No. But I'll find a way."

He glanced through the door frame to see the roiling sea quickly devouring its way up the deck.

"There's a cleat here," Jake said musingly. "Why's there a cleat?" He looked thoroughly confused, as though cleats should only be located on certain parts of ships. Likely as not, he'd never seen a cleat on the stern.

The sea breached the captain's door and swirled around the feet of the chair.

"Cleats are very useful things, Jake. A cleat on the stern might be used to tow a jolly boat, for example. But right now, we're going to use it to help me climb out of here."

Will glanced around for a rope for Jake to tie to the cleat. There wasn't one of those in here, either, though there was the one tied to the cleat outside he'd climbed on earlier. Probably now immersed in cold seawater. Then he saw the sheet he'd used to cover Jake with.

"Can you tie a figure eight, Jake?" he called up.

Jake looked almost comically affronted. "Yes."

The boy had, after all, lived the vast majority of his life on a ship, Will supposed. He grabbed the sheet and twisted it until it resembled a very thick rope. "Take the end here and tie it in a figure eight around the cleat."

He tossed it up to Jake. It took four tries, but the little boy finally caught it. He scrambled away, taking the sheet with him. God, Will thought, please let it be long enough.

Water was swirling around his ankles, quickly deepening until the cold shock of it covered his knees and then rose to his thighs.

Jake returned and tossed down the end of the sheet, and Will didn't waste any time. He scrambled up the sheet, feeling it tear as he did so. He moved faster than he ever had in his life, climbing the sheet hand over hand and then crawling to the top of the stern in just a few seconds.

He tore off his heavy wool coat, which would be no help in helping him stay afloat. Once again, he took Jake into his arms.

"Like a monkey," he reminded Jake, yelling to be heard over the sounds of cracking wood and rushing water. He scrambled to the edge of the ship—the starboard side, where the *Endeavor* had crashed. He chose an area of ocean that looked relatively calm and free of debris, and as the sea rose up to swallow Caversham's ship, he leaped off the side.

The water sucked him and Jake under. Goddamn, it was just as cold as the last time he'd dived in. How had Meg survived for so long in this? Keeping the squirming Jake tightly wrapped in one arm, he kicked to the surface.

They broke through, both of them gasping. Jake seemed to be doing well enough on his own, so Will let him go. They swam beside each other, wiping the water from their eyes and trying to find their bearings.

There was no sign of Caversham's ship. Men were swimming in the ocean around them, cursing, coughing, some of them grabbing on to bits of wood and other debris. Caversham's men. His own men knew what to do with them—they'd be locked in the hold and given to the law enforcement officials on land to sort through them when they arrived.

The *Endeavor* lay broadside to them, its ruined paddlewheel listing sadly to the side. Otherwise, though, everything looked shipshape. Men were running about on deck, and things were moving swiftly and surely. Excellent, Will thought, especially given that this crew was brand new and had never worked together before they'd left Liverpool.

"It's the captain!" he heard someone cry. He waved his arms overhead to identify himself, and moments later, the *Endeavor*'s jolly boat arrived, and men helped Jake and Will into it.

Will sat on one of the jolly boat's seats, trying to keep his teeth from chattering and holding an equally chilled Jake in his lap. The blankets wrapped around them weren't doing much good—they needed out of these cold clothes.

They reached the side of the *Endeavor*, a ladder was dropped, and Will helped Jake up before climbing up himself. As they headed toward his cabin to change, Halliday fell into step beside him.

"We're apprehending all the pirate's men, captain," he said. "Plucking them from the ocean and throwing them into the hold."

"Good," Will said shortly.

"We found the captain, sir. One of his men identified him."

"Alive?"

"Ah, no, sir." He flicked a glance toward Jake.

Will drew to a halt, looking down at Jake, who stopped, too, to stare over the starboard side of the *Endeavor* at the rolling sea where Caversham's ship had once floated.

Finally, he said in a small voice, "My papa drowned."

"Yes, son," Will said, placing a gentle hand on the boy's shoulder.

Jake exhaled slowly, and then he looked up at Will. "Will you be my papa now?"

Will swallowed hard and drew the boy close against him. They were both shivering wet and cold, but it didn't seem to matter.

"Yes, Jake. I'll be your papa now, if that's what you want."

Jake nodded, his expression solemn.

They watched silently as the *Endeavor*'s jolly boat collected the last of the straggling sailors from the sunken vessel.

With a sigh, Will took Jake's hand. "Come, son. Let's go dry off."

They turned away and continued walking toward the stern, Halliday following behind them.

"Steam won't be any good until the paddlewheel's fixed, sir," Halliday said. "And it can't be done at sea—too much damage."

"Very well, we'll proceed from here under sail. I'll have the paddlewheel fixed after we arrive at port."

"Will we be returning to Liverpool, sir?"

"Not yet," Will answered as they reached his cabin door. "First, we're sailing to Penzance."

Chapter Twenty-three

M eg?"

From her position at the chart table, Meg lifted her head and turned toward the voice coming from the doorway, blinking through her streaming, stinging eyes. "Will?"

She lurched up and out of the chair. And then she was wrapped in his arms, not caring that he was wet and cold, just happy that he was here, that he was alive, that he was all right.

She pulled back a little, looking up at him through blurry eyes.

"Jake?" Her voice was a rough squeak.

"Meg?"

She glanced down. Will was holding his hand—had been holding his hand the entire time. She dropped to her knees and gathered the dripping wet child into her arms. She looked up at Will. "Thank you."

He nodded.

She pulled back from Jake. "We have to get you out of these wet clothes," she said briskly, blinking back tears. "Both of you."

An hour later, Jake and Will were wrapped comfortably in blankets and sipping tea in Will's quarters while Thomas asked about their adventure, rattling off questions at the rate of a mile a minute. Drawing warmth from the teacup cradled in her hands, Meg watched the three of them—two little boys she'd grown to love, and Will, the only man she'd ever loved.

How could she have forgotten that? Forgotten him? She supposed she hadn't, not really. She'd just refused to be truthful with herself, and she'd used the excuse that they'd changed too much in the past eight years. They *had* changed, but change didn't make love disappear. How silly of her to think that it did.

"Boys," she said softly, seeing how Thomas was resting his face in his hands, his elbows on the table, and how Jake's eyes were growing droopy, a sure sign that he was exhausted. "I think it's time for bed for us all. Everyone is tired. It has been a long day."

Jake gave her a hopeful look. "Can I sleep with Thomas?" He waited in anticipation, his bottom lip trapped between his teeth.

She glanced at Will.

"They could have the second-mate's quarters," he murmured, "since no one is occupying that cabin at the moment. It is right next door."

Since Mr. Halliday was occupying the first-mate's cabin, that left the captain's quarters for Will...and for her.

She wanted to be with him tonight. More than anything,

she wanted to hold him and be held by him. And honestly, the time that she cared about what any of the sailors might think regarding her virtue had long since passed.

She released a long, slow breath through her teeth, then she nodded at Jake. "Very well. You may sleep with Thomas."

Jake shot up from his chair, raising his arms in victory. "Hoorah!"

Thomas stood, too, and grabbed one of Jake's arms. "I know where that cabin is. It's small, but it's got a window. I'll show you."

Rising, Meg smiled at Will. "Stay here, and keep warm," she said softly. "I'll put them to bed."

She dressed Thomas and Jake in extra clean shirts supplied by one of the sailors. Thomas's shirt reached his ankles, but Jake's draped over his feet and onto the floor.

"You better not run about too much in that, or you'll fall flat on your face," Thomas said wisely.

"I expect you to be sleeping," Meg said sternly. "Not running about."

With a noisy yawn, Jake agreed and clambered up into the narrow bed. One thing about Jake—he was more likely to agree than to complain about bedtime when he truly was tired. A bit more hesitant, Thomas crawled in beside him.

She kissed each one of the boys on the forehead, pleased when Thomas accepted her kiss and smiled up at her. Though his features were lighter than his father's, he reminded her so much of Will. Especially when he smiled.

"Good night, my darling boys," she murmured.

"Meg?" Jake asked.

"Yes?"

"What if I get scared?"

Her heart clenched. "I shall be right next door, and—"

But Thomas had turned toward him. "But you can't get scared, Jake!"

Jake frowned. "Why not?"

"Because I'm not going to let anyone hurt you. Not anyone!"

Jake turned to Thomas. "Do you promise?"

"I promise."

Jake let out a breath of relief and looked at Meg. "I won't be afraid, then."

She smiled at him. "I am glad."

She kissed them again, lowered the lantern lashed to the wall but didn't turn it completely off, and left the room. When she reentered the captain's quarters, Will was seated where she'd left him, still holding his teacup in his hands. He rose, gazing at her as she entered the small cabin and shut the door behind her.

"Come sit down," he said.

She sat, and he poured her more tea before he took his own seat again. The tea was still hot, and she cupped it gratefully in her hands and asked him the question she hadn't wanted to ask in front of the boys. "What happened to Caversham?"

"He is gone," Will said as she took a sip of tea.

She looked at him over the rim and carefully lowered the cup. "Are you sure?"

"Yes."

"How?"

"He went down with the ship. His choice. He'd rather drown than face the legal repercussions of his crimes."

Meg shuddered. That was a choice she'd never understand. But then, there were so many things about Caversham she'd never understood, and never would.

So she was free. Jake was, too.

She'd expected to feel a rush of relief when Caversham was finally gone from her life, a sense of joyous liberty. Instead, she felt numb.

He reached out, and she closed her eyes as his finger stroked down her cheek, warm and soft, bringing the nerve endings on her skin back to life.

"He's gone," she whispered. "He's truly gone."

"Yes. He is."

Another shudder racked her body. She'd never expected to be rid of him, not really. She'd expected she'd be running and hiding from him for the rest of her life.

Finally, *finally*, she was free. Body, spirit, and heart, she was no longer Caversham's captive. She was free to love Will again.

She opened her eyes and stared at Will for a long moment. Then she blurted, "Marry me, Will."

He didn't move, didn't change expression.

The words rushed out. "You once offered me your hand in marriage. My mother accepted on my sister's behalf, and it all fell apart once the truth came out. You offered me marriage again, but I was too afraid of Caversham finding us and ruining what peace we'd found.

"But I'm here now. I'm free of the man who kept me from living my life for eight years. You've saved us, Will. Because of you, Jake and I can finally start to live." She opened her hand, laying it palm up. "I know it might be far too late, but my hand is now free, and I am offering it to you."

Slowly, he removed his hand from his teacup and laid it over hers, his fingers curling over her palm. "Meg…"

The doubt in his voice made her chest hurt.

"What is it?" she whispered.

His hand was warm and steady over hers as the *Endeavor* pitched gently in the nighttime sea, its rigging creaking as the sails adjusted to the wind.

"I love you," he said softly, his voice achingly raw. "I always have loved you, and I always will. The eight years I spent without you—those were the darkest days of my life. The sheer knowledge that you're alive has brought the light back into my life."

He hesitated, then took a deep breath and continued. "But I told you this before. I cannot marry someone who merely feels gratitude toward me. Who is unable to open herself to me or share her darkest thoughts. Who is incapable of trust."

Grief carved harsh lines in his face. He had spent the past few months fighting for her, only for her to refuse to give him the trust he deserved. And now he'd finally given up.

She set her cup down on the table and rose from her chair. He rose, too, watching her with unfathomable dark eyes as she walked around the table and stood before him.

"I'm so sorry." She looked into his handsome face, her eyes stinging. "I was wrong."

He just gazed at her with that flatness of expression she couldn't interpret.

"But so are you," she continued. "You imply I cannot love you in return."

She reached up to cup his face in her hands, feeling the afternoon's rasping growth under her palms. "Nothing could be further from the truth, Will. I never stopped loving you, but I allowed my own fear to get in the way.

To protect myself, I convinced myself that my love for you couldn't be real."

Pulling him forward, she pressed a soft kiss on his lips.

"It is real, though," she whispered, tangling her fingers in the hair at his nape. "I have loved you since my first visit to London eight years ago. I'll love you forever."

Will's eyelids sank shut, and he released a sighing breath. "I want to believe you."

"Right now," she went on softly, "I'm going to share my darkest thought with you. My darkest thought is that I spent too long resisting trusting you ... and loving you. My biggest fear is that you have given up on me. That you've stopped loving me because I've been such a fool."

She let her hands slip from his neck. She wrapped her arms around his waist and laid her cheek on his chest. "I'm so scared you're going to mark me as the fool that I am and walk away. I'm so angry with myself for ever questioning you. I should have let you in, Will, but I waited too long. I made the worst choice in running away from Prescot. And now, I stand here pouring out everything to you, knowing I might be too late. Knowing that my own stupidity might have ruined my last chance for happiness."

His breath ruffled her hair. "I'll never not love you, Meg."

She closed her eyes, reveling in the warmth and firmness of the chest beneath her cheek. "Today, I was able to smash the last of the wall I'd erected between us. I was finally able to trust you completely. I worried and fretted and prayed ... but deep in my heart—in my soul—I knew you'd bring Jake back to me. That both of you would come back to me. A month ago, nothing could have kept me still with Jake on a sinking ship. But when the sailor told me you'd gone after him, I waited. Because I knew... and I trusted—I *trust*—you." She pulled back a little and looked up at him again. "Whenever I am afraid or in trouble or in danger, from now on, I shall turn to you before anyone else."

His fingertips touched her cheek. "Is that a promise?" His voice was gruff.

"It is my promise to you. For now and forever." She shook her head, a small smile forming on her face. "From my most recent experience, I doubt anyone would say that's not a wise decision."

"I don't want to rule your life, Meg," he said soberly. "I just want to be a part of it."

"That's what I want, too."

He drew forward, into another kiss. This one deep and commanding. His breath clashed with hers, scorching hot, as his tongue explored her mouth. Invading and conquering. And that was exactly what Meg wanted. She invaded and conquered in return, but it wasn't a competition, not a battle to see who was superior, which of them could conquer the other. It was a give-and-take, a sharing of power.

And that, Meg knew, would be how they would always be together. He wasn't the kind of man who would take her life from her and make it secondary to his own. It would be a partnership; a joint effort. They would raise the two boys they both loved together.

Will pulled back, his breathing harsh, his eyes glowing in the light of the lantern.

She blinked hard at that look of desperate vulnerability in his eyes. He needed to hear the words one more time. "I love you, Will. I love you so much."

He groaned, and his lips closed over hers once more. His hands moved over her, fumbling with the ties on her clothes. When only her stockings remained, he swung her up into his arms and took her to bed.

He was warm. Gentle. Soft, flowing pleasure. He touched her, kissed her, rousing every nerve ending over her skin and stoking the fire between her legs. She did the same to him, wanting to know every bit of this man, her man. Her hands skimmed the muscles of his arms and torso, the dips on the sides of his buttocks, the soft steel of his erection. He was a beautiful, honorable man. And he was hers.

Finally, he laid the hard length of his tall body over her, looking down into her face.

"Marry me, Meg," he said quietly. "Be with me forever."

She smiled at him. "I believe I asked you the same thing a little while ago."

He nodded. "You did. And I asked you eight years ago when I wasn't really in a position to ask and you weren't in a position to accept. I asked again two years ago, via a letter you were never able to read. I asked you two weeks ago, when you were still fighting the power Caversham had over you. But now I am asking you one final time, when we are face to face, flesh to flesh, and with a greater understanding of what love is than I was in possession of eight years ago...and even two weeks ago."

Those words sent a flush rippling through her, tingling and warm.

"I will marry you," Meg said, wrapping her arms around his bare shoulders. "There's nothing that I want more in the world than to be your wife."

He lowered his head and gave her an exquisitely tender

kiss, so lovely she didn't notice he was preparing to enter her until she felt his invasion into her body and the smooth glide of him inside her.

Oh, she thought as that honey-warm glow in her nerves spread and grew. It was beautiful and perfect. It was sweet and buzzing. It grew within her as he pressed over her, slowly at first, then more powerfully as their bodies moved in a synchronized motion of two people connected, not only by body but by mind and spirit as well.

By love.

The next day, they arrived in Penzance. Since the dock was currently unoccupied and the *Endeavor* needed prompt repairs, they were able to tie up rather than anchor in the small harbor. As they entered the harbor, though, Meg saw the *Freedom* anchored in the calm waters.

"Why on earth is the *Freedom* here?" she asked Will.

"I gave Briggs the order to search for more evidence against Caversham here," Will said. "And I told him we'd meet him here."

"I hope he found it." Meg knew Caversham was guilty of even more than what she'd witnessed, and she wanted the world to know about it.

"So do I," Will said quietly.

As the men hurried about, directing the docking process, Meg shaded her eyes and stared at the end of the dock. "My goodness," she said, now completely bewildered. "That young woman rather looks like my sister Jessica."

Will, who was standing beside her, frowned. "It certainly does."

They looked at each other, then spoke no more of it

until the ship was securely tied to the dock and it was time to disembark. Will lifted the boys down; then he helped Meg down the steps. When she was on the dock, Meg looked up to see Jessica running toward them, her skirts gathered in her hands.

"Meg!" she cried, launching herself into Meg's arms. "Thank God you're all right."

"Jessica, what on earth—?"

"Oh, there's so much to tell you. I'm so happy to see you! I didn't expect to see you here so quickly, but I'm so glad you're here! What happened to the ship? It looks rather... well, half destroyed. Were you attacked by pirates?"

"Yes," Thomas said, "a very horrible pirate, too. But we sank his pirate ship once and for all!"

But Jessica didn't seem to hear him. She kept rattling on.

Meg couldn't get a word in, so she just hugged her sister back, and when she finally paused for breath, Meg asked, "What are *you* doing here, Jessica?"

Jessica's eyes widened. "You haven't heard? Well, I suppose you haven't. I'm in a heap of trouble, according to Serena. But—well, you see, I stowed away on the *Freedom*—"

"You *what*?" Meg and Will asked in unison.

Jessica puffed out a breath, then glanced down at the boys and then around them. There was a small crowd milling about on the dock. "Perhaps we should talk in a more private location," she suggested. "David is heading—"

"David?" Meg asked with a raised brow.

Jessica had the grace to blush. "Um, I mean Mr. Briggs. He's heading to the inn, where Serena, Olivia, and Phoebe are staying with our brothers-in-law."

Meg's mouth dropped open. "All of our sisters are here?"

Jessica's pretty lips twisted, and her blush deepened. "Well, they just arrived this morning, you see. It appears that they came in pursuit of me. Although I don't know why, and having all three of them running across England after me seems a little silly, don't you think?"

Meg studied her sister for a moment, then said in a low voice, "No, Jess. It doesn't sound silly at all. They love you, you know."

Jessica heaved a long-suffering sigh. "I know."

Then she looked up at Meg, and her lips tilted into a beautiful smile. "They love you, too, Meg. And so do I." She wrapped Meg's arm in her own and pulled her down the dock. "They're all going to be so very happy to see you." She glanced back over her shoulder. "Captain Langley, of course you must come, too. After all that has happened, I have finally decided I can trust you. And"—she grinned at Meg—"David—I mean, Mr. Briggs—trusts you now, too, Meg. So come along, both of you."

An hour later, they were all sitting in the common room. Serena and Jonathan; Olivia and Max; Phoebe and Sebastian; Jessica and Mr. Briggs, who seemed to be doing their best not to look at each other. Thomas and Jake played with wooden wagons on the floor, and Meg and Will sat closely together as Meg recounted the story of what had happened to her after she and Jake had left Sebastian's house in Prescot.

Her story was followed by Will's, who told them how he'd predicted that Caversham would have taken Meg and Jake to sea. He told them how he'd first seen Meg floating in the water by the sun reflecting off something in her hand.

He turned to her, frowning. "What was that, anyhow?"

"I found a smashed mirror in the bilge where Caversham's men kept me. I took a shard, meaning to use it to protect Jake and me." She cringed. "I failed to use it in that respect, but when the whistle didn't work to capture the *Endeavor*'s attention, I pulled it from my pocket and tried to make the sun reflect from it. But I was so cold and so tired..."

He slipped his arm around her, and she leaned into him, uncaring that her entire family was watching.

"I found you just in time," he said, his voice breaking. "I jumped into the water...you had just started going under. I thought—I thought I'd lost you."

"But you didn't!" Jessica said brightly.

The darkness in Will's face disappeared, and he turned to look at Jessica. "No. I didn't."

"So," Jonathan said, "Caversham is gone."

Will nodded.

"But the Marquis of Millbridge isn't," Serena said darkly. She sat in a small armchair across from them, her arms draped protectively over her growing abdomen.

"And he's as much a part of this conspiracy as Caversham was," Mr. Briggs said. He was the only one of them who hadn't taken a seat. He stood, his hands clasped behind his back and his feet spaced apart, in a stiff, military posture. "In fact, I believe he was the mastermind."

"The mastermind of what, though?" Sebastian asked.

Briggs turned to Will. "We discovered a large cache of weapons in a druid cave not far from here. We have confirmed that Caversham wasn't only smuggling rum, but weapons as well."

"For what purpose?" Will asked.

"That's what we don't know."

"I know!"

Everyone's attention jerked to Jake. Meg hadn't even been aware that he was listening.

She slid off the couch and knelt beside him on the floor. "Jake, darling, do you know why your papa was collecting all those weapons?"

"He's not my papa anymore," Jake said, his expression blank. "He's dead now, so he can't be my papa."

Thank God, Meg thought. She didn't look at her family, but she could sense their distress. What a horrible thing for a child to say. And yet, Caversham had never, ever been a *father* to Jake.

Jake looked down at his wagon again and began to roll it on the carpet.

"Jake," Meg asked softly. "What was it that Mr. Caversham planned to do with all those weapons?"

Jake spoke flatly, concentrating on his wagon. "He's going to blow Princess Victoria to bits." He looked up at Meg. "But he's dead now, so he won't do that, will he? Princess Victoria is eleven, two times my age minus one. I don't want her blown to bits."

Chapter Twenty-four

The room went silent. Ten adults stared at the six-year-old boy sitting cross-legged on the floor.

Finally, Meg spoke. In a quiet voice, she asked, "Jake, this is very serious. Are you sure?"

Frowning, he looked up from the wagon he'd gone back to rolling on the wood floor. "Yes."

"When?" Max asked in a choked voice.

Jake shrugged and adjusted one of the wheels on the toy wagon, apparently finished with this conversation.

Meg looked up at her brother-in-law. "I think I might be able to answer the 'when.' Caversham said he needed to be in Oxfordshire by the end of the month. Perhaps it will be then?"

"In Oxfordshire?" asked Phoebe. "Why Oxfordshire?"

Jonathan made a low noise of distress in his throat. "The princess and her mother have just left London for a tour of the midlands. They'll certainly pass through the area."

"Damn," Max murmured under his breath. Everyone looked at him in shock—it wasn't like Max to curse in front of the ladies. He looked at them all, his dark eyes bleak. "The Marquis of Millbridge's seat, Barkwood Abbey, is in Abingdon...in Oxfordshire."

"It would make sense," Jonathan said, "for the marquis to invite Victoria and her mother to his country home."

Serena's hand moved from her belly to cover her mouth. "Do you truly believe he'll attempt to murder Princess Victoria in his own home?"

"But why would the Marquis of Millbridge and Caversham wish to murder an innocent child to begin with?" Phoebe asked.

David Briggs cleared his throat. "I might be able to answer that."

Everyone turned to him. "Go on, man," Will urged. "Tell us."

"When we first arrived, Miss Jessica and I found that the man who'd given me information on my previous visit to Penzance was...ah..." He paused to look down at the boys. "No longer with us," he finished.

He paused again, allowing the implications of that to sink in. Meg's stomach hurt. How many innocents had Caversham killed over the years? How many had she seen him kill? And he'd planned to murder a princess of England. Why hadn't she tried to stop him sooner?

"Though the elder fisherman was...er...indisposed, his son was forthcoming with information," Mr. Briggs continued. "He told us about how Caversham was against the Catholic Emancipation Bill Wellington passed last year."

Meg nodded. She remembered that well. Caversham had been furious when the bill had passed. It hadn't helped that Sarah was dying. She'd tried to keep Jake as far from him as possible during that time, lest he took his frustration out on his son.

"The Marquis of Millbridge lobbied extensively against that bill," Jonathan murmured.

"As did the Duke of Cumberland," Mr. Briggs said, "the king's younger brother."

"What are you getting at, Briggs?" Will asked.

"I think he wants to raise Cumberland to the throne once the king dies. And as we all know, the king is very ill. It could be any day."

"Impossible!" Serena exclaimed. "There are two people to prevent Cumberland's accession—William, the Duke of Clarence, is his older brother, and then there is Princess Victoria."

"But as the boy said, he has plans to assassinate Victoria. Perhaps he has plans to eliminate William, too," Mr. Briggs said.

"William?" Jake looked up from his wagon. "Captain Will?"

"No," Meg murmured soothingly. "This is a different William. This man is a duke, not a captain."

Jake looked at her, his blue eyes like saucers. He blew out a big relieved breath, his cheeks puffing. "That's good. Because Papa told me he was going to blow that William and Victoria *both* to bits." He shuddered. "And he said I could visit my uncle, the marquis, and that we would all watch it together. You won't make me watch them being blown to bits, will you, Meg?"

Everything went quickly from there. Mr. Briggs had set up spies at the cave he'd gone to with Jessica, and that day, they reported that a group of men had come with two covered wagons, into which they'd transferred the weapons and headed in the direction of Abingdon.

Upon hearing this news, Max had presented the evidence they'd accumulated to the local authorities. The magistrates rode out and stopped the small caravan that very night. They took the men involved in for questioning, and though they admitted an association to Caversham and that they'd been hired to transport the wagons—one to Abingdon and one to Bushy House, the home of the Duke of Clarence—they swore they didn't know what the weapons were to be used for.

Meg and her family rushed back to London, leaving Mr. Briggs with the *Freedom* and instructions to sail the ship to London, and Mr. Halliday with the *Endeavor* and orders to return to Liverpool.

In London, Will and her brothers-in-law presented the evidence they'd gathered to the Metropolitan Police, who commandeered the explosives in the warehouse at the London docks and sent officers to Barkwood Abbey and Bushy House on the last day of May. William, the Duke of Clarence and his wife, Adelaide, were in residence at Bushy House, but there was no sign of any intruders— the magistrates had stopped the intended attack back in Penzance.

However, the authorities found the princess, her mother, and the Marquis of Millbridge all in residence at Barkwood Abbey. The house was raided under a search warrant. The princess, her mother, and the duke were held in a safe place and Millbridge was questioned.

As Meg waited nervously with her sisters in London, the authorities found a hidden safe containing damning evidence in the form of receipts for contraband goods, the money for which Millbridge and Caversham had used to purchase the explosives and weapons.

It all came together in a clear story of conspiracy: Millbridge and Caversham had indeed intended to assassinate both Victoria and William, leaving the Duke of Cumberland as heir to a throne that would likely be vacant in a matter of weeks. They'd intended to burn Bushy House while the duke and duchess were in residence, and at Barkwood Abbey, Millbridge and Caversham had planned to "take a walk on the grounds" with their families as firebombs fell upon the marquis's house, destroying it and everyone—including Princess Victoria—inside.

Later, under questioning, the ten men arrested back in Penzance—all Irish Protestants recruited by Caversham two years ago—admitted that Caversham had paid them a thousand pounds each to destroy Barkwood Abbey and Bushy House. Their job was to ensure everyone inside was dead—most importantly the princess and the Duke of Clarence—then hide themselves and their weapons in a safe house in Oxford. The men were ex-Navy sailors. Now, instead of blowing an enemy ship apart in order to sink it, they intended to blow the houses apart and then burn them to the ground, while two snipers would keep an eye on each house, ensuring that the targets didn't escape alive.

No evidence was ever found that the Duke of Cumberland had been involved in the conspiracy to raise him to the throne. While he'd been acquainted with the marquis and had agreed with him on a political level, the duke had always believed the marquis to be overly fanatical about the Protestant/Catholic situation.

The Marquis of Millbridge held on to his claims of innocence until the end, blaming his brother Caversham for the entire conspiracy. He only broke when he was finally convicted of treason.

He said it had been worth it. He'd given everything for the cause. Now he only hoped that others would follow him.

He was hung for treason that autumn.

On a crisp morning in November, the Donovan sisters gathered in Serena's bedroom at Stratford House in Sussex. The sisters had all arrived at Stratford House last month for the birth of Serena's son, William. Upon learning the baby's name, most of society assumed he was named after the current king, for William IV, the old Duke of Clarence, who had taken the throne after the king died in late June. The family knew differently, though—Serena and Jonathan's baby was named after Captain William Langley.

It seemed right to Meg to have her wedding here, at the small chapel where her sister and Jonathan had been married two years ago.

The four of them—her, Will, Serena, and Jonathan—had decided that Serena would keep the name "Meg" and Meg would be "Serena" henceforth, to everyone but family. It would be just too difficult to explain all that had happened with the switch in their identities to everyone they encountered. It would be best for all if they kept their twisted stories a secret to the outside world.

There was still an element in both Serena and Meg that wanted to preserve their mother's reputation, as well. It was the final proof to both of them that there had always been something in their mother worth protecting, even as misguided as she'd been in forcing Serena to "become" Meg.

Meg's gown was simple but elegant—beautifully embroidered white lace over a white satin under dress, low-cut at the bosom with off-the-shoulder sleeves. Narrow around the waist, its two flounces made it wide at the bottom. She wore an emerald-encrusted bandeau about her head with a matching necklace, bracelet, and earrings—the jewelry had been a gift from her married sisters and their husbands.

"There," Olivia said softly. She'd just pinned the garland of white roses to Meg's embroidered lace veil, which fell almost to the floor. "Now it's Jess's turn."

"Please hurry," Jessica said. "We're going to be late."

"We are not!" Phoebe exclaimed. "We've loads of time."

Meg grinned. "Jess has been overanxious for this moment ever since Mr. Briggs returned to London on the *Freedom* and formally asked us for her hand."

Mr. Briggs, not knowing who to formally address for Jessica's hand, had asked the entire family, including Will, who was formally betrothed to Meg by this time, to meet him in Max's London drawing room. He'd faced them all and, in a shaking voice, had asked them all for the honor of marrying Miss Jessica Donovan. His nervousness alone had won Meg's heart—though she couldn't rightly blame him for it. She'd have been equally nervous facing so many potentially hostile Donovans.

No one had said no to Mr. Briggs, though the men had put him through some rather vigorous questioning.

"Do you intend to take her to sea?" Max had asked.

"If she wishes it," came Mr. Briggs's ready answer.

"How will you support her?" Sebastian had asked. That had been the primary concern when he'd married Phoebe.

"I have gone into partnership with Captain Langley. As the company grows, I shall continue to invest in it, and in other endeavors I believe will be profitable."

All three of Meg's brothers-in-law had great respect for Will's shipping business, so that had satisfied them.

"Where will you live?" Jonathan asked.

"I have a small house in London, but I've the funds to purchase another. I know Miss Jessica wishes to remain as close to her sisters as possible, so we'll decide together where we'll live."

They'd asked more questions. Mr. Briggs's answers centered around Jessica—around her desires and needs, and most of all, her happiness—impressing all of them.

Even Phoebe piped in. "How will you respond to her flighty moods and outrageous ideas, Mr. Briggs?"

He had to smile at that, making it clear to all of them that he had indeed been witness to Jessica's flightiness as well as her outrageousness. "I daresay it's impossible to control Miss Jessica. All I can say is that I'll do whatever it takes to keep her from danger."

Will asked the final question. "Do you love her, David?"

Mr. Briggs, who was already pale from nerves, grew even whiter. Tiny beads of sweat had broken out over his forehead, which he didn't seem to notice—because he didn't bother wiping them away with the handkerchief he clutched in his hand.

He swallowed hard. Then he said, in a very gruff voice, "I do love her. More than...anything."

Color had flooded his face. Her chest tight with compassion for him, Meg had been the first to speak. "I will gladly give you my permission to marry my sister, Mr. Briggs."

The others had chimed in with their permission as well, then they'd gathered around and congratulated him, the ladies holding his hands and kissing his flushed cheek, and the men slapping him on the back.

They'd called for Jessica—which didn't take long, since she was hovering outside the door and not in her room, where she'd been told to go—and they'd all hugged and kissed. They'd dined together, and at dinner, they'd agreed to have a double wedding in the autumn. Hopefully, by then, they'd be free and clear of the assassination conspiracy they'd uncovered, and they'd all be ready to begin again. What better way to begin than with a double wedding?

Smiling gently, Olivia worked on pinning Jessica's veil. Her dress and veil were twins to Meg's. Her jewelry was exactly the same, too, except for the stones—rubies rather than emeralds.

"Rubies suit you," Meg said quietly. The sisters stood side by side, gazing at themselves in Serena's large looking glass.

Jessica grinned. "And the emeralds suit you, Meg."

From her position on the sofa behind them, Serena gave a soft snort. "I daresay emeralds and rubies suit any lady."

Meg laughed. "You're probably right."

Ever since she'd returned to London with her family,

her relationships with her sisters had grown closer. It seemed that when she'd rid herself of the walls she'd built up to keep Will out, she'd allowed her family in as well. Now, her four sisters were what they'd once been to her—her friends, her confidantes, her *family*. Especially Serena.

Meg turned away from the looking glass to look at Serena, who was holding a dozing William in her arms. Meg had been present at William's birth, and she and Will had agreed to serve as his godparents.

"He's asleep?"

"For now." Serena gave a low laugh. "It never lasts for as long as I'd like."

"Well, that's true of any baby, I think," Phoebe said. "One would think they sleep all the time, but the truth is, they hardly do at all."

"But Margie is almost a year and a half old," Jessica said. "Surely she's sleeping enough now."

"Oh, hardly." Phoebe hesitated, then grinned at them. "Well, since we're all here, and since it's such a special day, I should tell you my news—"

"You're with child again!" Serena finished for her.

Phoebe's mouth dropped open. "How did you know?"

"Oh, I've watched you go through it once, Phoebe. You've a certain look about you, you know."

"A rather green look, I daresay."

Serena laughed. "No, not green at all. Glowing, more like."

Meg and Olivia went to their sister and hugged her. "Such wonderful news," Olivia said.

"I'm so glad you told us today, Phoebe," Meg said. "It makes the day that much more special."

Unable to get up without waking William, Serena blew her a kiss.

Jessica hugged her as well, but she said sagely, "If you're complaining about lack of sleep, it's only going to get worse."

Phoebe gave her an all-knowing grin. "Perhaps. But it's worth it, you know. Maybe you'll discover that soon."

"I certainly hope not!" Jessica exclaimed. "I wish to have many adventures, and plenty of sleep, before I'm tied down by toddlers scampering about."

"Oh, I have no doubt you'll have scamps as children, Jess," Serena said dryly.

Meg laughed.

"Oh, do hurry with my hair, Olivia."

"Why are you so impatient, Jess?" Phoebe asked. "You're so restless and fidgety."

"More so than usual, certainly," Serena added.

"The four of you cannot understand what it's like!" Jessica moaned.

"What what's like?" Meg asked.

"David...he's...Oh, he's such a gentleman!" Jessica said the word "gentleman" as if it were a curse.

"That's good, isn't it?" Olivia asked, her voice slightly slurred because she was holding a pin between her lips.

"No," Jessica said miserably. "It's wretched."

"Are you mad?" Phoebe asked, thoroughly confused.

"But why?" Meg asked.

Jessica closed her eyes. "He has refused to bed me until we're properly wed."

"What?" Phoebe exclaimed.

"The anticipation is going to kill me," Jessica said miserably.

Phoebe burst into laughter.

Meg fought her lips twitching into a smile. "Oh, Jess," she said softly.

Olivia's smile was broad. "He *is* a gentleman."

Meg glanced at Serena. She was doubled over her infant son, her shoulders heaving with laughter. She looked up at them, her eyes bright. "Oh," she gasped. "I'm so sorry, Jess. But I can't"—she gasped for air—"help it. It's too rich. That out of all of us, *you* should be the only one to wait until you were married to lose your virginity."

"You have always been the wildest of us all," Olivia said, "and the most beautiful."

"My innocent baby sister," Phoebe gasped through her laughter.

"It's not funny," Jessica groused. "And it's not my fault, it's *his*. Why does he have to be so blasted honorable?"

"Because," Olivia said, "he loves you, dear Jess. He wants to do right by you."

"He does indeed." Meg finally allowed her smile to bloom on her face. "I think it's lovely that he insisted you wait. This day will be so special for you, in the end, in so many different ways."

"Everyone thought it would be you who'd still be a virgin on her wedding day, Meg," Jess said, "because your character was so upright, so moral."

Phoebe snorted. "You fooled us all."

"You did, indeed," Serena said.

Meg just smiled.

"Are you finished?" Jessica asked Olivia.

"I am."

Jessica released a breath. "Good. Are we ready, then?"

Serena looked at the clock on the mantel. "It's still too early, Jess. All the guests won't have arrived yet."

With a low growl of impatience, Jessica flopped down into one of Serena's soft velvet armchairs.

"Don't worry," Phoebe said, "you'll be bedded soon enough. I'm sure David is equally impatient."

Jessica made an indecipherable noise.

"Oh, I imagine he is," Olivia said in her quiet way. "Have you seen the way he looks at you?"

"Oh, yes," Phoebe said. "I have. Rather like she's a slab of tender meat he wishes to devour."

"Phoebe!" the four sisters exclaimed.

"Well, it's true, isn't it?"

They looked at one another, all of them grinning like loons. "It is true," Serena said with a chuckle.

There was a knock at the door, and a maid poked her head in. "She's arrived, my lady. Shall I have her wait in the drawing room?"

"Uh..." Serena glanced around at the rest of them. "What do you think?"

Phoebe groaned. "I'd rather hoped she'd appear after the ceremony. I suppose the unfavorable winds didn't slow her ship as much as we'd hoped."

Meg glanced at Jessica, who looked into her eyes and nodded. "Have her come up," she murmured.

Serena held Meg's gaze for a long moment. Then she nodded to the maid. "Show her up, please, Flannery."

The sisters stood still and unmoving as they waited. Moments later, the door burst open.

The sisters didn't move as their mother came to an abrupt halt in the doorway, her hand flying to her mouth. "Oh!" she exclaimed. "Look at all my beautiful, lovely daughters!"

Then, her gaze latched on to Meg, and she burst into tears and rushed forward, holding her arms out. "Serena!" she cried. "My heavens. For so long I thought you were dead—drowned—and here you are, healthy and beautiful as ever, and still looking so very much like your sister."

Meg met Serena's eyes over her mother's shoulder. So, that was how it was to be. Even their mother wouldn't admit to what she'd done. Henceforth, the real Meg was to be Serena, and Serena was to be Meg.

Slowly, Meg smiled.

It didn't matter. She had Will. She had Jake and Thomas. She had Serena, and Olivia, Phoebe, and Jessica. All of them loved her and knew her for herself.

She pulled back and kissed her mother's cheek. "Mother." And then her own eyes flooded with tears. "I never... never thought I'd see you again."

And that was the truth. At least her mother was here, and Meg was no longer on the run from Caversham, afraid to involve her loved ones. She was free. Free to be with them again. Free to love Will.

Her mother clasped her face in her palms and kissed her lips, her own eyes streaming tears. "To see you... alive, my dear, darling daughter."

And then, Meg's sisters were surrounding them, even Serena, who had, for once, successfully transferred William to his cradle. And they were all hugging and crying.

"Meg," their mother said, turning to Serena. "You've done so very well for yourself. You're a countess."

"Yes, Mother, I am," Serena said, smiling.

"And Olivia, a duchess." She kissed Olivia on the lips.

"My dear, dear child. I knew there was a duke out there for you."

They all laughed at that. Olivia's health had been so poor when they were girls that their mother had despaired of her finding a husband at all—or living long enough to find one.

"And I shan't forget you, darling Phoebe. I knew you'd find a proper, honest gentleman to marry."

"That I did, Mother," Phoebe said. Then she added under her breath, "Even if you're the only person in the world who will ever call him a gentleman."

But their mother had turned again to Meg, and she took Meg's and Jessica's hands in her own. "I came just in time, didn't I? I told Geraldine's coachman that he must hurry, that he must rush all the way to Sussex so that I could reach my darling daughters' wedding in time."

"You're just in time, Mother," Jessica said. "We're just about to go downstairs and to the chapel."

"Oh, Jessica, my love, you're marrying a prosperous business owner. Well done, darling!"

Jessica widened her eyes at Meg. "Prosperous business owner? Where did you hear that, Mother?"

"Geraldine, of course."

"Of course," Serena said dryly. Aunt Geraldine was their mother's sister, who was just about as intent on having her nieces marry well as their mother was. Nothing was more important to the older women than their family's image in society.

"And Serena, at last," their mother said, turning back to Meg. "Marrying our dear Captain Langley after Meg jilted him for the earl. How gallant of you, Serena."

"Goodness gracious, Mother," Meg said, "Serena didn't jilt—"

Their mother released their hands and raised her own into the air as if praying in gratitude. "All of my dreams as a mother have come true at last. By the end of today, all five of my daughters will have married well."

They all stared at her for a second. And then Serena smiled broadly. "We *have* married well, Mother. We have all married for love."

The ceremony took place in the small chapel on the edge of Jonathan's property. The entire household had crammed into the narrow seats. The Donovans and their friends filled most of the pews, but David's six brothers and their wives had come, too, and took the pews at the back of the chapel. It was a solid first step in reconciliation between David and his family.

Beatrice served as a bridesmaid while Jake and Thomas and the three married Donovan sisters sat in the front row with their mother, wearing the utmost in fashion and her face glowing with happiness, as the couples made their vows: first Jessica and David, then Meg and Will.

"With this ring I thee wed," Will said softly, looking down at Meg, his eyes solemn and dark. The people around them seemed to blur, dim, and then disappear altogether. There was only the two of them here, joining together in this very special way that only would happen to her once in Meg's lifetime. "With my body I thee worship, and with all my worldly goods I thee endow."

There. He'd done it. He'd just made her another promise, and she knew, deep in her heart, that he'd keep it, just as he'd kept his last promise to her. "In the Name of the Father and of the Son and of the Holy Ghost, Amen."

He took her hand and cradled it for a moment in his larger, callused palm, and then he slid the ring on her finger. They had bought it in Brighton just last week, when Will had remembered that they would need a ring.

It was a simple gold band. It was a symbol of the endless nature of their love for each other.

It was perfect.

She smiled up at him. Her husband.

The vicar told both couples to kneel, and they all prayed together, then the priest sang a psalm and prayed again. Then he gave a sermon, and the congregation took communion.

Finally, the two couples rose and faced the people sitting in the pews. The vicar introduced them as Mr. and Mrs. David Briggs and Captain and Mrs. William Langley.

Organ music played joyously through the recessional. Meg went with Will first, her arm entwined with his. They walked slowly, smiling back at all the happy faces around them. Jake, the limits of his patience reached, rushed up to them as they passed where he was sitting with Phoebe and Sebastian. Thomas, not to be outdone, joined him.

Jessica and David followed, also arm in arm, then their sisters and brothers-in-law and their mother, and finally the rest of the congregation.

Meg and Will stepped out into the bright November morning, and they stopped on the lawn in front of the chapel. Meg looked up at her husband and smiled at him.

"We're married," she whispered.

He closed his eyes. "Tell me it's not a dream."

"I promise you, Will, you're wide awake."

"Thank God." He opened his eyes. "We are married. *Finally.*"

And he kissed her as all their friends and loved ones poured out from the chapel doors to wish them happiness.

Epilogue

M mm." Jessica wrapped her arms around her husband and brought him down for another kiss.

"I can't get enough of you, Jess," David murmured, his voice rough.

Jessica smiled. "Good, because I can't get enough of you, either."

The ship rocked gently beneath them as David's mouth moved across her jaw and down her collarbones to her breast. They were on the *Freedom*, heading south toward warmer seas for their honeymoon.

She arched up, giving him easy access to her breasts, stretching her body languidly. "I could never have imagined how good that would feel."

He chuckled. "No? You could have done it to yourself, couldn't you?"

"Heavens, no. There would have been no way for me to replicate your lips and tongue—"

His wicked tongue swiped over her nipple as if to

prove her statement, and she gasped and wiggled as pleasure wended its way through her. His hand came down over her bare hip, pinning her in place.

"And there would be no way at all for me to have the experience of your unshaven jaw moving over my skin."

He looked up at her, his blue eyes so dark they looked almost black. "Does it hurt?" he asked in a soft voice.

"It doesn't really hurt badly, but it does hurt...in the very best way possible."

His frown deepened into a scowl. "That makes no sense."

"But it does, David. Everything about our lovemaking is like that for me." She reached down and combed her fingers through his hair. "Pleasure with just the slightest edge of something else. Something *more*."

She shuddered as his chin rasped the side of her breast as his mouth lowered over it again. Then, he bit down gently on her nipple, and pleasure raced through her.

"Yes, like that," she gasped. "Just like that."

She felt his smile against her skin. "God, woman. I love you so damn much."

"Good," she said. "I wouldn't have it any other way."

And she loved him, too, more than anything. Life with this man was going to be a challenge she'd relish every second of every day.

His mouth moved back up her body until he was kissing her again, his lips so commanding as they moved over hers that her toes curled. He moved against her, and she could feel the hardness of him—of his erection—sliding against her thigh.

With a sigh, he drew back from the kiss. "It is after

noon. Your sister and Langley will be at the table for luncheon, wondering where we are."

"Oh, I doubt they'll wonder," she said saucily, pulling him to her again. "Make love to me, David."

And they made love again on the soft bed in their cabin, with the sea rolling under them and Will and Meg not doubting for a second what they were doing. They emerged to a starry sky, looking so engrossed and so in love with each other that everyone left them alone to stand on deck and enjoy the warm air as the ship clipped along in a brisk evening breeze.

Meg glanced at the bow of the *Freedom*, where David had his arm around her sister, and they were deep in conversation as they gazed over the moonlit sea. "They look so happy," she murmured.

Will's hand slipped into hers. "Are you happy?" he asked.

She turned to him. "What makes you ask that?"

He shrugged. "I know it wasn't your choice, to be at sea again. God knows you've spent enough time on the ocean."

"That was different. I was always in the cabin I shared with Sarah and Jake, then. I hardly dared go on deck. Being here on the *Freedom* is so very different from being a prisoner on one of Caversham's ships." She chuckled. "I think you named this ship very aptly, Will."

"Are you sure you're happy?" Will frowned down at her, worried. "We can go back to England... spend our time elsewhere. We don't have to take this tour..."

"Jessica wants this... And do you know what? I don't care where we are, or whether we're on land or on sea. All I care about is being with you."

He gazed at her, searching her eyes in the lantern light that splashed in a golden glow across the stern of the *Freedom*.

"So you are happy?" he murmured.

She leaned against him, and he slipped an arm around her like David's was around Jessica and pulled her close.

"So happy," she said, "I think I must be the happiest woman in the world." The warm, golden glow of happiness pulsed through her with every beat of her heart. How could a woman be happier than she was? How could Will not see it?

She had kept Jake safe and had grown to love Thomas, who was just as sweet and loving as Jake was. If anyone or anything could heal Jake from those horrible years he'd spent being abused by his father, Meg knew that it would be her and Will and the family they, along with Thomas and her sisters, would provide for them.

She had her family back—all of them. Her twin, Serena, the most important person in her life for eighteen years. Olivia, whose bedside she'd attended constantly when they were girls and whom she'd worried about incessantly over the years. Phoebe and Jessica, who'd grown into beautiful women. And even her mother, who loved them all in her way.

And she had Will. The captain everyone thought was perfect, but who had made a mistake he never repeated and was never likely to recover from. A part of Will would always be repentant for what he'd done to Eliza Anderson, and for his betrayal of Meg. But despite his mistake and in spite of all the years they'd spent apart, she'd never stopped loving him. He had always been the only man for her.

And...the most amazing, most miraculous bit of all was that he loved her, too. Unconditionally. Without hesitation. He'd part the seas for her, just as she would for him.

She glanced at his handsome face framed by dark hair ruffled by the breeze. "I'm not only the happiest woman in the world, but I'm the luckiest, Will. Because I have Jake and Thomas, and I have my family, and most of all, I have you."

He bent his head and touched his lips to hers.

And slipping through the waves and powered by the silent force of the wind, the *Freedom* sailed south toward sandy coves and warmer waters. But that didn't matter to the two newly married couples on board. What mattered was they were heading into new lives, together, strengthened by the power of their love.

After five years in the West Indies,
Serena Donovan is back in London.
But so is the one person she never
expected to see again…Jonathan
Dane—her very own original sin.

Please turn this page for an
excerpt from

*Confessions of an
Improper Bride*

Prologue

Off the coast of Antigua
1822

Serena Donovan had not slept well since the *Victory* had
left Portsmouth. Usually, the roll of the ship would lull
her into a fretful sleep after she'd lain awake for hours
next to her slumbering twin. Her mind tumbled over the
ways she could have managed everything differently, how
she might have saved herself from becoming a pariah.

But tonight was different. It had started off the same,
with her lying beside a sound-asleep Meg and thinking
about Jonathan Dane, about what she might have done
to counter the force of the magnetic pull between them.
Sleep had never come, though, because a lookout had
sighted land yesterday afternoon, and Serena and Meg
would be home tomorrow. Home to their mother and
younger sisters and bearing a letter from their aunt that
detailed Serena's disgrace.

Meg shifted, then rolled over to face Serena, her brow
furrowed, her gray eyes unfocused from sleep.

"Did I wake you?" Serena asked in a low voice.

Meg rubbed her eyes and twisted her body to stretch. "No, you didn't wake me," she said on a yawn. "Haven't you slept at all?"

When Serena didn't answer, her twin sighed. "Silly question. Of course you haven't."

Serena tried to smile. "It's near dawn. Will you walk with me before the sun rises? One last time?"

The sisters often rose early and strode along the deck before the ship awakened and the bulk of the crew made its appearance for morning mess. Arm in arm, talking in low voices and enjoying the peaceful beauty of dawn, the two young ladies would stroll along the wood planks of the deck, down the port side and up the starboard, pausing to watch the sun rise over the stern of the *Victory*.

What an inappropriate name, Serena thought, for the ship bearing her home as a failure and disgrace. She'd brought shame and humiliation to her entire family. *Rejection, Defeat,* or perhaps *Utter Disappointment* would serve as far better names for a vessel returning Serena to everlasting spinsterhood and dishonor.

Serena turned up the lantern and they dressed in silence. It wasn't necessary to speak—Serena could always trust her sister to know what she was thinking and vice versa. They'd slept in the same bedroom their entire lives, and they'd helped each other to dress since they began to walk.

After Serena slid the final button through the hole at the back of Meg's dress, she reached for their heavy woolen cloaks hanging on a peg and handed Meg hers. It was midsummer, but the mornings were still cool.

When they emerged on the *Victory*'s deck, Serena tilted her face up to the sky. Usually at this time, the stars cast a steady silver gleam over the ship, but not this morning. "It's overcast," she murmured.

Meg nodded. "Look at the sea. I thought I felt us tossing about rather more vigorously than usual."

The sea was near black without the stars to light it, but gray foam crested over every wave. On deck, the heightened pitch of the ship was more clearly defined.

"Do you think a storm is coming?"

"Perhaps." Meg shuddered. "I do hope we arrive home before it strikes."

"I'm certain we will." Serena wasn't concerned. They'd survived several squalls and a rather treacherous storm in the past weeks. She had faith that Captain Moscum could pilot this ship through a hurricane, if need be.

They approached a sailor coiling rope on the deck, his task bathed under the yellow glow of a lantern. Looking up, he tipped his cap at them, and Serena saw that it was young Mr. Rutger from Kent, who was on his fourth voyage with Captain Moscum. "Good morning, misses. Fine morning, ain't it?"

"Oh, good morning to you, too, Mr. Rutger." Meg smiled pleasantly at the seaman. Meg was always the friendly one. Everyone loved Meg. "But tell us the truth—do you think the weather will hold?"

"Aye," the sailor said, a grin splitting his wind-chapped cheeks. "Just a bit o' the overcast." He looked to the sky. "A splash o' rain, but nothin' more to it than that, I daresay."

Meg breathed a sigh of relief. "Oh, good."

Serena pulled her sister along. She probably would have tarried there all day talking to Mr. Rutger from Kent. It wasn't by chance that Serena knew that he had six sisters and a brother, and his father was a cobbler—it was because Meg had crouched on the deck and drawn his life story out of him one morning.

Perhaps it was selfish of her, but Serena wanted to be alone with her sister. Soon they would be at Cedar Place, everyone would be furious with her, and Mother and their younger sisters would divide Meg's attention.

Meg went along with her willingly enough. Meg understood—she always did. When they were out of earshot from Mr. Rutger, she squeezed Serena's arm. "You'll be all right, Serena," she said in a low voice. "I'll stand beside you. I'll do whatever I can to help you through this."

Why? Serena wanted to ask. She had always been the wicked daughter. She was the oldest of five girls, older than Meg by seventeen minutes, and from birth, she'd been the hellion, the bane of their mother's existence. Mother had thought a Season in London might cure her of her hoydenish ways; instead, it had proved her far worse than a hoyden.

"I know you will always be beside me, Meg." And thank God for that. Without Meg, she'd truly founder.

She and Meg were identical in looks but not in temperament. Meg was the angel. The helpful child, ladylike, demure, moral, and always unfailingly sweet. Yet every time Serena was caught hitching her skirts up and splashing at the seashore with the baker's son, Meg stood unflinchingly beside her. When all the other people in the world had given up on Serena, Meg remained steadfast, inexplicably convinced of her goodness despite all the wicked things she did.

Even now, when she'd committed the worst indiscretion of them all. When their long-awaited trip to England for their first Season had been cut sharply short by her stupidity.

"As long as you stand beside me," Serena said quietly, "I know I will survive it."

"Do you miss him?" Meg asked after a moment's pause.

"I despise him." Serena's voice hissed through the gloom. She blinked away the stinging moisture in her eyes.

Meg gave her a sidelong glance, the color of her eyes matching the mist that swirled up behind her. "You've said that over and over these past weeks, but I've yet to believe you."

Pressing her lips together, Serena merely shook her head. She would not get into this argument with her sister again. She hated Jonathan Dane. She hated him because her only other option was to fall victim to her broken heart and pine over him, and she wouldn't do that. She wouldn't sacrifice her pride for a man who had been a party to her ruin and then turned his back on her.

She'd never admit—not to anyone—that every time she looked over the stern of the *Victory,* she secretly hoped to see a ship following. And Jonathan would be on that ship, coming for her. She dreamed that it had all been an enormous mistake, that he really had loved her, that he'd never meant for any of this to happen.

She dragged her gaze to the bow of the ship. The lantern lashed to the forestay cast a gloomy light over the fog billowing up over the lip of the deck.

Smiling, she turned the tables on her sister. "You miss Commander Langley far more than I miss Jonathan, I assure you."

Meg didn't flinch. "I miss him very much," she murmured.

Of course, unlike her own affair, Serena's sister's had followed propriety to the letter. Serena doubted Commander

Langley had touched her sister for anything more than a slight brush of lips over a gloved hand. They danced exactly twice at every assembly, and he'd come to formally call on Meg at their aunt's house three times a week for a month.

In the fall, Langley was headed to sea for a two-year assignment with the Navy, and he and Meg had agreed, with her family's blessing, to an extended courtship. He'd done everything to claim Meg as his own short of promising her marriage, and Langley wasn't the sort of gentleman who'd renege on his word.

Unlike Jonathan.

Serena groaned to herself. She *must* stop thinking about him.

She patted her sister's arm. "I wager you'll have a letter from him before summer's end."

Meg's gray eyes lit up in the dimness. "Oh, Serena, do you think so?"

"I do."

Meg sighed. "I feel terrible."

"Why?"

"Because it seems unfair that I should be so happy and you . . ." Meg's voice trailed off.

"And I am disgraced and ruined, and the man who promised he'd love me for all time has proved himself a liar," Serena finished in a dry voice. It hurt to say those words, though. The pain was a deep, sharp slice that seemed to cleave her heart in two. Even so, Serena hid the pain and kept her face expressionless.

Meg's arm slid from her own, and tears glistened in her eyes. It didn't matter that Serena struggled so valiantly to mask her feelings, Meg knew exactly what she felt. Meg always knew. She always understood. It was part of being a twin, Serena suspected.

Gently tugging Serena's arm to draw her to a stop, Meg turned to face her. "I'll do whatever I can...you know I will. There is someone out there for you, Serena. I know there is. I *know* it."

"Someone in Antigua?" Serena asked dubiously. Their aunt had made it quite clear that she would never again be welcome in London. And Meg knew as well as she did that there was nobody for either of them on the island they'd called home since they were twelve years old. Even if there were, she was a debauched woman now. No one would want her.

"Perhaps. Gentlemen visit the island all the time. It certainly could happen."

The mere idea made Serena's gut churn. First, to love someone other than Jonathan Dane. It was too soon to even allow such a thought to cross her mind, and every organ in her body rebelled against it. Second, to love anyone ever again, now that she was armed with the knowledge of how destructive love could be. Who would ever be so stupid?

"Oh, Meg. I've no need for love. I've tried it, and I've failed, through and through. A happy marriage and family is for you and Commander Langley. Me? I'll stay with Mother, and I will care for Cedar Place."

A future at Cedar Place wasn't something she'd been raised to imagine—from the moment they had stepped foot on the island, the Donovans had told one another that Antigua was a temporary stop, a place for the family to rebuild its fortune before they returned to England.

But now Cedar Place was all they had left, and it was falling into ruin. Long before her father had purchased the plantation and brought the family to live in Antigua six years ago, Cedar Place had been a beautiful, thriving plantation. Nine months after their arrival, Father died from malaria, leaving them deeply in debt with only their mother to manage everything. And Mother was a well-bred English lady ill equipped to take on the responsibilities of a plantation owner. Serena had doubts Cedar Place could ever be restored to its former glory, but it was the one and only place she could call home now, and she couldn't let it rot.

Meg sighed and shook her head. "I just think—oh!"

The ship dipped into the trough of a wave and a boom swung around, trailing ropes behind it. A rope caught Meg's shoulders, and as the boom continued its path to the other side of the deck, it yanked Meg to the edge of the deck and flipped her over the deck rail.

Serena stood frozen, watching the scene unfolding before her in open-mouthed disbelief. As if from far away, she heard a muffled splash.

With a cry of dismay, she jerked into action, lunging forward until her slippered toes hung over the edge of the deck and she clung to the forestay.

Far below, Meg flailed in the water, hardly visible in the shadowy dark and wisping fog, her form growing smaller and finally slipping away as the ship blithely plowed onward.

After living for six years on a small island, Serena's sister knew how to swim, but the heavy garments she was wearing—oh, God, they would weigh her down. Serena tore off her cloak and ripped off her dress. Clad only in her chemise, she kicked off her shoes, scrambled over the deck rail, and threw herself into the sea.

A firm arm caught her in midair, hooking her about the waist and yanking her back onto the deck. "No, miss. Ye mustn't jump," a sailor rasped in her ear.

It was then that she became conscious of the shouts of the seamen and the creaking of the rigging as the ship was ordered to come around.

Serena tried to twist her body from the man's grasp, roaring, "Let me go! My sister is out there. She's . . . Let me go!"

But the man didn't let her go. In fact, another man grabbed her arm, making escape impossible. She strained to look back, but the ship was turning and she couldn't see anything but the dark curl of waves and whitecaps and the swirl of fog.

"Hush, miss. Leave this one to us, if ye please. We'll have 'er back on the ship in no time at all."

"Where is she?" Serena sprinted toward the stern, pushing past the men in her way, ignoring the pounding of sailors' feet behind her. When she reached the back of the ship, she tried to jump again, only to be caught once more, this time by Mr. Rutger.

She craned her neck, searching in vain over the choppy, dark water and leaning out as far over the rail as the sailor would allow, but she saw no hint of Meg.

"Never worry, miss," Mr. Rutger murmured. "We'll find your sister."

The crew of the *Victory* searched until the sun was high in the sky and burned through the fog, and the high seas receded into gentle swells, the ship circling the spot where Meg had fallen overboard again and again.

But they never found a trace of Serena's twin.

Two handsome rivals, one beautiful
Donovan sister.
The stakes run high…and the passion
runs deep.

Please turn this page for an
excerpt from

*Secrets of an
Accidental Duchess*

Prologue

She was an angel.

Maxwell Buchanan, the Marquis of Hasley, had observed many beautiful women in his thirty years. He'd conversed with them, danced with them, bedded them. But no woman had ever frozen him in place before tonight.

He stood entranced, ignoring people who brushed past him, and stared at her, unable to tear his gaze away. With her slender, slight figure, delicate features, and crown of thick blond hair, she was beautiful, but not uncommonly so, at least to the other men populating the ballroom. As far as Max knew, the only head that had turned when she'd entered the room was his own.

The difference, he supposed, the singular element that clearly set her apart from the rest of the women here, was in the reserved way she held herself. There was nothing brazen about her, but nothing diffident or nervous, either. It was as though she held a confidence within herself that she didn't feel any desire to share with the world. She didn't need to display her beauty like all the other unattached ladies present. She simply was who she was, and she made no apologies for it.

Her small, white-gloved fingers held her dance partner's, and Max's fingers twitched. He wanted to be the man clasping that hand in his own. He wanted to know her. He would learn her name as soon as possible. He would orchestrate an introduction to her and then he would ask her for a dance.

"Lovely, isn't she?"

Max whipped around to face the intruder. The man standing beside him was Leonard Reece, the Marquis of Fenwicke, and not one of his favorite people.

"Who is lovely?" he asked, feigning ignorance, curling the fingers of his right hand into a fist so as not to reach up to adjust his cravat over his suddenly warm neck.

Fenwicke gave a low chuckle. "The young lady you've been staring at for the last ten minutes."

Damn. He'd been caught. And now he felt foolish. Allowing his gaze to trail after a young woman, even one as compelling as he found this one, was an imprudent enterprise, especially at Lord Hertford's ball—the last ball of the London Season. If Max wasn't careful, he'd find himself betrothed by Michaelmas.

The dance ended, and the angel's dance partner led her off the floor toward another lady. The three stood talking for a moment before the man bowed and took his leave.

"Most people believe her sister is the great beauty of the family," Fenwicke continued conversationally. "But I would beg to differ with them. As would you, apparently."

"Her sister?"

"Indeed. The lady she's speaking to, the one in the pale yellow, is the youngest of the Donovan sisters."

Max looked more closely at the woman in yellow. Indeed, she was what most people would consider a great beauty—taller than her sister, and slender but rounded in all the proper places, with golden hair that glinted where the chandelier light caught it.

"The Donovan sisters?" he mused. "I don't know them."

"The lady in yellow is Jessica Donovan." Fenwicke murmured so as not to be heard by anyone in the crowd milling about the enormous punch bowl. "The lady in blue is her older sister, Olivia."

The angel's name was Olivia.

Due to his position as the heir of a duke, Max was acquainted with most of the English aristocracy perforce. Yet from the moment he'd caught his first glimpse of the angel tonight, he'd known he'd never been introduced to her, never seen her before. He'd never heard Olivia and Jessica Donovan's names, either, though their surname did sound vaguely familiar.

"They must be new to Town."

"They are. They arrived in London last month. This is only the third or fourth event they've attended." Fenwicke gave a significant pause. "However, I am quite certain you are acquainted with the eldest Donovan sister."

Max frowned. "I don't think so."

Fenwicke chuckled. "You are. You just haven't yet made the connection. The eldest sister is Margaret Dane, Countess of Stratford."

That name he did know—how could he not? "Ah. Of course."

A year ago, Lady Stratford had arrived from Antigua engaged to one well-connected gentleman, but she'd ended up marrying the earl instead. Like a great stone thrown into the semi-placid waters of London, the ripples caused by the splash she'd made had only just begun to subside. Even Max, who studiously avoided all forms of gossip, had heard all about it.

"So the countess's sisters have recently arrived from the West Indies?"

"That's right."

Max's gaze lingered on Olivia, the angel in blue. Fenwicke had said she was older than the lady standing beside her, but she appeared younger. It was in her bearing, in her expression. While Jessica didn't quite strut, she moved like a woman attuned to the power she wielded over all who beheld her. Olivia was directly the opposite. She wore her reserved nature like a cloak. She stood a few inches shorter and was slighter than her sister. Her cheeks were paler, and her hair held more of the copper and less of the gold, though certainly no one would complain that it was too red. It was just enough to lend an intriguing simmer rather than a full-blown fire.

Olivia's powder-blue dress was of an entirely fashionable style and fabric—though Max didn't concern himself with fashion enough to be able to distinguish either by name. The gown was conservatively cut but fit her perfectly, and her jewelry was simple. She wore only a pair of pearl-drop earrings and an austere strand of pearls around her neck.

Her posture was softer than her sister's, whose stance was sharp and alert. However, their familial connection was obvious in their faces—both perfect ovals with full but small mouths and large eyes. From this distance, Max couldn't discern the color of her eyes, but when Olivia had been dancing earlier, she'd glanced in his direction, and he'd thought they must be a light shade.

God. He nearly groaned. She captivated him. She had from the first moment he'd seen her. She was simply lovely.

"...leaving London soon."

Fenwicke stopped talking, and Max's attention snapped back to him.

Fenwicke sighed. "Did you hear me, Hasley?"

"Sorry," Max said, then gestured randomly about. "Noisy in here."

It was true, after all. The orchestra had begun the opening strands of the next dance, and laughing couples were brushing past them, hurrying to join in at the last possible moment.

Fenwicke gazed at him appraisingly for a long moment, then motioned toward the ballroom's exit. "Come, man. Let's go have a drink."

If it had been an ordinary evening, he would have declined. He and Fenwicke had a long acquaintance, and Max had always found the man oily and unlikable. They'd been rivals since their school days at Eton, but they'd never been friends.

He glanced quickly back to the lady. *Olivia.* At that moment, she looked up. Her gaze caught his and held.

Blue eyes. Surely they were blue.

Those eyes held him in her thrall, sweet and lovely, and sensual too, despite her obvious innocence. Max felt suspended in midair, like a water droplet caught in a spider's web.

She glanced at Fenwicke and then quickly to the floor, and Max plopped back to earth with a *splat*. But satisfaction rushed through him in a warm wave, because just before she'd broken their eye contact, he'd seen the first vestiges of color flooding her cheeks.

"Very well," he told Fenwicke. Tonight he didn't politely excuse himself from Fenwicke's company, because tonight Fenwicke appeared to have information Max suddenly craved—information about Olivia Donovan.

He turned away from her, but not before he saw another gentleman offering her his arm for the dance and a bolt of envy struck him in the gut. Thrusting away that irrational emotion, Max followed Fenwicke down the corridor to the parlor that had been set aside as the gentlemen's retiring room. A foursome played cards in the corner, and an elderly man sat in a large but elegant brown cloth armchair in the corner, blatantly antisocial, a newspaper raised to obscure half his face. Other men lounged by the sideboard, chatting and drinking from the never-ending supply of spirits.

Fenwicke collected two glasses of brandy and then gestured with his chin at a pair of empty leather chairs separated by a low, glass-topped table but close enough together for them to have a private conversation. Max sat in the nearest chair, taking the glass Fenwicke offered him as he passed. He took a drink of the brandy while Fenwicke lowered himself into the opposite chair.

Holding his glass in both hands, Fenwicke stared at him. "I gather you haven't had the pleasure of observing the Miss Donovans prior to tonight."

"No," Max admitted. "Do they plan to reside in London?"

"No." Fenwicke's lip twisted sardonically. "As I was saying in the ballroom, I believe they're leaving before the end of the month. They're off to Stratford's estate in Sussex."

"Too bad," Max murmured.

But then a memory jolted him. At White's last week, Lord Stratford had invited a few men, including Max, to Sussex this autumn to hunt fowl. He'd turned down the offer—he'd never been much interested in hunting—but now...

Fenwicke gazed at him. The man had always reminded Max of a reptilian predator with his cold, assessing silver-gray eyes. "You," he announced, "have a tendre for Miss Donovan."

It was impossible to determine whether that was a question or a statement. Either way, it didn't matter. "Don't be absurd. I don't even know Jessica Donovan."

"I'm speaking of Olivia," Fenwicke said icily. It sounded like Fenwicke was *jealous*, but that was ridiculous. As the man had said, the lady had been in Town for less than a month.

"I don't know either of them," Max responded, keeping his tone mild.

"Regardless, you want her," Fenwicke said in an annoyed voice. "I'm well acquainted with that look you were throwing in her direction."

Max shrugged.

"You are besotted with her."

Max leaned back in his chair, studying Fenwicke closely beyond the rim of his glass, wondering what gave Fenwicke the right to have proprietary feelings for Olivia Donovan.

"Are you a relation of hers?" he asked.

"I am not."

"Well, I was watching her," Max said slowly. "And, yes, I admit to wondering who she was and whether she was attached. I was considering asking her to dance later this evening."

The muscles in Fenwicke's jaw bulged as he ground his teeth. "She has no dances available."

"How do you know?"

"I asked her myself."

Max stared at the man opposite him, feeling the muscles across his shoulders tense as the fingers of his loose hand curled into a tight fist. He didn't like the thought of his angel touching Fenwicke. Of Fenwicke touching her. The thought rather made him want to throw Fenwicke through the glass window overlooking the terrace across from them.

He took a slow breath, willing himself to calmness. He wasn't even acquainted with the woman. Didn't even know the sound of her voice, the color of her eyes, her likes and dislikes. Yet he was already willing to protect her from scum like Fenwicke.

He wouldn't want Fenwicke touching any young innocent, he reasoned. He'd protect any woman from the marquis's slick, slithering paws.

"How is your wife?" he asked quite deliberately, aware of the challenge in his voice.

Fenwicke's expression went flat. He took a long drink of brandy before responding. "She's well," he said coldly. "She's back at home. In Sussex. Thank you for asking." His lips curled in a snarl that Max guessed was supposed to appear to be a smile.

Max remembered that Fenwicke's country home was in Sussex, just like the Earl of Stratford's. He wondered if the houses were situated close to each other.

"I'm glad to hear she's well."

"You can't have her," Fenwicke said quietly.

Max raised a brow. "Your wife?"

"Olivia Donovan."

Max took a long moment to allow that to sink in. To think about how he should respond.

"She's not married?" he finally asked. He knew the answer.

Fenwicke's tone was frosty. "She is not."

"Engaged?"

"No."

"Then why, pray, can't I have her?"

"She'd never accept you. You would never meet her standards. You, Hasley, are a well-known rake."

"So?" That had never stopped any woman from accepting his advances before.

"So, you're not good enough for her." Fenwicke's smile widened, but it was laced with bitterness. "No man in London is."

"How can you possibly know this?"

"She told me."

Max nearly choked on his brandy. "What?"

"I propositioned her," Fenwicke said simply. "In the correct way, of course, which was quite delicate, considering her innocence. I dug deeply—quite deeply indeed—into my cache of charm."

Max's stomach churned. He could never understand what women saw in Fenwicke—but obviously they saw something, because the man never needed to be too aggressive in his pursuit before capturing his prey, despite his marital status.

Yet it seemed Miss Olivia Donovan didn't see whatever it was in Fenwicke that all the other women saw. Intriguing. Without ever having met her, Max's respect for her grew.

The thought of how many times Fenwicke had abandoned his young wife in the country left Max feeling vaguely nauseous. How many times had he seen the man with a different woman on his arm?

Perhaps what left the sourest taste in Max's mouth was that everyone knew about Fenwicke's proclivities but continued to invite him to their social events. No one spurned him. He was a peer, after all, a member of White's, and an excellent dance partner or opponent at cards.

Long ago, Fenwicke had decided that Max was an adversary and had pushed Max into a constant competition. They'd competed over sports, women, their studies, and politics. It had all started in Max's third year at Eton, when his cousins had died of influenza and Max became the heir to a dukedom just like Fenwicke was—Fenwicke's father was the Duke of Southington and Max's uncle was the Duke of Wakefield.

Fenwicke even had the audacity to claim he'd be more of a duke, since he was an eldest son rather than a nephew. That statement had enraged Max—no one could vex him like Fenwicke could. Something about the man brought out the worst in Max, which was why he'd tried his damnedest to stay away from the marquis. Avoidance hadn't worked, however. Both he and Fenwicke had gone to Cambridge and now they belonged to the same gentleman's club. Max couldn't get rid of the man. And once they were both dukes and sitting in Parliament, they'd be required to see more of each other. Max had to come to terms with the fact that Fenwicke was a permanent fixture in his life, but that didn't mean he had to like it.

Now, thinking of Fenwicke's lascivious thoughts toward Miss Donovan in spite of his married state, Max's dislike of the man threatened to grow into something stronger. Something more like hatred. He closed his eyes and images of his father passed behind his lids. His mother...alone. The tears she'd tried to hide from him. Even at a very young age, Max had known exactly what was happening. Exactly how his father had betrayed his mother, how he'd hurt her, ultimately destroyed her.

Max would never do that to a wife—he'd never marry so there would simply never be a concern—and he'd never abide anyone who did.

Fenwicke set his empty brandy glass on the table with a sigh. "I'm afraid Miss Olivia Donovan simply isn't interested."

Max narrowed his eyes. "So because you failed to charm the lady, you assume that I'll fail as well?"

"Of course. She's frigid, you see. The girl is composed of ice as solid as a glacier."

Another of the many reasons Max disliked Fenwicke: He never took responsibility. If a woman rejected him, he'd think it was due to some defect in her character as opposed to a natural—and wise—dislike or distrust of the man himself. If a woman professed no attraction to the marquis, naturally she wouldn't feel any attraction to any man, because all other men were lesser beings.

"I sincerely doubt she's frigid," Max responded before he thought better of it.

Fenwicke's eyes narrowed. "Do you?"

Max met the man's steely glare head-on. "Perhaps you simply don't appeal."

Fenwicke snorted. "Of course I appeal. I'm a marquis, to begin with, and the heir to—"

"Perhaps," Max interjected, keeping his voice low, "she possesses no interest in engaging in an adulterous liaison, marquis or no."

At his periphery, Max could see Fenwicke's fists clenching. He braced himself for the man's lunge, but it never came. Damn it. If Fenwicke had attacked first, it would have given Max a good reason to throttle him.

Fenwicke gave him a thin, humorless smile. "I would beg to differ."

Max shrugged. "Perhaps we should agree to disagree, then."

"If she did not succumb to my charms, Hasley, then rest assured, there's no way in hell she'll succumb to yours." Fenwicke's voice was mild, but the cords in his neck bulged above his cravat.

Max shook his head, unable to prevent a sneer from forming on his lips. "You're wrong, Fenwicke."

Fenwicke's brows rose, his eyes glinted, and a sly expression came over his face. He leaned forward, greedily licking his lips.

"Would you care to place a wager on that?"

THE DISH

Where authors give you the inside scoop!

❤ ❤ ❤ ❤ ❤ ❤ ❤ ❤ ❤ ❤ ❤ ❤ ❤ ❤

From the desk of Kendra Leigh Castle

Dear Reader,

I admit it: I love a bad boy.

From the Sheriff of Nottingham to Severus Snape, Spike to Jack Sparrow, it's always the men who seem beyond saving that throw my imagination into overdrive. So it's no wonder that this sort of character arrived in my very first Dark Dynasties book and has stuck around since, despite the fact that most of the other characters either (a)wonder why he hasn't been killed or (b)would like to kill him themselves. Or both, depending on the day. His name is Damien Tremaine. He's a vampire, thief, assassin, and as deadly as they come. In fact, he spent much of *Dark Awakening* trying to kill the hero and heroine. He positively revels in the fact that he has few redeeming qualities. And I just. Couldn't. Resist.

Writing SHADOW RISING, the third installment in the Dark Dynasties series, proved an interesting challenge. The true bad boy takes a special kind of woman to turn him around, and I knew it would take a lot to pierce the substantial (and very stylish) armor that Damien had built up over the centuries. Enter Ariane, a vampire who is formidable in her own right but really remarkable because of her innocence, despite being hundreds of years old. As a member of the reclusive and mysterious Grigori dynasty, Ariane remembers nothing of her life before being turned. All she knows is the hidden desert compound of her kind, a place she has never been allowed to leave. She's long been restless...but when her closest friend goes missing and she's forbidden to search for him, Ariane takes matters into her own untried but very capable hands. Little does she know that her dynasty's leader has hired an outside vampire who specializes in finding those who don't want to be found—and that once she crosses paths with him, he'll make very sure that their paths keep crossing, whether she likes it or not.

All of the couples I write about have their differences, but Damien and Ariane are polar opposites. She's sheltered, he's jaded. She longs to feel everything, while Damien's spent years burying every emotion. And she is, of course, exactly what he needs, which is the first thing to have actually frightened Damien in...well, ever. Damien's slow and terrifying realization that he's finally in over his head was both a lot of fun to write, and exactly what he deserved. After all, redemption is satisfying, but it's not supposed to be *easy*.

Between Damien's sharp tongue and sharper killer instincts, Ariane has her hands full from the get-go. Fortunately, she finds him just as irresistible as I do. Like so many dark and delicious bad boys, there's more to Damien than meets the eye. If you're interested in finding out whether this particular assassin has the heart of a hero, I hope you'll check out SHADOW RISING. I'll be honest: Damien never really turns into a traditional knight in shining armor. But if you're anything like me...you won't want him to anyway.

Enjoy!

Kendra Leigh Castle

Kendra Leigh Castle

♥ ♥ ♥ ♥ ♥ ♥ ♥ ♥ ♥ ♥ ♥ ♥ ♥ ♥ ♥

From the desk of Jennifer Haymore

Dear Reader,

When Meg Donovan, the heroine of PLEASURES OF A TEMPTED LADY (on sale now), entered my office for the first time, I mistook her for her twin sister, Serena.

"Serena!" I exclaimed. "How are you? Please, take a seat."

She slowly shook her head. "Not Serena," she said quietly. "Meg."

I stared at her. I couldn't do anything else, because my throat had closed up tight. For, dear reader, Meg was dead! Lost at sea and long gone, and I'd written two complete novels and a novella under that assumption.

Finally, I found my scrambled wits and gathered them tight around me.

"Um," I said hopefully, "Serena...that's not a funny joke. My income relies on my journalistic credibility. You know that, right?"

She just looked at me. Then she shrugged. "Sorry. I am Meg Donovan. And though the world might like to pretend that I am Serena, I know who I am."

"But...but...you're dead." Now I sounded like a petulant child. A rather warped and quite possibly disturbed petulant child.

She finally took the seat I'd offered Serena, and, settling in, she leaned forward. "No, Mrs. Haymore. I'm not dead. I'm very much alive, and I'd like you to write my story."

Oh, Lord.

I looked down to rub the bridge of my nose between my thumb and forefinger, fighting off a sudden headache. If this really was Meg, I was in big, big trouble.

Finally I looked up at her. "All right," I said slowly. "So you're Meg. Back from the dead."

"That's correct," she said.

I studied her closely. Her twin Serena and I have become good friends since I wrote her story for her, and now that I really looked at this woman, the subtle differences between her and her twin grew clearer. This woman was about ten pounds thinner than Serena. And though her eyes were the same shade of blue, something about them seemed harder and wary, as though she'd gone through a difficult time and come out of it barely intact.

"So who was it that rescued you, then?" I asked. "Pirates? Slavers?"

Her expression grew tight. Shuttered. "I'd like to skip that part, if you don't mind."

I raised a brow. This wasn't going to work out between us if she demanded I skip all the good stuff. But I'd play along. For now. "All right, then. Where would you like to start?"

"With my escape."

"Ah, so it *was* pirates, then."

She gave a firm shake of her head. "No. I meant my escape from England."

"That doesn't make sense," I said. "You'll be wanting to stay in England. Your family is there." I didn't say it, but I was pretty sure the man who loved her was there, too.

"I can't stay in England. You must help me."

I clasped my hands on top of my desk. "Look, Meg. I really like your family, so I'm sitting here listening to what you have to say. But I'm a writer who writes happy, satisfying stories about finding true love and living happily ever after. Is that what you're looking for?"

"No!"

I sighed. I'd thought not.

She leaned forward again, her palms flat on the desk. "I need you to write me out of England, because I need to protect my family, and..."

"And...?" I prompted when she looked away, seemingly unwilling to continue.

"And...Captain Langley. You see, as long as I stay in England, they're all in danger."

I fought the twitch that my lips wanted to make to form a smile. So she did know about Captain William Langley...and she obviously cared for him. Whatever danger she was worried about facing meant nothing in the face of the depth of love that might someday belong to William Langley and Meg Donovan.

"I see." I looked into her eyes. "I might be able to make an exception this time. I will do whatever I can to help you protect your family."

Note that I didn't tell her I'd help her to escape. Or to get out of England.

A frantic, wonderful plan was forming rapidly in my mind. Yeah, I'd write her story. I'd "help" her keep Langley and her family safe. But once I did that, once I gained her trust, I'd find a way to make them happy, to boot. Because I'm a romance writer, and that's what I do.

"Thank you," she murmured, glassy tears forming in her eyes. "Thank you so much."

I raised a warning finger. "Realize that in order for this to work, you need to tell me everything."

She hesitated, her lips pressed hard together. Then she finally nodded.

I flipped up my laptop and opened a new document. "Tell me your story, Miss Donovan. From the moment of your rescue."

And that was how I began to write the love story of Meg Donovan, the long-lost Donovan sister.

I truly hope you enjoy reading Meg's story! Please come visit me at my website, www.jenniferhaymore.com, where you can share your thoughts about my books, sign up for some fun freebies and contests, and read more about the characters from PLEASURES OF A TEMPTED LADY.

Sincerely,

Jennifer Haymore

Jennifer Haymore

♥ ♥ ♥ ♥ ♥ ♥ ♥ ♥ ♥ ♥ ♥ ♥ ♥ ♥ ♥ ♥ ♥

From the desk of Jill Shalvis

Dear Reader,

Ever feel like you're drowning? In FOREVER AND A DAY, my hero, Dr. Josh Scott, is most definitely drowning. He's overloaded, overworked, and on the edge of burnout. He's got his practice, his young son, his wheelchair-bound sister, and a crazy puppy. Not to mention the weight of the world on his shoulders from taking care of everyone in his life. He's in so deep, saving everyone around him all the time, that he doesn't even realize that *he's* the one in need of saving. It would never occur to him.

Enter Grace Brooks. She's a smart smartass and, thanks to some bad luck, pretty much starting her life over from scratch. Losing everything has landed her in Lucky Harbor working as Josh's dog walker. And then as his nanny. And then before he even realizes it, as his everything. In truth, she's saved him, in more ways than one.

Oh, how I loved watching the sure, steady rock that is Josh crumble, only to be slowly but surely helped back together again by the sexy yet sweet Grace.

And don't forget to pick up the other "Chocaholic" books, *Lucky in Love* and *At Last*, both available wherever books and ebooks are sold.

Happy Reading!

Jill Shalvis

Jill Shalvis

♥ ♥ ♥ ♥ ♥ ♥ ♥ ♥ ♥ ♥ ♥ ♥ ♥ ♥ ♥

From the desk of Kristen Callihan

Dear Reader,

I'm half Norwegian—on my mother's side. If there is one thing you need to know about Norwegians, it's that they are very egalitarian. This sense of equality defines them in a number of ways, but one of the more interesting aspects is that Norwegian men treat women as equal partners.

Take my grandfather. He was a man's man in the truest sense of the term. A rugged fisherman and farmer who hung out with the fellas, rebuilt old cars, smoked a pipe, and made furniture on the side. Yet he always picked up his own plate after dinner. He never hesitated to go to the market if my grandmother needed something, nor did he complain if he had to cook his own meals when she was busy. My grandfather was one of the most admirable men I've known. Thus when I began to write about heroes, I gravitated toward men who share some of the same qualities as my Norwegian ancestors.

Ian Ranulf, the hero of MOONGLOW, started out as a bit of an unsavory character in *Firelight*. All right, he was a total ass, doing everything he could to keep Miranda and Archer apart. So much so that, early on, my editor once asked me if I was sure Ian wasn't the real villain. While Ian did not act on his best behavior, I always knew that he was not a bad man. In fact, I rather liked him. Why? Because Ian loves and respects women in a way that not many of his peers do. While he feels inclined to protect a woman from physical harm, he'd never patronize her. For that, I could forgive a lot of him.

In MOONGLOW, Ian is a man living a half-life. He has sunk into apathy because life has not been particularly kind to him. And so he's done what most people do: He's retreated into a protective shell. Yet when he meets Daisy, a woman who will not be ignored, he finds himself wanting to live for her. But what I found interesting about Ian is that when he begins to fall for Daisy, he does not think, "No, I've been burned before; I'm not going to try again." Ian does the opposite: He reaches for what he wants, even if it terrifies him, even with a high possibility of failure.

While Ian certainly faces his share of physical battles in MOONGLOW, it is his dogged pursuit of happiness and his willingness to love Daisy as an equal that made him one of my favorite characters to write.

Happy Reading,

Kristen Callihan

Find out more about Forever Romance!

Visit us at
www.hachettebookgroup.com/publishing_forever.aspx

Find us on Facebook
http://www.facebook.com/ForeverRomance

Follow us on Twitter
http://twitter.com/ForeverRomance

NEW AND UPCOMING TITLES

Each month we feature our new titles
and reader favorites.

CONTESTS AND GIVEAWAYS

We give away galleys, autographed copies,
and all kinds of exclusive items.

AUTHOR INFO

You'll find bios, articles, and links to personal websites
for all your favorite authors—and so much more.

GET SOCIAL

Connect with your favorite authors, editors, and
other Forever fans, and share what's important to you.

THE BUZZ

Sign up for our monthly romance newsletter,
and be the first to read all about it.